GETTYSBURG

Also by Kevin Morris

White Man's Problems

All Joe Knight

GETTYSBURG

A NOVEL

KEVIN MORRIS

Grove Press
New York

Published simultaneously in Canada
Printed in the United States of America

First Grove Atlantic hardcover edition: July 2019
First Grove Atlantic paperback edition: July 2020

Library of Congress Cataloging-in-Publication data is available for this title.

ISBN 978-0-8021-4904-6
eISBN 978-0-8021-4739-4

Grove Press
an imprint of Grove Atlantic
154 West 14th Street
New York, NY 10011

Distributed by Publishers Group West

groveatlantic.com

20 21 22 23   10 9 8 7 6 5 4 3 2 1

For Rocky, Dulcie, and Gaby

DAY 1

CHAPTER 1

Man of Action

In his dream, John Reynolds Stanhope held the fine and fabulous gun, the giver and taker of America. He held it sideways and ran his hand from the very butt of the stock, over the comb, past the percussion action, along the forty-inch barrel with ramrod underneath, to the tip of the bayonet. It seemed so rudimentary and beautiful now, the same way the soldiers and the generals seem when you look at the gone-to-yellow daguerreotypes. When he closed his eyes, he was with them; they were not of a different world. They were of this world, but they were long gone. In that small difference everything lay. They were not as foreign as they seemed, they were just here long ago. Before we knew the things we know now because of what they went through.

He was semiconscious. It was the flip side of magic hour, the time between day and night when the movie directors say they get the best light. Scenes filmed in that light crackle with life. He peeked with one eye at the television at the foot at the bed and saw his reflection in the flat screen. He had not surrendered to the idea that he couldn't sleep, so he put his head back on the pillow.

He knew the time between night and morning had a magic hour as well. Night or day, he knew what the directors were talking about. He thought of the films he loved, of British Olympians sprinting along the beach, of gangsters stopping to buy oranges. He wondered if they'd been shot at night or in the morning. It didn't matter to him. Not as someone caught up in the narrative flow of a story: a viewer, a filmgoer. Or did it matter? Would it cheapen things if you learned that a romantic scene set in the early evening was filmed at five in the morning? He could lie around like this for hours, mind half-alive, somewhere between sleep and consciousness, thinking about fact and fiction.

He opened his eyes. The master bedroom with just him in it. The girls were gone. He looked out the glass doors to his left, to the east, a vast yard—rare in Malibu to have such a yard—surrounded by a canyon creating a rocky amphitheater around the property. It was dry here, even with the beach less than a mile away. He rubbed his forehead and then felt his beard, two months old and thick.

Reynolds found the remote, and the TV came to life. His reflection was overpowered by high-definition graphics. He had entered one of the Lifestyle channel's six-minute commercial breaks. He squinted. The commercial that was on had a rendering of a male human torso depicted in profile against a graph with the torso's spine along the x axis. The torso turned slowly to face the viewer as the narrator said, "Do you suffer from abdominal fat?" With that, the stomach grew in the same slow steady pace at which the polar ice cap melts over the earth in films warning of global warming, resulting in a neck-down, waist-up view of a pre-cardiac-arrest man. A quick graphic of the lifetime evolution of Boris Yeltsin's body.

He walked past the entrance to his wife Stella's bathroom to his own, smaller bathroom in the back. He looked in the mirror at his own abdomen and saw the resemblance. He stared at his image, as he did every day. He didn't like waking up any more than sleeping. He had learned to accept this state as well, but some days were worse than others, and with the insomnia this figured to be a bad day. He looked at the bags under his eyes. He surveyed the beard. It was beginning to resemble a patchy coat. Most of his attempts at facial hair had been harebrained schemes, and this one was looking to be more of the same. He tried to decide if it was different this time, whether he could grow it beyond the comfort zone of a well-insured man. He heard lyrics.

Come out West.

It was from a Lucinda Williams song he couldn't get out of his head, and like many songs, it was having an effect on him long after the last time he'd heard it. He had come west almost without thinking about it. And he had stayed. And here he was. Twenty-five years gone by, a small fortune made, a family built. A wife for his best friend, many good people in his life, a daughter for whom his devotion towered.

It was Friday. Bella was off with her friend Heather, and Stella was on an overnight set visit in Vancouver. They were both coming home today. They expected him to be on a golf weekend in the desert. It was all going as he'd planned. He just didn't know whether he had the balls to do it. His mind clouded again, before he snapped into purpose.

He headed to the garage. It was overflowing with the necessities of their Malibu life: luggage, beach chairs, surfboards, a horseback-riding helmet, boogie boards, old golf clubs, a croquet set, lacrosse sticks, a softball helmet with a face mask—he could never get used to the softball mask. He mounted a stepladder and reached to the back of the upper shelf and pulled out the hidden long black case. He sat cross-legged on the garage floor to open the bag, removed its contents, and stood up. The first thing that someone watching surveillance video would notice would be the rifle's length. Standing on its end in front of him it reached his chin. It smelled like high school metal shop. Next, he fixed the bayonet. Reynolds knew a lot about this gun. It weighed nine pounds, and the most expert riflemen could reload and fire it three times in a minute. More than seven hundred thousand had been made at a time before there were paved roads, electricity, or light bulbs. The gun was real, not a cheap facsimile made for folks who didn't have the money to get a real one. He had chased it for six months until a collector in Seattle had agreed to sell it. The man was in his seventies, and he said it had been his father's. They had both kept it locked up except for an annual firing and cleaning.

And now it was here in his garage in Malibu. The genuine article. A killing stick. He had no way of knowing where it had been, what action it had seen, but he could tell it was real. He'd seen enough of the rifles to know by the age of the wood, the imperfections of the trigger, the wear on the grooves of the barrel. He detached the bayonet and set it in the case, followed by the rifle. He popped the trunk of his Mercedes and put the long case in.

Next came the wardrobe bag and a small suitcase on rollers. Both were innocuous; it looked like the luggage any middle-aged man would take on a weekend trip with the boys. Inside, though, was the most authentic reproduction of a Union general's uniform money and Internet searches could yield. Quietly over the past year, he had been acquiring the elements, mainly through eBay, a few from vintage-clothing sites, businesses operated by interested-in-history types. He'd found First Corps tunic and trousers from a buff in Maine, a cap sold on a site based in Murfreesboro, Tennessee. The perfect riding boots, which he spit polished when no one was home, that he'd overpaid for on an eBay auction.

Inside the house, the phone rang. They still had a landline. Four extensions in total: one each for Stella, Reynolds, Bella, and the housekeeper.

"Hi." It was Stella.

"Hi," he said.

"How are you? Did you watch?"

"The Globes? I did. I turned it off."

"Who thinks that English guy is funny?" Stella said. "Why do they do that?"

It was January, and January was the worst of times in Hollywood: awards season.

"He's horrible." The Golden Globes had been on this past Sunday, and they had recorded it on DVR.

"I know. Why do I hate it so much?" she said.

"Horrible people in a fake world making the rest of the world feel excluded," he said.

"Yeah."

"And we're not there because we are too old to be relevant anymore?"

She laughed. "OK, you've made me feel better."

"When are you getting back?" he said.

"Leaving in an hour. Are you coming home first or driving straight from the office?"

"From there. We can play nine if we get there by four thirty."

"OK. I talked to Bella. I'll take them somewhere for dinner."

"Did they have fun?"

"They were in Rosarito," Stella said. "What do you think?"

"OK," he said. "I'm cringing and hanging up."

He put a robe on and walked to the front gate to get the papers. The delivery kid, or guy—whoever it was that threw newspapers out of a truck at five thirty in the morning—always tossed the papers same way. They lay right outside the gate at the base of the containing wall that circled the property. The kid must throw them hard and fast, he thought, because they hit the wall and go straight down to the ground. They were always right at the foot of the gate, at the base of the wall, as though placed there, like pitched pennies.

He was a fat guy in the morning, like Tony Soprano. He looked the papers over as he made coffee. He took in the front page of the *New York Times*, noting the president's shifting position on clean air and a subcommittee vote on net neutrality. More chaos in Syria. He followed with a story about Connecticut quadruplets admitted by Yale, then skimmed the op-eds, weary though he was of the daily drumbeat of the *Times* columnists. The *LA Times* was next: with nothing but a casual look at its front page, he moved on to its business section, which covered Hollywood.

It was a lifelong instinct, this immediate and urgent desire, once he got lucid, to start consuming information. This was the influence of his father, who taught English and read three papers in the morning. Unlike most academics, his father was not into politics or finding news that fed self-righteous anger or kooky theories *about* politics. His dad read the papers for real estate prices, stock prices, local tax breaks, government auctions, foreclosure sales, and sways in the value of the dollar. He always had a new get-rich-quick strategy that would rocket the family beyond the limits of an English professor's salary.

They had lived in Gettysburg, Pennsylvania, the site of the great battlefield of the Civil War. Their house was right next to the battlefield. Everything in Gettysburg was right next to the battlefield. It dominated life there the way chocolate owned the town of Hershey or the Johnstown Flood dominated Johnstown. His mother was a graduate student when she met his father, Robert Reynolds, then a young professor. Both were single and in their twenties, so the affair was scandal-free. They became the much-loved husband-and-wife team of the Gettysburg College English Department. His dad was the big gun, teaching the survey course, 101, covering Shakespeare to Steinbeck. His mom tended to Jane Austen and ran the Film Club.

English at Gettysburg College was like baseball at Ohio State: not what people came for. While giants in the field of American History came to the school for its proximity to the grounds and sense of place, for the possibility of finding a minié ball with every turning of soil, whether from plowing or touch football. Literature was off to the side, what the devastated turned to. His dad was a gifted teacher, preparing for lectures as if they were Broadway performances, practicing well into the night, his stage voice rumbling from the attic. But his wife and son suffered as Robert blew money on one idea after another, often forcing them to put their plans for the summer or the semester break in abeyance to support him, like vassals to the king.

The summer when he was fourteen, his dad had the idea to purchase a Dairy Queen franchise on Hagerstown Road. Robert depleted their savings account to the tune of ten thousand dollars and used it to buy the exclusive right to sell Dilly Bars in Gettysburg County. When Reynolds expressed his doubts to his mother, she said, "C'mon, it'll be fun." The small building was next to the

Little Dutch Family Inn, an eighteen-room motel fronted by a big neon windmill. The *[No] Vacancy* sign was in a jarring red that stood out more as the night came, while the painted figures of the little Dutch boy and girl holding wooden buckets in green grass disappeared.

Now, in Malibu, he shook his head, thinking about how his mother had washed the pots and blenders and ice-cream machine components every night after closing. She would drive Reynolds out to open around two, then returned home or to her office to grade papers for her summer-session courses. Business was completely drive-through, and he started each day with change for a twenty—a ten, two fives and a one—in the register. He read novels and waited for customers, worrying both about the lack of customers and his lack of change.

He got hungry after an hour or so from boredom. All packaging for the hot food had the trademark *Brazier* emblazoned on it—one of the weirdnesses of the Dairy Queen milieu Reynolds never understood. The brochure from HQ said that DQs served only "Fine Brazier Foods." Neither his father nor his mother could explain how Brazier fit into the Dairy Queen picture. He spent hours wondering how it worked, whether Brazier was part of the Dairy Queen family. For that matter, he wondered whether the Gettysburg-Hagerstown franchise and, ultimately, his family—Drs. Robert and Susan Stanhope and son, Reynolds—were themselves members of the Dairy Queen family, *when it came right down to it*.

He loved popping Brazier frozen hamburger patties into the mini-oven. His dad hadn't bought the standard grill that DQ franchise rules called for, which made Reynolds nervous. The rolls came in plastic bags with a slice of cheese inside, which you weren't supposed to open before heating. When the timer went off, he took the meat patty and the plastic-wrapped bun out with metal DQ tongs. He tore the plastic open, doused each side of the bun with ketchup from one of the squeeze bottles his mother made him wash out and refill each day, separated the melted cheese from the wrapper, and put the whole combination together. The burger roll browned a bit at the corners and its sesame seeds toasted when he did it just right. He closed the sliding-screen service window, put his feet up, and watched the cars drift by, knowing in his gut they wouldn't stop and worrying, there in the shadow of the windmill, that his father's Don Quixote syndrome would doom them all. To make matters worse, he was eating up any pitiful profits, one frozen Brazier cheeseburger at time.

Robert arrived at five each day to check in on things. He asked about business and fretted when Reynolds showed him how little there had been. "What is wrong with these people? They're Americans for Christ's sake. And they're tourists. *And it's hot outside.* Why wouldn't you stop for ice cream?" Around six the old man would calm down and sit behind a desk in the back corner, away from the service window where Reynolds waited for customers. Robert would go through the inventory ordering forms provided by Dairy Queen corporate and make sure they were supplied with soft-serve mixture and cups and straws and strawberry topping. He brought Whitman or Wordsworth or some other dusty book with him. They had a transistor radio, and as the sun went down they listened to the Phillies game. Like a valve loosening, Reynolds felt his dad drift away as the dinner hour passed, free verse and sonnets sweeping him away.

Susan Stanhope would arrive at seven-thirty, with dinner in a Crock-Pot, or sandwiches, or salads or other foodstuffs in Tupperware containers. "Comin' in with Fine Brazier Foods," she said, to try to cheer his father up, and most days it worked. They were corny like that. On her birthday that summer, his dad wrote on her card, "To my once and forever Dairy Queen." Post-cheeseburger, Reynolds wasn't hungry. So his parents ate together at the little desk amid the invoices and bills, laughing about faculty gossip, while Reynolds manned the window by the windmill, on the look-out for an army that never came.

From that summer on, Reynolds spent his free time reading books. He was interested in everything. He read nonfiction for fun, eating up biographies and business and sports books in one or two sittings. But his main passion was fiction—it went back to his days as a kid. He loved the Pennsylvania authors, especially John O'Hara and Updike. He read about the lives of all the writers, and worried that he liked their life stories as much, even more than, their fiction.

Stella and Bella knew Reynolds's true nature was artistic. Norman knew it too. But to everyone else he was a lawyer—Norman's law-yer. And he was an excellent lawyer. Deep down, he had always felt that practicing law was a temporary thing, a stopover he was making to earn some money until he moved on to something else more to his liking. Lawyering was not in his heart. But this had a different effect than he thought it would. He found he was a very good negotiator and, because he was more aggressive than the opposing side, more willing to walk away. He was not attached, not worried all the time, not scared—after all, this was not what he wanted to do. In spite of all the screaming and bravado that went on between Hollywood lawyers, the real secret was indifference.

Reynolds made a lot of money and changed jobs, and in that new job he made a crazy amount of money. The same happened to Stella—who went from assistant to producer and landed a giant production deal at Paramount, where she produced a spy picture with Brad Pitt that was now shooting the third sequel. Reynolds and Stella had become very rich from their combined success, and for twenty years now when he talked to the accountants to ask if he could afford one scheme or another, the answer was yes, and he thought of his father. It made him well up, and soon he was crying.

Reynolds thought of his dad's morning papers, which Reynolds picked up when Robert was done. When he was a boy, his father read the Gettysburg paper, the *Pottstown Gazette*, and the *Philadelphia Inquirer*. On Sundays his father would bring home the *Philadelphia Inquirer* with a dozen Dunkin' Donuts. Reynolds read about Nixon and Watergate, about fights in the Philadelphia City Council, about Abscam. He knew everything about sports, from the NBA to Penn State football to the Gettysburg College varsity lacrosse standings. He read movie reviews and book reviews and comics. He could tell you the names of the little kids in *Family Circus* and the college kids in *Doonesbury*.

There was nothing new in this morning's papers, just gradations of newness, this not being one of the days when a few actual new things happen, a fresh story line that, depending on the force of the wave, spawned days, weeks, or months of further stories. He sat at the French farm table and picked at a bran muffin, the kind of sawdust food the girls ate for breakfast. He became wistful. I am, he thought, a sneered-at character from a book: a well-insured man standing by an SUV, dropping my kid off at a college on the hill. As you look at that long line of other people dropping their kids off, you don't think that they have stories, are interesting, have had life happen to them. They are just blank, boring faces. But the truth is you are the same, just like anyone else in the line. What about that? Turn around, and you're not that man who has done things. Turn around and look up, and you're an insured man with secrets and regrets.

Reynolds walked outside and surveyed the Astroturf putting green in his backyard, situated where the Santa Monica Mountains stop just short of the beach in southern Malibu. The putting green was the size of a volleyball court. Reynolds placed ten balls in a circle, ten yards in diameter around the pin.

"Chambersburg," Reynolds said. He brought the club head to a backswing and hit though the ball with a click. Without waiting for the result, he moved to the right and set up over the next, "Emmitsburg." Click. Move, set up. "Baltimore Pike." Click. "Taneytown." He pronounced it the correct way: "Taw-ney Town." Next came Biglerville, then York. He holed it at Hanover. Table Rock. Hagerstown. Click, click, click. A circle of routes leading to the goal. He looked at his phone.

"Get up fat boy," It was a text from Jim Mulligan, his neighbor.

Reynolds thumbed a response. "I'm up. Where U?"

"Coming over in five."

Reynolds set his circle of putts again and was beginning when a voice called to him. "To be a truly bad golfer you have to be a truly bad putter." It was Mulligan, who appeared with two paper cups of coffee, the green of the label matching the green of the grass. Mulligan did not use cardboard hand protectors.

"Shut up. I'm concentrating," Reynolds said.

Mulligan watched and then rendered a verdict. "It could be worse."

"I'm done. Let's go in."

Mulligan wore professional-caliber sports gear: a San Diego Chargers rain-resistant poncho and mesh running shorts with a pair of those nylon leggings that look like tights that athletes and amateurs who think they are athletes wear to work out. He moved with the tanned energy of someone predetermined by good genes to be slim and in shape.

"What happened to you?" Mulligan said, as he took the lid off.

"What?"

"You were supposed to meet me. To run."

"What?"

"Yes. We said it Tuesday."

"Shit. Sorry."

"What's with that beard?"

"Trying something new. Sorry, I was up on Tuesday and everything," Reynolds said.

"Don't worry about it. I knew you'd forget." Mulligan looked around. "No girls?"

"Stella went away for the night, and Bella is coming back from Mexico." Reynolds headed to the kitchen. "What do you want to eat? We have these awful fucking muffins."

"Just some water."

Reynolds returned and handed him a glass. He gestured at Mulligan's legs. "Really, man? With the yoga pants and everything?"

"Shut up," Mulligan said. He worked the remote until ESPN's college football coverage came on. "I'm watching the Washington game later." Mulligan oriented his outlook on sports, and to a certain extent on life, in relation to UCLA football. The world divided into camps. Either you were for UCLA or you weren't. Mulligan was born in Connecticut and had been a monster linebacker and fullback at high school near Hartford. After college at UCLA, he blew through business school at Stanford before returning to LA, where he became an investment banker at the time when junk bonds and leveraged buyouts were making investment bankers lots of money and Beverly Hills was part show biz, part West Coast, and part Wall Street. Mulligan put together banking deals between banks, as far as Reynolds understood it.

Reynolds loved Mulligan. When Reynolds and Stella and five-year-old Bella had moved to the neighborhood, they'd felt the usual isolation from their neighbors. Reynolds had struggled enough with the oppression of Hollywood types when they'd lived in Brentwood, and when they'd moved here, to Madera, the horsey and secluded estate-filled canyon tucked just east of Surfrider Beach, he'd realized they could be in for more of the same. There were five houses on their road; two were occupied by movie stars and two by directors of special-effects-driven event pictures. Mulligan and Lucy lived a half mile away with their twin girls, who were the same age as Bella. The girls became close and the parents followed course, and before long the two families were very close, enjoying a constant flow of communication and no-permission-necessary sleepovers.

Reynolds and Mulligan became friends because of, rather than despite, the lack of business intersection. After years of obsessing about everything and everyone in Hollywood—the comings and goings of studio executives, the latest firings of talent agents by actors, how "unwatchable" or "unreleasable" a new movie was—Reynolds found talking to Mulligan as fun and relaxing as taking a Xanax. Mulligan and Lucy were removed from Hollywood, lived a different life, and had different politics and social circle. They belonged to the LA Country Club, which was so Waspy that no one from Hollywood was even allowed to apply. That said it all.

Reynolds looked at Mulligan's football outfit again. "Um . . . Jim . . . the UCLA-Washington game was in November. It's January."

"So what," Mulligan said, "it's a recording but I watch it like it's live. Come over and watch with me. Lucy and the girls are gone for the weekend."

"Nah, thanks. I got to go do something."

Mulligan studied him. "Like what? What do you have to do that's more important than watching football with me?"

Reynolds did not want to repeat the phony golf trip story to Mulligan. "Just a thing I got to go do."

"What, like a kid thing?"

"Sort of. Well, not really."

Reynolds thought about how the two men existed within a zone of familiarity that in Los Angeles can be shared only by guys who have played—really played—contact sports at a major level. There was an exclusivity to the way they could deal with each other that in previous eras was shared by men who had been in the service and fought together. Though Mulligan had more of the kill-or-be-killed banker's personality and Reynolds was more easygoing, they both knew the other could take a hit. And this knowledge manifested in respect, and that respect led to true friendship.

"What are you up to?" Mulligan said, not satisfied with what he'd heard.

After months of secrecy, Reynolds decided to open up. "Let me show you something," he said. He grabbed his iPad, typed in a few words, and found a YouTube video. Holding it where Mulligan could see, he hit *Play*. The chords of "The Battle Hymn of the Republic" started to play over a shot of an old American flag, the kind with many fewer stars, blowing in the wind. Then it cut to a title card: *The Battle of Gettysburg, Enchino California.*

Mulligan didn't say anything as he watched the six-minute video of guys with heavy beards dressed up as soldiers fighting back and forth. Interspersed were still shots of these impersonators around campfires, in bleached white tents, drinking from tin cups, and shooting rifles.

When the video ended, Mulligan stared at Reynolds. "Jesus," he said.

Reynolds smiled back at him, a little too eager.

After a moment, Mulligan said, "Wait. You're not . . ."

Reynolds nodded, smiling. "Yup," he said.

Mulligan started to get up from his chair. "You're going to *do* it? Like . . . be *in* it?"

"It'll be kind of fun. It'll be funny."

"You're signing up for it?"

"I've *signed* up for it," Reynolds said.

"In Enchino?" Mulligan said.

"This weekend. Starts today."

"You drive out there?"

"Yup.

Mulligan paused, ducked his head and rubbed his hair with both hands, and then stepped in close and looked at his friend. "Reynolds," he said, "Let me be very straightforward with you." His hands were now clasped in front of him as though in prayer. "No fucking way in hell, you fucking jackass."

"Oh, c'mon."

"Look, I know you're from back around there somewhere . . ."

"I'm from *there*, literally." Reynolds said. "Gettysburg. You know. My name? Remember? John Reynolds."

"Who's John Reynolds?" Mulligan said.

"*Me*. My name, remember? It's the guy I'm named after."

"Right, right. Sorry. The soldier?"

"He was a general."

"Right. Was he, what, your ancestor?"

"No, butthead, I'm just *named* after him—my dad just liked him. He was very cool." Reynolds could see Mulligan was struggling. "He was shot at Gettysburg. I was thinking, you know, that I could, I don't know, that I can honor him."

Mulligan did not seem to be getting any more sympathetic.

"Look," Reynolds said, "I know it's, like, not exact. The event takes place out here, for one thing, in California and not in Pennsylvania."

"No, Reynolds, it's not exact."

Reynolds looked away. "I don't know. It's where I'm from, you know?"

"No man, I don't know," Mulligan said. He waited for Reynolds to bring his eyes back to him. "From there, whatever. Doesn't matter. You have to understand something. We—you and me—we are normal people. We have normal families. We play golf, watch sports, lease foreign cars. This thing you're talking about, this is *weird*. Not our kind of weird. Our kind of weird is being left-handed, or rooting for the Bengals, or some shit. This, this Civil War reenactment kind of thing is for serious nuts. Whatever is going on with you, you have to stifle these thoughts, and whatever you do, don't vocalize anything. Tell *me*, fine. But don't fucking repeat this. Have you told anyone else?"

"No."

"Thank God. Because given your background, people will pigeonhole you with lightning speed as nothing more than one of these bearded kooks. They'll say, 'Oh yeah, Reynolds, he grew up with that kind of thing. He's like an avid reenactor. I've heard he flies around the country doing it.' Next thing you know, it's all over. You have a lifetime tattoo on your neck just below your jaw that says 'For the Union' or something. Is that what you want for your family?"

"You don't want to go, then? I know it's kind of last minute, but I thought maybe . . ."

"No, I don't want to go." Mulligan stood up and made like an umpire calling safe. "No one is going to go. Not you, not me. Get it out of your head."

Reynolds broke into a smile, like he had been joking. "All right, relax."

Mulligan smiled back. "Say it, dickhead. Promise me."

"OK, whatever. I promise."

"All right. Let's go out back and putt."

They walked through the kitchen, where Mulligan picked up one of the muffins and took a bite. "Jesus Christ," he said, throwing it into the trash can. "Really, Reynolds. You're a grown damn man. How are you going to get control of your life if you can't get control of your own breakfast?"

Once outside, Mulligan asked, "How's business?"

"You know," said Reynolds. "There's show, and there's business."

Mulligan picked up Reynolds's putter from the grass and took his stance over an eight-footer. "Hey, how's that *Gargantor*? I kind of want to see it."

"I heard it's unwatchable," Reynolds said.

Mulligan snorted. "Such a fucking snob."

"Hey, who's your insurance guy?" Reynolds asked.

Mulligan kept putting. "For what?"

"I don't know. Life."

"Life insurance?"

"Sure."

"You don't have life insurance?"

"Of course I have life insurance. But I read that you can do it like an investment."

Mulligan looked up. "Who's selling you life insurance policies as an investment? Tell me you didn't do that."

"I didn't do anything. I just want to know who your guy is."

Mulligan handed him his putter. "OK, big boy. I got to go get ready for the game."

"It's in two hours," Reynolds said. "What do you do, get into a uniform? Put a helmet on when the game starts?"

"Funny," Mulligan said, not smiling. "I'll send you my insurance guy's name."

He jogged across the lawn, thumbs by his waist and up, just like a wide receiver, and was gone. Reynolds, alone now on the turf, in shorts and sandals, lined three golf balls up on the turf and tried to focus. Golf was just about being consistent. Stroke it the same each time. He had a perverse relationship with consistency. He wanted to wake up every day in a different place, but he hated flying. He wanted variety, yet as he aged he found himself preferring a morning routine: newspapers, coffee, information gathering. He had a dream job, but he wanted to quit. His phone buzzed.

It was Mulligan. "Are you OK?"

"Yeah, why?" said Reynolds.

"I don't know, you're fucking buying life insurance, talking about Civil War impersonations, acting crazy in general. What's this all about?"

"Nothing. It's Civil War *reenactments*. The people are *reenactors*."

"Glad that we've got that straight," said Mulligan.

"Let me ask you something. Do you remember the name of the first Playmate you loved? I mean, like *really* loved?"

"Wow, you're completely insane today."

"Just answer. Don't think."

"Patty McGuire. August seventy-seven."

"Ooh, good one," said Reynolds. "She married McEnroe or something."

"Jimmy Connors."

"Right. OK. You answered my question. What time is your game? Maybe I can get there."

"It's at one sharp. I wish you would come. You're squirrelly."

"All right. Later."

With Mulligan off the line, Reynolds put the golf balls in his pocket and looked around. He was a well-insured fat man putting outside his mansion. The house was beautiful. It was a single-story Mediterranean with a red-tile roof and two ancient oak trees in the yard. A two-bedroom guesthouse with lounge chairs covered in terry cloth sat on the side. He walked toward the pool, thinking of a swim. But he needed to get ready: he had breakfast with Norman at ten thirty. He saw a copy of *Vogue* on one of the poolside recliners. On the cover was a dark-haired beauty with a red hat and black-mesh veil, looking like Audrey Hepburn crossed with one of those French actresses with multiple names that ran together who seemed to erupt into stardom every few years. The kind of ageless, unattainable woman who would reemerge later, now Reynolds's age, doing art films with the New Wave directors who were still around, married to the president of France or to one of those dashing, uncompromising writers living on the Left Bank in a fabulous, rambling apartment full of books.

He went inside to dress.

CHAPTER 2

Breakfast with Norman

The hardest thing for Reynolds about moving to LA was that there was nowhere to arrive. LA has no center you can touch. New York has Times Square; London has Piccadilly, and so forth. All cities have hearts, except LA. It has areas: Beverly Hills, Hollywood, Santa Monica, Downtown, West Hollywood, Los Feliz, South Central, and on and on. There is no focal point. It evolved into this—it was not always this way—Reynolds knew. It was a sad truth of history, the way the center had not held. In Nathanael West's time there had been a central location—call it Hollywood and Vine—where people coming to California got off the bus to try their luck before dying. But now, there is not one place the pioneering youngster, the starlet, the Sooner from the Dust Bowl, or anyone, can drop their bags and say, "I'm here."

During the summer, hundreds of tourists and local day-trippers realize the same thing about Malibu. They come looking to touch something, but there's no fulcrum, no main location, no heart. Like LA itself, Malibu is spread out. Reynolds remembered traveling to upstate New York as a kid with his parents. His mother said they were going to the North Pole, and after a day in the car, they'd arrived in North Pole, New York, just outside Niagara. Satisfying the East Coasters' innate sense of destination, in the dead center of town was positioned an actual fake North Pole. It was a fine, icy cylinder about eight feet high. It looked like the goddamn North Pole *should* look. When you set out for something, Reynolds thought, you should be able to find it when you get there.

He considered Malibu to be a miniature Chile, a skinny strip of land running north–south along the coast. All visitors heading north on the Pacific Coast Highway are informed of the length of its shoreline by a sign that says, "Malibu: 27 Miles of Scenic Beauty." It was in truth a set of beaches strung together like a series of links golf courses: Topanga, La Costa, Carbon, Surf Rider, Colony, Puerco Canyon, Ramirez, Paradise Cove, Queen's Necklace, Zuma, Broad.

Reynolds got dressed and turned everything in the house off—the coffeepots, lights, computers, printers, iPads—he had an obsession with turning everything off. He did not like leaving a house with anything running, because he couldn't relax once he left thinking there were still things buzzing while he was away. He got caught up in that a lot, that kind of thing. Or with thoughts about Bella's life compared to his—how the movie of her experience would be so different, how the camera inside her head would play back a different tape than his. Only now in life was it dawning on him that the camera in his mind was not recording the world's sole experience. There were millions of movies, TV shows, talk shows—all manner of entertainments—going on. Each one had a different narrator, a different style, a different language, diction, idiom. Different tones, different casts.

The PCH paralleled the beaches and had intermittent commercially zoned stretches with motels and restaurants and gas stations. The few centers to speak of were shopping centers. Land-side Malibu life was conducted in a few upscale strip malls closer in, meaning closer to Santa Monica and Westside. Retail shops, restaurants, bookstores, and banks. Each had a Starbucks and a Coffee Bean. (The place was well-caffeinated.) Locals avoided tourists as they do in any beach town, making a few dressed-down places hip until they became classics.

He went into Joey's Restaurant and saw Norman sitting with a newspaper at their table in the corner.

"What happened to you?" Norman said.

"Sorry," said Reynolds. He looked at his watch. "I'm, like, five minutes late. How long have you been here?"

"Not too long. I started my walk a little early today. I didn't realize it. She was making me crazy. Whaddya want? I'm starving." He looked at the waiter, standing a few tables away. "Luis, get your ass over here. We're ready."

The woman at the table next to them looked startled. Luis laughed to let her know it was OK. "Sixteen years he's been yelling like this," Luis said. Then he continued to their table. He nodded at Reynolds with a smile. "Hey, man."

"Hey, Luis."

Luis looked at Norman. "Why don't you stick to baseball?" he said.

Norman closed his eyes. "Shit. What was the score?"

"Two–one."

"Son of a bitch," Norman said and reached into his pocket and pulled out a wad of bills held together by a rubber band. He peeled off two hundreds. "Here," he said.

Luis pocketed the money, looked at Reynolds. "What can I do? Tell him to stop betting *fútbol*."

"Fucking Barcelona," Norman said.

Luis said to Reynolds, "What you are having today, *chico*?"

"Egg whites, turkey bacon, no potatoes."

Luis looked at Norman. "*Jefe?*"

"Same. But give me tomatoes." He held the menu back when Luis tried to take it. "Who's back there today? Manny?"

"No. Tomás."

"OK, he's the one. Tell him, *from me*, that tomatoes are supposed to be red—not yellow."

"OK, OK."

"No yellow in the center. You got it?"

Luis said, "I got it, I got it. Stay calm, man. You going to have a heart attack. Then I got no one to bet with." He sped away from Norman, who had reached out to grab him.

Reynolds looked at Norman and said, "You bet on soccer now?"

"I watch it on Sundays sometimes—in the mornings. The Russian guy up the beach likes to bet on it. I take money off him all the time." He blew into his coffee. "But these guys," he gestured at Luis, who was now at the coffee stand with a few of the other waiters, "they're at another level."

Reynolds chuckled at him. Even with all the passage of time, whenever Reynolds sat with Norman he was surprised at how big he was. By all rights he should have been a little guy—what one would expect from a seventy-five-year-old comedy writer. But sitting next to him, one was taken over by Norman Daley. He was big and handsome and funny and charming, a cross between Leonard Bernstein and Ted Williams. But today, Reynolds noticed, Norman had a black eye. A deep purple darkened the lid on his left side.

"You look terrible, what's the matter?" Norman said.

"Me? Nothing," Reynolds said. "I was going to say the same thing to you. What's that?" He pointed at Norman's face. "You have a shiner."

"I was at the kidney doctor yesterday."

"Did he punch you in the eye?" Norman, who didn't laugh easily, chuckled, much in the same way Reynolds had chuckled at him moments ago. Now Reynolds smiled and said, "What's the deal? Are you OK?"

"Fine. Forget it. And don't change the subject. Why do you look so tired?"

"Dunno," Reynolds said. "I slept fine."

"Don't bullshit me," Norman said. "Look, happens all the time. It took a lot of courage, what you did."

"You're crazy," Reynolds said, waving his hand. "I have too much other shit on my mind."

"Yeah, well, let me tell you something, put your mind at ease. It doesn't matter. All that matters is that you keep going. If it had been picked up, if you were warming up for a full order with a good time slot, it wouldn't matter." Norman was talking about Reynolds's pilot that had just been rejected by A&E.

"Ah, I know," Reynolds said. "I mean, I don't *know* know, you know that. But I know."

"Look," Norman said. "It *was* a pilot about sleep. Sleep's a hard sell."

Reynolds never once thought it was a bad idea. And other than two braindead executives at Lion's Gate, everyone he pitched it to—including Stella and Norman—got behind it. It was a tailor-made hour for cable, maybe HBO, even for network if it turned out right. What was more common, more universal, or more pressing than sleep? Everyone had trouble sleeping, but it was unexplored on television. A well-made program that explored selected individuals' sleep issues could work in the warm void of television—pure, relaxed, and distracting voyeurism.

He also believed it could be *his* thing. A form of the medium that would allow him to get out from under the life-sustaining but identity-squelching influence of Norman. It would not be a narrative—not a procedural. Unscripted. Not serial. A reality show, to use the overused term. *Sleep with Me*. It would be about ordinary people. Once established, later episodes and then full seasons, or even spin-offs, could focus on athletes, celebrities, chefs. The possibilities were endless. *A franchise*. That's what Ted Carlin from Comcast had said when Reynolds pitched it. With one show, Reynolds could escape the network scripted world he'd so nicely benefited from on Norman's coattails. But that bored him more each day. And quickly he was in the world of non-scripted cable, which he was convinced was more creative, the place where the real energy of the business was. And as he had learned so well from Norman, any producer could leverage a hit—a *sleeper*, no less—into a classy scripted series. His own *Sopranos* or *Band of Brothers*. His own *Game of Thrones*. After years behind the scenes, he could come into his own. It had happened before for plenty of people.

The show had lain down in front of him from the moment he first thought about it. A subject—a person—would be selected each week, someone who had some kind of sleep problem. The first fifteen-minute segment would be documentary-style, giving the audience the basic information: who, what, where, why. Basic setup interview intercut with on-location pickups of family life, daily pressures, discussion of habits and attitudes toward sleep. The segment would wrap up with one of the show's four rotating sleep doctors. (The network would like this idea because it meant the show would not become contingent on any one individual doctor's personality, thereby avoiding a renegotiation headache. This was an example of the added value of an experienced entertainment lawyer.)

The doctor would identify the problem, explain it, and tell the subject what he or she proposed to do to treat the condition. Then right to commercial.

After the jump, the focus would return to the subject, now prepping for bed. The crew would spend several nights with the subject, so the subject never would know which night was being used in the show. (In fact, footage from all the nights could be intercut.) Presleep habits—TV watching, game playing, putting kids to bed, reading, interaction with spouse (even sex), listening to music, drinking, late night cigarette, masturbation, eating, telephone calls, texting, booty calls—it would all become normal after a while with the growing familiarity between the subject and the crew. Good stuff would be used for promos and teasers and so forth as the show took off.

Past the bottom break, the third segment would pick up with a recap of the story line and then get into night-vision hidden-camera footage of the subject sleeping. The edited cut would contain a combination of stop-motion, close-ups, and intermittent body measurements before, during, and after the night's sleep.

The final fifteen-minute segment would reunite the doctor with the patient, and they would discuss attacking the issue first with a change in habits. Then there would be a transcending moment when the subject talked about the benefits of more sleep. As more episodes rolled out, the producers would throw in a failure, a subject whose sleep doesn't change at all, to keep the audience guessing. Over time, the show would be spellbinding, addictive. Because, to Reynolds's mind, there was nothing out there like it. "Because," to use the promo line he'd come up with, "everyone needs sleep."

At the restaurant, after a pause, Norman said, "Listen, you'll recover." He stared at Reynolds a second more, possibly satisfied. "Did you watch the Golden Globes?"

"I looked at it last night," Reynolds said. "I turned it off."

"I know. Horrible. That guy is not funny. The British guy." Norman blew into his coffee again. "How's my college girl?"

"She's good," Reynolds said. "She's coming back from Mexico. Before she left she said she's sending you something to read."

"I know. I just got a text from her a little while ago."

"Then you've talked to her more than me," Reynolds said.

Having thought of the device, Norman put his glasses on to check his messages. He loved to catch the newest gadget whenever it came out. Norman told Reynolds, as if it were a secret, that staying in touch like this as you got older was the kind of the thing that kept you from getting Alzheimer's. "I'm waiting," he said.

"For what?" said Reynolds.

"Her Person," Norman said.

"Oh, that," Reynolds said. "Who is it?"

"Jackie Gleason. That'll be good for her."

"Probably right," said Reynolds, after a moment.

"You know, we're doing an experiment," Norman said. "I gave her Jackie a long time ago. It's the first time I've ever repeated. She doesn't know it, but I have the old one."

Norman had been giving Bella biographical writing assignments since she was eight, in a running flow. There were no fixed time schedules, and she loved to do them, without fail. He chose a subject, which Bella came to call her "Norman Person." When she was bored or grumpy, Stella would say, "Do your Norman Person."

Over the years, Norman had her cover everyone from Kermit the Frog to Tallulah Bankhead to Jack Paar. He suggested the approximate length of each report and gave her research hints. When Bella was nine, she made Reynolds dig out his *Encyclopedia Britannica* set, and she pored over it, making sure not to crib, because she knew that was wrong. Whenever an assignment was finished, Bella left Norman the report in his mailbox in the Colony, and that same weekend, without fail, Norman took her to breakfast. When Bella went to high school they changed their regimen to frozen yogurt or coffee, since she hated getting up in the morning, and they were both worried about their weight.

From what Reynolds could tell, when they met for the discussion, Norman didn't focus too much on the writing, though he complimented Bella, which was easy and appropriate, since she did a thorough and clever job. (Reynolds would find Bella's reports and read them with delight.) Norman talked about what the subject meant to him, where he put the Person in his map of the world. Norman started with a historical perspective, then, no matter the Person, brought it down to some personal anecdote or another. Then Norman quizzed Bella a bit, and she answered. Then the Person report discussion flowed into a general conversation about anything. It was, at center, a great pretext for their relationship. Sometimes they spoke about the Person for two hours and even on the phone later or via e-mail. Then again, sometimes they got right into whatever was going on in the very eventful mind of Bella G. Stanhope.

Bella grew up having a constant tutorial with Norman Daley, the preeminent television showrunner of the sixties and seventies, one of the country's most cherished filmmakers of the eighties and nineties, and, in these twilight Malibu years, author of glorious works of fiction. As Bella grew older, the conversations could get intense—for example, she didn't talk to him for a month after Norman said Che Guevara was a dope. The real point, of course, was that Norman, ever the strategist, knew it was a way of keeping in touch, of having regular contact with his surrogate granddaughter. The relationship was unusual, but it endured on both ends, and the way they kept it up made each of them—Norman, Bella, Reynolds, and Stella—happy.

"Did I ever tell you about him? Jackie?" said Norman.

"Yeah, maybe. Wait, I forget. Someone did. Must have been you. Didn't he take a party train to Florida or something like that?" said Reynolds.

"I was on it a few times. From Miami to the city and back. He was *the best*. Don't listen to what anyone says. He was the best to be with. Bar none. Drink all night, women, play music, poker. The whole works."

"God, you can't say that in front of Bella, you know. She'll call you a pig."

"Ah, don't worry about her. I got her under control." Norman looked at Reynolds. "You're fat. You're gonna drop dead one of these days. Why don't you call that guy I told you about? Niemeyer. The weight guy."

"OK, all right," Reynolds said. He needed to change the subject. "C'mon, we got to go over a few things today. I have to get back to Doug on the Universal thing."

Norman had heard about Niemeyer during his card game. Once a month, Norman had a gathering of his pals from the real old days—the NBC days. All those guys had to talk about anymore was doctors. One of them, it might have been Leon Bremmer—Reynolds couldn't remember—lost thirty pounds with this Niemeyer. Norman had met Leon in 1952 when they were both writing jokes for radio. It was around that time Norman had an idea for a new show and made an appointment with David Sarnoff. At the end of the meeting, Sarnoff had said to Norman, "I don't know about the pitch, but I like your balls."

Norman half-listened to Reynolds go through the business issue, which was a skill Norman had developed over forty years of dealing with the entertainment business. It wasn't Reynolds. Norman loved Reynolds. He had been Norman's lawyer and right hand for over twenty years, his Tom Hagen. Norman let Reynolds run everything. Everything that needed running, anyway. It worked on its own at this point—in truth, it had been working like this for fifteen years, at least. Monitoring the money coming in, approving reuses, renewing deals with syndicators, and all that garbage. The man was a full-time job.

Norman Daley was born in 1924 in the Bronx to an Irish family. After serving in the army's communications corps, he gained an honorable discharge in 1946 and, armed with a set of connections at NBC he gained during the war, he headed for the world of show biz. His big break came in the form of a gig as the gofer in the NBC building in Rockefeller Center, which had a slew of writers who went on to become an integral part of American culture for the next sixty years. Norman was funny and sharp, and the writers liked him because he always came up with just what was needed, whether it was for a radio serial or one of NBC's productions in the expanding world of television.

The show Norman created after his meeting with David Sarnoff back in 1952 was *Artie in the Army*. It ran for eight seasons, its life coinciding with the length of the Eisenhower administration. It was a vehicle for Bobby Bank, the beloved comedian who played Artie, the rascally unit commander who always found a way to outwit the Germans and the Army brass alike. Norman's strategy was to get the show on the air to Phil Silvers's audience, which all the networks desperately wanted to do, and to make it new by expanding the program's world in terms of both writing and conception as well as visually, in the scope and camerawork allowing more depth of field and more close-ups. As a result, *Artie* was the first comedy on TV to do outdoor shots. Bobby Bank joined George Burns and Milton Berle in the ranks of America's favorite funnymen. But it was Norman who supplied the genius of the show, finding the right blend of Bobby's Borscht Belt style and the high jinx of Artie's crew of enlisted men (mainly other writers who Norman stuck in front of the camera) in the burgeoning format of the half-hour comedy. Later (but way before *M*A*S*H*) Norman created heartwarming and heartbreaking endings as the soldiers were sent home or, in the cases of Sergeant Buddy Jaworski from Brooklyn (played by Sam Simpson) and Private Mel Harris from Memphis (played by Warren Berg), to unexpected deaths. By the end of the run, no other show in the short history of television had come close to accomplishing such emotional story arcs during one program.

Norman moved to LA when *Artie* finished and ensconced himself in the bursting television landscape. He began developing several shows at a time, realizing that volume would be the name of the game in the burgeoning business. By 1971, he had six programs on the air in prime time, on three of which he was the main writer. He kept offices at the studios at Sunset and Gower and had a group of writers from every program at his disposal. Not only did this make him a legend and a power within television circles at the time, it put him in a position to begin the careers of dozens of other creators, all of whom credited Norman with their start.

Norman remembered the first time he'd seen Reynolds. It was in the late eighties and Norman had been at his lawyer Irv Toffler's office in one of the new buildings in Century City. Irv was laying on so much bullshit about the expansive investments the networks were making—as an excuse for less money showing up in Norman's bank account—that it became too much. Norman noticed that Irv's young associate, Reynolds, couldn't keep his eyes open. Norman watched with amusement for the next twenty minutes as Reynolds tried to fight off sleep.

When the meeting was over, Norman had gone across the meeting room and, to Irv's shock, asked Reynolds to lunch. They went to Jimmy's, where Norman ordered a scotch. Reynolds did the same, and over the course of the next three hours, Norman had extracted from the young lawyer the ins and outs of Irv's shenanigans. Reynolds was amazed that Norman, who the other lawyers in Irv's office always figured was out to lunch on financial matters, knew the games Irv had been playing. But Norman was on to how the game worked: how the agents carved pieces out of broadcast license fees for themselves; how the agents teamed with the television studios—Lorimar, Warner Brothers TV, Universal—to fuck with the networks *and* their own clients by using two different financial models for each show, one that said the program would never make money, and one that showed the program would never stop making money; and how, through a blend of selling and fixing, lots and lots of money ended up in the wrong hands.

Norman was not unaware of the risks of financing and always appreciated the sunk costs and gambles that were taken by others. But nor would he be taken, and when his representatives were no longer representing him, when he was no longer the product but the stooge, he took action. At that lunch in Century City, Reynolds had balked at talking at first, but Norman had been overwhelming, alternately charming and tough. After learning about Reynolds's background, Norman had said, "You like the business, but you don't like the bullshit, right? You can't stand the way these fat cocksuckers go over to Universal or to Warners and cut up the shows and the airtimes and use the unions one way or another to get what they want, am I right? I'm sure this is confusing. It would confuse me. You like television, right? You watch the shows. You like going to the pictures too, I'm sure."

Reynolds had nodded like a prisoner hoping to join a jailbreak. And at that instant, Norman knew he had his guy. Norman had known for years he was getting fucked. He had turned things over in his head for months and finally come out with a plan, and when he saw Reynolds in the meeting, he'd seen his opportunity. Norman knew all he needed was an honest, smart, and ballsy young lawyer who couldn't be controlled by the agents of the studios. He needed such a guy to help him take it all back.

Norman had spoken of his plans with Fred MacMurray, with whom he liked to talk business because no one worked those guys over better than Fred. Bobby Bank had played in a golf game at Riviera with Fred years ago, and Fred had told Bobby he'd like to meet Norman, that he was a fan. Norman made a friend out of Fred, and at the time he met Reynolds, Norman was still going up to Fred's ranch to see him a few times a year. Fred had more money than anyone and had done it by keeping his distance and buying real estate. William Demarest, who had played Uncle Charley in Fred's late-career vehicle *My Three Sons*, said Fred brought hard-boiled eggs in a brown paper bag for lunch. Fred would still be eating dyed Easter eggs two weeks after Easter. Fred had told Norman what to do. Find your guy and go get the bastards. At lunch in Century City, with Reynolds in his sights, Norman decided to unleash his plan.

"Look," he said to Reynolds, "I'm going to fire Irv Toffler when I leave here—that's a given. The question is, what you are going to do? So, spill. Tell me something I don't know."

And so, for the next two hours, Reynolds confirmed to Norman the specifics of Irv's mishandled and shady dealings. In fact, the kid made Norman realize that not only were his fears well founded, he had not been suspicious enough. From *Artie* through *John Iron* and *Crenshaw Ten*, Norman had written more than four hundred television episodes. And while he now had more money than he once thought existed in aggregated world currency, Norman realized that the suits had just been keeping him happy, giving him just enough not to raise his suspicions. But the agents and lawyers and other older men in whom he had put his trust were slowing down, and as they did, their hands began to cake with mud. Plus, the times were now charged with the energy of change and drugs and greed, and Norman didn't like the idea of heading into a shaky time with his career in shaky hands.

Norman never lost the confidence that his next idea would change it all, and this was foremost in his mind in Century City the day he hired Reynolds. He wanted to be ready; he had fed the machine enough, met all of them, had dinner with all of them, gone to Vegas, gone to bar mitzvahs, drunk with union heads, and played golf in the desert with the whole lot. The part of this that was going on at Norman's expense would go on no longer. He knew his move. As Jimmy's emptied, Norman told Reynolds he wanted him to come work for him. "One thing you need to know that Irv Toffler or Tony Riggi or any of these pricks will not ever understand: I'm smarter than all of them. I'm willing to give up a lot to write what I want and make shows people want to see, but I've had enough of this."

Reynolds never forgot that day and how Norman had begun their new relationship. Norman was already the most prolific writer in the history of television, but it was Reynolds who came up with the name for his company: Mandale Productions. The name would roll off the tongue of every agent and D-girl and business-affairs person in the business for decades to come. Norman Daley's prime was the period of the old Frank Sinatra and the young Warren Beatty. The highlight reel of America from that time would show hippies and Woodstock and Nixon and Jimmy Carter, but what made up the workaday substance of the country in that era, Norman knew, were the television programs made in Los Angeles over the course of the past two decades: *Dragnet*, *Bonanza*, *The O'Hara Family*, *My Favorite Martian*, *I Dream of Jeannie*, *John Iron*.

Mandale had more shows on the air than anyone else. Norman and Reynolds worked out of an office on the MGM lot in Culver City. *John Iron*, Norman's detective show for NBC, was shooting its fourth season when Reynolds moved in. Norman finished the pilot script for *The Fauntleroys* at Christmastime and told Reynolds the pilot had to shoot in the spring, period. Wondering why Norman gave such an order, Reynolds coaxed the first draft out of his boss. It was a comedy about an interracial family in a Manhattan high-rise. Reynolds knew they were in for a fight. Norman had enormous clout with the management at Paramount at the time. Mandale had three programs on the air, and the company's international unit was being launched on the back of many of its syndicated half hours. The concept of the foreign value of American television programs was in its infancy, but already the suits in New York and Burbank knew that if set up right—that is, with the right programming—these systems would become a cash and cultural gusher. So there was yet another reason they wanted to keep the most dependable supplier in television happy.

As much as they needed him, the men of television did not want to let Norman make *The Fauntleroys*. No network or studio wanted to touch it. Norman's agent from William Morris drove to Mandale's offices as soon as he read the script to rail against it. But Norman's mind was made up. After the agent left, Norman said to Reynolds, "Looks like we're going to have to do this ourselves." And with that he told Reynolds to call Marvin Fludheim, the Austrian chief of Eastern Oil, which owned Paramount.

"Tell him that if *The Fauntleroys* is not green-lighted for a full season order, Mandale will not be doing any more shows for his fucking studio."

Reynolds told his boss to stand right there while he dialed New York. To Norman's amazement, Reynolds got Fludheim on the phone and delivered the message and hung up.

"We'll get it," Reynolds had said when he put the receiver down. "Fludheim doesn't care about anything but the growth. He needs us to approve any foreign deals."

"How's that?" Norman said.

"Because it's in your contract," Reynolds said.

Then Norman had an idea. He would make the neighboring white family British, thereby enabling the studio to presell the program to the BBC and Australia, which would cut its cost.

The Fauntleroys went on to become the number-one rated comedy in the history of television, maintaining a stranglehold on the Thursday eight p.m. slot from 1981 to 1988. Its value to NBC was immeasurable, since Thursday was the biggest night of the week for advertisers looking to push weekend sales of everything from Buicks to blenders. Such was *The Fauntleroys'* domination of the eight o'clock lead-in that it allowed NBC to build its other shows into hits. Thus, shows like *Worcester Rules* and *St. Mary's* flowed from Norman's brain into slots at eighty thirty and nine and became megahits. And when Lorimar convinced NBC to put its signature hospital hit, *Medical Man*, in the ten o'clock slot, it had no choice but to appease Mandale with five points off the top.

As they ate their breakfasts at Joey's, Norman said to Reynolds, "Tell me again what the issue is."

"What issue?" Reynolds said.

"The question you have for me. You know, syndication or affiliates, whatever you said. Whaddya you gots?"

"Oh. It's a digital deal for the CBS shows—the whole library. Ten grand up to fifteen, with bumps over five years."

"Is that what they're getting now?"

"Well, when you consider that kids are streaming them for free whenever they want. And that some of them are twenty years old, yeah."

"What, twenty-year-old kids?"

Reynolds looked at him. "No. The shows are twenty years old."

"Right. Yeah, do it. Hey, Tommy called me."

"Yeah, how's he doing?"

"He's good. He wants me to introduce him at his AFI thing."

Tommy was Tom Mack, the movie star. Norman had given him his first break, on *St. Mary's,* as the sympathetic young teacher at an inner-city school. He also let him out after three seasons to do a movie for Spielberg, and from there Tommy had blown up as a matinee idol of the modern day. Reynolds knew that though Norman downplayed it, he loved it when he heard from Tommy. And Reynolds was happy when he saw Norman pleased. Norman was a good man, the rare man whose reputation fit his character, perhaps better than people even knew. Though Reynolds was not objective, as a beneficiary of Norman's largesse, Norman's achievements and the respect he'd gleaned from decades of relationships with people in every area of the business—executives, studio heads, grips, gaffes, actors, agents—set him apart. He was like a father to Reynolds. And he was still the smartest, funniest guy Reynolds knew.

"I gotta go," Reynolds told Norman.

"Into town? What the hell for? Come over the house with me. Or let's go to the track," Norman said.

"Can't," Reynolds said. "I have a lunch. Can't get out of it."

"One of your projects?"

Reynolds couldn't help but feel the sting of that. He was a producer now, had been for the past ten years. The Mandale stuff was so automatic—at this stage it was just collecting checks. Reynolds had been drifting since Norman's retirement. In his heart, he never wanted to practice law. Norman had rescued him from that life. So Reynolds had tried putting together a few movies. Norman had even backed one and convinced Paramount to pick it up. It was a film version of Reynolds's favorite book, *Appointment in Samarra*, by John O'Hara. The book was a fictionalized rip on the town in the twenties. For Reynolds, it captured all the nuance of America between the wars, drunk and dancing but with one eye on the papers. The book read like a screenplay, and he collaborated with a young writer named Alan Bloom, whom Paramount fancied at the time, to adapt it. After much hand-wringing, and against Reynolds's wishes, the kid was allowed to direct it. Norman warned him against it, but the studio wanted it, and Stella made a deal on the inside to ensure Norman's money would come back if Alan could direct.

But the distributor went with a mid-September release, and a bad review in the *New York Times* sealed their fate, that of another bomb in the long history of bombs. Reynolds didn't have the stomach to try the movies anymore. Next he took a deal with a management company, with the idea being that he would be their TV expert, get involved with their actors, and help package new shows for them to produce. Though Norman and Stella both warned him against working with actors, he'd convinced himself it would be fun. Hollywood was a place where you always envy how the other side lives. He had been fascinated with the sell side, the agent's and the manager's role: massaging egos, shepherding careers, collecting clout through the ability to get the ear of the stars.

"Yeah," Reynolds said. "Trying to get something going."

"What is it?

"It's just general. Too early to even talk about." He motioned to Luis for the check.

"Put your wallet away," said Norman, pulling out a gangster's wad of hundreds. "Go do your thing." He pointed to Luis. "I'm going to get my money back from this collection of goniffs. Call me later."

CHAPTER 3

A Report from Bella

Dear Uncle Norman,

Here is my report you asked for on John Wayne. John Wayne was not his name when he was born. It was Marion Robert Morrison. He was born on May 26th, 1907. As a young boy he had a dog name Duke and that's the name he liked more than Marion. He was a famous movie star. He was in cowboy movies. I think it is funny that a cowboy like John Wayne was named Marion because Marion is a girl's name except it is usually spelled MariAn with an A instead of O. I don't like cowboy movies because they are boring. But I think I would have liked John Wayne because he was nice. He died in 1980 when he was of 73 age.

His famous saying is WELL PILGRIM because he called all the people PILGRIM

I LOVE YOU,
By, Bella G. Stanhope

CHAPTER 4

Reality

Reynolds hadn't dared tell Norman about his meeting. Three days earlier he'd received a call from an agent he knew from the old days, Scott Stein. Scottie was a good guy, a TV hustler who handled writers, always trying to slap together shows. Like everyone, he had turned to reality. The non-scripted shows had taken over the business, and front liners such as Scottie had to adjust. So there wasn't any surprise—or, Reynolds thought to himself, shame—when Scottie said, "Would you and Norman ever do reality?"

"Norman wouldn't," Reynolds said.

"What about you? I have something that might interest you," said Scottie.

"How could reality interest me?"

"It should interest you when it's good. Check it out. I have a former Playmate—one that was Playmate of the Year and was almost married to Hef. She's famous."

"What's her name?"

"Delaney Bedford."

"You're kidding," Reynolds said.

"She's a good lady. There might be something there."

"What's the show?"

"She has some ideas, but that's why she needs a producer."

This is how it goes, Reynolds thought. Deteriorate and advance. That's how the world works. All he could see was a beautiful ass. July 1979. He was thirteen and exploding with hormones. His Uncle John had *Playboys* under his bed. Reynolds would sneak in to his and Aunt Tchally's bedroom, pull one out, and smuggle it home, where he looked at it for hours. He studied every angle of the Playmates' bodies. He read the profiles, marveling at the handwriting, how they dotted their *i*'s with little circles, sometimes even hearts. The summer he was fourteen he realized he could get away with buying the magazine himself at the pharmacy. He waited for all the other customers to clear away before he approached the register. The girls behind the counter always gave him half-cracked smiles, like they were watching him undress. One even said, "Don't go blind." They weren't embarrassed at all; it was a one-way street of humiliation.

Delaney Bedford. Hers was the only centerfold picture he could recall taken from the rear. The photo spread, as it were, had a camping motif. In the first few shots, she was outdoors, in a red lumberjack coat with nothing underneath. The coat slipped off, and she was shown in various stages of camping activity. In the centerfold picture, she was lying down, tilted to the right a bit. Her whole aura was blonde, but on close inspection the hair, the skin, the stockings, even the tint of the rouge on her cheek—were all beige and brown. She had large, outstanding breasts, but they were pressed into a sleeping bag and only the side of the right one could be seen. The tent was lit by a kerosene lamp in the background; the sleeping bag was white, and all around her were rough green camp blankets. One pillow tossed to the bottom of the frame had an elk motif on it, its horns pointing to the thing that got him: the just-detectable hint of tawny brown pubic hair running through the divide where her legs met her back.

He devoured the rest of the pictorial, of course, at each view-ing, but he returned to the centerfold spread. He thought he had a type, and she was not it: Texas blond, with all that comes with that generality. His type, even then, was the brown-haired, green-eyed girl. This one, though, Delaney Bedford, took over his mind, changed him. She represented something wholly different, some-thing beyond his range. Her mouth was open, the large, white gleaming teeth hinting that she would have looked gawky two years before.

The thoughts Delaney Bedford put in his head made it inev-itable that he would come out West. He knew when he sat in his room fantasizing about her that he would have to leave Gettysburg, that there was something inside him that could not sit still while this was out there.

The way her thigh turned to hip, to a C-curved, pure white pad, was just the camel's nose under the tent. It started in him a desire to get to the center of things. This was only inflamed as he followed Delaney's progress: she was named Playmate of the Year and moved into the Playboy Mansion. Nearly all issues of *Playboy* from that period had a reference, a picture of her at a party or something about her. It was as if Hef had seen the same thing he had, the dirty bastard. Even he, with the ten million girls and a new one each month for decades, had recognized something in the frosted-feathered-haired open-mouthed bosomy brown blonde on her tummy on the sleeping bag.

Yes, indeed, Reynolds thought. He was meeting her at Ivy at the Shore, which was right on his way to Enchino. The restaurant was the kind where the waiters wear pink shirts and white aprons. It was loud even when it was quiet, silverware clinking in the recesses, Ella Fitzgerald's voice covering the room, a fixture of the restaurant as much as the paint on the ceramics. Reynolds had been there a million times. There was a funny thing about Hollywood restaurants: they lived for awards season, the time when actors and writers and directors were on a perpetual cycle, either as nominees or presenters—a constant flow from the ridiculous Golden Globes to the nonsensical Screen Actors Guild Awards to the boring, socialist Writers Guild Awards to the angry Directors Guild Awards to the callow Spirit Awards (Hollywood's annual opportunity for the parents to drink with the students), all leading up to the sploogie fest of the Oscars.

Reynolds had long since tired of it all. He had seen, in person, Roberto Benigni jump on the chairs and David Letterman do his "Uma, Oprah" bit. Going to the shows was like going to work, no exaggeration. Horrible. He would try to keep it in perspective— mathematical, no emotion—and then the perspective shattered, and he descended into hatred. He wondered why or how he'd got there. Why he cared. Why he didn't care. Why he was working himself up. It was all part of the game. An expensive game but a game. The hunt of it had propelled him in younger days with a desire to provide and protect. As with anything, the luster had worn off. This was somehow more shattering, though, because Hollywood, in all of its obvious falseness, still managed to promise the never-ending fulfillment and reward of art and artistic process, special among all businesses as the one that is more fun, interesting, and good for the soul. It was lonely to find out it was not.

Reynolds deduced but never let on that one's ability to be excited by hype corresponded in proportion to one's ambition for fame. If he had none, he would not have been there in the first place, so there was Original Sin and shame and so forth. But he did quite honestly tire of it. Reynolds had a teenager's ability to romanticize and live his life by the wisdom of song lyrics. So, he reasoned (internally—advertising or shouting it would be stupid) that he was interested in Hollywood the way Hurricane Carter was interested in the fight game: less and less. *It's his work, he'd say. He did it for pay. When it's over, he'd just as soon be on his way.*

As Norman said, things get fucked up when you mix fame with money. It was no surprise that no one—no committee, no awards show, no benefit—could pay Norman enough to show up in the past ten years. He had already received lifetime achievement awards from the various television, movie, and writing worlds. He told them he was not doing these things anymore, or, more often, Reynolds told them. Even Stella would get calls from event producers and charity groups begging for help, and she would get them off the idea.

It could not be called misery, and that was the bitch of it. There were moments of redemption. He and Stella and Norman tried to keep conversations limited, as best they could, to nice stories about people, or nice recollections, tried to keep their relationship to the town genteel. Foreign stars or kids, nominated before anyone knew who they were, came and went so many times. Reynolds sought encounters with anyone offbeat and brilliant. Years ago that meant John Cassavetes at a little bar in the living room of a house on Coldwater. He coupled that with appreciating the ordinary: he caught things, took an interest in things, tried to be outside-in. He noted kids who had been brought up in red states, with small-town lawyers and doctors for fathers and mothers, rather than in Studio City. Reynolds would not respond at first if one of these kids spoke, testing to see if the kid was for real, and often he or she was not. Even so, he had a weak spot for any actor whom he saw getting his shy and uncomfortable dad a beer, as Jeremy Renner had done at an after-hours party attended by Jack Nicholson and Madonna.

Reynolds headed from Malibu to Santa Monica, where he was scheduled to meet Delaney at Ivy at the Shore. Unless on the phone, he zoned out in the car. It was a hazy state, car-mind-zone-fade, he called it, checked out of life. For Reynolds, it was also a time to assess all that was wrong, undone. He headed south on the PCH as he did every day, ignoring the surfers, hugging the left lane when tourists slowed to watch them at Topanga or Carrillo. Natives had nothing on him when it came to car-mind-zone-fade. He was a pro. If there were a league of car-mind-zone-fade players—say, subway riders from New York and London, taxi riders from Paris zooming in and out of tunnels—all lined up for a showdown, he, Reynolds, would be one of the best. If there were scouts, they'd go nuts for him.

Riding south out of Malibu was very good for the zone. It provided contextualization in real time, because the zone required the smashing together of self-loathsome nostalgia and insecurity-driven anxiety, and it was better if external stimuli could conjure both. Thus, as he drove his black-on-black S63 AMG Mercedes past the pier, past the thirty-foot stucco statue of a taco-eating Mexican in front of Las Chacas, and alongside the cement-colored sand, he thought of sitting in his room looking at the back cover of the Beach Boys' *Endless Summer*, which he'd bought despite not having a record player, regarding the investment as sound because he could look at the album art and play it at his friend Arthur's house.

He never wanted to surf. And he never thought he'd meet Delaney Bedford. Yet in some corollary to the Warholian fifteen minutes, if you lived long enough, that's what happened to you—sudden brushes against the impossible. He wondered what she would look like, and he started to get a little hard-on. There it was again. He could not believe how much craving for sex he had. He rubbed his hands. He had become like the real Homer Simpson, the one from *The Day of the Locust*, not the cartoon. At least not yet like the guy from the cartoon. The guy from the book was kinder.

A Billy Bragg song from his Spotify playlist came on:

Ingrid Bergman
Ingrid Bergman
Let's go make a picture
On the island of Stromboli
Ingrid Bergman

Ingrid Bergman, you're so perty
You'd make any mountain quiver
You'd make fire fly from the crater
Ingrid Bergman

If you'll walk across my camera
I will flash the world your story
I will pay you more than money
Ingrid Bergman

Scottie had told him Delaney still looked like she looked in the magazine, just older. Reynolds replied that was a line good enough to qualify Scottie for the agent hall of fame. Reynolds arrived and left the car with the Argentinean kid at the valet; somehow the Ivy had these tall, great-looking Argentinean kids, come to America to park cars, an upside-down American Dream. He went inside, and George said she was already there. And there she was, sitting at the good table, the one in the back left-hand corner under the ten-foot Ed Ruscha painting of a clipper ship with big, bold white letters running top to bottom: BRAVE MEN RUN IN MY FAMILY.

Delaney Bedford gave him a little wave. Scottie was right. The same, just older. She stuck out her hand and said, "Hiiiii." He could tell the way you can tell that she was friendly; that she had been scooped up by Hef because she was so extraordinarily attractive; that she'd lived her twenties in a blaze of mirrors, cameras, travel, access, and petty jealousies; that she woke up not knowing what hit her, met a business guy who loved her underneath, married him, went into isolation, and raised the kids; that she got divorced; and that she was now in Enchino and trying to figure out what to do. She was battered by life, beaten down by the clock, but she was still hot. That's what life is like for these women, he thought. Like they had to overcome their beauty.

"So nice to meet you," he said, in his friendliest tone. As if he were a kid at the top of a waterslide, the waiter pushed him in. His head fogged. He had been to class reunions, which were weird, he later deduced, because multiple things were happening: old emotions revived, passage of time clocked, new impressions made, new events occurring. Now he was going through the same thing with Delaney Bedford, except his relationship with her, while it had gotten physical, was solely in his own head. He told himself it was not any different from meeting any of the ten million movie and television stars he encountered daily, in offices, on sets, at restaurants, concerts, ball games. He'd perfected the Hollywood ability of being bored by it all. First you're amazed by it, then you bask in it, then you take it seriously, then you think it has something to do with you, then you start to worry that it has nothing to do with you, then you make a new plan and tell yourself you're over it all and decide to use it for your own purposes. And that's all this was. In his pocket, a call came in on his iPhone. He had it on silent and it went to voice mail.

In the great tradition, Reynolds and Delaney broke the ice by talking about someone else, in this case the one they had in common, Scottie.

"He says such nice things about you," said Delaney.

Upon closer inspection, Reynolds saw she had dressed up for him. This was a girl who knew clothes, no matter how long she'd been in the Valley. Reynolds did not have a bone in his body for fashion, but marriage to Stella and a life of materialism had had their effect on him. At forty-seven, he could take a woman in and assess the jewelry, the top, the nails, the shoes, and the bag the way Jason Bourne took in an empty room with high ceilings somewhere in Europe after waking up with amnesia. She had on a silky blouse showing a discreet amount of cleavage, diamond stud earrings, not too big, not too small, and a Cartier Tank watch—that was all he could see from the table up.

"He's the best," Reynolds said.

"How long have y'all known each other?" Delaney was leaning forward, as though Reynolds's response would be the most important thing she'd ever heard. But not in a dumb way—more in a Southern way, the way Southern girls always made everyone feel so special.

"Oh God, let's see. Wow. You know, I think I've known Scottie for twenty years." He was nervous. He felt like he was on a first date. The waiter was there to take drink orders. "Would you like some wine?"

"Ooh. Of course. My kind of guy."

Thrilled, he ordered a bottle of chardonnay.

"So, thanks again for meeting me," she said.

"Oh, it's my plea—"

She lifted her eyes to something toward the entranceway and put her hand on his forearm. "Oh, there she is." She stood halfway in her chair and waved. "Marisol . . . Marisol, over here."

She sat back down and looked at Reynolds. "I hope you don't mind, I asked my friend to join."

"Oh, OK," said Reynolds, not sure what to say.

In a moment, an elegant and tall Latina in big black sunglasses was being escorted by the maître d' to their table. Reynolds rose from his chair as Delaney embraced her friend.

"I'm sorry for being late, *cara*," Marisol said.

"Oh, don't be silly. Mari, meet Reynolds. Reynolds, this is Marisol Ocampo de Campos."

They shook hands and all sat down. "Reynolds, as I was starting to say, Marisol is my partner. She's just the best."

"Oh, stop," said Marisol. "You know these days you can't say that, Laney. He will think the wrong thing," and she gave Reynolds's arm a little smack in laughter. Then she directed his attention at Delaney. "Will you look at this girl, she's still like a Bunny."

"What this girl won't tell you," said Delaney, "is that she was Miss Universe in 1975. From *Es-pan-ya*."

Reynolds's eyes widened. "Oh, wow."

Marisol gave Delaney the same little slap. "Oh stop, you." They giggled.

Reynolds tasted the wine and told the waiter it was fine.

After the wine was poured they toasted. "Here's to success," Reynolds said.

"And new friends," said Delaney.

"Even better. To new friends," Reynolds said, and they all took noticeable gulps.

"So, Mari," Delaney said after a moment, "Reynolds is a producer, of course." She returned her look to Reynolds. "Scottie told us all about you. He said that you were an agent, before, or a manager?" They both now looked at him with their heads tilted a little sideways, just a touch, a cue that he should start talking about himself.

"Oh, no, no. I was never an agent. Everything else but," Reynolds said, with a forced laugh.

"So now, you are a producer?" said Marisol. Like Delaney, she was acting as though she was on an audition. Reynolds got the panicked feeling that Scottie had promised them more than he could deliver.

"Well, yes. I guess so." He forced himself to focus. "I run Norman Daley's company."

Delaney interrupted for Marisol's benefit. "You know Norman Daley. The writer. He did *The Fauntleroys*." Marisol jolted a little. "And *It's All in the Air*. And so much else."

"Oh, yes, of course," said Marisol. Reynolds would have bet everything he owned and every penny he could borrow that Marisol did not know what *The Fauntleroys* was. The girls were listening closely. Reynolds had marveled at this quality for years; the transparency of a person's affected interest was usually correlated in some way to the lack of brain waves behind their eyes. But these ladies were nice. And they didn't have to be smart. After a bit more chitchat, he refilled their glasses, noting Marisol's breasts as she held out her glass.

"More wine?" Reynolds said, looking for the waiter.

Marisol said, "Know what? It is a special occasion. Laney, let's have that special drink . . . you know, the gim-let." Reynolds noticed that she pronounced s-words with an extra syllable, "eh-special."

"Oh, lord have mercy, girl," Delaney said, Texas-style. "You gonna get me drannnkin'."

"You want to have Ivy gimlets?" Reynolds was amazed. Those were goblets full of vodka with a bit of mint and sugar. "Sounds great."

"Go ahead, please, Reynaldo. I don't mean to interrupt," said Marisol.

Reynolds listened to himself talk. He took the girls through his background with Norman, all their famous and successful shows. It was a canned speech, something he did on autopilot. But his internal voice, already feeling the wine, ran through a series of debates. *Am I really doing this?* Aside from being on the receiving end of a few strenuous lap dances over the years, he had never been unfaithful to Stella. *But this is—like, literally—your fantasy girl. Should I try for Delaney? What does that even mean? What does "try for both of them" even mean? Is this how a threesome happens?*

He realized he was talking through his daydream. "But let's not let me ramble on. I'm here to learn about you two. How do you know each other?"

The girls exchanged looks. "You tell him," said Marisol. "I'm too shy."

"Ha!" said Delaney. The drinks came, and they all took a sip. Reynolds tried not to wince at the taste of the vodka. The girls didn't flinch.

Delaney rolled her eyes. "Wellll ... where do I start?"

"Start with the Italians," Marisol said.

The girls cracked up again. All three took another sip of gimlet. *Good lord*, thought Reynolds.

Delaney sighed, put her glass down, and set sail. "We married brothers. Italian brothers: Stephano and Silvio. Do you know them? The Rinaldis? They make blue jeans."

"Designer jeans. Motto Royal jeans?" Marisol said.

"Sure," said Reynolds. "I've read about those guys."

"Well, we married them," said Delaney. The two laughed again.

"Didn't they sue each other?" Reynolds said.

"Oh, my goodness, they sure did. Took nine years," Delaney said.

"Oh God," Reynolds said.

Marisol grabbed his forearm and said, "They are animals."

Delaney went on, "We all met around the same time, in 1983. I had, you know, retired, shall we say, from the mansion and all that. Anyway, I was at a party, and this dashing Italian man starts talking to me. Now, honey, I was used to a lot of money by then, but everyone was kind of, you know, cheesy. This was like a fairy tale. He sent me roses, took me to dinner, flew me to Paris ..."

Reynolds reflected on the notion of something being too cheesy for the young Delaney Bedford. He took another drink.

"They did everything together," she continued. "Whenever I went out with Silvio, Stephano was with us. Always a double date. Stephano always had some bimbo or another. Then out of the blue one night, he shows up with *Señorita* here, and she and I hit it off like that." Delaney snapped her fingers.

"We were like sisters," said Marisol, and she snapped her fingers.

"We did everything together. We got married on the same day, honeymoons, vacations."

"Had kids same time."

"That's right. Our kids are the same age."

"But you're both . . . not with them anymore?" said Reynolds. "The brothers?"

"That's right. This terrible, terrible fight started about ten years ago." Marisol's accent became more intoxicating as she got more intoxicated.

"Ugh, it was awful," said Delaney.

"They no talk to each other anymore."

"But," Delaney said, indicating a bond between her and Marisol, "we told them, 'No way is this affecting *our* friendship.' I said, 'Silvio, if you think I'm not going to see Marisol, you've got another thing coming, *paesan*.'"

Marisol nodded. "She did. She did that. And when I find out, *lo mismo por* Stephano."

Delaney showed the palms of her hands. "So, we all got divorced. They had to let us keep the houses—we're down the street from each other in Enchino."

"And they keep fighting each other," said Marisol. "They spend everything on a fight with each other."

"Fascinating," said Reynolds. He tried to remember whether he'd read about the Rinaldi brothers killing anyone.

"So anyway," Delaney said, "there we were in the Valley raising these kids and homeschooling them and everything."

"You homeschool them?" Reynolds said.

They nodded in unison. "Is very important," said Marisol. "We use the Secret."

"So," Delaney said, "the boys are in college, and our girls are tenth-grade level, and we have these funny, crazy lives. And everyone is always coming up to us and saying, 'You two should have a reality show.'"

"Is crazy," said Marisol.

"More drinks?" said the waiter. They all agreed, without disturbing the flow of the conversation.

"And I know Scottie for a million years," said Delaney. "Do you know he represented Hef for one of those contest shows years ago?"

"I never knew that," said Reynolds, kind of impressed by Scottie, who he thought just chased three-episode arcs on *How I Met Your Mother*.

"He did so much bad things," said Marisol, talking about Hugh Hefner, Reynolds realized after a moment. "On television. So many stupid shows."

"So, I asked Scottie what he thought, and he flipped over the idea. We went in for a meeting with him, and—" She showed her palms again. "Well, he just thinks it's a great idea. 'We just have to find you a producer,' he said."

Delaney looked at Reynolds. Marisol looked at Reynolds. Not knowing what else to do, Reynolds lifted his eyebrows and turned his palms up too. Marisol did the same. The three sat with their palms up and their gimlets in front of them.

"And here we are," he said. They giggled. "Terrific." The waiter returned.

"Ready for something to eat?"

"God, yes," said Delaney. "I'm getting smashed."

"I missed something," Reynolds said, after the waiter left. "What do you mean when you say you have 'the secret'?"

"The *Secret*," said Delaney.

Marisol leaned closer. "You know, the *Secret*."

"You know," said Delaney, "The program, the books. *The Secret*."

"Ooh," he said. "And how do you do that?"

"Well, it takes a long time to explain," said Delaney. "But basically we follow the principles of the Secret in everything we teach them."

Reynolds did not want to betray his lack of knowledge of the Secret, so he nodded.

Marisol had put on a pair of sexy-librarian-style glasses to read the menu. "Scottie said the Secret is a big hook for the idea."

Delaney nodded. "Said we could work that in there." More drinks came, and they both asked for Cobb salads with no bacon, and at Reynolds's insistence they ordered crab cakes to share. Reynolds said he would have the swordfish.

"So, what do you think? Are we just a couple of suckers? Please, you have *got* to tell us if we are being silly," Delaney said.

"Yes," said Marisol. "Look, Reynaldo, we both have seen a lot."

"A lot," said Delaney.

"We have been boolshitted by the best."

"You can just tell us straight."

They were staring at him. Reynolds couldn't tell who was more beautiful. He grabbed a piece of bread, because his head was starting to spin from the vodka. And then nerves took over again, and he took a sip of his drink while he tried to think of what to say.

He cleared his throat. "OK. Here's what I think." He leaned in. "One of the most important things I've learned from Norman— that's Norman Daley, of course," he said—looking at them both, like a speaker at a TED conference trained in eye contact—"is the importance of genre."

"That is so true," said Delaney. Marisol nodded in agreement.

"He was—is still—a genius at ushering in a style of television just as—or even just before—the public realizes its appetite for such a program. So, you see, *Artie in the Army* was one of the first half-hour situation comedies, *John Iron* one of the first hour-long Westerns, *Ten Sector Red* an old cop show, and so on."

"God, I loved *John Iron*," said Delaney. "That man was so sexy." Marisol lifted her eyebrows at Delaney in mock surprise at her randiness.

Reynolds went on. "Cut to today, and now, of course, we are in the age of reality."

"Yes!" said Marisol.

Her vigor threw Reynolds off his rhythm for a moment, but he recovered. "The important thing with reality, or non-scripted programming, as it's sometimes called, is to know which niche you are approaching."

Delaney put her elbow on the table, set her head on her palm and nodded. "My gosh, Scottie was right about you. Wasn't he right, Mari?'

"Um hmm," Marisol said. "And he didn't say he was so cute."

Reynolds continued quickly to show the girls he couldn't be distracted. But inside he was freaking out. "So I think we just have to bang it out a little—find our genre. Once we do, we can figure out our target distributor and go from there."

Delaney put her hands together like she was about to pray and gave a little clap. Marisol grabbed Reynolds's upper arm and looked at Delaney and said, "OK. So now we bang it out a little?" They laughed. "Laney, we have to lighten him up a little, no?"

"Seriously!" Delaney said. "C'mon, Reynolds, tell us more about yourself. What shows are you working on now?"

"Well," he said, "you're getting me at a good time. I've taken a break for the past several months. To tell you the truth, I've been looking for the right vehicle to get back in."

Marisol said, "We can be your vehicle, no?"

"Oh, keep your claws off him," said Delaney. "What have you been doing while you've been off?"

"Well, I keep things going with Norman. He has a lot of legal needs, of course. And, I don't know, I spend a lot of time reading, I guess. I have a daughter in college, like you guys."

"Aw. How cute." Delaney tilted her head to the side a bit. "So, you ended a show last year?"

"Yeah," Reynolds said. "Well, it didn't get picked up."

"What was it?"

"It was sort of an experimental show about sleep."

"You are kidding me," Delaney said.

"Sleep is so important," said Marisol. They all nodded.

"What do you like to read?" Delaney said.

He took a drink. "These days I read a lot of history."

Delaney dropped her fork. She stared a Marisol, who broke into a smile. "Marisol and I *love history*."

"It is *absolutamente* our favorite."

"*Verdad?*" said Reynolds.

"God's honest," said Delaney. Marisol widened her eyes in delight and lifted up a little, as if she were tasting something delicious. Delaney said, "And I will tell you something else." She paused and grabbed her purse and started to stand up.

"Yes?" he said.

"Smart men are so sexy," she whispered, as she started to squeeze by. "Lemme get through you, I gotta go to the little girls' room. Don't you go anywhere."

"I come with you," said Marisol.

Delaney slid past him, and the two glided away. Reynolds was awash in vodka. He watched them walk. And there it was. The rear end of Delaney Bedford. The Holy Grail of his youth, like a sacred religious relic in a Dan Brown novel. She had kept it up. Yes, he could make the connection between the butt walking away from him and the image from thirty-five years ago. How was that possible? And yet it was true. There was a particular dimensionality to it—not flat, not circular. It was just shaped damned well. Exceptional. He felt like he could see the top of Everest.

As impossible as it was to compete, Marisol was nothing if not also compelling from the rear. Who'd have ever dreamed that when Delaney Bedford actually came into his range he would at the same time meet her Spanish doppelgänger? With Marisol, it was like watching the Spanish-language version of a favorite game show. There was the fundamental appeal of, say, *Who Wants to Be a Millionaire?*, with its pot-roast-like comfort, and underneath it the sensation of consuming something ridiculous through a foreign language. Different and yet the same. It was a bonanza of head-splitting proportions.

They moved through the restaurant like tall ships tacking to harbor. He had seen a lot of women head to the bathroom mid-meal, actresses, models, hookers, the gamut. But those had been nothing like these two at a late Friday lunch at Ivy at the Shore. *And what is even crazier*, he thought, as he tasted mint on the tip of his tongue and swallowed the last piece of crab cake in spicy Thousand Island sauce, *they are my age. Even a little older.* They weren't young idiots. In his now drunken state of mind he reasoned that this was better than what other middle-aged guys were up to. While it would be a disaster to be found out, if this came to anything, he wouldn't have to worry about the scorn of his contemporaries, the shame in front of his mother, the additional sense of letdown and anger and disgust from Stella and Bella that would accompany any kind of interaction with twenty-five-year-old models. No, sir. Delaney Bedford and Marisol were *older* women.

In truth, they reminded him of the older girls he'd flirted with in high school and college. Those moments with the babysitter or his neighbor's girlfriend or the TA for chemistry class—or one drunken night with a grad student that had been close to against his will. Not typical moments for the male, but they existed in his memory nonetheless, always submerged. But wow, what could have been had been great to consider.

The waiter was refilling their water glasses. "Another round?"

"Why not?" said Reynolds.

"Right away," he said, clearing the dead soldier gimlets.

Reynolds could see the guy was enjoying waiting on this table. "Pretty phenomenal, huh?"

"Sensational," said the waiter. He bent a little to Reynolds's side. "Who are they?"

"Playmate of the Year in 1979, and the other was Miss Universe. Way before your time."

"Wow." He shook his head. "Like, from Sweden?"

"What?"

"Like Miss Universe from Sweden?"

"No," said Reynolds, whispering, because they were coming back from the restroom. "She's from Texas."

"Ooh, so the blonde was . . . ?"

"Playmate."

"Wow. And the Mexican lady was Miss Universe?"

"She's Spanish."

"Got it."

"OK, scram," Reynolds said, smiling. He was in that gauzy place. The girls sauntered back to the table like a couple of floats from the Rose Parade.

He stood as they sat down. "Marisol, I haven't asked you what part of Spain you are from."

"Barcelona."

"Oh, I love Barthelona," Reynolds said.

"You've been?"

"Oh, yes. I am a huge fan of Gaudí."

Marisol stared at Delaney as though she'd seen a ghost. They broke into laughter.

"What?" Reynolds said. "What's so funny?"

"I tell Laney . . . I tell her all the time . . . I say the first man in America who knows who Gaudí is—I will marry that man!"

"But he's mine!" Delaney said.

The waiter returned with more drinks.

"Ay, no!" said Marisol. "Ray, you gonna get us drunk."

"Ah, you two can handle it," Reynolds said.

"What is your favorite about Gaudí?" Marisol said.

"Oh . . . let me think. Isn't there a park in Barcelona that was his dream project, which didn't get finished?"

"Yes. The cemetery . . . you've been?"

"Oh yes. I spent a day there."

"You see, this is the kind of thing Laney and I want to do with the show. The people will think, 'Here is two stupid, you know, bimbos who look at nothing but fashion magazines and were beautiful when they were young, but now they have no life and they just get old and divorce and die.'"

"Exactly," said Delaney. "But we can come in and surprise them all. We can talk about art and history and architecture and the Secret and all of this deeper side."

"And we can speak to all the women out there who feel the same way. There is a big market out there in the women who feel this way, Ray," Marisol said.

"They want to be deeper. Y'all men don't get it," Delaney said.

Reynolds nodded in agreement. He thought Marisol looked like a younger Sophia Loren. He thought Delaney was a cross between Ingrid Bergman and Loni Anderson—young Loni Anderson.

"OK, so let's think this out," he said. "What other show could it be compared to?"

"That is the thing," said Marisol. And she held her head up in a regal manner. "There is no show that has ever been like this."

"It's unique," said Delaney.

"Well, OK," said Reynolds. "What channel do you see it on?"

"Fox," said Marisol.

"OK," said Reynolds. Like Jodie Foster as Clarice Starling speaking to Hannibal Lecter, he was jarred out of the manipulated state he'd allowed himself to get into. He remembered he was the one outside the cage. "Maybe FX. Or FXX. In fact—" He snapped his fingers. "Guys, you know what? This must be a cable show. Like Lifetime, or Discovery—maybe A&E." He considered what he was saying. "Maybe."

"Well, that's why we need *you*," said Delaney.

Reynolds chewed a bit of swordfish. He noticed that the ladies were not eating, just pushing around their salads. *They must be smashed*, he thought. *How can they not be smashed?* He thought about what Norman would say right now. He put it out of his mind.

"OK, tell me about the Secret," he said. "What's *is* the Secret?" He paused. "I mean, I don't know a thing about it. I want to know."

Delaney brought her napkin to her lips. "Well, it's not really a one-lunch, wham-bam-thank-you-ma'am kind of thing."

"It's very complicated," said Marisol.

"But it's also very simple," Delaney said, as much to Marisol as to him.

"*Sí*. Is very true," Marisol agreed. Reynolds noticed Marisol's Spanish was coming out more as she got drunker.

"But it's complicated, she's right," said Delaney.

"*Sí*."

"OK," said Reynolds, "but what *is* it?"

"It is a program developed by these fab-ulous people. They are doctors, for the most part," said Delaney.

"Men?" Reynolds said.

"And women," said Marisol.

"One main woman and a prominent doctor, who is a man. And many other doctors," said Delaney.

"Yes, and another group of man and woman," Marisol said. Realizing it sounded a bit convoluted, she waved off the explanation, "*Es* a little *confuso*. But look, *papi*, the basics are that it is a book, and there are DVDs. You follow their program, and you begin to see the most wonderful things happen."

"Your life, it goes through so many wonderful changes," Delaney said. "Things just start happening for you."

"The sex life gets much better," Marisol said. They giggled at this.

"The key is: you have to believe," Delaney said.

The girls were staring at him, nodding. He was hammered. Ella Fitzgerald was in the background, and the restaurant was emptying. The busboys and waiters in their shirts and white aprons were setting up for dinner. Delaney Bedford was staring into his eyes. He returned the look, just as he had at fourteen when she was looking back at the camera, with her back arched, next to her standard issue green blankets and sleeping bag. She was right there, in the flesh. Just older. Above, the stars moved and stayed put; simultaneously static and in motion, moving or not moving, all within a super crazy gigantic box of space and time.

"Do you want to go have a cigarette?" Delaney whispered.

"Fantastic," he said. "I haven't smoked in twenty-five years."

"Good," said Marisol. "We gonna live a little."

CHAPTER 5

A Report from Bella

July 24, 2002

Dear Uncle Norman,

The Person of this Report is Elvis Aaron Presley, born January 8, 1935 died August 16th, 1977.

Elvis, as he is known to millions of fans around the world, was the (first singer of rock and roll.) He was American. He wore big white suits and I don't understand why but girls screamed when he sang his songs. He is in lots of movies, that's what my mom told me. My dad told me he ate peanut butter and banana sandwiches that were fried like french fries. I think that is (disgusting,) don't you? some of his songs are Hound Dog my favorite, blue suede shoes, Are you Lonesome Tonight and Jailhouse Rock my Dad's favorite. what is your favorite? It is very sad that Elvis died because we can't hear him sing and I think I would have like to hear him sing. He got in trouble for shaking his hips on Ed Sullivan's show. That is very funny and is not something I think you would get in trouble for now. But times have changed.

His famous saying is You Aint Nothin But a Houndog. Roof Roof.

By, Isabella Great Reynolds

p.s. ha ha Isabella Greta Reynolds did you get it??? Xoxox

CHAPTER 6

On the Road to War

Ninety minutes later, the threesome was hunched on the heavy stools at the Ivy's small bar with a fresh round of gimlets. Reynolds was in the middle. They had not wanted to leave one another when the check came, and the waiter signaled they should adjourn to the bar. Aside from a few vacationers having tea over on the patio, they were the only customers left in the restaurant.

"The last thing anyone will expect," said Reynolds, "is that this show will have substance. A real level of depth to it."

"That is so true," said Delaney.

"He so smart," said Marisol. "How can we do that?"

"But we still want it to be sexy," said Delaney.

"Yes, sexy. It must be, more than anything else, sexy."

"Well, the two of you are so sexy," said Reynolds.

"Raynahldo!" said Marisol.

"Reynolds!" Delaney said, mock slapping him at the same time.

They all had sips of their drinks. There was a long pause as they each went up into their heads.

"Life is so funny," Reynolds said finally.

"I know," said Delaney. "Wait, how do you mean?"

"I don't know," he said. "I grew up on a battlefield, you know? It's so far away now. I used to study the great generals. I knew so much about it. I was a tour guide."

"You were a tour guide?" said Marisol. The girls cracked up.

"With the hat and a uniform and everything?" said Delaney.

"Oh, shut up," he said. "What hat? Who wears a hat?" The girls crumbled in laughter. He kept going. "No, I wore a white shirt and tie. It was in the old days, when guides didn't wear uniforms. I tried to look like a professor."

Delaney recovered. "Was it a place from Revolutionary times? Like George Washington?"

"Did you talk about James Madison?" Marisol chimed in. They were like a weird chorus in a show in a gay bar. Reynolds paused for a second. *Where did she get James Madison?* He let it pass.

"No, I grew up in Gettysburg. The Civil War."

"Abraham Lincoln," said Marisol.

"Very good," he said.

"All y'all Yankees love Abraham Lincoln," said Delaney.

"You don't?" he said.

"Oh, I'm just trying to be funny, Mister Man," said Delaney. "You *have* to tell us more."

He fell into memory. He thought about long afternoons with families from Ohio or Maryland, a mother and a father with two or three kids, sometimes the neighbor's kid. He had learned the art of the canned speech there, which would serve him well, first with girls in high school, then in college, then in law school, and most of all with women in Hollywood. Reynolds remembered it as a time before he got cynical; when he gave his best every day because these people had spent their hard-earned money to come see their heritage. They hadn't gone to Ocean City or the Poconos; they were there, at

Gettysburg, at the crossroads. They were using their limited time, their week of vacation from the insurance company or the phone company or Honeywell, to pay homage. He took that seriously.

Each tour took three hours. Larger groups moved through the park on a bus. Reynolds could do private tours, where he just jumped in the station wagon with the family and told the father where to stop. The National Park Service was very loose back then—once you passed a test, you were thrown on the schedule. The park gave him general rules to follow, but as long as Reynolds kept the tours on time and went on a more or less chronological path, he could direct the tour around the battlefield as he wished. His vast knowledge had been gained the way most boys learn the infield fly rule in baseball or the concept of a first down in football —that is, by osmosis, by just being conscious.

Reynolds's goal was to make the people feel as though they weren't getting the same old boring history lesson. He showed them the site just off Little Round Top where the soldiers, North and South, had congregated around a campfire the night after the second day. He brought a canteen with a dent in it that his parents had given him for his fifteenth birthday. He ended each tour in the trees to the west of Cemetery Ridge, where the Confederate soldiers had gathered before Pickett's Charge, on the third and final day, just prior to the hour of combat that would decide the battle, the war, and the future of America and the world.

Delaney and Marisol watched Reynolds talk and nodded along. The story flowed out of him, and he was surprised to learn he didn't feel intimidated or strange telling it. They made him feel comfortable in a familiar way. He ignored the fact that he was drunk.

"It's so nice to meet with you two," he said, in the sappy way that comes with being blitzed. "It's so nice to meet two people who are in it for the right reasons. We are all the same, in a way."

"I was just thinking the exact same thing," said Delaney.

There was such a disconnect between the past and now. How had it gone so . . . weird? How had things progressed to this point? Deterioration and advance, the way Grant moved at the end, taking the one-step-back-for-two-steps-forward deal every time. Sacrificing troops but with unstoppable, ineffable movement forward. With Sherman, Grant's grim little brother, paying a horrible price in men and inflicting terrible destruction but driving to the sea. Again, how had it become this way? It had all sped up so fast, he thought, that the white noise of light took over. It was not really his theory, of course. It was from his reading, this knowledge that the audio-visual onslaught of consumerism and frivolity had taken us over. Sports stars and teenage actors had replaced orators and folk music. Airplane engines, radio static, the blogosphere, and just the constant yam-yam-yammering of everyone drowned everything else out. Television, television, television. He was drunk. He looked at the two awesome creatures beside him. Maybe they *were* his future.

"We should start getting you guys on tape, right away," he said.

"I am a mess," said Marisol.

"He doesn't mean now," said Delaney.

"Yes. No. Not right now. But we should get going on it right away."

"We have to be doing something, don't we?" said Delaney. "That's the idea: that we're always doing something interesting."

"Exactly," Reynolds said.

"Yes. Ray, *una cosa*. One thing. I want to tell you one thing. We don't want to look like we are making it for YouTube."

"Understood," he said. "That is the last thing we want." Reynolds noticed that a new hostess was coming into the restaurant for her shift. "Wait," he said. "What time is it?" He looked at his watch. It was almost five. "Shit. Excuse me, I have to make a call." He went outside and dialed his cell phone.

"Robert Houpt," said the voice on the line.

"Robert, it's Reynolds."

"Hi, Reynolds."

"Hey, man, are you busy this afternoon? I need you."

Robert had been driving Norman for twenty years. Among the many luxuries of show business, Reynolds had gotten used to the convenience of a chauffeur. Norman and Reynolds hired Robert for more than airport runs—for Reynolds this meant when he was drinking or had to go to a premiere deep in Hollywood and didn't want to drive. Robert was a burly guy. He was equal parts happy and quiet. Reynolds told him his whereabouts and his plans.

"Jesus," Robert said.

"I need you, man."

"OK. Pick you up in twenty-five minutes. I'm just getting out of LAX."

Reynolds started back inside, and again his mind wandered. The Battle of Gettysburg was a locked-down commodity to the world. But not for him: he knew it not just as a linear concept but as a three-dimensional experience. *His* awareness was formed in the physical space, not just of its memory but of its ghosts. Writers, historians, social studies teachers—they were anthropologists on a dig. Reynolds knew the battle more than they ever would. It was, to him, like water to fish.

He knew the lead up, what it was like to walk twenty miles down Chambersburg Road, as Lee and the Confederate forces had. He'd got his first hand job in a car parked on Baltimore Pike. Reynolds knew the rolling hills of green and yellow in the summer and fall, the cannons in the snow, the long drives out from each of the ten roads into town. He knew the exact place where General John Reynolds of the Union First Corps, the Iron Brigade, had been shot after marching to the rescue of John Buford's cavalry company, on the first day. He knew what happened between the historians' reference points. Reynolds's home was Gettysburg, and he lived in its tent, breathed its air, lived its song.

"I have an idea," he said, when he returned to the bar.

"What?" said Delaney.

He looked again at her face. The thing about beautiful faces is they keep you looking at them. Look at a beautiful woman. There are surprises each time; when apart, he thought, a man can't remember if he has it right. Delaney's face was an image deep in his cerebral cortex—and now come to life. It was as clear as a fire alarm. It was the opposite of the white noise of everyday life.

"Forget it. It's stupid," he said.

"Ronaldo," Marisol said. "You must tell us. Nothing is stupid."

Marisol was the excitement of the new: undefined, unfamiliar, off the map that he knew. Not like Delaney. Together they were a perfect combination. The duality. They knew the Secret.

"OK," he said. He felt like a high diver springing off the cliffs in Acapulco on *Wide World of Sports*. "This is going to sound crazy. But I am going somewhere today—at least I was thinking about it." He stopped again. "No, it's too crazy."

"What is it?" they both said. "Tell us!"

"Out in Enchino . . . about seventy-five miles east of here . . . do you know where Enchino is?"

"'I set out from Enchino, I was trailed by twenty hounds,'" Delaney said.

"Deadhead?" Reynolds said.

"You know it."

"Jesus. Just when I thought you couldn't get better."

"You are going to go to a concert?" Marisol said.

"No. Well, kind of. No, not exactly. Not at all. But it is an event," Reynolds said. "There is this event out in Enchino this weekend. I can't believe I am saying this out loud. I was thinking of going . . . I mean, I'm going."

Delaney giggled and looked at Marisol. "Well, what is it?"

He took a long drink. He stared at them, one after the other. "It is a Civil War reenactment."

Their faces didn't register any reaction.

Reynolds went on. "They are doing the Battle of Gettysburg, which is where I grew up. Where I was a tour guide."

"But that was in Virginia or something," Delaney said.

"The Civil War was in California?" Marisol said.

"No, no," he said, shaking his head. "It was in Pennsylvania, where I grew up. Or at least this part was. But they do the reenactment here. They do them everywhere. It's sort of a way of honoring things—like a big, out-of-control parade."

"Ooh, sounds like crazy fun," said Delaney.

"What do you do?" said Marisol. "Do you shoot guns? Oh my God, Laney, I am drunk."

"Me too," Delaney said. Then she grabbed Reynolds. "It sounds great. We want to go."

"Sí," said Marisol, clapping. "We are coming!"

"Do you really want to?" Reynolds said.

"Yes!" said Delaney.

"You're not just saying it?" Reynolds said.

"It will be great," Delaney said.

"My driver is coming in twenty minutes. If it's too weird, we can drive you home."

The girls gave more hand claps. Reynolds ordered one more round of drinks.

"It goes on all weekend. The people arrive tonight and get organized. They come from all over."

"Do you stay in Palm Springs?" said Delaney.

"No." He cringed for a second. "You stay in little tents, like the soldiers had."

"Sleeping bags?" Marisol said.

"Marisol, it was the eighteen hundreds," said Delaney. Back to Reynolds, she said, "Does everyone dress up?"

"I think so."

"It sounds fabulous," said Delaney. "Mari and I were saying we were looking for an adventure."

"You're sure?" Reynolds said, repeating himself.

"Reynolds, remember: I was an actress. And so was she." Delaney waved at Marisol. "We loooove this kind of thing."

Reynolds's phone buzzed. It was a text from Robert. Reynolds clapped his hands. "OK then, ladies. Our ride is outside."

The girls jumped up in a fuss. "Let us pee really quick," Delaney said. "This is gonna be aaaawesome," she said, grabbing Marisol's booty.

"Oh my God," said Marisol. "There will be so many men. *Loco* men."

Reynolds was too hammered to think to ask them if they wanted anything from their cars, presuming they had driven in the first place. He paid the check and headed into the afternoon sun. Robert was standing in front of a stretch SUV limousine.

"Oh Christ," said Reynolds. "You have a stretch?"

"What can I tell ya?" said Robert. "I had to take a band to the airport. Then you call with an emergency."

Robert was a hale and hearty fellow-well-met. He had wavy gray hair and a beard that he let get bushy because it made him more intimidating, which his job called for when he needed to get a client through a barricade or a crowd.

"Any bags?" Robert said.

Reynolds gave his ticket to the valet. "Will you get my car? I need to get something out of my trunk."

As they waited, Robert said, "Enchino? Really?"

"Enchino."

"Civil War?"

"Civil War."

"Are you drunk?"

"Paralytic."

The girls came bounding out of the restaurant. Reynolds continued. "And they're coming with us."

"Wow. What do we have here?" said Robert.

"I'll fill you in as we drive. We have to stop at a liquor store." The girls were chewing gum and smiling. "Ladies, this is Robert. Robert, Delaney and Marisol."

"Hello," said Delaney.

"Roberto," said Marisol, rolling her *r*'s.

"Hello, ladies," Robert said.

"Shall we?" said Reynolds.

"*Vámonos*," said Marisol.

Reynolds opened the door, and the girls climbed in. He was behind Delaney as she stepped up into the SUV, her backside rising right in Reynolds's face.

* * *

Forty-five minutes later, after stopping at a liquor store on Lincoln, they were in traffic on the I-10. "Reality programs have three basic forms," Reynolds said. He had a red plastic cup filled just below halfway with champagne. They were on bench seats in the limo. "First, you have the game or contest show. Think *Survivor*."

"You want to make us a contest?" said Marisol.

"A MILF contest?" said Delaney.

"Not a bad idea." The girls fell onto the floor in stitches. "You guys are fun," Reynolds said. They were normal. "You guys are so normal."

"So why you no marry us?"

"Maybe I will."

"That'd be a great show," Delaney said.

"God, everything is a show with you guys. OK, get serious, I'm trying to teach you something here."

Marisol stuck out her tongue. "Oh, teach me, Reynolds," Delaney said in a sultry voice.

"I'm ignoring you," he said. "The second kind of reality show is the family show. Think Osbornes."

"Or Kardashians?" said Delaney.

"Or Kardashians or the Mormons with twenty-five kids. *Real Housewives* falls into this. Any kind of basic cable novelty show fits this. So *Queer Eye*, *Flip This House*, all of them. Any kind of non-contest following people is in this category."

"So, that is what we are?" said Marisol.

"Well, now, wait a minute," he said. "That's where I'm headed. The third kind of show is the high documentary. These have been mainly on Discovery and A&E. Here, we are thinking stories about people with dangerous jobs or who try to climb Mount

Everest—things that go beyond the bitchiness and shallowness of everyday life in suburbia—things that avoid stars, or former stars, or reflected glory or selling houses to stars or any of that crap."

"What shows are that?" said Marisol.

"I'm talking *Deadliest Catch, Ice Road Truckers, Survival Man, 1800s House*, stuff like that."

"What does that have to do with us?" said Delaney

"Well . . . that's what I'm thinking." The girls were once again enraptured. He went on. "The show *sounds* like a dumb relationship show—a category two show."

"Because we are supposed to be bimbos," Delaney said.

"Exactly," Reynolds said. "And *Pow!* We change it up on them, and it moves across genres into a serious show. We make a category three. You go into serious subjects."

They looked at each other and grinned. "*Qué bueno*," said Marisol.

"I love it," said Delaney. They drank champagne from their red cups. Delaney lit a cigarette and cracked the window.

"OK, back to the show," Reynolds said. "Aren't you going to ask me what serious subjects?"

More laughter. Marisol fell onto Delaney's lap. "We are the bimbooos, Ray," she said from below.

Delaney collected herself. "No, hold on," she said to Marisol. She pretended to be formal, like a student in college. "We're sorry. What do you think the other topics will be, Mister—" Before she could finish she snorted with laughter, and she and Marisol fell into hysterics again.

He leaned into it. "Think about it. We can go to DC. Take you guys around the Smithsonian. We can go to the White House."

"And we can do weird stuff," said Marisol. "We can go to, like the star conventions with the autographs and the outer space suits."

"Mari, we can go to Spain!" Delaney said.

"Spain. Wow. That's right," said Reynolds. "Now you're talking. Give me a cigarette."

Marisol produced a small plastic container from her purse and shook a joint out. "Laney . . . look what I haaaaave."

"Oh God, yes. Light that," Delaney said, snatching it from her. She lit it and handed it to Reynolds. He checked the front of the car; the screen was up. He wasn't sure whether Robert would mind them smoking pot. Then again, Robert had seen everything.

He tapped on the window, and Robert put the screen down halfway. "How you doing up there?" Reynolds said.

Robert kept his eye on the road. "Doing fine," he said. "But this is the worst possible traffic time—it is going to take another hour." He looked at Reynolds. "How are *you* doing back there?"

"We're progressing, progressing," said Reynolds. The window closed, and Reynolds took the joint and inhaled.

Reynolds began talking like a producer again. "I want to make a show that they don't expect, you know? Hit the audience with something that comes at them out of nowhere. That's what it takes to make a franchise, you know. That's what Norman has always told me." He watched them nod. "I think we can blow them away."

They were going about three miles per hour. Delaney and Marisol began asking him technical questions, like how many people were on a crew and whether they could get decked out and do occasional interviews commenting on any disagreements they had with their ex-husbands.

"How bad is the stuff with the Italian brothers?" Reynolds asked.

"Bad," Delaney said.

"Worse for me," Marisol said. "I can't go anywhere."

"You can't *go* anywhere?" Reynolds said.

"She's exaggerating," Delaney said. "But we do talk a lot about how we got here, how we got to this point in our life. Those kind of conversations, those will be good in the show."

"How did we do all of this to ourselves," said Marisol.

The car's lack of motion momentarily quieted them. Reynolds looked at his champagne. Marisol's philosophical question took him by surprise, and he felt swept away by it. He was unhinged, holding a joint. He blurted, "I know. Me too. The truth is I'm so monumentally unhappy. I never wanted to live in Los Angeles." He leaned back and thought and flicked the roach out the window, something he would not have done if he were sober, and if he were sober he would not be smoking a joint, all adding to the out-of-body, wild-eyed nature of the speech. "Check that, yes, I did. Sure, I did. I didn't want to go to New York, and I didn't know what to do, didn't know where to go. So, hey, what the fuck, a job in LA, sounds great, exciting. A job anywhere in Pennsylvania was boring."

"What about the big city?" said Marisol.

"Philadelphia?" Delaney said.

"No. Wasn't interesting to me."

"Pittsburgh?"

"God, no."

"Harrisburg?" said Marisol

"No," he said. Then he scrunched his face. "Wait. Harrisburg? How do you know Harrisburg?"

"It's a capital." Delaney shrugged. "We teach homeschool, we do capitals."

Reynolds said, "Well, no, not Harrisburg or Shippensburg or Scranton or any of those shitholes."

"And why not New York?"

"New York was just so much about making money, everything set up to make money off of making money. Bankers helping people with money make more money, so much that the bankers get most of the money, so it's an ever more rigged game. I don't know. I don't know how the hell that works. Hollywood seemed more ethical." He gave a drunken noise into the air and laughed. "Puh," he said.

Marisol nodded her head and looked forward. "Life is funny like this."

Delaney said, "Oh, you guys, fuck this. Let's keep up the good vibe." She lurched forward and tapped the window. "Robert, can you turn the radio up?"

"It's back there," Robert said, looking in the rearview mirror.

"Hey, man," Reynolds called up to him. "Can you find a gas station?"

CHAPTER 7

Introducing Stella

Stella Stanhope hated when Bella corrected her. It was the only downside for Stella of the fabulous relationship Bella had with Norman, whom Stella adored. Norman's tutelage of Bella had started so early, and he had taught her so much, that by fourteen Stella couldn't get a goddamn thing by her. So, when Stella told her in an argument that, "as P.T. Barnum said, 'there's a sucker born every minute,'" Bella told her mom that although the remark was often attributed to Barnum, he never said it. When Stella went to *Wikipedia* to check, she found, as usual, that her daughter was right.

Bella had occupied a middle ground that other Westside children couldn't find. Half of these kids were disconnected, sleepwalking, nonverbal. The ones in Malibu surfed, the ones in Brentwood went to Hollywood at night. They all lost their sweetness. That's what scared Stella the most: the lack of sweetness. She always thought that when the kids Bella's age reached that awful period—the horrible teenage years, fourteen to sixteen, say—that she would still find them lovable. But that didn't happen. The kids were not still lovable. Other than Bella's friends who were at the house all the time for sleepovers and such, Stella hated most of the kids Bella's age. The short shorts with half of their asses hanging out. The stoned-out ones held nothing for her. She thought them all cretinous wastes. She wanted to smack them all with a rolled up *New York Times*.

Part of the population she preferred, but they too were annoying. These were the achievers; the ones at Harvard-Westlake and John Thomas Dye who were stepping on one another's necks to get into Princeton and Brown and Stanford. The mothers who stayed home and consolidated the unleashed combustion of all their manic, crazy energy—which could have been pointed at winning project bids or seeing patients or cold calling for charity—toward one early-decision letter, to come in November of the senior year, after the 4.1 GPA, the captainhood of at least one team sport, at least two significant nonathletic achievements (one charitable), and the selection of which school to make said early application to. That decision would come at a big sit-down at the dining-room table, where factored in would be all the metaphorical wind conditions: standardized test scores; grades; the racial and gender leanings of the schools ("we have to be realistic about this"); and the number of Harvard-Westlake kids that were accepted each year. They played out every scenario but, like TV executives who start each year of development looking for something new, at the end of the process they reverted to the traditional choices. After they got out of their systems how *pretty* Colby College was or how *nice* the girl who gave the tour at Emory was, they knew they were talking only about Stanford and Harvard.

It was at these moments she hated Los Angeles most. But most of the time she loved it and was happy it was her home now. The other moms would invite her to their houses for coffee. In those half-real, passive-aggressive, no-cooking-smells-coming-from-the-kitchen moments, Stella thought California—Los Angeles, really—might just be a set after all, like the one in *The Truman Show* or in that Gary Ross movie with Tobey Maguire. God, how she had chased that script for months before Nancy fell out of love with it. But Stella held onto the notion that when confronted with California's plain and vapid culture, rather than confronting it, filmmakers and writers just came up with stories involving characters in a "fake" reality, with a manipulative and true reality behind it.

Stella lived in the constant tension between thinking herself chronically unique and commonly boring. She felt her Italian DNA wanted her to become a lady in a tomato sauce commercial, with black lace and an ever-expanding mothering body. She could not recall Don Corleone's wife's name. That told you something: to be in the greatest film ever made and not have a name—this is the abyss you step into. But she also wanted to be thin, thin, thin, in that Upper East Side way. She wished for the sinewy arms and creaseless forehead of the women who appeared in the society ball pictures in the *Times*, growing older into Patricia Buckley or Brooke Astor. She wanted to be an X-ray.

Stella loved her job. It was exciting. She was inundated with great material. She discovered great young artists. She developed projects in the same way as a literary editor—the only other job she'd ever wanted to have. She hired directors, most of them at the very top of the market. She hired casts, which made her the object of great affection to the town's top agents and managers. As such, she was wined and dined and invited to the most exclusive parties at Cannes, Berlin, and Venice during awards season and to small salons with the president. She was integral to the decisions about the movies the world would see.

Her mind continued to wander. The worst part of life, she had decided, was the internal pain that one suffers alone. It wasn't any more about looking good to men, who were, let's face it, idiots and babies. Men feared they were disappearing, all of them. That was the curse of the male. The female curse was much worse, she maintained. It was the curse of nullifying, dying on the vine, growing fat when such was unaccepted, with its attendant drying of sex parts, failure of breasts. The endocrinal grind down. It was not about sex; it was about being strong and maintaining the balance between femininity and art versus competition and equality. Her mother said that women combatted the curse by having children, that that is where she should take her solace, fortify her mind. That is where a woman defends against the men, in the end, when they leave her, like a paper-chip bag, open, the snack gone, only the wrapper with its colors and promises left.

It was then that Reynolds came into the picture. He'd been her neighbor and had tried to wend his way in, asking for a date for months, waiting for her occasional trips back to the condo on Texas Boulevard in Westwood to grab clothes before her next trip. He was funny and not bad looking—a nice body, she realized, when she walked behind him when he was helping her with groceries. He wasn't square, really, that was too sixties. But he was too boring and too *young*.

Stella told him to go away when he pounded on the door three days into her post-miscarriage Valium binge. Reynolds stood in the doorway and would not leave. Within an hour she'd told him everything. She was unhinged, and he was safe, though which mattered more to the telling she did not know. He didn't leave till she was asleep, and the next morning she called him to say thanks.

Over her protests that it was not necessary, Reynolds said he was coming over, soon.

Stella looked out the front door and saw a young woman come out of Reynolds's condo and get into a Honda across the street. Her heart sank. And then she told herself not to be crazy. She didn't have a thing for the *neighbor* guy. Good to nip thoughts like that in the bud.

She took her time coming to the door when Reynolds knocked. She opened it a crack. "I'm OK, you know," Stella said. "I just wanted to say thanks."

He was taken aback, hurt.

"You seem like you're busy anyway," she said.

"I was, I'm not anymore," he said. "Let me in."

"Ha. You're sweet. But, seriously, no worries. I'm sorry about last night. I was upset. So, thanks, but I really have some things I should do."

The Honda returned to the spot across the street, and the girl jerked the emergency brake and got out. She reached into the passenger seat, grabbed two bags, and headed toward Reynolds's condo.

"Have you eaten anything?" Reynolds said.

"Go ahead," Stella said. "Your friend is back."

"Dianne, over here," Reynolds said. He motioned for her to come to the doorway of Stella's place. She handed him the two bags and dug into her pockets and handed him a few dollars change.

"Thanks," he said. "See you Monday."

"See you Monday," Dianne said. She looked at Stella through the doorway. "Bye," she said, and gave a little wave.

Stella looked at Reynolds, incredulous. He watched Dianne go and turned back to the door.

Stella stared. He held up the bags. "Bagels. You said you liked." When she didn't say anything, he held them up again. "Lox and everything. C'mon. Let me in."

"She's very subservient," said Stella.

Reynolds looked confused. "She's my secretary."

Over time, Reynolds wore Stella down. It wasn't overnight, and it wasn't without work. Looking back, she wondered at the inverted course they had taken. In those first days, she had been the complicated one, her life bearing down on all fronts with opportunities for love and advancement. Everything seemed to have value, and her job with Nancy Beveridge afforded her access. The world of *Mad Men* was gone; the women older than Stella—aside from Nancy, who was always an anomaly—were secretaries, and there were no women younger than Stella. She and her friends realized they were in the right place at the right time. Working at the studio, she had opened the door and if you were pretty and loose and ambitious you could go places.

Reynolds was the simple one. He'd held little interest for her in the early years, as she bounced between semi-famous actors and divorced producers. He was just Reynolds, her neighbor. He was cute but not in any kind of game. When she thought about him, which wasn't often, it was when she needed to fix up one of her friends or a new girl in town. But mainly she shot him the occasional "hi" and tried to avoid him.

It wasn't supposed to happen this way. Nancy filled up space between script meetings with speeches to her and Pam about how they would be the first generation that had it all: sex, careers, money, kids. Careers had not been available before. Nancy and the very few like her had put their noses under the tent at the expense of having children. Nancy made no bones about how jealous it made her. Stella and Pam did not demur when they received these optimistic projections. They knew it was true.

Stella had been taken by surprise when Reynolds told her he was working with Norman Daley. She had adopted the Hollywood habit of not being happy for anyone, ever, no matter how small or unimportant the promotion. Luckily, she hadn't succumbed to the related Hollywood sleazeball tradition of claiming to be responsible for a promotion or new client for someone the Hollywood sleazeball barely knew.

She had learned to be awful in so many ways. She remembered the golden retriever look on Reynolds's face when he'd tried to nonchalantly deliver the news that he was now Norman's guy. She'd delivered an acidic "I'm so happy for you" that would have made Nancy proud.

It was she, not he, who settled down. Not so much just after the miscarriage. She still had a few bridges to burn. But she looked up six months later, upon returning home once again from New York, after one more set of all-nighters at the New York Film Festival, with Jack and Bobby and Dustin. They were shits, all of them, but she loved it. Stella thought anyone who pretends it's not fun rolling around with movie stars is lying.

Her weariness was growing because of the changes in the business. Eastern Oil was in charge of Paramount after a byzantine set of mergers no one could understand. This made her mad, and in her inner monologue she noted it spelled doom. She watched Pam in the meetings and could tell she hadn't a clue either when the lawyers started coming in and discussing projections and the new distribution fees and overhead charges that were to be charged to the talent.

It had all made Stella tired. At thirty-three, she'd found it was no longer as fun to take a limo to JFK straight from Elaine's. She still to this day perked up when she heard the gossip, still spent five to eight nights a year getting smashed in Toronto or Paris or Pittsburgh when she was with a fun and hip group for whatever accidental reason.

But the worm turned at that time. Stella started to accept Reynolds's glances when they ran into each other; gave him the green light to flirt. They went to the movies on the weekends, and she stayed in on Sundays and made him tacos. They smoked a joint before dinner and ate and laughed while they watched a VHS tape of some picture she'd brought home from the office. She let him kiss her and take her to bed.

The rules were clear enough—not stated, because that wasn't necessary. She was the prominent one, whose name was in the trades, who took lunches and dinners with the big agents, who was expected at Nancy's dinner parties. When she was mad at Reynolds or felt like flexing, she disinvited him to a party or dinner or premiere she knew he was looking forward to. She ignored him during the Independent Spirit Awards, when he insisted on going even though he had a seat at a very bad table. She handed him, or withheld, access and invitations like a cruel stepmother.

But that was when Stella was mad, and eventually her anger subsided. Reynolds's simple loyalty became more and more appealing, whereas the splash and reflected glory of her job became less so. Not being 100 percent on fire for her job for the first time began to bum her out all the time, and she came to want to just be at home. And being at home meant being with Reynolds.

Stella and Norman had already been friends for years—ever since he'd made her sit and have a drink with him at the bar of the Beverly Hills Hotel, where they were both taking a break from the crowd at John Calley's third wedding. Stella could tell Norman liked her the moment he saw her arriving at the bar like a fugitive. They were thick as thieves after ten minutes.

Soon, Norman and Carol were having Reynolds and Stella out for weekends every so often. Reynolds was proud of being able to deliver fun events and access to Norman to her, and she was pleased to take all she learned from Norman back to Nancy. It helped, especially as her partying, and therefore her access to information, dropped off. It was nice to be able to say she heard such and such from Norman Daley.

CHAPTER 8

Norman and Carol

"You never stop with that goddamn thing," Carol said. She was pointing at the iPhone in Norman's hand.

He considered her. "Who does? It's taken over the goddamn world." Turning it left and right he said, "It's fascinating."

"Big deal," she said.

"Big deal? It's in the hands of a billion people—probably more. It's glued to the hand of every single person *everywhere*."

"Yes. Big deal. You get your e-mail. It's a phone. You listen to songs. I get it. It's a little gadget."

Norman stared.

"You act like some goddamn kid," Carol said. She put a lid on a Tupperware container and looked in the fridge for a place to put it.

"Grumpy," he said. "I'm going."

It was their code. They'd promised long ago they would stop each other from getting grumpy. They both had grumpy parents who lost whatever sense of humor they'd had for life—and it hadn't been much—in their eighties. Norman and Carol had moved the four of them out to LA. And as their four parents rode out their time in California, their lives coalesced, and they fed off one another's complaints and ailments. His father, Sam, was the quietest. He sat for hours and listened to Norman's mother and Carol's mother gossip and reminisce about the Bronx as they handed newspapers back and forth and watched CNN and true-crime stories and waited for dinnertime. But Sam was the exception. He never complained about them or about his lot. Sam always made himself useful. Carol doled out a steady supply of things that needed fixing or assembling, and Sam completed every task. He was proud to be Norman's father and Sam dispensed advice almost never.

Carol told Norman once that the reason he liked Reynolds was because he reminded him of Sam. Not in a heroic way but in the comfortable way Reynolds went about his business without bothering anyone, self-sufficient and uncomplaining. Norman had thought this right, but he also thought—and maybe Carol had meant this all along—that there was a sadness to Reynolds that could remind one of Sam. Because the thing they had in common was that their quiet manner did not have as its basis a fundamental happiness or contentment. They were both soothing without being soothed; they resolved things for others without being resolved themselves.

Carol was the opposite. Funny, diplomatic, and a softie, Carol started each day with a walk on the beach at five thirty, not out of service to a fitness compulsion but rather because that was when she woke up each day and, once up, she wanted to take a walk on the beach.

Her efficiency came from having any number of people within reach who were happy to fix things for her. She had her fingers into everything—the charity world, the art world, the Hollywood world, the Malibu world, the political world, and the private-school world. She had accomplished this by being ever-cheerful and possessing a call-it-like-it-is sense of humor. From eight to eighty, one and all came to Carol with their secrets and problems, and she called in favors, had a word with involved parties, and dispensed stern advice to get things fixed—much like Norman.

CHAPTER 9

Starting to Wonder

Stella thought of her mother, how she never would have had such negative thoughts about her father. Bella was like this too. Like baldness, the gene skipped a generation. Her mother, Minnie, was undefeatable, talking to everyone she met, leaving a wake of good cheer behind her for seventy years, from Stuyvesant Town to Dix Hills to Malibu. Stella went nuts for the first two hours of every visit because she had to hear about whosoever it was her mom had sat next to on the plane. The most interesting young guy from Nova Scotia, he was an editor—did she know him? When Reynolds talked Minnie out of giving out their number to other passengers or limo drivers with screenplays, there was no conflict—but when Stella told her not to do it, Minnie told Stella that she should stop being so mean to her.

Mean. Stella had written the word off long ago as a hobgoblin, used by anyone against any woman who was successful in Hollywood. Her boss at Paramount, Nancy, was mean, she would grant that. But her generation, Stella and Pam, they shook off *mean*. They didn't start out as secretaries and thus never had to learn the inside game. Their generation at Wellesley and Barnard—the Hillary diaspora—assumed they could get it all. The boys they went to college with had the condescension learned from their fathers beaten out of them in gender-bias classes. The men her father's age and just below—the last set of patriarchs—wanted women Stella's age as their mistresses.

No one would ever have called her mother mean. Stella remembered the disgust she felt when Minnie brought her father a cup of coffee or a glass of wine when he asked. It was subservient, plain as day. She made it clear to Reynolds from the jump that there wouldn't be any of that bullshit. She didn't want a house husband—she wasn't an egomaniac. She was connected enough to reality to see the disadvantages to *that*. But there was to be a partnership in full, with no exceptions and no expiration date. That was the deal. It did not need to be signed.

Stella pulled out her phone and called Reynolds.

"Hi," Reynolds said.

"Where are you?"

"Uh," he said. He adopted indignation at being quizzed. "Coming back from golf. Where are *you*?"

"I'm home. You left a bit of a mess."

"No, I didn't," he said.

"I'm kidding. I like coming back when you've been here alone."

"How's the coed?"

"Coming back soon. She's with Heather."

"My third favorite.

"You sound busy," she said.

"No," he said. "What's up?"

"I just wanted to make sure you will be home by Sunday." She cringed. She knew he would see through that, since it was the kind of detail she could have covered in an e-mail.

"Sure," he said. "Anything else?"

"Nothing else. What are you doing tonight? And where are you staying, anyway?"

"We're just at some motel near the courses. It's not far from Rancho Mirage. Little pool in the back. Haven't decided what I'm doing tonight. Just gonna go play some big course they're all excited about today and then probably read."

She decided that it would be worse now to sound as if she were prying. "OK, have fun. We'll all be here tomorrow when you get home. Bella and Heather will be back, and they say they want us all to cook something."

"OK. Great. Say hi."

"Bye."

"Bye."

CHAPTER 10

The North Came from the South, and the South Came from the North

At 8:40 p.m., Robert and his crew pulled off the Pomona Freeway at the Enchino exit and drove past a small commercial shopping center, one of the ubiquitous brown-stucco developments off any exit anywhere in California, with a McDonald's and a Chili's and a Sav-On. Robert followed the directions Reynolds had provided and presently came upon what appeared to be a large park with softball backstops and infields and soccer goals.

"Look for a sign-in desk," said Reynolds, over Robert's shoulder through the partition. "Wait, there it is."

They poured out of the limo next to a brown (they came to realize that all the buildings in the park were one shade or another of brown) concrete structure that housed restrooms.

"Laney, look," Marisol said, pointing to the outfield of the closest softball diamond. Dozens of beige-white tents covered the area in rows.

Reynolds approached the two men who sat at a table with a sign that read: "Welcome to soldiers of the Blue and Gray."

"Howdy," said the larger of the two. He wore a blue Union Army soldier's uniform.

"Hello," said Reynolds. "The reservation is under Stanhope." Then he looked both men over and added, "Fantastic uniforms, both of you."

"Thank you kindly," said the Union infantryman who was checking them in. "Give me just a second here."

"You have a reservation?" Marisol said to Reynolds.

"Oh yeah," he whispered. "You need one. I got a tent."

"Just the one tent?" said the Union check-in guy. He gestured at the ladies.

"Yes, that's all I requested. But, do you have more available?" Reynolds said.

"No, sir," said the Confederate check-in guy, shaking his head. "We are plum filled up." This Confederate officer wore a threadbare gray tunic with gold trim. He looked to be the same age as his Yankee counterpart.

"Are you in the show too?" Delaney asked the Rebel.

"Yes, ma'am. Twenty-fourth Alabama."

"But the suit," Marisol said to Reynolds. "It is so . . . unimpressive."

"No, Marisol," Reynolds said. "By the time of Gettysburg, many of the Southern soldiers' uniforms had become very ragtag, and the Confederacy did not have enough money for many supplies at all, let alone new uniforms. This gentleman's uniform is incredibly realistic. Bravo," Reynolds said with a nod.

Marisol whispered to Delaney, "It's like Raynoldo is changing into a professor."

"Are there motels nearby?" said Reynolds to the men of the Blue and the Gray.

"No vacancies," said the Confederate guy.

"Oh, it's OK," said Delaney. "It'll be fun. I love camping."

"Are you ladies reenactors?" said the Confederate.

"We are actors," said Marisol. "Does that count?"

"I am kind of showing them the whole deal," Reynolds said.

The Southerner said, "Do you have gear? Reenactment stuff?"

"No, we didn't get a chance to dress," said Delaney. "This was a last-minute thing."

"Well, check out the dress shop tomorrow. It has lovely vintage wear."

"Your tent is all the way down this first row," the Confederate said.

A different Yankee officer with a robust beard said to Reynolds, "Will you be needing a uniform?"

"No, I'm all set."

"Which outfit you with?" said the man. Reynolds saw he was smoking a corncob pipe.

"First Division, First Corps, Army of the Potomac," Reynolds said.

"Iron Brigade. Very good."

Reynolds leaned toward the corncob-pipe man and asked, "What can they *be*? I mean, who are they going to dress as?"

"Oh, leave that to the ladies," said the man.

Reynolds noticed that Delaney and Marisol were greeting some women who wore nineteenth-century frocks.

"My wife is back there," said corncob-pipe man. "She's been Jennie Wade about thirty times now."

"No kidding?"

"And the other lady is Mary Lincoln all over the West Coast," the man said, adjusting his pipe.

"Really?" Reynolds realized that Delaney and Marisol had wandered off somewhere.

"Yes, sir," said the man. "Not too many other Marys this year. We always get a lot of Lincolns. Even saw a black one. Light-skinned guy. Looked more like Obama." He started to clean his pipe. "To me at least."

They talked about the schedule. Tonight would be general socializing and making camp. Saturday was to be a full day, with battles starting early in the morning and continuing till dusk, when a big bonfire and party were scheduled. There were five hundred people expected from all parts. After the bonfire, there would be a cotillion at an off-site location. "Everyone wears their best getup to that," the man said.

Reynolds felt his buzz fading. These people were intense. "OK, then. I'm going to go get dressed," he said. He walked toward the limo, where Robert was sitting in the driver's seat, looking on in bewilderment. He turned around, and Delaney and Marisol were back.

"Lady who owns the store was gone. Something about her tent being a twenty-minute walk away."

Marisol said, "We can get clothes tomorrow. Now, let's get wasted. These guys have tequila somewhere."

"I am *so* down." Delaney said. "Let's go find it."

"Jesus Christ in the morning, Abel, do you see that guy?" said the Union infantryman at the table.

They both stood up. "I'll be damned."

They were looking at Robert.

"What?" Reynolds said.

"The Old War Horse, as I live and breathe," said the Alabaman. He was pointing at Robert, sitting behind the wheel.

"What?" said Reynolds.

They approached the limo. Robert lowered his window.

The Confederate officer guy took his cap off. "Are you coming out, General?"

"Excuse me?" said Robert.

"What is going on?" said Reynolds.

"I thought you knew the war," said the Confederate. "That man is the image of General Longstreet."

Reynolds looked at Robert through his glassy gaze. Shit, it was true. With the beard and the gray hair. He was the goddamn spitting image of James B. Longstreet, Lee's right hand. The Old War Horse.

"Let's get you over to the outfitters," said the Confederate.

"Robert, call your dispatcher," said Reynolds. "I'm gonna need you all weekend."

"Mercy," said the Union soldier. Then he pulled Robert up out of the limo and gestured to a nearby Union colonel, whose uniform was completed by a thick white moustache. "Cyrus will take you to your tent," he said to Reynolds, "while I find what we have for General Longstreet."

Cyrus led Reynolds, Delaney, and Marisol toward the field. The ladies tiptoed around the mud as they walked. They passed a rope divider, which ran the length of the field. At the opening, a sign read: "Entering Town of Gettysburg, July 2, 1863." Outside the tents, men were making fires and sitting on canvas seats. A few lawn chairs and barbecue grills were set up beside plastic coolers of beer.

"If it were up to me, there'd be none of this current-day material allowed," Cyrus said. "There's a lot of guys who are not very good."

Marisol said, "Yes, Cyrus, what is that? They should be only like it is the time of the Civil War."

"Amateurs," said Cyrus. He slowed and looked at the numbers stenciled on the tents. "Here we are. North 362." They stood outside a simple canvas tent situated amid a long row of other simple canvas tents. The soldiers camped on either side of Reynolds's tent took in the sight of Marisol and Delaney. Reynolds was aware of the staring, but he realized the girls didn't care. They were like little kids playing make-believe or actors in an acting class—or ex-models from the Valley. He noticed that a group of six Confederate soldiers, who were from the camps to their left, had stopped talking and had now stood up and taken off their caps.

"Howdy," said Delaney.

"Hello, ladies," said one of the soldiers. "You just improved this camp one hundred thousand percent."

"That's all?" said Marisol.

Reynolds ushered them away from the soldiers and into the tent.

There was barely room for the three of them. Reynolds rolled his sleeping bag out, and they staggered around and plopped down on it. Marisol produced a coke bullet and passed it around.

"What do we do now?" said Delaney.

A Confederate campsite neighbor stuck his head in. "Hi there. Y'all want to join us? Would you like a glass of wine, ladies? I brought a few bottles of Cab."

"Ah, I need wine," said Marisol, and she followed him.

Reynolds noted that the light inside the tent had a mellow look, as though a flashlight were held close to the side of a brown paper bag. He began to struggle to his feet, but Delaney, who was lying next to him on top of the sleeping bag, pulled him down and kissed him. She tasted like cigarettes and gimlet mint. He lifted up and looked at her face. It was the same as the one in memory, turned at the corners a bit by age but the same. The eyes were gold, and she was just a tiny bit buck-toothed, enough to notice but still be unique and cute, beautiful and distinctive all at the same time. Like her body, her face was curvy but not chubby, angled enough to achieve alchemy. She pushed him off, saying, "Let's go see what they're doing."

He tried to keep her down, but she giggled and was up and out in a flash.

Next door, he saw they were equipped with tin cups. Marisol was sitting on a white plastic chair. She was eating Triscuits from a box.

"First time?" said the leader of the Rebels.

"Yes," Delaney said.

"Well," Reynolds said, "I did a fair amount of battles when I was younger." Delaney looked at him warily, like he was showing a fake ID at a bar. He shrugged, and said to her, "*What?*"

"Glad to have you," said a Confederate officer who had joined the conversation. "Name's Clayton. We're part of General Pickett's brigade." He waved his hand at the other soldiers, drinking from the tin cups. "Don't get many ladies like you all."

"We're doing a TV show," said Marisol.

"And we're the hosts," said Delaney.

The soldiers nodded at one another.

Reynolds went with it. "It's like a documentary. Where are you guys from?"

"Sacramento."

"*Dios mío*, you come from Sacramento for this war?" said Marisol.

"Oh yeah. This is the big battle. We wait all year for this."

Reynolds felt a sudden desire to establish his credentials. "Like I said, I did a fair amount of stuff when I was . . ."

Clayton wasn't listening. His eyes went over Reynolds's shoulder, and he jumped to his feet. The other Rebels did the same.

"What?" Reynolds said.

"Reynaldo!" Marisol said.

Robert approached the tent. He wore the full uniform of a brigadier general, Army of Northern Virginia. His gray flannel was set off by a golden-yellow shoulder rope, and on his head was a Stetson.

"Reynolds, look at this shit," Robert said, looking down his left sleeve and his right.

"Evening, General," said one of the Confederate kids.

"Uh, evening. Company dismissed . . . at ease," said Robert. All the soldiers sat down after a respectful moment. One offered Robert his lawn chair, but Robert declined.

Instead, he grabbed Reynolds by the arm. "Who the hell do they think I am? Who's Longstreet?"

"You're, like, the number-two guy in the whole Southern army. Lee's right hand," Reynolds whispered.

"I need a drink," Robert said.

One of the Rebel soldiers had a boom box blasting the Rolling Stones. Delaney got into the music and within a few moments was dancing. Clayton, who looked like he spent a lot of time playing softball and working on cars when he wasn't doing reenactments, started a mini Mick Jagger strut.

"Reynaldo," Marisol said. "Get dressed!"

Reynolds went inside the tent, where he had set down his gear. It was getting dark. He stepped into the trousers and donned the tunic. He heard Delaney laughing and looked outside the fold of the tent to see that she was leaning on Robert, also laughing. Reynolds returned to his uniform.

Reynolds's emotions were all over the place. This was supposed to be a secret, his way of returning to something—as Van Morrison might say, of getting down to what's really real. He'd planned it for months, changed his mind a dozen times. For him, Reynolds Stanhope, unlikely Hollywood lawyer, agent, manager, producer, this was all just so . . . weird. Yet, that was what made it perfect. It was an escape from the horror. It was not just the horror of the bitchiness and the shallowness and the culture of lying. Not just the baseless relationships and the shallow lives lived in pure heedless, ambitious greed. Not just the disgusting sucking up to thirty-eight-year-old studio heads but the relentless drive to star-fuck, every minute of every day, and consider each incident of star interaction a notch on one's scoreboard, keeping precise records of the time you were close to Clooney at a dinner party, when you partied with Jen at the Miramax after-party at the Hotel du Cap, when you got drunk with Johnny and Leo at secret poker games.

This trip to Enchino was supposed to be his little secret fling. In truth, it was maybe more than that. He had been coming around to something: he was going to give up on doing creative things for other people. He was not going to be another in a long line of people coming to California to die. He was not going to be Nathanael West's Homer Simpson—or the cartoon character they'd made of the iconic literary figure.

He was going to return to his authentic roots and get involved in the living version of the historical battle that informed so much of his orientation—and the orientation of America and Americans. Gettysburg is everyone's home. Without Gettysburg, all the history of the Union would be different—our very gene pool would be completely different. And Gettysburg was what he knew best. It was a way for him to be authentic.

Yet he had fucked up the whole plan. The presence of a real live icon of his youth had blown his highfalutin ideals out the window. Was it sex? *You betcha* was the only answer. In his defense, almost no unresolved, death-fearing man his age could resist this set of challenges. In any event, regardless of the excuses and the extenuating circumstances, the truth was he had—with shady intent—let himself invite two polite and sweet women who happened to be bona fide, grade A, five-star smokestacks. His high thoughts were out the window, and he now found himself the proprietor of a five-by-six-foot tent in Enchino, California, with Delaney and Marisol after a full day of chaos and alcohol and even some drugs. Instead of a journey to the sanctuary of his memory and to the calming effects of this anonymous pilgrimage to his roots he had envisioned, he was no longer anonymous and he was far from the sanctuary of his memory. He was in a raucous gathering with five hundred or so weirdos and Delaney, Marisol and Robert.

"Let me look at you, Soldier Boy," Delaney said, coming back inside the tent, her bust once again leading the show.

"Hello, Scarlett," he said.

"Wrong side of the war for you," Delaney said. "And Rhett was a blockade runner. You look like cavalry."

"You're close. Infantry. I'm a general. I command the cavalry too."

She came up next to him and kissed him. He reached for more, and she glided away.

"These guys are insane," Delaney said, taking his hand. "C'mon. Let's go do some background research on what it was like back then."

It was dark by now. Drawn by the magnetic force of Delaney and Marisol, a crowd of soldiers had amassed. It was like a college kegger and the girls were at the keg. Reynolds looked for Robert but couldn't find him.

Cyrus was in front of him all of a sudden. "Delaney says you're from Virginia. What part?"

"She said that?" Reynolds said.

"Been to the courthouse?" Cyrus said.

"Appomattox?" said Reynolds.

"What else?"

Reynolds closed his eyes, like a prissy casting director. "I've been to Appomattox Courthouse, but I'm not from Virginia. Are we supposed to be talking in character?"

"Sure, but it's loose," Cyrus said.

"What I mean is, is it 1863 as far as we're concerned?" Reynolds said. "You know, are we *in* 1863?"

Cyrus sighed. He pointed toward the ground. "Well, they had no boom boxes then," he said. "It's a matter of how serious you are. To me, historic accuracy is the essence of this thing. On the other hand, see these guys?" He pointed at a bonfire to the left. "They just drink moonshine." Reynolds saw the jug. "They get blown away in the battles."

"Jesus. But you drink Cabernet?" said Reynolds.

"Yeah, I'm not a fanatic."

After a pause, Cyrus said to Reynolds, "So you're not from Virginia?"

Reynolds got right next to Cyrus and whispered in his ear, "I'm from Gettysburg."

Cyrus stood back. "No shit?"

"Don't tell anyone. Please."

"*Noooo shit!*" Cyrus grinned like he'd met D. B. Cooper.

Reynolds gave the nod of an old pro. "It's a long way from here."

A shotgun went off.

"Oh, Christ, here we go," Cyrus said. A Rebel yell—the famous bloodcurdling war cry the Confederates issued when they were on the attack—went up. The blast came from a group of eight or so graycoats moving in from the south side of the park. "It's the idiots from San Diego."

"Southern?" Reynolds said.

"Yeah, but they're terrible."

"Yeah, boys," one of the Rebs yelled out. "Get ready, all you Yankee sons of bitches."

To Reynolds, they looked like mechanics, maybe air-conditioning guys. With gray coats and Confederate hats. Lots were in the shade of yellow called butternut. They had not much more than actual Confederate soldiers had, Reynolds thought.

Cyrus pointed at a tall man in the incoming group. "That's Rooster. He's the ringleader."

"Alabamians?" Reynolds said, squinting at the uniforms.

"They don't know what the hell they are. They change every battle."

The tall guy in the Confederate uniform walked up. "Hello, Cyrus."

Cyrus looked him in the eye. "Evening, Rooster."

Rooster doffed his cap. "With any luck, Providence will be on our side in the morning."

"Can it, Rooster," Cyrus said. "The men were not as God-fearing as that fucking nutball Stonewall Jackson. You don't have to pretend to be so devout."

"Oh, spare me your lectures, Cyrus."

One of Rooster's men came up and said to Cyrus, "Where are your whores?"

"What?" Reynolds said.

The soldier spied Marisol and Delaney, who were now outside a neighboring tent, and led a few of his fellows over toward them.

Cyrus was focused on Rooster. "Have you learned anything since last year?"

"Did the Battle of the Wilderness in Ojai. Didn't see *you* there," Rooster said.

"I had back surgery."

"Shoulda been there. We had a helluva time," Rooster said. "You need a new sash, by the way."

Reynolds's tin cup that he got on eBay was empty, and he felt his teeth grind. He headed over to the Cabernet bottle. While he had been listening to Rooster and Cyrus, the crowd of San Diego Rebels had circled around Marisol and Delaney.

"You ladies trailing the battle?" said one, a handsome surfer type.

"Must be some good trade," said another. Boozy laughter went up.

Marisol was enjoying the attention. "You boys look very good. Right, Laney?" Reynolds thought Marisol looked a little cross-eyed.

"For sure." Delaney took the surfer's cap and donned it. "How do I look?"

"Mighty fine, ma'am," the surfer said, a little more in character than the rest.

"Delaney, Marisol, come here," Reynolds said, hissing.

Marisol leaned into a husky Confederate. "What are you, *chico*? Are you an officer?"

Before the kid could answer, Rooster went over and put his arm around Delaney. "Hello, darlin'." Then he looked at his nemesis. "I got to hand it to you, Cyrus. This is pretty good, bringing your own tail."

"Hey," Reynolds said.

"How much for three of us?" Rooster said.

"Excuse me?" said Marisol.

"We got Confederate scrip and three silver dollars," said the young one, crowding in.

"What'll that get us?"

"Hey, that's a little too far," Reynolds said.

"They's whores, ain't they?" said the husky one.

"Ha!" Delaney said. "Nooo. No. We're making a *TV show*. You guys can be in it."

"Come on," said Rooster, pawing Delaney.

Reynolds stepped in. "Hey, knock it off, Rooster."

Rooster pushed him. "What the hell, man?" he said. "They're here, and I'm making a business proposal."

"Reynaldo, what in the fuck is this?" said Marisol, ready to fight now.

"How about I give you a good rogering," said the young husky Confederate to Marisol.

"A what?" she said.

The three Confederates were now enclosed around the girls; Reynolds tried wedging his way in. Cyrus and his Union soldiers stood back about ten feet, not knowing whether to help or find something else to do.

"Raynoldo!" Marisol yelled.

"Get off me," Delaney said, pushing Rooster away.

"Stop it," Reynolds said. "What's wrong with you guys? This is a reenactment! Not every woman is a hooker! Then *or* now, I might add."

"That sign over there says it's 1863," said Rooster. He grabbed at Delaney's breasts.

"Hey!" Delaney said.

"*Cabrón!*" Marisol said.

The shoving was now in full force. The surfer had his arms around Marisol's waist. Rooster hung on to Delaney. Reynolds was beginning to panic.

Then a booming voice rang out. "*What is all this?*"

Rooster and his boys stopped and looked up. The crowd parted, and Delaney and Marisol were unhanded.

There stood Robert, in the large gray hat and the full-on regalia of a Confederate general. He was coming back from the bathroom.

"General Longstreet," said someone in the crowd.

"Dude, that's fucking *good*," another voice said.

Robert addressed the crowd. "You men—what is the meaning of this? Desist immediately." He strode in and shoved them away from the girls. "Who is your commanding officer?"

"I am, General," Rooster said. "Sorry."

"Back to your tents, all of you," Robert said.

As the group broke apart, Robert addressed Delaney and Marisol. "You ladies OK?"

Marisol made a motion with her hands as if brushing away a fly. "They just a little horny. Like all soldiers before a big battle," said Marisol.

"I'll tell you what. They know their history," said Reynolds. "I can't believe how scared they are of you, Robert. They know exactly who you are and why you're so powerful."

"Tell me about it," Robert said. "Guys are saluting me all over the goddamn place."

"Let's get in the tent," said Delaney.

Inside the tent, the light reminded Reynolds of Delaney's *Playboy* centerfold. Robert said he was going back to check on the car; Reynolds suspected that, drunk with power, he wanted to wander around camp a bit more as General Longstreet. Reynolds lay on the ground. He was so tired. Tired, drunk, much on his mind, and still a bit stoned.

Marisol sat on the grass in the corner of the tent. She took off her bra and turned toward Delaney, momentarily giving Reynolds a full-frontal view.

"Stop, Mari," Delaney said. "Not in front of our producer." They cracked up.

"I'm so sleepy all of a sudden," Marisol said.

Delaney followed Marisol in becoming topless. Seeing Delaney's breasts, Reynolds was transported in time. Her nipples were just as he remembered, just as in the centerfold, the silver-dollar kind, with a button on top. He was on his side, just as he had been so many times in his youth.

Delaney raised to *her* side, facing Reynolds, brought him in for a kiss, and reached over and massaged him through his authentic britches. Reynolds made a mental note to himself to remember this moment: he was in a Union Army general's uniform, at Gettysburg—in Enchino—with his all-time favorite Playmate, getting masturbated.

"Do you like that, baby?" Delaney said. "Do you like me?"

"I do," he said. "I do."

"Are you going to put me on TV, Reynolds?"

"I am."

"Tell me." Delaney moved her mouth right next to his ear and whispered, "Tell me what you're going to do. Make me wet. Tell me, Reynolds. Tell me."

"I'm going to make you a star," Reynolds said.

"Again, right, baby?" She rolled on top of him, holding her breasts from each side with her arms.

"Yes."

"Again, right?" She bent closer to him. 'You're gonna make me a star again, right?"

"Yes." Reynolds said, his eyes closing, her amazing breasts in his face. "I'm gonna make you a star again."

DAY 2

CHAPTER 11

Did We Do Anything?

"Wake up, sleepyheads," said Marisol. She parted the flaps of the tent, balancing four Venti coffees from Starbucks. Reynolds realized his head was on Delaney's breasts. For a moment, he knew contentment, awake but still in the realm of dreamless sleep. The light from the tent opening split his head. He and Delaney both lifted their heads, smiled, and averted their eyes. She set about tending to her face and hair; he looked for something, anything, to mask his breath. He knew to do this from the many times Bella snuck into his and Stella's bed, and when he woke and tried to pull her close, she recoiled, telling him, "Ew."

Reynolds tried to remember what had happened. He managed a quick look at Delaney again. She was still beautiful, even in a tent, even after a ridiculous night. Had it all been just a dream? He felt the texture of the ground. There were little gravelly rocks in the dirt. The composition was familiar: infield. He looked to the other side, and there was Robert, sleeping on his back in full uniform. He looked like General Longstreet in his coffin.

Marisol nudged Robert. "Wake up Mister General. Your troops must be waiting for you." Robert stirred, had a moment of recognition, and closed his eyes again.

Reynolds took his coffee. "*Gracias.*"

"Thank you, *chica*, you are the best," said Delaney.

There was silence. Reynolds considered the deep brown liquid. He thought of what coffee meant to the soldiers in Gettysburg. They were crazy for it, both sides, making it every morning. Most of the time, they didn't have actual coffee beans, so they made it from anything they could find: peanuts, chicory, huckleberries, used grounds.

"It's time to fight, no?" Marisol said.

Delaney was looking at Reynolds as he put his phone in his sack.

"Lots of messages from Bella," he said. "Kids, you know."

"Oh brother, do I."

"I'm sorry about last night," he said.

"What for, sugar?"

"I don't know. It was such a crazy day. And now I brought you here." He opened his arms and turned to the right and then the left.

"No, it's fun," Delaney said. "Last night was fun."

"Did we . . . do anything?"

She laughed. "You're cute in that uniform."

They were walking ahead of the others, toward the cluster of municipal park structures at the center of activities. He and Robert were in full colors, but because they'd both slept in their uniforms, they weren't as crisp as those of the other officers they saw. The center of the octagon—the space where the eight home plates met each other—was also home base for the SCCWA event. The restrooms, and snack bar were in the center of octagon, while a line of little shops and souvenir stands were aligned in the space between the chain link fence backstops of Field One and Field Eight. This weekend, instead of softball players in white breeches carrying aluminum bats, Confederate and Union soldiers in blue and gray breeches with hundreds of old-time rifles were on the fields.

"Oh God, Laney—I just remembered our idea. Muffin tops."

"That's *right*," Delaney said. "Reynolds, what do you think of this? One of the things we could do, too, you know, is like an episode on how people can fight the muffin top."

"What's a muffin top?" Reynolds said.

Marisol grabbed his waist. "Stop for a second." She held the part of his skin above his hips at the waist.

"See that," said Delaney. "That's a muffin top." She grabbed at Reynolds's muffin top with both hands.

"Women have the same problem," Marisol said.

"It is a real opportunity because no one talks to the body issues," Delaney said.

"Like Martha Stewart used to talk to the home issues, but no one on those shows talk right to the audience about these kinds of issues. *Nada.*"

"Also, like dishes and cooking—" said Delaney, stopping as she saw something. "God, look. They all have beards, all the soldiers. Was that a thing?"

"Yes. That was a thing," Reynolds said.

"Is that why you grow a beard, Ray?" Marisol said.

"They're all from the South, it looks like," Reynolds said.

Then he saw Cyrus sitting at a stone picnic table with his Union troops: three young guys, a ragtag bunch. Reynolds walked over to them. "Hey, man," he said to Cyrus. "Lots of greycoats going to fight, it looks like."

"Yeah," Cyrus said. "It's always that way. Fucking weird. It's like they all like the Southern thing."

"It's a way of going against blacks without saying it," one of the kids, Bob, said.

"You should see the Mexicans," said a skinny kid, whose name was Stevie. "They all go for the South."

"Do I have to, like, leave you guys?" said Robert, looking down at his Confederate gray.

"Of course," said Cyrus. "What the hell do you think?"

"You need to find the Third Brigade, right next to Lee," Reynolds said.

"Hey, good," Cyrus said, impressed. To Robert, he said, "Should be over by the soccer fields."

"Where do the fans sit?" said Delaney. "We need shade. It's hotter than Texas out here."

"Y'all need to get up over there where those ladies are heading," Cyrus said. "You can watch from the grandstand on the side of the parking lot near field three. All the little stands and shops are there. They have one of them Mexican food trucks that comes around to construction sites."

"Robert, can we have the keys?" said Marisol.

Robert, his sense of professionalism jarred out place by major force majeure events, like, for example, a hurricane, tossed the keys to her.

"Have a good day of battles, boys," said Delaney, and she blew them kisses.

"Jesus Christ, how many Jeb Stuarts can there be?" Reynolds said to Cyrus after the women left. Scattered throughout the congregating masses every few feet were soldiers with the hip boots and wavy hair of the young Confederate cavalry officer. It was like an Elvis convention

"Tons," Cyrus said. "You have to remember, most of these guys are amateurs."

"I would think more would be Stonewall. He was the interesting one," Reynolds said.

"How so?" Bob said.

"Religious nut," Reynolds said.

"Well, I mean, so was Lee," said Cyrus.

Reynolds agreed. "Never more than at Gettysburg."

"Ever wonder why Lee didn't move back?" Cyrus said.

"He couldn't," said Reynolds. "You know when you watch poker on TV, and the guy starts losing and gets more and more frustrated until he just throws all of his chips in?"

"Um hmm." Cyrus said, chewing a blade of grass. The other guys were listening too.

"Lee was 'pot committed'—beyond the point that he could fold. He wanted to end the war then and there, at Gettysburg. I think he was tired. Anyway, he threw it all in. He told everyone that God wanted him to end it on those fields, amidst those trees, on those rocks, and over those stony ridges," Reynolds said. His tour-guide speeches were coming back to him. "Lee decided to bet it all on a charge right up the center of the Union Army. He got greedy. And impatient. He lost his sense of reality."

"On poker shows they say that's 'going on a jag,'" said a third kid assigned to their crew, who was younger and pudgy.

"That's exactly right," Reynolds said, pointing at the pudgy kid. "He was on a jag." They walked in silence, Reynolds thinking, remembering the dead. "And it was a helluva mistake." Cyrus and the boys nodded.

After walking quietly for another minute, deep in thought, Reynolds tuned in to a conversation that had begun among the kids, off to the side.

"Yeah ... no. I mean, it is really fucked up," the pudgy kid was saying. "I go and do this thing and I'm proud of it and all. Like it shows something I'm passionate about, and I spent a lot of time and whatnot. Lots of work went into it, I'll tell you that. And shit, there I am at lunch one day, you know, at La Salsa, and this fucking same kid is staring at me. Like a real creepy kid. He says, 'Hey, you wrote a book, right? About Charlemagne? Middle Ages, knights and all?'"

Reynolds and Cyrus looked at each other, surprised. The boy went on.

"I was kind of impressed—like, blown away that someone I didn't know had actually seen it. So, I'm like, 'Yeah that's me. Thanks, dude. Did you like it?' And he just laughed at me and said 'Yeah, it was pretty cool.' Like that. But I could tell he didn't mean it—like a fucking little asshole. Next thing I know, he's finding me anytime I go to the food court in Calabasas or anywhere. This little pimply-faced kid is there giggling at me, dragging his friends over, pointing and shit."

"Well, ignore him," Cyrus said.

"What's your name?" Reynolds said.

"Nicely," he said.

"Nicely?" Reynolds said.

"Whatnthefuck?" Cyrus said.

"Nicely," said Nicely.

Reynolds considered that for a moment. "Tell me about your book, Nicely. It's about Charlemagne?"

Nicely nodded. "The period between AD 754 and 810."

"Is your father a little on the queer side?" said Cyrus.

Reynolds stared at Cyrus. "Really, Cyrus? Just because of *Guys and Dolls* you go right to that place?"

Cyrus shrugged.

"You're an amazing combination," Reynolds said to Cyrus. He shook his head and looked back at the kid.

"My dad sells insurance," said Nicely.

"What about your mom?" said Cyrus. "I bet she listens to a lot of show music."

"Shut the hell up," said Reynolds. "Listen, Nicely, I want to hear more about this book. What made you do it?"

"Passion."

"For Charlemagne?"

"Yup."

"A whole book about Charlemagne?"

"Sixty-seven pages with illustrations."

"Oh Christ," Cyrus said.

"No kidding?" Reynolds said. "And now you're here."

"What's that supposed to mean?" Nicely said.

"Means you're a freaky little history nut," Cyrus said.

"What are *you* then?" Nicely said to Cyrus.

"Son, I've been wearing this uniform for twenty years. Just because you went to the fucking costume store and bought that terrible outfit as soon as you got to an unpassable level of Saxonic boredom doesn't mean you can waltz in here and start inhabiting the soul of a man from the Iron Brigade."

"OK, Cyrus, take it easy," said Reynolds. "Nicely, how's school going? Are you still in school?"

"I was at Mount SAC Tech, but I dropped out." He pointed at Cyrus. "What's wrong with him? Why's he such a dick?"

"Mount SacTech? That's a school?" Reynolds said, and right away felt bad for being such a snob.

"Yeah, online school." Picking up on Reynolds's concern, Nicely said, "Doesn't matter. I don't need it."

"What are you going to do with yourself if you quit?" Reynolds said.

"I'm gonna write books."

"Here we go," said Cyrus.

"You can make enough money doing that?" Reynolds said.

"Absolutely," Nicely said. "I'm doing one on this here—the Battle of Gettysburg—right now. Then I'll write the next one on the next thing. It'll add up."

"Impressive," said Reynolds. "Charging ahead, I guess?"

"I'm also making a brand of whiskey—with musk oil."

"Hmm . . ." Reynolds said.

"You're an idiot," Cyrus said to Nicely. "Musk oil is not a tempting taste."

"Then what would you make, Cyrus? Like blackberry wine or something gay like that?"

Stevie broke in. "Hey, OK, you guys are such great experts, let me ask you this: Where are the slaves? If the Civil War, if this whole fucking hoo-ha was about freeing the slaves, where are they? What kind of shitty reenactment is this?"

"Well, *Stevie*, what the hell do *you* think?" Cyrus said. "That the slaves just sat there on the side like some goddamn prize that would be presented to the winning team? Like the refs would unlock them when the scores were in if it showed that the Union side won? We try to recruit Africans, but we don't do well, for understandable reasons. But still we try."

The other boys had been curious along with Stevie, but after Cyrus drilled him between the eyes, Bob and Nicely treated Stevie like an unclean asshole. When Reynolds gave Stevie a second look, he saw that the kid appeared to be bursting out of an out-grown Boy Scout uniform, at least the shirt, with the patches and the troop number on the sleeve. Stevie's pants could have been plain blue britches from Walmart. It was so blistering hot—and absurd—in the park that Reynolds began to go a little blurry. He decided he had bigger fish to fry than the realism of the cannon fodder's uniforms. They all had the right headwear, though, so he tried to lighten the tone.

"Where'd you guys get such good . . ." he circled his head with his finger. "You know, such good stuff?"

"They're like smashed down felt baseball hats," said Nicely, who had on a black Stetson that wasn't realistic at all.

Cyrus spat out tobacco juice. "I don't know how we let these fucking freelancers have a party at the bleeding-heart sacred Jesus Christ Battle of Gettysburg."

"OK, I'm going," said Reynolds. "Cyrus, the term is *African Americans* not Africans. Do you, like, live in the world, man?"

Reynolds kept walking, passing through one of the outfields, then along the side of the parking lot, which was blocked off every-where by traffic sawhorses placed by an overzealous/delusional park war-game organizer. Stevie came with him as walked.

"If you and Bob don't like this, why do you come?" Reynolds said.

"Oh, we like it. We just like to break Cyrus's balls."

"What do you do for Cyrus?"

"Used to run three different trades. Now Cyrus has made me project manager," Stevie said.

"That's great. For someone your age especially. How about Bob?" Reynolds said.

"Bobby's a cop."

"No shit."

"Yup. A good cop. Gentle giant but a badass. Always has been."

"I thought you guys might have been troublemakers," Reynolds said.

"Oh, we *were* trouble makers," Stevie said. "But after it got too stupid, Bobby and I joined the army. When we got out, I started to do construction—learned framing, roofing, sheet rock installation. Bobby became a cop and I went to work with Cyrus. He liked that I was in the service. Tell you the truth, he's been very good to me, even though he's a Civil War kook. I don't mind coming to these things with him, even though I bust his balls. And Bobby just started coming with us too. Actually, it becomes like a hobby. It's good to have a hobby, my dad always said."

Reynolds gave a friendly but guarded greeting to the woman in front of the boutique named the Covered Wagon. Once up the steps, his path took him past two potted palms and then onto steps going right back down to the ground. The wood and canvas and the giant wagon wheels were just a cheap movie-set front opening into a tented area in which sat three trailers, the kind used to house movie stars—contractually locked and cleaned daily, no individual to receive better. First-dollar-gross-level star wagons. The tented space opened into what looked like a mini lobby, with regular grass for a floor. At the far end of the covered area were three separate parallel-parked RVs. Each had an open door, up which the lucky customers stepped into spaces replete with costume racks full of nineteenth-century ball gowns.

Two women who appeared to be reenactors' wives were right in front of him. He followed them into one of the trailers and eavesdropped as he looked around.

"Oh wow. Terri, look at this," said one.

"That's darling," said Terri. "I wonder where they get it all from."

"They can't make it, can they? It's not, like, an all-handmade Civil War boutique, right? It's one of hundreds that all get their clothes from a central place where Mexicans and stuff are making everything look old?"

Terri yelled, to no one in particular, "Are there any prices on these?"

A voice replied, "On the sleeve."

Reynolds slipped away and headed back to the confines of the visitors' dugout, on the third-base side, where Cyrus and the boys were looking at their guns. They all had their tunics open. Stevie and Bob were wearing old-fashioned undergarments, which impressed Reynolds.

"What happened?" said Cyrus, when Reynolds sat back down in the dugout.

"It turned into a regular store astonishingly fast," Reynolds said.

Beyond them from one of the softball fields rang the warning beeps of a truck moving backward.

"LRT skirmishers please go to sector seven-A and seven-B congregation point," said a voice on the loudspeaker. "Field is ready." The loudspeaker sounded more like a megaphone, with plenty of distortion.

"What is LRT?" Reynolds said.

"Little Round Top, what else?" Cyrus said.

"Oh Cyrus, Jesus," Reynolds said. "If I know anything it is that the Battle of Little Round Top should never be called LRT."

The men grabbed their guns. Reynolds watched Nicely and the other boys fix themselves.

"OK, let's get out in front here on the double. Prepare for single-line march!" Cyrus commanded, standing next to Reynolds with his arms crossed. "Can't coddle these kids," Cyrus said.

After Cyrus, with Reynolds's half-hearted help, tried but failed to get the boys to march in formation, he said, "I'm going to take a leak before I get out there, so I don't piss my britches." Reynolds agreed and joined him.

After hitting the urinals, they moved to the sinks and began to wash their hands. Reynolds hit the soap dispenser and a giant blast of pink soap and white foam shot out A tall man with a thick broom mustache emerged from one of the stalls. He was in a Confederate uniform.

"Hello, Cyrus," he said.

Cyrus turned and looked at him. "Charles. I'll be goddamned. Reynolds, meet Charles."

The man stuck out his hand. "Charles Oakley, how do you do."

Reynolds was fumbling with paper towels, trying to get the foam off his hands. "Hi . . . hi, sorry."

"So, how ya been?" Charles said to Cyrus.

"Can't complain. You fixed up here?" Cyrus said.

"Twenty-seventh Alabama this weekend."

"Ah. You're gonna come up the rocks?"

Charles was about six foot three. He shot them both a resolved look. "I'm looking forward to it."

"I bet you are. Think Reynolds and I are grabbing a soda. Till we meet again?"

"Yes. Count on it." Charles turned to Reynolds, nodding at his uniform. "Nice to meet you, General."

Reynolds felt a shot of pride. "Thank you, Charles. Those were brave men, those Alabama boys. Under John Bell Hood, right?"

"That's my man," Charles said.

"You kind of look like ol' A. P. Hill," said Reynolds, speaking of a different Confederate general.

Charles was not too happy with that. He touched his hat and left.

Cyrus gave Reynolds a dirty look.

"What?" Reynolds said. "C'mon, man, he's bald. John Bell Hood had hair. Long, flowing, gigantic hair. And an insane beard. *You* know that, Cyrus."

"Charles has been around a long time. Don't be a show-off."

"Show-off?" Reynolds said. "All of you guys are show-offs! Every single person at this . . . this softball field . . . is a show-off! He looks like Richard Ewell. He's playing John Bell Hood, Cyrus, for Christ's sake. You wouldn't want him looking like John Bell Hood and playing Richard Ewell. Would ya?"

"This is important to us."

"I know," Reynolds said, now upset that he had offended Cyrus. It was good that there was a hard-core group of pseudo-historians who took time out of their lives to keep the tragedy of the war alive.

Cyrus lightened up. "I guess Charles *doesn't* look very much like Hood, does he?" he said. "I might have to bring that up in San Luis Obispo."

"What's there?"

"Shiloh. Next month."

The woman behind the snack-bar window said, "Next." Cyrus looked at the menu scrawled on a piece of poster board to her right.

"Give me two hot dogs and two diet Dr. Peppers" To Reynolds, he said, "That OK?"

"Fine. That's a fine breakfast."

Cyrus paid the woman and tipped her a dollar. They moved to the pickup window and retrieved their order.

Reynolds tried to change the subject. "Does everyone have a name that becomes their cultural reference point?"

Cyrus thought about that. "Well, look at you."

"I know. I do feel at home," Reynolds said. Then, "And that's bad."

Cyrus, who was focused on putting what looked like his third packet of ketchup onto his hot dog, said, "What?"

"Never mind," Reynolds said.

They were back with the boys after a few minutes.

"What do we do in the afternoon?" Reynolds said.

"Wheatfield," Cyrus said "But we got LRT square in our sights now.

"Chamberlain. Alabamians and Maine men."

Cyrus nodded. "We got an ass-load of Chamberlains."

"Explain something to me. It's day one right now, we are going to Culp's Hill on that softball field—that I suppose is well enough. But it happened on day one. The Battle of Little Round Top was on day two . . . July second, eighteen sixty-three. We are ready to begin reenacting day one."

Cyrus looked at him. "So what?"

"It's not right," Reynolds said. "Little Round Top was on the second day. *You* know that, man."

"Yeah," said Stevie. "You kind of gotta roll with it. I mean, the first day of the Battle of Gettysburg was really on a Tuesday. In July." They were walking forward, and Reynolds stared straight at what was apparently their theater of war. Stevie used his hands a little as he talked. "In *Pennsylvania*. A hundred and fifty years ago." The kid let it sink in. "I mean, technically, yesterday was day one, and then they just scheduled all of the big battles for today and are calling it day two. It's all fraudulent at some point." He pointed at Bob. "Me and Bob aren't Union soldiers. I install tile for Cyrus, and Bobby fights crime, for shit's sake."

Everyone marched in silence for a few seconds.

"It requires a little imagination, is what he's saying," said Cyrus.

CHAPTER 12

GPS

Two weeks earlier, using their nickname for each other, Bella said to Stella, "Myrtle, let me see your phone. I just learned the coolest thing." Bella worked on it for a few minutes, reciting small things to herself. Then she looked up and said, "Well, he should never be a spy."

"What?" Stella said.

"Well, Myrtle, you can find Dad whenever you want. There's a function on the iPhone that allows you to find any other iPhone on your account—if the other phone, Dad's phone—hasn't been turned off."

"Ours *are* connected," Stella said.

"Well, then, old girl, you can always find where he is," Bella said.

"Oh, I would never do that," Stella.

"Sure, Mom," Bella said. She handed Stella back her phone, smiled, and left the kitchen.

Saturday morning, around nine, Stella looked at the phone. To date, she had resisted stealing Reynolds's iPhone to check his e-mails, to read any of his texts—from whom, about what, she didn't know. At first, she resisted because she thought it an improper action of mistrust toward her soul mate. But as the years passed, Stella didn't do it because every divorce seemed to involve someone or other looking at their spouse's phone, and Stella didn't get divorced.

But now, since she had become so concerned, she figured it was not snooping. Stella looked at her phone and selected the GPS application. Instantly, there was a little red phone figure on the map showing Malibu, inland of the Cross Creek shopping center. Her location.

Stella couldn't resist. She hit *Search* on the tracking application, and a new map popped up, showing a second red dot. The second red dot was tiny. She hit the directional arrows, but then the image was too far out, showing all of southern California. She zoomed in again. He was inland somewhere but not in Palm Springs. He was in . . . Enchino? What the fuck was in Enchino? He must be going to Vegas, she thought. Maybe he was going to Vegas, but he didn't want to tell her because . . . because why? Because he didn't want to tell her what?

Whatever. She went to the bedroom and lay down. It was nine a.m., and she was already bored. She had done twenty-five minutes on the treadmill and been to Starbucks. She had a stack of scripts to read, so she might as well get to it. She thought of how the movie business sapped her strength. It spoiled the excitement, took away her passion.

After thirty years in the business, the color of the movies had been reduced to a pile of black-and-white screenplays on her night table. It was the life she'd chosen, the life she'd grabbed by the throat and not let go of once she'd realized it was available to her. Everyone in the game had signed over their movie souls—their

Cinema Paradiso selves—in a heartbeat. The price, the Faustian bargain, of being in the movies was that you lost the thrill of being at the movies. These days, if you weren't careful, being part of a successful release became something akin to being part of a winning team at a corporate 10K. Still, years earlier, when she'd had her first premiere of a movie she'd produced, at the Chinese, she'd brought her dad and it had been a glamorous, fabulous night.

Sure, there were a few "childlike geniuses," who constructed great playgrounds around themselves and were the focus of *New Yorker* and *Vanity Fair* articles about how they kept the magic, how it was the very essence of what kept them going, of what made them special and *better* than the other heartless douchebags of Hollywood who had lost the "childlike wonder." But when you scratched the surface—as in worked with them every day for two years or got a little too wasted and slept with them after a long night in Toronto or Venice—you found those guys to be the worst, mainly because their attitude toward everyone and everything was, in fact, so "childlike."

No, for most of the ones like her—the multiyear, multimillion-dollar-guarantee, just-below-mogul, if you think about it, super-stars—there were retreats in Santa Barbara and Newport Beach discussing noninvasive placement and the opportunities afforded by cloud computing. She left hotels with mini duffel bags full of branded studio swag and the latest handheld device from the latest Silicon Valley frenemy. There was to be another retreat in a week, the mere thought of which made her jump out of the bed in a panic.

After thirty seconds, Stella jumped up again. She put a few magazines in her bag and then went to her dresser. She picked a different scarf than last time. She didn't know when it had started, this secret habit she'd adopted, which was akin to smoking by yourself or looking up crushes on Facebook but more insane. She and Reynolds kept an old white '57 Chevy Bel Air convertible in their garage. It was the kind of thing they had done when they were happy, buy that car. Neither of them was a *car* person—one of the things that made their being in Hollywood so ironic. It was her suggestion; they saw it on a lawn in Glendale when they were coming back from visiting the set of one of the studio's pictures in Palmdale. She'd said, "Oh, c'mon, let's get it."

Mostly it sat in the garage. There was a phase when Bella liked it, so Reynolds would take her out and let her sit up front, which Stella said he should not do because of all the front-seat safety issues one heard about. It aged Reynolds in her eyes when he'd said, "Christ, Stella, when I was a kid we used to ride around in the front seat all the time." It wasn't consistent with his usual approach of measured consideration, the acceptance of the logic of science and the advancement of it all. Stella loved Reynolds for his sense that things were getting safer and improving with time.

She didn't know when Maria had crept back into her mind. Stella tied the scarf around her head and took the top down. She rolled the windows open with the crank handle and adjusted the rearview mirror. Stella loved slipping into Maria's character when she needed to work something out. It wasn't until she pulled out of the Shell station at Cross Creek that Stella put her Wayfarers on, and upon doing so she felt as if she was taking the first sip of the martini, like she was slipping into a booth with a good friend and taking up the menu. Driving north on the PCH in a Bel Air convertible was a timeless escape—a relaxing drive. The only way to react to the cinematic viscera existing between those southern-facing beaches and the rock walls was to develop a machine to traverse it. But it wasn't just the machine, that was the key part. It wasn't just the car any more than it was just the horse in *Lawrence of Arabia* or *High Noon*.

Maria, the character also had to evolve. This is what the movies were for: to help conjure the human riding in the car. Don Quixote was a man on horseback, but he was more than that. When you got in the car in Los Angeles, you got to play the part. You got to escape into the part. Everyone could be a star. You could wrap a scarf around your head and put the glasses on and drive down the PCH and you could be Audrey Hepburn, you could be Tuesday Weld.

The first time she'd snuck away in the car by herself, she'd driven north to Oxnard. Once there, she'd looked around the parking lots and Mexican restaurants and found nothing, so she drove back to Malibu. She had been so excited, but she was scared. She'd felt a little silly, so she'd stopped and gone back in the house, grabbed her bag and her phone. She'd snapped out of it and gone to work. But it stayed in her mind, like a good book or a good movie. She drove into town in her normal car, the BMW. She didn't need the big one, the seven hundred or nine hundred or whatever. She always got a five hundred. She felt it was not too obnoxious, a dick car, the kind men got; nor was it too small and cutesy, the little two-seat three hundred coupe that the D-girls and assistants from rich families drove. Little bitches in their three series convertibles, driving around looking for married men to distract. Did they think they were the only ones to ever have no fat on their thighs?

The Bel Air had a radio, but Stella didn't play it. She watched for surfers. Surfers don't let themselves be governed by time; somehow construction guys from all over LA get to the water anywhere in Malibu when there is a swell. She looked at those guys parking their pickups on the stretch between Topanga and Leo Carrillo, where there was free parking. No different from the time of the Beach Boys or Steve McQueen or Peter Fonda—you could park right here, right in front of the most famous beaches in the world, just like that—no traffic meters, no parking cops.

She thought of her favorite literary character: Joan Didion's Maria, from *Play It as It Lays*, feeling the sun and the wind in Technicolor, a camera car in front of her, the director and DP looking out the back, driving in the movie in her mind, on the road in the sun and the wind. It was the guiltiest of pleasures. It had the feeling of being out of control, different than an affair or a sneaky act requiring GPS. She was not sure anyone—Reynolds, Bella, or anyone else—would have given two hoots about what she was doing. There were far worse things than putting the top down on the old car and going for a ride. Today she even had a purpose: she was going to Enchino to spy on her husband. It was like filling her head with the sweeping gray and brown and bleak parts of Joan Didion. She filled up with gas at one of the stations in Malibu, got in the Bel Air, scarf in the wind, and began to drive.

As a rule, Stella didn't respond to guys in wraparound sunglasses, especially outside the gross bathrooms at an Exxon station off the 71 freeway outside Enchino. Then she stopped dead and realized what the guy had said. He was walking into the bathroom now.

"Excuse me. Excuse me," she said,

He stuck his head back outside the door.

"Did you say 'war show'?" Stella said. "Like an air show?"

"No," he said. "It's one of them old-time things. Where they dress up. Like in the Civil War. They come all done up. They do it every year."

She watched him.

"Pain in the ass," he said. "They block off the roads and every-thing. Bunch of wackos."

"Like a Civil War reenactment?" she said.

"Exactly."

"Oh." She moved her head backward like she had been hit in the forehead.

"I know, weird, right?" he said.

She thanked him, and he shut the door. She drifted over to the convertible. Reynolds had come to watch a Civil War reenactment. She was relieved. While it was weird, it wasn't as bad as it could have been; he could have been involved with a meth lab, say, or a hooker who was blackmailing him. Reynolds had come to watch one of those idiotic things where the people dressed up like the Civil War? Wow, he was losing it. What the hell was bothering him?

But it was strange. Reynolds never talked about Gettysburg—she couldn't remember the last conversation she'd had with him about it. She'd never been there. His parents had moved to Mon-mouth, New Jersey, by the time Stella and Reynolds had met. Stella was aware of his childhood in Gettysburg only through rare references he'd made and the photos his mother had shown her when she and Reynolds had visited his parents, driving down from New York City to say hi, bringing Bella when she was a baby.

They were good people, Reynolds's parents. Removed, smart, scholarly. Stella often thought that Reynolds's challenge in life was to grow past his interior life and develop into the more out-going spirit of someone who is not obligated—self- or not—to the world of the mind. Bob Stanhope was a difficult man. Ever since Stella had come into the picture, Reynolds's father had pestered

Reynolds—and by extension her—about his screenplay on Dvořák. Reynolds's charming personality came from his mom. While they were never close enough for Stella to say she loved his mom, she admired her resilience and cheerfulness. Still, Stella didn't understand his mother's subservience to the brooding man in the other room—this was Stella's issue with most women of Susan's age. And Susan was a woman who had a PhD, who'd lived through the sixties.

Stella had learned more about the Stanhopes' life in Gettysburg from Reynolds's mother than from him. Susan told Stella about how he stood out among the Gettysburg College professors' kids—not the easiest bunch of kids to be in school with—for his love of history. His father didn't love that Reynolds had been like this—he felt an animosity toward the History Department, which Reynolds's mother laughed off. Despite his father's disapproval, as a boy Reynolds had loved to walk around the battlefield, she said, and the park had made an exception for him when he'd wanted to become a guide, hiring him though he'd been underage. His mother was amazed at the amount of tip money Reynolds had brought home his first day.

Once, his mother snuck into one of Reynolds's tour groups. She told Stella she couldn't get over what an entertainer he was. He kept two bullets that had met in midair during the battle. He talked about his favorite commanders the way other kids talked about sports superstars. He took the group around the rocks at Devil's Den, climbing up and down the boulders with them.

Yes, it was weird how Reynolds never spoke of Gettysburg all these years, almost like it was a secret, or something embarrassing. A wave of emotion caught Stella off guard. He didn't tell her, she realized, as if for the first time. He'd come here to see his Civil War, that's how lost he was. The wave came rushing over her the way it did when she thought about an old aunt she didn't visit, though this was worse. Reynolds was her husband. She knew he was in some kind of funk, but she didn't indulge it. It was pathetic, she thought. And so cliché. As she drove down the 71, she realized her eyes were getting wet. God, maybe he *was* lost. He had to be lost to be doing this.

She got off the freeway and saw a sign that said, "Southern California Civil War Association Parking." She followed the road to a municipal lot and paid five dollars to a Boy Scout.

"Where is this thing taking place?" she said.

He pointed out the man-made hill in field seven. "There's a battle about to begin now. The crowd sits over there on the side."

She needed to see him. Or would she freak him out? He must have had his own reasons for not telling her he was doing this. She would have to make up an excuse for how she found him. Bella told her? She decided to deal with that if she had to; now she wanted to find him. Just ahead of her, grandstands had been set up, and she could see what looked like a big green construction site, a hillside. *How did they make that?* she wondered. It was huge. Two kids in Metallica T-shirts walked in front of her. A woman in a bonnet and old-fashioned dress was selling lemonade from a pitcher. It was like a show, like Disneyland, or the medieval fairs she'd heard about. There was a food truck and huts selling swag. She saw a sign that said, "Black Gunpowder and Black Gunpowder Vouchers." Who *were* all these fucking people?

Stella had to reach him, to get him back from all this. Maybe he would laugh when he saw her. She vowed to herself to be nice, to tell him not to be embarrassed, and to not ask him to explain it to her right away. They could spend the day, and then she would ease him home. They could go to the Ivy in town on their way back and drink margaritas and leave the cars if they had to. They could get a room at the Four Seasons, or even the Bel-Air. They hadn't done that in ages.

A cannon went off. *Jesus, that's loud*, she thought. Was this going to be like one of those air shows she'd read about, where the planes crashed into the stands? Would a cannonball hit their seats? How nuts was this? Was it run by people competent on issues of public safety? She took in how massive the whole project was, and she reasoned that it was about the same size and scope of a Soccer Saturday at Moorpark. God, she needed to find Reynolds. He must be so sad to be doing this. She wanted to see him. She began to run toward the stands. The battle was starting: soldiers in gray started up the ridiculous hillside. Smoke from guns filled the air. She needed to find him. She approached the crowd and searched the faces. The train-station scene from *Reds* flashed in her mind. She was Diane Keaton. She imagined Reynolds, sad and beaten senseless, standing in the crowd in Enchino watching a Civil War reenactment. Where was he? Where was that Warren Beatty face that comes into view just as you've given up hope, just as you thought he was dead? He wouldn't be dead, Stella convinced herself, just exhausted and needy and, thank God, alive.

Stella wound through the crowd, looking desperately for Reynolds. The people were white, lots of them in T-shirts and sweatshirts emblazoned with the names of colleges. Some wore Civil War pins and other memorabilia, and there were lots of flags, Confederate and Union alike. A lot of the guys were war veterans, it seemed, retired, wearing VFW caps and baseball hats with the names of aircraft carriers. The sounds from the battlefield were earsplitting. A loud cannon burst went off. *Jesus Christ*, she said to herself.

She reached the end of the crowd and didn't see him. She doubled back, heading the way she came. She glanced toward the fighting for the first time. She saw the men in the misfit uniforms—they must be the South. She remembered from some history class that their uniforms were much more ragtag than those worn by the North. A different look: the thrown-together kind versus the put-together outfits of the Union. Ever since Stella went to work at the studio, she'd been much more in favor of the put-together. She resented the thrown-together types. *Where the hell is Reynolds?* she thought. She was beginning to get mad. What the fuck was he doing all the way out here at this stupid thing? Stella looked at the GPS again, and it showed he was right here. She sighed and looked out to see the war. The South guys were fighting their way up the hill. One big guy was almost at the top. She thought that weird, because it looked like the South was going to win the battle up there. A nerdy guy in front of her pointed at the hill and said, "Look, hand-to-hand."

At the top, a soldier in blue hopped out in front of the barricade and went at the guy on the attack. The big gray soldier swung his rifle at the Union soldier. *Very real*, she thought. *I wonder if these guys are stunt men in real life?* The blue soldier ducked and then brought his rifle up and into the big guy's chin. An astonished sound went through the crowd, followed by cheers and a few boos. "Niiiice," said a voice.

The Confederate collapsed into a pile. "Did he really hit him?" the nerdy guy in front of her said. In the foreground, the Union soldier stood at the top of the hill, framed in the sun. A perfect cinematic moment, like in a Terrence Malick movie.

Then it hit her: it was Reynolds.

It was Reynolds out there in the battle. Stella's jaw dropped. He was hatless, and his hair blew a little with the wind. He was tall and blue and valiant. The buttons of his coat gave off a glint in the midday sun. Stella gasped. My God, it *was* him. The noise of the battlefield died down, and all she could see was Reynolds, triumphant in battle. She lost all sense of where she was. She was looking back in time, transported somehow. He took a step forward, and he was Gary Cooper, he was John Wayne. She felt a wave of emotion she didn't recognize. An American flag was planted behind him. She became transfixed on the man; he was such a *man*. Her head tried to stop her. A voice in her head said, *Come on, it's so corny.* The flags, the male silliness of it. She fell into a swoon. She felt the sense of doing something wrong; for so long she'd been trained not to feel this way—inferior, worshipful—about men. It was an artificial weakness forced upon women by a patriarchal society. But it subsided instantly, so strong was the force of what she was feeling. This was all of it: lust, admiration, the feeling of protection. She felt protected. Reynolds was a man. He had all of this inside him.

"Look, it's Reynolds!" someone said. Two rows down to her left, a blond woman was doing little jumps and pointing, talking to another woman. Stella stepped down to see who it was. She saw their faces. Two pretty women in cheap clothes.

"*Sí, sí!* Oh my God, Laney. *Es* Reynolds," said the other one. They were both Stella's age. Very pretty, in fact. Too pretty to be out here at this thing. Stella felt a wave of jealousy.

The blonde squealed, "Go, Reynolds!"

"Ray-nahldo!" said the brunette.

Stella stepped toward Delaney and Marisol and said, "Excuse me, do you know that guy out there?"

Delaney smiled and said, "Yes. He's our friend. We're here to watch him."

The Mexican girl looked at her too. "Do you know him?" she asked.

Out on the battlefield, a group of blue soldiers pulled Reynolds back behind the barricade.

"Look, Mari," said Delaney. "They're pulling him back. It is all so *real*."

"And crazy."

CHAPTER 13

The Battle of Little Round Top

Cyrus and the boys walked along. Reynolds saw that Stevie was looking a little sleepy.

"Kind of tired today," Stevie said to Reynolds's look.

"Hmm," Cyrus said.

"I got a lot of shit to do, you know," Stevie said.

"Here we go," Bob said.

Just then, Reynolds looked at the audience in the viewing area and saw Delaney and Marisol on lawn chairs. *Christ*, he said to himself, *anyone else would have left.*

Cyrus planted himself in front of Stevie to block his path. "Do you know how far the Twentieth had to walk the three days before the Battle of LRT?"

Stevie looked like a teenager getting a lecture on pregnancy prevention. "I know."

"Tell me," Cyrus said. "Humor me. How far?"

"Like a hundred miles or something."

"Eighty miles in four days! Eighty miles in four days! Eighty miles in four days! You've never done anything like that in your life—in or out of the Army!"

Stevie stomped the ground with his foot in protest. "I'm not saying I have."

"Of course, you're not. Because you *haven't*. You *haven't* done anything like this."

"C'mon, now, calm down," Reynolds said.

"It's true," Stevie said. "But, everything you know is from that Ken Burns documentary, and that stupid movie with Ted Turner in it."

"That's not true!" Cyrus said. "I've been studying this war my whole damn life. Bastards. You can ask me anything. Go on." Cyrus stomped away for a second. Aggravated, he stormed back and pointed at Stevie. "Ted Turner paid for that movie, for your information. He could place himself any-damn-where he wanted."

Bob said, "What's that have to do with anything? The point is we do this because we are paying respect to something. You are always saying that yourself, Cyrus."

"I'm tired, that's all," said Cyrus, now moving slowly, like Stevie. They marched on toward the rec center.

"Look," said Reynolds, wading into the quiet. "This is actually something I know about." He felt them look at him. "I know I told you guys last night, but to say it again: I grew up there. Maybe I can explain that a little better to you.

"This place can remind you of Gettysburg." He looked around. "Well, not really." He saw that he was losing them, so he got it together. "It's hot enough, I'll say that. That's a good place to start." He closed his eyes. "Yes, that's exactly the place to start. In Gettysburg on July 1, 1863, it was approaching a hundred degrees. It was dusty too. Out there, it was pretty much farmland. People seeing it for the first time think it looks like Kansas or something when they see it, though I've been to Kansas and it looks like South Dakota to me, but that's a whole other story." Again, he saw them looking at him as though they didn't know what he was talking about. "It looks like it's going to take a while to start. Let's go back to the tents."

The company liked this idea and headed that way.

"OK, so it was hot like this. You should understand that Pennsylvania was not just part of the North, it *is* the North. Philadelphia is a hundred and fifty miles away from Gettysburg—almost as close as LA is to San Diego. You must also understand what it felt like to people in the North that the Southern army was in Pennsylvania. Now came a battle. Now came a battle for the soul of the country. Imagine that you don't have any of the preconceptions you have today about the Union or freedom or slavery—none of that. None of that had to be the way it turned out. It all could have been different."

Cyrus said, "That's what I tell these guys."

The outfit arrived at the tents, and all took a load off. Delaney and Marisol were there and had bought a bunch of beer and put it on ice for the guys.

"It's true," Reynolds said. "Lee had spent the first few years of the war kicking the Union's ass. In the summer of 1863, both armies were heading north, out of northern Virginia and the swampy areas around DC. The Union Army was much bigger and much slower than the Confederates. Some of the stuff about that army is funny. For example, do you know who the general of the Union was before the Battle of Gettysburg? Joseph Hooker.

That's right. Well . . . he was an idiot. Stonewall Jackson took fifteen thousand men all the way around his right flank at Chancellorsville and sneak attacked in broad daylight. Yup, Old Joe Hooker. He was famous for all kinds of reasons. Do you know where the word *hooker* comes from?" He nodded in the direction of Delaney and Marisol. "Comes from Joseph Hooker—he let prostitutes follow the troops and come into the camps at night." He gestured toward the girls again. "That's how they got their name."

"Didn't know that," said Cyrus. He looked at Delaney and Marisol, as did the rest of the men.

"Oh Jesus, Cyrus," said Delaney, throwing her arms in the air. "We were wearing costumes."

"Oh, I'm sorry," said Cyrus.

"Is like Thousand Island dressing," said Marisol.

"What?" Reynolds said.

"Like Thousand Island dressing. In the fifties. I saw it on the TV. A documentary. The man, McCarthy, had the people so scared of the Russians and the *comunistas*. They change the name of the salad sauce to Thousand Island—not Russian." Everyone stared at her.

"*Es* true."

"Oh," Reynolds said. "Yeah, kind of like that."

"I love things like that," said Marisol. "That is why I like history eso much."

"Perfect," said Reynolds.

"But we're not being hookers again tonight," Delaney said.

Robert came up just then, and leaned over to Reynolds and whispered in his ear, "Are we staying here again *tonight*?"

"You can leave if you want," Reynolds said.

Robert sighed and rolled his eyes, resigned. "No, I'm staying," he said. "I canceled all my shifts."

Reynolds tried to get back to his story. "So anyway, by the beginning of July, Lee thinks he is invincible."

Bob said to Stevie, "Fuck. More Lee."

Stevie made like he had a pistol and put it in his mouth and pulled the trigger.

Reynolds said, "He is a deeply religious man, and he is certain that God is on his side and will not let the South fail." Reynolds felt the rhythms of his past grab him. The guide in him started to come out. He found his voice. "But Lee has one problem: he has no eyes. You see, back then the cavalry was an army's eyes and ears. Generals like Lee used reports from the cavalry to ascertain where the other army was and where it was heading."

Marisol said to Delaney, "They were not all on horses?"

"I guess not. I don't know. Shh."

"So, the leader of the Confederate cavalry, J.E.B. Stuart, got himself lost a long way from Lee. Lee didn't know where the Union Army was, see. On that first day, Lee thought he could just blow into town and take the high ground." Reynolds held up his right hand to indicate high ground and moved his left in toward it. "But Buford had backups coming from just eight miles away, and they got there in time to reinforce his troops. And commanding those troops, in the Civil War's most gallant ride: John Reynolds."

An announcement came over the loudspeaker, "Attention, reenactors. The engagement on Little Round Top will begin in thirty minutes on field number seven. Little Round Top, field seven."

"That's us," said Cyrus. He started away from the tents toward the ball field.

Delaney grabbed Reynolds's sleeve. "Reynolds, Mari and I are gonna go to Starbucks. We'll catch you over there. You want anything?"

"No thanks, honey. I gotta go fight this battle. It's a bloody one."

Reynolds caught up with Cyrus and the boys heading over toward field seven. "How are they going to do this?" Reynolds said "It's flat as hell out here. We're on cotton-pickin' little league and softball fields. That fight was up and down a hill."

Cyrus pointed to a huge green monstrosity three fields away. "See that? That there's the hill."

"What, we stand on that?" Reynolds said.

"Yeah, that's Little Round Top. Each session, there's one of the hill fights over there in field seven, where we're headed."

As they approached it, Reynolds came to realize how big the edifice was. The reenactment association had placed a tremendous structure that reached about thirty, thirty-five feet high—life-size, to Reynolds's eye. The faux Pennsylvania hillside was green and rocky. It undulated and had rocks, trees, and little places to take cover.

"What the fuck?" said Reynolds.

Cyrus stood next to him, arms crossed. "The SCCWA built it three years ago. We sized out what we needed to do and built a polyurethane structure—almost like a massive jungle gym— covered in asphalt and then three layers of sod, with a lot of land-scaping on top."

"They got serious people out here," Stevie said.

"Lots of guys in the building trades are reenactors," Bob said

"Lot of waste-management guys too," Stevie said."

Reynolds kept staring. "It looks like a hazardous waste dump with sod and rocks and trees on it."

* * *

"Let's go, we're supposed to line up over yonder," Cyrus said. He gestured to the other side of the man-made hill, a distance about the length of a par three. They passed Rooster and his Confederate troops.

Rooster came out smiling. "Better get over there, Cyrus. They might think you're one of the ladies."

"Stick it up your ass, Rooster."

"We'll see who's talking at the end of the weekend," Rooster said.

Reynolds and Cyrus and the boys walked on.

"Don't they know what happened in this battle?" said Reynolds. "There's a real 'I'm gonna kick your ass' thing going on. It kind of defies the whole idea—on multiple levels."

"Course they do," said Cyrus.

"How's he thinking he's going to win? Or might win?"

"Oh, he knows they get killed. But I think he has some fantasy notion each time out that the South will win. The South will ride again, that kind of bull crap. The South will rise again. But he's also operating on another level: his more concrete goal is to win the award on Sunday for best reenactor, best company, best everything."

"We won in best brigade in Sacramento last year," Bob said. "Shiloh."

"We kind of had that rigged though," Stevie said. "The judges were the teachers from our old high school."

"Rooster likes this battle because he gets to take the lead as he runs up the hill," Cyrus said.

"Thinks he's a good dier." said Bob.

"Got it," said Reynolds. "He's right that there were a lot of Rebel officers that ran up Little Round Top that day."

"We got a bit of a situation today, though," said Cyrus. And he pointed to the gathering Union troops. "We got a lot of Bufords and Black Hats."

"So we do," said Reynolds, knowing what he meant. He counted six reenactors dressed as John Buford, the leader of the Union cavalry division that held off ten thousand Confederates. There were also dozens of guys dressed in the uniforms of the Iron Brigade of the First Corps.

"What do you do about that, Cyrus?" Reynolds said, "when multiple people come for one part?"

"They'll draw straws for the true Buford. As for the soldiers, they try to stay organized by division and hit the battle in the right order, but . . . well, it kind of breaks down a bit, if you know what I mean. We do our best."

"You can't be fucking perfect," Bob said.

Reynolds walked over to a cluster of John Bufords. *Where am I?* he thought for a moment. The whole thing had a bit of an Elvis-impersonator feel. But as he looked at the care each of the others had put into his outfit, he felt a wave of admiration. He thought of Buford. He thought of all the days on the tour when he would bring the tourists to tears when he told Buford's story.

Buford was a professional soldier. By the time of Gettysburg, he was tired of the war. The incompetence of the Union high command and the bureaucratic nonsense of Washington had driven him to disgust. It was all compounded by the way the Confederate cavalry commander J.E.B. Stuart was becoming a legend because of his daring rides at Chancellorsville and Fredericksburg. Stuart wasn't half the man Buford was, as Stuart would show over those few days. Looking at all the reenacting Bufords, Reynolds thought about how, in life, some asshole ends up getting more credit than he deserves, and the deserving party ends up getting screwed. He should do a piece centered on that.

It all would have been different if not for Buford. On the first day of the battle, Buford and his cavalry troops were up on a ridge in front of the hills north of the town, while the Confederate Army gathered around them in the late afternoon. Buford assessed the situation and posted his twenty-five hundred troops along the stone wall on Seminary Ridge. There was a brick church with a clock tower—a cupola—from which he could survey the whole area. Standing in the cupola, Buford knew he was surrounded. Yet he made the decision to stand and fight.

General John Reynolds was John Reynolds Stanhope of Malibu's hero, and now the man from Malibu wore his hero's uniform. As he'd grown up, and the logistics and story of the battle were imprinted on him, he gravitated toward Buford. Reynolds identified himself at his deepest core as Union. Pennsylvania was in the North, after all. More than that, though, the North had been right. His people had stopped slavery and saved the Union. And that saved America. It didn't have to go that way. Real men won that battle; real men changed the world in those few days. And if you learned anything growing up in Gettysburg, it was that everything, every single blessed thing, could have been different.

"Here, take a straw," said an old-timer in a very authentic gray beard and a brigadier general's uniform. He appeared to be in charge.

"Thank you, General, but I'm John Reynolds," Reynolds said. "Sir, where are the horses?"

A nearby Buford looked at Reynolds like he was an alien. "It's *horseless*. Didn't you look at the website?"

"No, apparently he didn't," the brigadier general said. "We got two horses for the day, the Rebels get two, too. Today on the Yankee side General Buford gets a horse and so does Colonel William Gamble."

Haven't heard that name in a long time, Reynolds thought. Gamble had been in charge of the Eighth Illinois, on the crucial left flank.

"So, this is McPherson's Ridge?" Reynolds said.

"We're a three-day battle jammed into two days," said the old-timer with the beard. "So many things are out of order chron-wise. And it's kind of all fucked up in terms of landmarks and locations."

Reynolds took that in.

"John Reynolds was a damn fine man," said the brigadier general to Reynolds.

When they revealed the straws, the Buford next to Reynolds had the long one and was congratulated by the others, and the brigadier general led him to get his horse. The rest of the Bufords and Reynolds gathered up and headed back to their outfits.

Reynolds found Cyrus and the guys.

"Cyrus, I want to fight with the guys," Reynolds said.

"Take off your stripes, put on a cap, and come with us," Cyrus said. "They called us to position."

"OK. You're meat like the rest of us, now," Bob said.

"When do we get killed?" Reynolds said.

"Cyrus got us a good number out of the pot, so that means we stay alive to the end. Then you can die during Pickett's Charge. If you want to."

Ten minutes later, Reynolds crouched behind a long chain-link fence in between Bob and Nicely on top of the Astroturfed and sodded covering on the polyurethane structure. Stevie was a few feet back.

"They'll be comin' up from down there in a few minutes," Bob said.

"Wow, this is kind of just like it happened," Reynolds said. To the boys he said, "Tell me something. I don't mean this the wrong way, but you guys are into this just to be rank-and-file soldiers?"

"What do you mean?" Nicely said.

"Well, it's just that . . . it seems like if someone were to be into the reenactment stuff so much, you would kind of like to be a general or a colonel or something like that. You know, pick a historical figure that you can impersonate."

The three kids looked at one another.

"Cyrus got us into this," said Bob. "Him?" he said, gesturing to Nicely. "I don't know about him, about why he does it. Strikes me he's a few bricks short of a load. But me and Steve, we just came with Cyrus one time because he wanted us to. And it was a real goof, and we had a lot of fun. Got drunk, met some other guys, did all these pretend fights. Now we're into it. Being a police officer and all, it's a good solid hobby."

"It's a lot of work to do that general shit," Stevie said.

Bob said, "Cyrus goes to SCCWA meetings all the time. Spends weekends out at national parks and softball complexes training other guys. Fuck that."

"Yeah, fuck that," Stevie said. "We specialize in getting a little high and fighting for the Union."

Reynolds didn't say anything for a few moments. Then he said, "You want to hear about the soldiers, the guys who were in the battle we're doing?"

"Sure," they all said.

Reynolds said, "They were cavalry. Buford's cavalry. There are three ridges in that part of Gettysburg: Herr Ridge, McPherson Ridge, and Seminary Ridge. Buford put one brigade on each ridge."

"Which is bigger, a brigade or a regiment?" said Stevie.

"Regiment," Nicely said.

"That's right," Reynolds said.

"It's a very strange place to be from, Gettysburg," Nicely said, out of thin air.

Reynolds nodded. "It's a very troubled place to be from."

"You know, Eisenhower moved there when he retired," Nicely said.

"I know. A lot of affectation there, I think."

"You think? It wasn't just fun for him?" Nicely said.

"Fun is getting your cock sucked, son," said Cyrus. "Gettysburg is not fun."

"Then what are you doing here, Cyrus?" Nicely said.

Cyrus pointed at him. "Remembering the men."

A moment passed.

"It's good to remember the men," said Reynolds. "I like that, Cyrus."

"Back at ya." He raised his tin coffee mug. "Here's to General Reynolds."

"You're a general?" Nicely said to Reynolds.

"No."

Cyrus took over, "There was a famous commander named John Reynolds. Union. First Corps." He indicated his own uniform. "Iron Brigade."

"So, are you him?" Nicely said.

"No," Cyrus said, and then indicated Reynolds. "But I think *he* is. Show some respect."

Nicely and the other boys looked at Reynolds, who opened his palms. "My parents named me after him."

"Cool," said Nicely, holding his paintball gun.

Reynolds felt the need to tell them about his namesake. He told the boys, who sat there as if they were in a Cub Scout den meeting, that the great John Reynolds was from Pennsylvania, attended West Point, fought on the same side with Lee and Grant and Stonewall Jackson in the Mexican wars. Reynolds went on to say that, by all rights, General Reynolds should have been in General Meade's place. General Reynolds had secretly been to Washington to meet with President Lincoln three weeks earlier, at which time the president offered General Reynolds command of the whole U.S. Army. Reynolds told Lincoln that he would refuse unless he was given free rein to fight. The young general had felt that the preceding commander, Old Joe Hooker, had been hamstrung by Lincoln and his armchair generals in the capital. In the end, John Reynolds left Washington and resumed command of the Iron Brigade. And Lincoln named George Meade the new major general, and Reynolds ensured no one was the wiser."

Reynolds raised his hand to eye level and lowered it as he spoke. "It goes: corps, then division, then regiment, then brigade. The brigade that was on this hill was dismounted cavalry guys under Colonel William Gamble. That's what we are, a brigade."

"Where are we from?" Bob said.

"We were from Maine. And the guys coming up this . . . ter- rain," he gestured at the sod and Astroturf decline in front of him, "were from Mississippi."

"A. P. Hill," said Cyrus.

Reynolds met his eyes. "That's right."

A cannon went off and made them all jump. "Here we go," Cyrus said.

"Where do you want us?" Reynolds said.

"Stevie, come with me to defend the breastworks over here," Cyrus said, indicating the trench and fenced-off section to the left. Reynolds and Bob and Nicely jumped in the trench and aimed their rifles down the hill. Reynolds began to realize the terrain had of bit of location integrity. Then a piercing Rebel yell came from below and was followed by dozens of Rebel yells as the Mississippians from Hood's division started up at them.

"A few of them will bust through, they always do," Cyrus said. "We'll get up and give them some hand-to-hand when they do. Remind these fuckers why the Union won!"

At an unannounced moment, Rebels down the hill started to scream and shoot their Winchester 57's. Reynolds and the boys returned fire, and Reynolds felt a thrill discharging his gun for the first time in battle. Reynolds aimed at a big boy with a yellow undershirt climbing toward them. A puff of white air left the barrel, and he reached to reload. Bob and Nicely were doing the same. Behind him, Cyrus moved back and forth behind the line, serving as the commanding officer for the entire line on this side of the hill. Reynolds and the two boys were in the extreme left position. Off to his side, Reynolds could see the crowd sitting in the grandstands. There were a lot of people. He looked down the hill again. There were more of the Rebels now. The uniforms were pretty good. They captured the disorganized yet organized feel of the Rebel army. They were some tough men.

Reynolds had always felt they were the enemy. It came from being part of the North. These people had wanted to tear the Union apart. The seceded states of the South wanted to keep owning slaves. That was the bottom line for him. He always maintained a sense of right belonging to the Union side. A sense of the true America. He felt a swell of pride. Something profound was surging up in him, and contrary to what he would have thought, it was pleasant. He remembered all the long hours in the museums, walking up Cemetery Hill or along the Peach Orchard. He could lose himself, back then, in the feeling of what it was like in 1863. He was born exactly one hundred years after the battle, at the time of the centennial. The obstetrician had had to come in from a huge gala at the main museum when his mother started labor. A teacher had said to Reynolds in fourth grade, "Maybe it was a sign of something that you were born that day." It was so long since he had thought of it all. How connected he was to it. He understood the battlefield the way other kids know every part of their neighborhood or their block. It was in his DNA, a natural part of him.

The charge was getting thick now. They guys in gray did a great job of dying. They were moving a little and dropping. The ones who were shot overdid it a little, but who cares, he thought. The Confederates were gaining ground. He'd always wondered what it must have felt like, being at the top of that ridge as crazy-ass Rebel soldiers came at you. With the boys in the Eighth Illinois, off their horses, unable to run, thinking the whole Southern army was coming up that hill. Union Colonel William Gamble rode up and down the line behind them, ordering soldiers to shift and fill the line when and where it appeared to be giving out. He was a rock. Even if a soldier didn't panic, he couldn't run away anyway, because there were no holes in the line with these officers behind you. The men had no other reason to believe in the high command, after Fredericksburg, after Chancellorsville. Their generals were idiots compared to Lee. Until now. They were fighting from the high ground.

Jesus, I'm really feeling this, Reynolds thought. He felt fear rise in him as a big greycoat with a yellow shirt began coming toward him, now ducking under sod forty yards below. It was amazing how real these guys were. They were damn good at the Rebel yell. Amazing how the Confederates were so romanticized. Where else in the world would the losing side of such a bloody event be given such treatment in the minds of the people, its culture, and its scholars? It angered him sometimes as he was growing up. The Confederacy tried to break this country, this land of freedom. It all could have broken apart if not for Reynolds, for Hancock, for Meade—Pennsylvania men.

He would have to stop the big Rebel leading the charge up the hill. *Get him*, he thought. *I must stop the big crazy fucker. Take the wind out of their sails. This guy won't stop unless I take him down.* "I got the one in the yellow," Reynolds yelled. "He's mine."

"Stay down," yelled Stevie from the breastworks. "They'll carve you up."

But Reynolds was certain. He rose up from behind the fence and the earth and hurdled over toward the Rebel. Seeing Nicely, the Rebel took his rifle by the butt and jabbed the bayonet at the kid, tearing the arm of the long-sleeved T-shirt hanging out beneath his tunic. The blade just missed Reynolds's arm.

"What the fuck?" Reynolds said. He held his own rifle across his chest and lunged forward, smashing the butt up against the Confederate's jaw. The Rebel went down with a groan. Reynolds stood over him, victorious. He felt his blood rush through his veins in triumph. Adrenaline made his eyes pop out; he stood like a boxer after a knockout, Ali standing over Liston, a big-game hunter over his prey, David over Goliath. He couldn't think straight.

Bob was at his arm. "Jesus, Reynolds. You smashed him?"

The Rebel soldier held his jaw. "What is wrong with you, man?" He checked his nose for blood. "Take it easy."

Cyrus rushed over and helped Bob pull Reynolds back behind the fence while Stevie helped the guy up. In the background, the fighting continued, the shots and cannon fire didn't let up. They leaned their backs against the wall of the trench, winded. Cyrus laughed, "Damn, man, you let him have it." Bob let out a chuckle. Stevie joined them, looking at Reynolds with a growing smile.

"What happened?" Stevie said.

"I don't know," Reynolds said. "He got too close to Nicely, and I lost it." Reynolds started to get up. "Shit, do you think that guy is OK?"

The guys pulled him to the ground. "Stay down," Cyrus said. "You can apologize to him later. If you go out there now it will cost us points."

"Well, at least my insurance is good," Reynolds said to himself. "Least I think it is."

Bob held his fist out for a bump. "Good job. I hate that guy."

"You know him?" Reynolds said.

"Yeah. He's a roofer. Fucking asshole."

"I wonder if he's going to go on a killing spree now?"

"Don't worry. If he does, I'll arrest him."

CHAPTER 14

Lunch and a Big Secret

"He's my husband," Stella said to Delaney and Marisol.

The women's eyes got big. Marisol turned to Delaney with her brows raised and the corners of her mouth turned down. She was wearing high-waisted jeans, very tightly cinched with a belt, and a pink polo shirt.

"Oh, duh," Delaney. "Hi. You don't know us, but we are working with Reynolds." Delaney looked at Marisol for help. "It's all happened so fast. I'm Delaney. This is my friend Marisol."

Stella shook hands. "You're working with Reynolds? On a project?" Stella wanted to twirl the two of them around like flamenco dancers.

"Yes," Marisol said. "We're doing reality."

Stella looked to Delaney, who put her hand on Stella's arm. "It's so exciting for us. Your husband is *such* a nice guy."

"And eso smart."

"So, you all came out here together?" Stella decided to give up all pretense of playing it cool. The three stood staring at one another as the cannon blasts and rifle shots rang over the ball fields. "I'm confused. Did you *plan* this?"

"Oh God, no," said Delaney, bending toward Stella and grabbing her arm again.

"Oh, no," said Marisol. "This is research for the show."

"What *show*?" said Stella.

"Oh my goodness, that's right," said Delaney, rolling her eyes. "You probably don't know anything about us."

Stella recaptured her practiced superciliousness. "Yes. No, I don't know anything about you."

Marisol responded with a minuscule recoil and a tiny, aristocratic pursing of her lips. "Did Reynolds not call you?"

Delaney tried to defuse the tension. "It's been a whirlwind. We met for lunch yesterday to discuss our project—he probably didn't tell you about it—at the Ivy at the Shore, and we all just fell in love. Well, not *love*, of course, but professionally in love. Anyway, he flipped over our idea, and we just got to talking, and he told us about this weekend down here, and he called Robert, and the next thing we knew we were here at the Battle of Gettysburg."

"And sleeping in a tent," said Marisol. And they both giggled.

"That's why we look such a mess," said Delaney.

"And in these *bobo* sneakers," Marisol said, flexing her foot up and down.

Delaney stage-whispered, "We took Robert's keys and went to the *Walmart*."

Stella just nodded, punch-drunk, still reeling from the impact of seeing Reynolds on the hill.

"Did you see Reynaldo kick that guy's ass just now?"

"I just got here when I saw him," Stella said.

"He looked so handsome, if you don't mind me saying so," Delaney said.

"Yes. He did look very . . . authentic," Stella said. "Gallant." She looked out, not knowing what to say. "Wow, they're really fighting now, huh?"

On the hill, the gunfire was reaching a crescendo. Southern troops were running up the man-made hill and falling in piles. They were tripping on turned-up sod and gouging so many holes they could see the hill's polyurethane frame. The crowd was cheering as the battle noise increased. It felt to Stella like the grand finale of a fireworks display. The last few of the chargers went down like cowboys in a Western, and a great cheer rose up from behind the blue line.

"Fans of the Blue and the Gray," came a voice from the loudspeaker. "This is the end of the morning battle of Little Round Top. Please join us for lunch in the picnic area adjacent to field two. Only day-two vouchers will be accepted. Reenactors' lunch will be held in the field. No spectators at the reenactors' lunch please. And this is a reminder: the battle of the Wheatfield will begin at three p.m. on the outfield of field number sixteen. You can find it because it looks like a wheat field. It's actually left field of field sixteen. But the organizers have done a good job of making it look like the Wheatfield, where so many brave men died."

"What happens now?" Stella said.

A man with a USS *Alabama* hat on said, "They've got a lunch line over by the concession stand." His wife, in a pink hoodie with "Juicy" across the breast area and eyeglasses with large, dark rectangular frames said, "And they have a flea market with all kinds of stuff."

"Where do you meet up with the soldiers?" Stella said.

"Oh, you don't see the soldiers till the end of the day," the man said. "They have to set up over by where they're doing the Wheatfield battle."

"No problem," said Marisol. "We just will get them excited for later—right, Laney?" They giggled once more. Marisol smiled at Stella. "We were whores last night. You should have seen it."

Stella stared.

"Shall we get some lunch?" said Delaney. "I only have two vouchers but I'm sure we can manage."

They began to follow the crowd to the concession area. "Laney," said Marisol. "Can I ask you a question? That man says we go to 'where they do the Wheatfield,' no?"

"Yes. That's where the next fight is. The afternoon show."

"I know," said Marisol. "But why didn't he say, 'over to the Wheatfield.' You know, to where it is? And why they build a hill like this? With the fake grass and the *futbol* field?"

"I don't understand what you're asking me, honey," said Delaney.

"Why don't they not just do it on the hill where it happened? Where the Wheatfield and the Round Top that they have the first war on? If this is a battle, why not make it true?"

"Well, that was the hill battle this morning," Delaney explained. "And they set up the Wheatfield battle in the afternoon, over by another ball field." She looked at Stella. "Isn't that right, Stella? That's what he said, right?"

Stella came out of her daze. "Yes, I'm pretty sure that's what it meant."

"I know that's what *he says*," said Marisol, getting frustrated. "But where is the *real* thing. The real places? Do they knock it down to play baseball?"

Delaney looked confused, but Stella figured it out. "Where is it *here*? In *this* park? Is that what you mean?"

"*Ay!* Yes, *exactly*, Stella. Thank you."

Stella stopped and took her arm. "Oh, no, Marisol, it didn't happen *here*. It was in Pennsylvania." Marisol looked at her blankly. "In the *East*. Far away."

Delaney shook her head. "Oh God, Mari, no. It didn't *happen* here."

"Not here?" Marisol said.

Both Stella and Delaney shook their heads.

"They no fight the battle here?" said Marisol.

"No," they said.

"Is made up?"

"It's made up that they fought it here, yes," said Delaney.

"It's like a set in the movies," said Stella.

"Not here?"

"No. Right. The battle was real, just not here, remember? It was in Pennsylvania."

Marisol couldn't believe it. "Nooo."

"Yup," Delaney said.

Marisol whistled. She started walking again. "Boy oh boy." She looked at the other women with a big smile and gave a shake of the head and another whistle. "*Estos chicos están locos, ¿no?*"

The three women walked to the next site of the action, trailing the crowd, which seemed to know where it was going.

"You know," said Stella, "I can't believe this whole thing. I mean, I've seen some weird stuff in my days, trust me. But, God, who are these guys?"

"It's pretty odd, I guess," said Delaney. They kept walking.

"*Pretty* odd?"

"Hmm," Delaney said.

"I'd say," Stella said. "You got five hundred guys dressed up as soldiers from the Civil War. It's pretty goddamn odd."

"I don't know. I think it's kind of sweet," said Delaney.

"Sweet?"

"You know . . . *men*. They're all little boys inside. They're just playin' dress up out here. Bunch of big old weird guys playin' dress up. Honey, there's worse things in the world."

Stella didn't say anything.

"And Reynolds seems to like it."

"Yes," said Marisol. "He like it very much." Then she changed the subject. "Laney, I want to go over to the store again and check on our dresses for the party."

"Oh, that's right," Delaney said. "Good idea."

"Party?" said Stella. "What party?"

"They have a big party tonight. It's the big gay ball," Marisol said.

"The cotillion, sugar. I think it can be called a gala," Delaney said.

"What *es* 'gala'?"

Stella thought about it and realized she didn't know the answer. "It means big, I guess," she said.

"Come get dresses with us," said Delaney to Stella.

Stella said, "I'll go with you guys. But I'm not getting a dress."

Marisol's phone rang. "*Hola, mi amor. Dónde estás?*"

"Is he with Lance?" said Delaney.

"*Estás con* Lance?" Marisol said. She looked at Delaney. "Yes."

"Tell them to come!" Delaney said. "Tell them we will get them uniforms, and they can fight!"

Marisol agreed and started rattling away in Spanish.

"Our sons are both eighteen," Delaney said to Stella. "They will *love* this."

"Really?" said Stella.

"Of course. It's so crazy," Delaney said. "Our boys are two months apart. They're like brothers."

"My daughter is the same age," Stella said.

"You're kidding!"

"Going to be a sophomore," said Stella.

"You're kidding! Same with our kids," Delaney pointed at Marisol. "Well, you know, graduating from home." Then she grabbed Stella's arm. "Tell her to come!"

Stella looked at her. "Graduating from home?"

"Yes, we homeschool."

"You mean, they don't go to a school?"

"That's right," said Marisol. "We've taught them at home from the principles of the Secret."

Delaney, Marisol and Stella pulled salads and bottles of water out of a long display case packed with ice. They sat at a picnic table to eat.

"Those shoes are sooo cute," said Delaney after they finished eating. "What are they?"

Stella looked at her shoes for a second, then said, "You like? They're Prada. I do love these."

"Oh, me too. Look at you, girl. You are just too much."

"Oh, Delaney, stop."

"No, I'm serious. You're *fierce*. I love fierce. It's impossible to do, but you do it. The straight hair, the leather jacket, the Prada, mmm." Delaney took hold of the lapels of Stella's jacket, looking her up and down. "This top, classy, the black jeans and the shoes. Fierce."

"You're hilarious," Stella said. She changed course. "I'm curious. Tell me about the show again? What are you doing with Reynolds? It's about you guys?"

"Yes," Stella said. "We talked to Reynolds, and he thinks we can do something great. You know, not the usual crap. Something that is . . . what was he saying, Mari?"

"Breaking. Like we're going to break it all it up. Break the ground."

Stella nodded. "Groundbreaking. Cool. And it will be based on you? I mean, it will follow you around?" Stella said.

"Yes" said Marisol. "And we will do interesting things. That's what Reynaldo says the idea is. Right, Laney?"

"Exactly. He was saying he wants us to go to different places. Like museums. Things of that nature. Well, he didn't really say museums."

"And it will show us teaching the Secret," Marisol said.

"Oh, that's right." Stella said. "Let me ask you, so you teach the Secret?"

"*Qué?*"

"It's something you *teach*?"

"Of course," said Delaney. "We are certified."

"I see," said Stella. "God, I guess I just never spent any time looking at it. Can you give me an idea of what it is? The Secret?"

"*Es* not that easy," said Marisol. "It is . . . well, you know . . . it's Secret."

"Here it is," said Delaney. "The basic concept is that the Law of Attraction can be extrapolated to a point where you believe you can do anything you set your mind to. It's much more complicated than that, of course. But that's it."

"I see," Stella said. "That's concise and straightforward."

"For example, Mari and I decided we should do a show. And we set about it, and here we are."

"Fact of the matter," Marisol said, "that is what the Secret is all about. Since I been doing it, all my dreams come true. Every single one."

"True or coming true," said Delaney.

Stella wanted to run, but she stopped herself. For all she knew, Reynolds *had* promised these women a show. He was stupid enough to do that. Lost enough. She told them she needed to make a call and excused herself.

Stella got well out of sight and put the phone up to her ear.

"Norman, it's me," she said.

"How are you making out down there, toots? I hear you're looking for you husband."

"What, you know already?" said Stella.

"I just got a call from my driver. Where are you?"

"I'm there."

"Where?"

"I'm *there*. At the battle. The war. I am at the war. In Enchino," Stella said.

"Oh boy," Norman said. "You're *there*? What's it like?"

"They're fighting up and down a four-hundred-foot jungle gym with sod on it, to start with. I haven't been able to talk to him yet."

"What can I do?" Norman said.

"I think you have to come help me. Bella is going to come here tonight, to go to the cotillion."

"What's that, a big dance?"

"Cotillion. They have a cotillion on tonight. It's a whole week-end of events."

"Fantastic."

"Would you? What about your walk with Tom? I know how much . . ."

"Stop, toots. I'm coming."

"You sure?"

"I'm sure. I'm sure."

CHAPTER 15

Bella and Heather

"Hi, I'm picking up from number thirty-eight." Bella was at the Colony gates. The security guard came back with a clipboard.

"Name."

"Heather."

"Do you know where it is?"

She nodded and thanked him and drove the span of the short feeder road to the main avenue of the Colony, Malibu's most exclusive neighborhood, paralleling the beach. She knew by memory the names of the residents of each of the mansions she breezed by. They were mostly executives in the film business—some in television, a few in music, though most of those were gone because of the massacre brought by digitization. Norman and Carol lived toward the north side. There was also a healthy share of movie stars and rock stars. Sting was in one of the houses. Bella had learned the order of the buildings as she grew up, based on which kids lived where—this kid from soccer, that kid from her third-grade class. At any point she could recall, at least two of her best friends lived in the Colony. As she grew older there were boys and parties. With the divorces and the rentals and the rising and falling fortunes of show business, the houses started to blend together. She had been in almost all of them by the time she graduated from high school, knew their floor plans, the ones that had pools, the ones that had tennis courts.

Bella's classmates at Brown liked to ask her about Malibu. It occupied a mythic place in their minds. She found she was repeating the same lines and then realized she needed to turn it into a spiel—or *schpiel*, as Norman would say. She got her spiel down after a few months and gradually educated the girls in her hall that Malibu was just like any other place except it had movie stars and rock stars and the ocean and sick mansions. Every interaction and the beginning of every potential relationship involved an explanation of the Malibu of it all. But although she knew she should just be patient—it wasn't foreign to her, after all—she found she gravitated more toward the girls who understood her desire to move past it. She couldn't help it if those girls were the ones from Manhattan or who had money. She didn't like it, but it was easier.

She was careful not to be a snob in any way. Bella got that from Reynolds. From her mom too, but in a different way. Left to her own devices, her mom could end up a snob, not because she thought she was better than anyone else but because she was less sensitive. Reynolds was the sensitive one, more considerate than Bella or Stella—or just about anyone. Bella worked hard at being a "good" kid. It was part of her identity that she was one of the good kids, something she'd homed in on when she was very young, once it became clear to her, as it did to all good kids, that the road through adolescence into young adulthood in Malibu would diverge, with the stoners and the surfers and the druggies and the disaffected slackers going one way, while the college-bound achievement-oriented good kids went the other.

The truth was, it wasn't hard for her. She had no overwhelming desire to rebel, and she wasn't attracted to the kids who did. It wasn't like Bella judged; she just felt it was a waste, that they were wasting something. This, too, she credited to Reynolds—though, she thought, that sounded too tough on her mom. She was very close to her mom—they had no major problems. They were good. It was her relationship with her mom that let her have such a good relationship with Reynolds—he didn't have to be the bad guy. But it wasn't that he was always able to be the good guy, nor was it that her mom was any worse by comparison. It was subtle, and it was all understood. They were both great heroes, especially when she looked around. They were cool, Reynolds and Stella. They were a good unit, the three of them. Nothing corny, just a family. And her mom was the center point.

But Bella did have a special thing with Reynolds, a closeness earned over a lifetime of long talks and little jokes. He tucked her in at night and took walks with her in the afternoons when she was bored. He helped with math homework and went on her class trip to Washington, DC. She could bring him anything—any problem, any curiosity—and he wouldn't think she was crazy, not for this idea for a show or that idea to write a letter to the *New York Times*, wouldn't cut her off, wouldn't make her feel embarrassed. Reynolds would always answer, comfort, help her put on a play or shoot a movie with her iPhone. He would always drop everything to go on a run with her.

Heather was sitting on a bench in front of her house, back for winter break. She and Bella had been best friends since elementary school. They had styles that pleased each other, liked the same things for the most part, did not compete for attention or recognition, and were each happy for the success of the other. Bella knew enough growing up near Hollywood not to care who anyone's mother or father was. Heather was also a year into college, at UC Santa Barbara. They were enjoying comparing notes, and Bella was happy they had been able to return to their groove so quickly—like there was ever any doubt.

"My mother's insane," Heather said as she got in the car.

"My parents are the ones who are at a Civil War show in Pomona."

"I thought you said Enchino," Heather said.

"Enchino. Whatever. What did your mom do?"

"She just wants to talk . . . and talk . . . and talk. About my dad. She wants me to play marriage counselor."

"Again?

"She's trying to make up for lost time."

"What is it?"

"What is it ever?"

Bella pulled the little BMW through the Colony gates and onto the PCH.

Heather went on. "He is having a crisis on what he wants to do next, says he might not do anything, and she can't stand to be around him. It's boring. I told her she made her bed and she should lie in it. What's she going to do, *leave*? She won't last one day."

"She might make it two," Bella said, and Heather laughed.

"I know, right? She's so full of it. My dad is crazy, but, I mean, he gives her everything. I think she is bored."

"But Jack's still at home."

"He's not much company. He doesn't talk. He just grunts at her. At me too. He's horrible. He only comes out of his room to leave. And he's disgusting. When he goes out he's just hair and zits in a Dead Kennedys T-shirt."

"Ick. But very poetic."

"Thank you, I try. OK, can we talk about this for a second?"

Before Heather could continue, Bella pointed to the double drink holder by the gearshift, which had two Starbucks cups.

"Bam. Double vanilla latte, nonfat milk," Bella said. "Who's your bitch?"

"Oh, you are a real one, girl." Heather tasted it. "Mmm. Now: What in the hell are we doing?"

"All I know is she called me—"

"Stella?"

"Yes. Stella. She called me and said my dad is at a Civil War reenactment and he didn't tell her. She had a GPS tracker on his phone and followed him there."

"Ooh. Go Stella."

"Courtesy of yours truly. I showed her how to do it. Anyway, he's down at this thing and she said I needed to get out there to help her."

"Why does she need help?"

"Because she's afraid he's losing his mind. I don't quite understand it myself. She was kind of laughing too. She said we don't want to miss it."

"I can't even understand."

Bella let out a suppressed laugh. Heather was so good at stunned disbelief. "I know," she said.

"Well, so he's watching it. Big deal," Heather said.

"Nooo! That's the point. He's *in* it."

"He's in it?"

"Yes!"

"With a gun and all that shit?"

"It's insane."

"Aw," Heather said. "It's so cute. He went out there with a gun and an army suit and everything?"

"I know, it *is* cute, isn't it? Poor Reynolds. At first, I think my mom was freaking out. But then she called me again and I think she was feeling better. And you're never going to believe the other part of this."

"What?"

"They have a barn dance or something. A square dance. And we're going."

"What kind of square dance did they have during battles in the Civil War?"

"Fuck if I know. But the whole thing is insane. It's a made-up thing about a war a hundred years ago, so why can't they have a dance too?"

"It must be how they try to get their wives to go."

"Right," said Bella. "That's what I thought too. And guess what?"

"Tell me."

"My mom is going to buy us dresses."

"Shut up."

"Swear to God. We have to wear hoops and petticoats."

Heather slapped her. "You are lying to me."

"Nope. We're going to the ball with the soldiers."

"Oh my God. This is not . . . that's crazy. Do you really want to go to a square dance in a hoopskirt?"

"It might be fun."

"Wait a minute." Heather turned and faced Bella in the car. "You're telling me that your mother is going to put on a hoop dress and pretend like she's some old-fashioned lady?"

"She said she's not doing it, but that she will get dresses for us."

"We have to do it and she doesn't? No way."

"I'm going to make her do it."

"Will there be any young guys there?"

"There will have to be, don't you think?"

"What kind of dork would go to this thing? Ew, I bet they're all like *Dungeons and Dragons*."

"It is not promising, I agree. And we're sleeping in a tent."

"Tell me again, *why* I am doing this?"

"Because you're my best friend and my mother called me and said, 'come help me get your father out of here.' And you love my father too."

"Yes. Best reason so far."

"And we were going to go out tonight, but we don't have anything to do, so we were just going to sit around my house or your house and get stoned and watch a movie."

"Wouldn't that be better?"

"How many chances will we ever get to go to a Civil War cotillion?"

"True." She considered it for a moment. "What kind of shoes do we wear?"

"I have no idea. Here, let's call my mom." As she made the call, she said, "Have you taken anything like this yet—like American history?"

"Next semester I'm taking American literature from Hawthorne to the present. But I guess the Civil War doesn't count much?"

"Well, since you haven't taken it yet and since Hawthorne wrote in the 1880s, no it doesn't count much." They laughed.

"Look, bitch," Heather said, "Don't make me do my kung fu on you."

"Girrrrl, don't make me stop this car," Bella said.

Now they were hysterical.

"Oh, check it out," Heather said. She turned up the radio. "'I ain't no hollaback girl, I ain't no hollaback girl . . .' Remember this?"

"Of course I remember this," Bella said. They moved their shoulders in the rhythm of the song.

"What's it called when you still like something even though you have outgrown it?" said Heather.

"What do you mean?"

"Like, you know, when you hear this song, 'Hollaback Girl.' And you see yourself at an earlier age, or whatever, and you put yourself back in that place."

"Memory."

"Shut up. I'm serious. It's like an art thing."

"Self-parody."

"No. It's like a Warhol thing, with the soup cans."

"Nostalgia? Are you talking about nostalgia? That's not Warhol. The soup cans were about reproduction and consumerism."

Heather sat back and thought. "I feel like the soup cans are more about what is real and not real. How everything is like a reproduction."

"That's what I just said."

"Oh, right. You did just say that." She giggled. Then she put her face in Bella's face and sang with the radio. "I ain't no hollaback girl."

"Get away from me," Bella said, moving her face. "You're a freak."

They moved on to the 71. They were making good time.

"Crystalline? What is crystalline?" said Heather as they watched the road signs go by. "Like what does it mean when someone has crystalline eyes?"

"T'onno," said Bella, mouth full, taking a sip of her latte. "I would guess it's like you smashed up crystals and dipped the eyeball in them?"

Heather looked at her. "You blue-haired weirdo." She took a bite of a muffin, and as she was chewing said, "What were you saying before you said that Deondra said his eyes are crystalline?"

"That was the main thing," Bella said. "It was just at the end of the litany about how perfect he is."

"Good use of *litany*," said Heather.

"Thought you'd like that. Wait, is that right? What did I say?"

"You said, 'a litany about how perfect he is.' Like that."

"Right, so is litany a list or a sermon?"

"It's a litany if it's a list, and it's a sermon if it's like a speech," Heather said. "So, was it a list or a speech?"

"I guess it was a list with a lot of bullshit about each item. Like 'his room is so cool, it just feels cool, all the stuff in it is natural, like not made up, not too clean . . .'"

"Oh, kill me."

"Right?" Bella looked at her friend, whose Wayfarers were propped up on her forehead. "That is something I definitely got from you: saying 'right?' after someone agrees with you. "Like, I say, "It is so hot."' And then you say, 'I know, right?'"

Heather said, "It's called being around morons."

"It's true." Bella said.

"No, I know. Is it bad?"

"Yeah, Heather, it's terrible."

"Wait, so get back to the story. What else was Deondra saying?"

"Oh yeah, he never criticizes her, she said that too."

"I don't know if I would like *never* criticizing," Heather said.

Bella shifted lanes. There was a car in her blind spot. The guy blew his horn as other cars ripped by. Bella scrunched her shoulders and waved in the rearview mirror. "Sorry, sorry . . . dude, I'm sorry."

Getting back to the conversation, Bella said, "But too much criticism is bad."

"Right. It's a fine line."

"Exactly." Bella became drifty. "Like, what is too much and what is not enough?"

Heather drifted with her. "I always do the fridge test."

"What?"

"The fridge test. When you're sizing up a guy you do this exercise: you try to imagine how he would handle his refrigerator."

Bella made a fist and slammed it on the steering wheel in mock urgency. "Oh my God, tell me this right now."

"That's it," said Heather. "You ask him how he organizes his fridge. First you ask if he organizes his fridge at all."

"First you ask if he even has a fridge," Bella said.

"Right. I am assuming you've gotten past the guys with no fridge. I can't help you unless you're at a certain level."

"Bitch. No, I'm just kidding. Ha, love you," said Bella.

"Ha. Love you," said Heather. Both made a kissy face at the other. "Back to the fridge. You find out if he has it organized, like *at all*, that's the first thing. You can smoke out whether he does, because if he's the kind who doesn't, he will look at you like you're crazy."

"Uh-oh. I think those are my type." Bella said. "Is that bad?"

"Yes, it's bad," Heather said. "What do you expect from a guy who just throws stuff in the fridge herky-jerky?"

"Herky-jerky?" Bella said. At this, Heather started laughing, and in response, Bella burst out giggling. A fit ensued. Heather was the kind of young woman who, when in extreme hysterics, began fanning herself with her hand, as though she were holding her breath. Their faces both turned red. They broke through the regular laughing to the point that the mere sight of each other sent the hysteria to a new level.

"OK, OK, stop," Bella said as they stopped at Joey's for lunch. Heather smiled at a couple who had driven up in a Peugeot with what looked like three bikes on the back. They also had top notch—or so it seemed—biking duds on.

"Ask them if they're in the Tour de France," Bella deadpanned. Heather slammed her hands down on the dash, bracing herself for the lung-heaving ahead. Seeing this, Bella cracked up again.

"*I'm all about that bass, 'bout that bass . . .*" The song was loud and came from somewhere close.

"Wait, it's my mom," Bella said, looking at her iPhone, which had the song playing and a picture of Stella wagging a finger and the words "Myrtle Mom" flashing.

"Hello, Myrtle," Bella said.

"Myrtle, where are you?" Her mom sounded a little panicked.

"We're on our way . . ."

"Hi, Myrtle," Heather said.

"Oh, hi, honey. I can't wait to see you. Sorry it's in the middle of this crazy thing."

"We're a little late because we smoked a joint," Bella said.

"Very funny. Get here now, please," Stella said.

"What's the matter?" Bella said. They had a talk-about-anything-in-front-of-Heather agreement.

"Besides the fact that Dad's been lying to me for months?"

"Mom, he's not necessarily lying."

"Oh, goddamnit, he has too been lying."

"Easy, tiger," Bella said. "How's the thing?"

"So weird. You guys have to get here. You have to help me bear witness."

"All right, hold tight, we'll be there soon."

CHAPTER 16

A Report from Bella

April 18, 2004

Jackie Gleason

Well, after eight years of torturing me, you are finally getting to the good stuff. After Norman Vincent Peale and Martin Luther, it is a relief to do someone normal. I suggest you do more of these in your assignments to me. A rock star occasionally would also be appreciated.

Jackie Gleason (b. Feb. 26, 1916—d. June 24, 1987) was a comedian, actor and he was also a very good musician. He was the quintessential American everyman as English teachers would say.

(Like I have told you before, I know it is not right to copy from the internet sites like Wikipedia. I have made this into my own words as much as I can but cut me a break if you see some stuff that looks the same. Remind me to talk to you about this. It is very impossible to say basic things like when he was born and what someone is famous for without sounding like you are copy9ng.)

He was born in Brooklyn, New York. He is most famous for playing the bus driver named Ralph Cramden in the television show entitled The Honeymooners. But as famous as it was, The Honeymooners, is not the only thing he should be remembered for.

First of all, he also did a lot of movies. The one that pops up most in all of the information about him is the movie The Hustler that he did with Paul Newman (handsome and CUTE!)! he played Minnesota Fats which is a funny name and I think pretty interesting because he was pretty fat in real life. Like I said, Jackie was also a very good musician, which from what I've seen and read is the least well-known thing about him since everybody only thinks of him as the guy in The Honeymooners and maybe they think of him a little bit as Minnesota Fats. He played jazz music. He had ten albums that sold over one million copies and that was in the days before CD's and iTunes when people played records on a record player with a needle etc etc.

I would like to say a few things I discovered in my research about Jackie Gleason. First, did you know (or do you remember is more like it) *The Honeymooners* was first a sketch on a show called *The Cavalcade of Stars* and the lady who played his wife was named Pert Kelton. She was kicked off the show because they said she was a communist. Remind me to ask you if she was a communist)

Second, like I said, he played music. (Did you know that?) He did a record called Music for Lovers which was on the charts for 153 weeks which is still the all-time record.

The other thing I would like to say about *The Honeymooners* after watching the old episodes is that he always has a big scam going. He always wants to get rich and he always gets in trouble for it. He is not happy being a poor bus driver and he wants to be a millionaire. His wife gets mad at him and they have big fights which are funny. But I think it is a little sad that he is not happier with life just as he has it. He also is not nice about Norton, but he is a dope so that joke is always funny. The best is when they are playing golf and he tells Norton to "address the ball" and Norton goes "Hellloooo Ball."

You know I always wonder why you give me different people to do. Like why you pick them. I am most interested in why of all the TV people in the world after all these years you never gave me a giant TV star. And why is Jackie Gleason the first one? I have a philosophy about this which is that you like him a lot and that maybe he is someone you think was very good at making TV shows. All this watching of *The Honeymooners* gets me thinking about how simple it is compared to all of the shows nowadays. And that is why I think you have picked him. You are always telling it me why people are important. It always boils down to the same kind of things, like there was something special about them usually one thing like they were smart or pretty or they did something brave at one time. There is the other category you talk about where they were truly great over a lifetime. The other category is that they sto0od for an important rule that then became very important to the world. I don't think Jackie Gleason is in any of these "columns" like you say it. I think he is in all the columns. I want you to tell me what you think about all of this when I see you.

Xxxooo I love you,
Bella

CHAPTER 17

Belles

Stella was standing in front of the dress shop when Bella and Heather saw her. The girls ran to her, and the three hugged like reuniting army buddies.

"Oh my God, what took you so long?" Stella said. She had known Heather since she was a baby. "Heather, you look cute," she said.

Gesturing to the store, Heather said, "Look at this. Can you believe?"

"No," Bella said. Then, to her mother, "I thought you were getting a dress?"

"Funny. Haha," Stella said. "I can't bear to go in there. Reynolds's new friends are getting done up now."

"Oh my God," Heather said. "What are they like?"

"They're nice, actually, and pretty ironic," said Stella. "And they're both beautiful."

"We looked them up. Their sons played football at Westlake," Bella said.

"Must be rockheads," Heather said.

"In other news," Stella said, "Reynolds told the ladies he's going to produce their reality show."

"What reality show?" Bella said.

"That's what I'm trying to figure out," Stella said.

"Like the Kardashians?" Heather said.

"No, not at all. It will be a show about us going different places and guiding the audience through. We will also explain the Secret more and more with each episode."

"I love the Secret," Heather said. "Well, I mean, I loved the book. My grandma had it, and I read it—a little. I can't say 'I love it'—that's an exaggeration. But I know people who love it."

"What is the Secret?" said Bella.

"Yeah, what the hell is it?" Stella said. "We passed on it, but I didn't read it. It came back around as a book. I couldn't understand it."

"How do you even do that with a book?" Bella said.

"It's like buying a foreign movie and taking license a little bit."

"With the Secret, they kind of don't tell you what it is," Heather said. "That's the genius part."

"Like a fricking secret. I get it, Captain Clarity," Bella said. "But what is it? Do we think these ladies are crazy, Scientologists, soft-porn stars, or do we think they're reality-show moms in on their own joke?"

"Were Playmates soft-porn stars?" Heather said.

"No, of course not," Stella said. Then she thought about it. "Well, in a way, but not now. I mean they wouldn't be now. You guys don't get how complicated it was then."

"Oh, OK, but we do get some things, Myrtle. Let's return to the matters at hand. Dad ran away here in a Civil War uniform with strange people. There's talk of a self-help soft-porn, fly-on-the wall TV show called *The Secret Girls*."

"No doubt. I still don't understand the Secret," said Heather.

Stella said, "Don't ask me. Let's go inside."

They walked into the costume trailer and were directed behind a curtain, where the Secret Girls were changing. Behind the barrier, Stella, Bella, and Heather found Delaney and Marisol in petticoats and corsets. Both had their breasts sticking out of the tops of their bustiers.

"Oh, hey, there," Delaney said. "These must be your girls! Well, hi, y'all, come in. We're trying on all kinds of stuff. This is Gail, she's helping. It's her place."

"Hello, ladies," Gail said. She was in her mid-fifties, had gray-red hair, and wore knee-length denim shorts and a blue sleeveless blouse with flowers on it. She had a red pincushion in her hand. "Let me know if y'all need help. I'm kind of in shock, though, because Miss Lovely Delaney is here."

"I still can't believe you know who I am," Delaney said. "From all those years ago?"

"Lord, are you kiddin' me? You were the most beautiful thing— *are* the most beautiful thing—to come out of West Texas *since* the Civil War."

"You are too sweet."

"Stella, *ven acá*," said Marisol. "Look what I find for you." She reached down and held up a midnight-blue dress made of satin.

"It belonged to the wife of the governor of Georgia," Gail said.

"I hope she had a big fat ass," Stella said.

"Mom, stop. It's beautiful," said Bella.

Stella looked at it. It was, in fact, beautiful, and the next thing she knew she was being dragged by Gail and Marisol to the section of the trailer that held all the undergarments— "the Petticoat

Junction," Gail said—but she stopped enjoying the pun when she saw the miles of nonrecognition on Marisol's face. The boas and the light made Stella feel like she was with the whores on *Deadwood*. And she was still distracted by Delaney's and Marisol's chests. She'd seen hundreds of actresses and body doubles and was a professional and jaded expert in this field. But here, both of their sets seemed to defy gravity; supported by the underwire of the corsets, they protruded into the light as proud and firm flesh. Neither woman was the least bit self-conscious; they were ladies who were used to having their tits out.

For the first time, Stella was worried about what Reynolds's role with these two had been, was, or would be. Boobs like that change men's minds, she thought. Breasts like that can make a depressed man whose last creative endeavor was a sleep-provoking reality television show about sleep reconsider all decisions. And Stella also saw the opportunity that Reynolds's head was seeing: they were hot and flirtatious; cougars, MILFs, whatever. Dumber shows than theirs were working. She *watched* dumber shows than that. Having them in a world that showed their dingbat nature in high society or other ironic formats was maybe not a bad idea. Then you throw in a little skin and a little personal life—who knows? Lots of ideas sprang to mind. Aging demographics. Cross-promotions with Victoria's Secret. Even Playboy might buy in. There was a guaranteed Univision presale with a Miss Universe from Spain. Also, Mexican, Latin American, and Spanish TV. Asia was becoming a buyer. The English-speaking world—the UK and Australia—was a lock. And then they'd find deals in France, Italy, and Scandinavia. Germany as well.

She looked at Delaney, trying to discern what kind of boob job she'd had, because no woman her age had those tits. She looked for scars around the areola but could not see any. She wanted to see underneath, to look for that darkened line in the shape of a U and concluded that beyond furnishing underwire, the corset was concealing the evidence of the breast enhancement surgery. The same thing with Marisol, and it wasn't out of the question that they'd had their operations together. Stella began to recover. Not saying anything, she looked at the first lady of Georgia's dress again.

"Stella, put it on," said Heather.

"How do I even start?"

"Let her strap you into your undies, first," said Delaney. "It's suffocating." She indicated the strings of her own bindings. "I'm getting out of this thing."

"What about you two?" Stella said, gesturing at Bella and Heather.

"I have enough for everybody," said Gail. "First, get your petticoats." She sized the teens up and began handing out white undergarments. Stella and the girls began to undress. Marisol was struggling to unlace Delaney's bodice.

"This is so fun, no? Stella, you gonna look beautiful."

Bella and Heather reviewed the dress options Gail put in front of them. "I hear you guys are going to be on TV," said Bella.

"Oh, yes, thanks to your dad," said Delaney. As she spoke, Marisol pulled the lace through the last eyelet on Delaney's corset and the support fell away, unleashing her breasts. Normally, this would have created one of two possibilities. If Delaney was unenhanced, which Stella doubted, her boobs would adhere to the laws of gravity and aging and would move down and to the outside. If they were aftermarket, as Stella suspected, they would stay pretty much cemented in place. They did neither. Delaney's breasts gave a slight yield, like a strong hammock taking on a young child, and then stood firm.

"Jesus," said Heather. "Nice rack."

"Oh yeah?" said Delaney. She nodded at Marisol in front of her, whose laces she was undoing. "Look at these." She pulled the brace away from Marisol's brown back, and the same action, like a tiny acrobat falling into the safety net, happened. Marisol's pair was as perfect, but larger, even more ample. Rather than dark brown, as might be expected, her areola and nipples were pink, contrasting in a muted way next to Delaney's, who was behind her and to the left. Stella was flanked by the two younger girls. All three stared.

"I thought the pencil test was to see if your boobs hold a pencil *up*," Heather said.

"Who's ready?" said Gail.

"Me!" Heather said.

As they watched Heather struggle into her ball gown, Stella tried to collect her bearings. "Delaney, have you guys talked with Reynolds about what actual events you will be doing on the show?"

"Well, not exactly. We ran through some brainstorming ideas in the car on the way down here. But it's been so hectic. We're doing a battle like this."

"And the car races," said Marisol.

"Yes. NASCAR, for sure," said Delaney. "And a bullfight."

"We're going to my country," Marisol said.

Bella was perusing jewelry items in an ornate walnut case to the side. "Wow, look at this. Mom, you have to see this." Stella and the others looked over her shoulder at a silver necklace with a large open locket, displaying two small photos side by side. One was of a young woman, the other of a Union soldier who appeared to be the same age.

"That's my finest piece," Gail said.

"Do you know who they were?" Bella said.

"Yes, they're quite famous."

"Is it the girl's locket? Of her and her boyfriend?"

"No. It's a curio that someone put together after the war."

"They're so young," said Stella.

"It's such a sad story. These two were in love. They grew up in Gettysburg, which was a very small town. Jack Skelly and Jennie Posey. They also had a friend named John Wesley Culp, who right before the war moved to Shepherdstown, which today is in West Virginia. When the war started, Wesley Culp joined the Confederate Army and Jack Skelly joined the Union Army. The fighting was in Virginia those first two years, and Jack sent Jennie loads of letters, which she loved so much she kept them in her apron."

"Wow," Bella said.

"A month before the Battle of Gettysburg, Jack Skelly was wounded in Springfield, Virginia, and taken prisoner," Gail said. The women stopped dressing and undressing. Marisol and Delaney each held camisoles up against their chests to cover themselves. Heather's dress was more or less pulled on, and Stella and Bella, in petticoats, stopped lacing their bodices. Gail adopted a lyrical and literary tone, speaking as though she were reading from a book.

"He was laying on the ground as a group of Rebel soldiers passed by. One of them was Wesley Culp. He saw Jack and fell out of line. And then Wesley gathered Jack up and spoke to one of the officers to request passage to the nearby field hospital in town. On the stretcher, Jack asked Wesley to deliver a special message to Jennie if he was ever able to return home."

"What was the message?" Heather said.

Gail ignored her for now. "Wesley Culp never would know, but Jack Skelly died later that day at the hospital. Wesley marched with the Confederate Army to Gettysburg and was on the front lines for the first two days of the fight. He snuck into town to see his sisters, and hopefully Jennie, on the second night. He found his sisters at home, but he couldn't find Jennie to give her the message. He returned to his outfit late that night, and they were told they would attack a first light. Wesley was killed around eight a.m. on Culp's Hill. And later that same day, while she was baking bread for the soldiers, a stray shot killed Jennie in her kitchen. Through two doors and pierced her heart."

The girls remained silent. Gail held the locket, and they stared at the two pictures.

"Yep, it's some story. Three friends in a small town. Sweethearts, just kids. All dead within a few days." The group sat lost in the story's atmosphere. Gail broke the silence herself. "Well, I'll be damned. It's about happy hour around here. Who wants a little rosé wine? I got that and Coors Light."

Heather whispered to Bella, "Do you think we can smoke a joint in here?"

"Let's wait till we're outside," Bella said. She looked at the others. Delaney had tears in her eyes. Marisol held her fingers below her own to stop her mascara from running. Bella turned to check her mom, and to her amazement, Stella's eyes were watering too.

"I'll take some wine," Stella said.

"I have to run and get some cups," said Gail. She said, over her shoulder, "The message Jack gave to Wesley was, 'Jennie, I love you.'"

After a collective "Aw," the women continued with their dressing. In a minute the others noticed Stella had pulled on the blue satin gown.

"Oh my God, Mom, you're beautiful," Bella said.

"Bam," Heather said.

"They're right," said Delaney. She held a mirror for her.

It *was* good. It played to her best parts: high cheekbones, fine features, long lines. The corset was slimming, her hair for some reason looked good for late in the day. With all the ruffled business below the waist there was nothing to worry about in the fat ass department. The *Deadwood* hooker vibe lessened. She felt like a pretty, rich, old-fashioned woman and not as ridiculous as she had expected.

Gail returned, and Stella accepted a plastic cup of wine, and after she took a gulp she made like she was giving up. "OK. I'm in. What the hell happens at this party?"

"Cotillion," Heather said.

CHAPTER 18

Reynolds and the Boys after Little Round Top

When the shooting was over, Reynolds and the boys stood behind the breastworks. The other Union soldiers ran and hugged and hollered like they had just won the World Series. Bob and Stevie ran and joined in. Reynolds and Cyrus walked toward the crowd and shook hands with the other officers. The guy who had been picked as Buford came over on his horse and said, "Good work, gentlemen."

"What now?" Reynolds asked Cyrus.

"We'll grab lunch over at the mess and then set up for the afternoon. It takes about forty-five minutes to get the cannon moved, so we shoot the bull for a while."

Reynolds followed Cyrus and the boys. The squad was happy, chattering away, the kids gesticulating with their hands the way young boys do when they talk about video games. As they headed down the man-made hill, Reynolds felt good. It was a combination of things. He had the endorphin rush from a good workout, but he was relatively used to that. And though he didn't play softball or basketball with his buddies anymore, and though it had been a very long time since he'd played for his college lacrosse team, the Gettysburg Bullets, he remembered the feeling of winning. And then there was the thrill of the performance and the afterglow of the theater, the backstage, post-premiere excitement of having pulled off the show.

The electric mood sustained him as they walked several ball fields over to the picnic lunch for soldiers. The Federals and the Confederates mixed together in the buffet line. The food preparers were in uniform and stood behind tables ladling out beans and rice and pieces of pork. Most of the men had their own tin plates and forks. Lacking the right equipment, Reynolds had to bear the indignity of using a paper plate and plastic utensils. They sat together on the stone picnic tables and talked about the battle. It reminded Reynolds of lunch on a movie set with extras. Many of the men had blood all over them, having used their time-release capsules and other mechanisms of injury. He imagined these guys waiting all year to get the right bloodstain on their leg.

Rooster and a few of his boys appeared, and Cyrus invited them to join. Reynolds noticed that Cyrus and Rooster had given up their Seinfeld and Newman thing—it was as though the struggles on the battlefield had caused them to abandon their petty differences.

"What I love about this," Cyrus said, when he came back to the table with a piece of peach pie on his tin plate, "is that in some small way, I'm honoring the past. We take for granted all that's been given to us."

"Goddamn right," said Rooster. The younger guys all around the table nodded in agreement. "These men died for us. All of them."

Reynolds started to say something and then thought better of it.

"Are you ready to take me on, Cyrus?" Rooster said.

"You bet your ass. Let's add soldier boy, here," he said, gesturing to Reynolds.

Reynolds gave Cyrus a questioning look. "A little game we play at every show," said Cyrus. "We quiz each other on the war. First one to stump all the others wins."

"OK," Reynolds said.

"Here you go, Cyrus," said Rooster. "Which Confederate commander was between Pender and Early at the end of the second day?"

"Easy," Cyrus said. "Rodes. Who was across from him?"

Rooster smiled. "Winfield Scott Hancock." Reynolds gave a big nod. Rooster looked at him and said, "All right, Cyrus, let me try your friend here. Reynolds, where were John Bell Hood's men from?"

"Well, which ones?" Reynolds said, cat with the canary. "Hood, as you know, was in a lot of action in the war." A few laughs came up from the boys, as if they had heard an effective taunt.

"The one here—Little Round Top," said Rooster.

"OK. Hood had seven brigades at Gettysburg. And I know you know all this, Rooster, you old rascal. For the most part, they were Alabamians. The five brigades under Hood the second day of Gettysburg were from Alabama and two were from Texas. From right to left as you look up Little Round Top—so as we look down from the top of the hill that we'll be holding—it was the Fifteenth, Forty-seventh, and Fourth Alabama, then the Fifth Texas and the Fourth Texas, then the Forty-eighth Alabama, and then in front of Devil's Den it was the Forty-fourth Alabama."

"Ha," said Cyrus. "That'll shut you up, Rooster."

Stevie spoke up. "Reynolds, tell us something we don't know. Something about all of this shit that maybe we don't get."

"Yeah," said Cyrus. "Tell us something these amateurs can't get from just watching PBS."

Reynolds blew out of his mouth. "OK, let's see. I hated that picture, by the way."

"The movie or the documentary movie?" said Rooster.

"The *movie* movie," Reynolds said.

Stevie said, "Then, can a picture also be a documentary, or does a picture mean a regular movie?"

"Good question," Bob said. "I always wondered that."

"A picture means any kind of movie. And a movie can be a picture or a documentary, you fucking morons," Cyrus said.

"Oh yeah, Cyrus?" said Nicely, standing up. "Well, what about a film?"

"Films are just movies."

"Oh yeah, you're going to call *The 400 Blows* a movie?"

Silence. Reynolds grinned. The other guys stole glances of non-recognition at each other.

"Didn't think so, bitches," Nicely said.

"Well, anyway," Reynolds said. "I was talking about the Gettysburg movie. The one with Martin Sheen and . . . like, Tom Berenger in some crazy beard."

"They all had crazy beards," said Stevie.

"Anyway, I hated that movie," Reynolds said.

"So two-dimensional," said Cyrus.

"What about the documentary?" said Stevie.

"I liked the documentary," said Reynolds. "But even that's just a movie." He saw that they were disappointed that he didn't love the documentary. "Anyone ever been there? To the battlefield?"

"I took my kids," said Rooster. "Twenty years ago."

"Where'd you stay?"

"Motel. There was a cannon out in front. Had a history professor ride in the car with us for three hours."

"What do you remember about the trip?"

"Everything. It was glorious. Best vacation of my life. What I took away was freedom. Every goddamn day since, I try to remember that someone gave me this freedom I have." The great memory seemed to shrivel as he looked around in the present. "Doesn't look anything like this here memorial service we try to pull off." He had become almost embarrassed. "But I guess everyone knows that."

"Well, everyone here is trying very hard," Reynolds said. "Stevie, I still haven't given you one thing that isn't well-known. I guess it's that after Pickett's Charge, when the Confederate soldiers were retreating from Cemetery Ridge, Robert E. Lee rode out of the cover of the trees and said to them, "This is all my fault, boys. This is my fault alone."

CHAPTER 19

A Note from Bella

From: Bella G. Stanhope < bonmotonemillion@gmail.com >
To: Norman Daley < bigfliar@mandaleproductions.com >
Subject: Wake up, time for breakfast with me

Queridoio Chumly—
    Hola from Argentina!
    (Sorry, there should be an upside down explanation mark before *Hola*, but I don't know how to make my laptop do that yet—which is a serious dilemma if I'm going to be doing Spanish papers on it—for now it will have to suffice that I just use italics for any Spanish—as we say to each other on email now, note the *Querido*, querido.)
    And I'm sorry I haven't written earlier, but I've been all caught up with getting adjusted these three weeks. They seem to have gone by in a moment's flash.
    So listen up, Old Buddy Old Pal: like last year, some of these dispatches are going to double as both letters home and reports. Why the hell not?
    Letter Part:

I love this City!!! Classes are good, and my Spanish is improving. The City is so beautiful— '*que linda, Buenos Aires*' the Portenos say, particularly the taxi drivers (don't worry, I'm not being all like, Westside Malibu brat and taking taxis everywhere—but a girl needs to jump in a cab in this town every once in a while, I've learned . . . AND . . . they stay up all night here! You warned me about that and you were right). For the rest, see Report below, section 2.

Report Part:

Section 1. (Where, having called you out for what you are trying to do, out of fealty [good new word from MacBook thesaurus (is thesaurus like dinosaurs for any reason?)] I give you the meat and potatoes aspect of the report.)

I'm now mini-obsessed with Mavis Gallant, thanks to you. She was born in Montreal in 1922. (She's still alive.) She was married and divorced by 23. She worked as a journalist in Montreal and decided, crazily (at least uniquely) to go to France in 1950. Although this shows up exactly nowhere, I think it was because she had a broken heart. Because that's the way she writes.

She spent most of her time in Paris, but wandered around Europe, spending a lot of time in Madrid and Capri. She established a "relationship with The New Yorker Magazine" that sounds like it was a great thing to have, and she published a bazillion stories there. But she was always broke, it seemed. I found a couple videos on YouTube of her giving readings and doing Q and A's, which are pretty interesting. She seems great— still kicking. My favorite is at a book signing in Paris when someone asks her when she decided she had enough confidence to become a writer and she says, "It never even occurred to me to be anything else." Kind of what we've talked about. What you've said.

Section 2. (In which we get to the bottom of your heavy-handed assignment, and I sprinkle in details of my life here on the run. My focus of late has been to ruminate, investigate and speculate as to why you hand me the subjects you hand me. Not to mention interrogate, but we both know why that doesn't get me far, because you obfuscate and prevaricate.)

OK, we find me, young Bella, just out of high school, far from the intellectuals and ganja of Berkeley down in Buenos Aires—Palermo Hollywood (nice irony, btw). You give me the curious assignment of Mavis Gallant. Interesting. Some theories, fragments, observations: she is Canadian and a woman. You are catching two birds with one stone here, playing on my sense of alienation. I am an outsider by nature and currently you are coupling my physical plight with my nature to dwell on that sense of alienation. Now, from what I've read and studied, you've picked the perfect subject to get me good and alienated, and, thus, in an outsider's state of mind. I am old enough, as I've told you for the past few years, to be hip to your strategies. Yes, I am an outsider currently, as you might expect, even in this fabulous city (more about that later). So, here I am an outsider and you are supplying me with someone who is ostensibly outside of myself (a Canadian) who is however similar enough (she is your, away from home, writes stories (in English) and is hell bent on being free and alone, like me). So, look Chum, I get it, I GET IT. We did alienation in tenth grade. (Kids are not kids so there goes your proof. Can you guess that reference?) Once again, you are relating by superimposing upon me a figure who will appeal to some aspect of my personality which, in turn will cause me to reflection my own plight and how it relates to my art, all in a metamanipulation to get me to follow the path we've discussed for so long or, put a nicer way, a metamanipulation to get me excited about living a writer's life. I love you for it, I really do, I especially love you the way you've tried to expand the simple early assignments, which, let's face it, were a grounding in American popular culture which you thought—quite rightly—as it turns out—would give me a bit of a leg up on my schoolmates with respect to the chum (!) of the California Public School system.

OK, updates. I am pretty much in love. Before you get all worked up let me tell you it is not what you expect . . . not some Argentinian dude. (Though the boys down here are *gor-geous*. Sorry.) It's a guy in my program named Donovan. He's sweet and he's smart and funny and wtf he is FROM MALIBU. We can't figure that one out, how we missed each other. He was only there for two years before graduation and then he moved to Ventura. You would like him. He's cynical. But not with me. We know we are both young and everyone hooks up so it's chill. TMI, I know. I'm being nonchalant and in keeping with that I will tell you more later. And don't tell my mom, or my dad, can you please just this once keep a secret? If you don't I won't write any more. :)

I'm still in the apartment with Becky and Petra with the family in Belgrano (they are totally OK, but not that interesting, and very religious) and still we are in classes at the Center for a lot of the time during the day. The combination of Spanish class and the general populace speaking Spanish has improved my Spanish considerably. It's one thing to try to figure out past subjunctive on a test and another thing when you are eating dinner

with a bunch of friends (Argentinians eat dinner all night, and
yes, even though I have a boyfriend I find myself at big crowded
tables with lots of chicos often) and someone says *he hacido*
something or other (I might have done something or other).

The first semester classes ended well—good marks in
LatAm Lit (read *El Aleph* in Español . . . holy shit . . . you try
that, big boy) and a 17th through 19th Century Argentine
History class that was a touch blah blah but I did pick up some
good stuff—it was a good appetizer for this term, because
now we're in 20th Cent Politics Economy and History, which
is just crazy. This is I guess why you go somewhere to learn
about a place. Walking around Plaza de Mayo (pronounced
Mazho, that's the only way I can try to 'splain how it sounds)
seeing Casa Rosado where all that great black and white
footage of Eva P we always see is, and through San Cristobal
and San Telmo and Barranca and Recoleta—all the different
neighborhoods—while reading and discussing them in class
and at night in real time is just, well, it sounds queer (gushy),
but exciting. This place is a puzzle. A big beautiful puzzle.
There are days when I can walk for hours around the Recoleta
looking at the French buildings with the fabulous arched windows, all made from limestone, all the doormen looking like
actors, the security guys in front of the nice hotels even like
movie stars. Sometimes Becky and I will just say, did you *see*
that guy who is just putting people in taxis? And there is not
a woman in the whole country who goes out in sweat pants.
Even the girls we see at school, who should look shitty the way
you're supposed to look when you roll out of bed to class, are
like pow—kablam—good hair, bag, shoes. You should see the
old ladies walking down Montevideo or Arroyo, each one in

purple or yellow or maroon—any color—suit with gold buttons and matching fringe on the shoes, or bag, sometimes a hat that is part of the outfit. So much of this is like Paris or the time Dad took me to Spain—but I think it is too easy to say that. It is all part Mexico too. Not very American. The people seem to me like Italians, actually—and there are so many Italian names, that is probably the deepest impression you get. Hardly any feeling of the English, except with Borges—he feels like he had some of the English stuffiness. But it is all, like a puzzle. My lit teacher likes Andre Malraux a lot (did you ever read— we never talked about him)—but Malraux said Buenos Aires is the capital of an Empire that never existed. I like that.

I'm trying to write a series of one-acts. It would be pretty fricking awesome to put something up down here (up/down, did you notice?) Bet you didn't know Buenos Aires has the most theaters per capita of any city in the world? The main street is Corrientes. There are tons of big houses playing what look to be big exuberant shows. There also seems to be an unlimited desire for drag queens and aging singers who we never heard of up in the States. It is like you took Broadway at, like, 49th and 7th Ave—in there. That feeling for a whole long Avenue. Where this is going is that there is also a large amount of spaces for plays. And a really vibrant place for experimental stuff. I have one and I really think if I can get the second and third pieces done the school or another little theatre where my friend Pilar is part of the company will workshop it—at least for a few weeks.

OK I'm rambling *he ramplcito* - or some such. And I've mixed up my report and my letter. I am mysterious what can I say. Okie doke and all that rot. Feel weird about the playwriting.

Maybe you can advise. gtg. I hope you are good and well and tell Carol I am in the middle of a letter to her about food.

Besos, b

P.s. By the way Mavis Gallant doesn't have a saying but I read a great story about a young American or Canadian girl living with three other young adults in Madrid. Nothing happens and I think that means everything happens . . . but, I should work on what it means.

CHAPTER 20

Monkeying Around

Norman hung up the phone and shook his head.

"What?" said Carol.

"That was Stella. She's in Enchino."

"What? Out in Palm Springs?"

"Toward the desert, yes. She followed Reynolds down there. He didn't tell her where he was going but she found out somehow and followed him."

Carol said, "Strange."

"I haven't even started yet. He's there doing a Civil War reenactment. In the uniform and everything."

"What?" she said, her voice in that unique pitch of a crow protesting that is reachable only by New Yorkers born between the two world wars.

He gave a small laugh. "A Civil War reenactment. Battle of Gettysburg. You know, when they get together and do a reenactment of the whole thing."

Carol grimaced. "With the guns and the cannon?"

He was laughing harder now. "Yeah."

She sat down next to him, trying to fight back a smile. "And Stella's there too?"

"Yes. And she wants me to come help her talk to him," Norman said.

"Are you?" Carol said.

"Yes."

"When?"

"Tomorrow." I'm going to drive out there after Tom and I walk."

She took all this in. "What's Reynolds doing there?"

"Fighting, I guess," Norman said. "Reenacting. How the hell do I know?"

"I guess it is in his blood."

"That's what I was thinking. You know, we've talked about it. He was a tour guide in high school. He knows everything. We make bets. I look shit up on the Internet and ask him. I would give him questions like: Which general was from Florida?"

"And Stella didn't know?"

"The general from Florida?"

"Oh, stop it, Daley."

"She got home Friday night and Reynolds wasn't there. But he had said he was playing golf with the boys."

"At least he wasn't monkeying around," Carol said.

"What do you call *this*?"

"This I call weird. But not monkeying around."

They were quiet for a moment, both of their heads spinning. Then she stood. "It's *fakakta*. That whole business about the Civil War. Never understood it. Remember, we went there for a weekend when you were with NBC?"

"Oh God, remember?" Norman said.

"It was boring. And we stayed in a red motel."

"I kind of liked it."

"Oh, you say that now, but we were bored. It was just killing, killing, killing."

"There *was* a lot of killing."

She became reflective. "Not that I know anything about it, but I could never understand these people who get dressed up and pretend to do battles. A national park, I can understand. You need to have that. But why pretend to do it again? What the hell is that? Why would you re-create something so horrible?

"All right, enough," he said. "It's not the same. And by the way, remember that re-creating the army has been very good to us. It's how we bought this house."

"What, *Artie?* Don't be ridiculous. That not the same thing. That's *comedy*. Nobody believed he was in the army. And you didn't kill anybody." She stood and walked into the kitchen, waving him off.

Maybe she was right. As Norman sat he thought about it. Why would you re-create the goddamn Battle of Gettysburg? In Enchino? Is that a worthwhile endeavor? On the one hand, it was the glorification of a horrible event. On the other, it was preserving something. But *were* they preserving anything? He stood and walked into the kitchen.

"Maybe it's like community theater," he said. "They just want to put on a show. You know, how everybody must be in a show, the inner performer comes out in everybody. Like reality TV."

"It's true that he never talks about it," she said.

"Well, except he talks to me."

"So he's going through a phase."

"I guess. But I'm getting worried."

She dried her hands on a dish towel. "At least he's not monkeying around."

CHAPTER 21

Father's Son

Yes, Reynolds thought, everyone here was trying very hard. He looked at the troops sitting around him. A small group had gathered to listen. A few of the younger kids had their iPhones out and were texting. One kid put his headphones on and looked away, another held his phone up and took a picture of Reynolds.

So, my picture in this uniform will be transmitted somewhere, he said to himself, *and maybe somewhere a thousand years from now, someone will think I was in the Battle of Gettysburg.* He felt the dark wave coming up, the disgust from so long ago. The business of the town had been tourism. They shuttled the people through as fast as they could, but the one thing about growing up near the battleground was that there was nothing else to do in Gettysburg but serve the battle. It was all about the battle. "There ain't no more," his mother always said, with her pretend Southern accent and a smile.

He could tell from the way the soldiers around him were dressed where they got their inspiration from. There were the usual: Lees and Grants and Shermans and Jacksons, even though three out of those four weren't even at Gettysburg. But even more troublesome to Reynolds was that every fourth guy was dressed like Chamberlain. A lot of Longstreets too—it was obvious they had read *The Killer Angels* or seen *The Civil War* on PBS and that had hooked them. They might as well be Trekkies at a Star Trek convention. It was shades of shades, wheels inside wheels.

The Killer Angels was a novelized version of events covered in Shelby Foote's Civil War history and Douglas Southall Freeman's *Lee's Lieutenants*. Then Shelby Foote himself was in the PBS documentary—the Ken Burns miniseries. The names ran through these histories like cult figures. Some of the guys around Reynolds, the unfortunate ones, looked as if they had found their inspiration in the New Line movie that Ted Turner had paid for, called *Gettysburg*. He groaned inside. That was the worst. You could almost see the fake beard hanging off Tom Berenger; he was sure he could see Jeff Daniels's mustache almost blow off during a take on Little Round Top.

"You know, guys, the Civil War was a terrible thing," Reynolds said. "I'm not so sure it's worth celebrating like this."

"Why not?" said Cyrus.

"It's the most important thing an American can do, if you ask me," said Rooster.

Reynolds felt his father coming out in him. "Why?" He realized he had raised his voice. The crowd recoiled a bit. He went into his challenging mode, which existed underneath his profound and genuflecting mode. "They were nuts. Crazy. Lunatics. *Religious* nuts. Robert E. Lee? *Robert E. Lee?* He was a religious fanatic. Do you realize what the day after the battle was?"

"Judgment Day?" Bob said.

"No!" he yelled. Then he stopped and looked at Bob again. "*Judgment Day?*" He regained his train of thought. "No, not

Judgment Day. It was the fucking fourth of July. Do you know why Lee slaughtered all his own men like that? Because he had a premonition from the Lord that he wanted the South to become free on Independence Day. So, Lee sent twenty thousand men toward a clump of trees in the face of the whole Union Army."

The crowd didn't say anything.

"It was butchery. It was insane." Reynolds was yelling louder now. "The stuff we see—the movies, the books—it's all fifty times removed from the truth. It happened a hundred and fifty years ago all the way across the country. It wasn't romantic. It was evil. Believe me, I lived there."

"But it was real," Cyrus said.

"And the body count was nothing compared to the Crusades or World War II," Nicely said.

Reynolds stared at them and said, "You're right. It was real." He felt a headache coming on. "But it's not real today. Now it's what we make it. The further away it gets, the further from the truth it gets. Let me tell you a story. When I was a tour guide, there was a well on the way from town to the battlefield, which is outside of where the shops and downtown are. Now, this well was dug and made in the 1920s. Because of the route I used, my tours would go right by it. One day a lady asked me, 'Is that well from the time of the battle?' And you know what? I didn't have the heart to tell her no. I told her it was famous because the two sides drank from it together. I even told her that Buford himself took a drink from it. Then on the next tour I said that Lee himself took a drink from it. I made it a game. I found the name of a Union commander who had been killed at Chancellorsville a month earlier—Edward Hooper—and I told them all that it was called Hooper's Well. They loved it."

"So, what's your point?" said Rooster.

"That we don't know what's real!" Reynolds said. "All that was left after the battle were army reports and letters the soldiers sent home to their wives and sweethearts. No one knew the truth because no one saw it all. Historians study those letters and those reports and write books about it. Then other historians write books about those books. Then more guys write books about the books about the books. Now we have movies based on the books about the books. I bet all of you guys know about Joshua Lawrence Chamberlain, right?"

Everyone nodded.

"What do you know about Chamberlain?"

"That he led the troops on Little Round Top," Cyrus said.

"And he charged down the hill when they didn't have any ammo left," said Rooster.

"And how do you know that?" said Reynolds.

"It's documented fact," said Cyrus.

"It's in the goddamn *Killer Angels*, that's why," Reynolds said. "He's Jeff Bridges. It is in half the books. But who knows? Do you know who Holman Melcher was? Is anybody being Holman Melcher today?" When there was no response, he said, "Holman Melcher was in the Twentieth Maine with Chamberlain. Now, Melcher went to his deathbed saying he was the one who had the idea to run down the hill with bayonets. Chamberlain himself said he never gave the order. Chamberlain was a great guy, but no one knows whose idea it was."

"That kind of thing always happens," said Rooster.

"Yeah," said Stevie. "It makes it interesting. And why does the arguing over the details make it not important?"

Reynolds didn't know what to say.

"You never were in the service, were you?" said Rooster.

Cyrus and Rooster exchanged a look.

"Well, I think if you'd been in the service you might feel different. And you're in the Hollywood business, right? Isn't that what you told me?"

"Yes."

"Cool," said Nicely.

"Well, excuse me for saying so," Rooster said. "But you people there are all fucked up. You never give enough credit to the military. You never do anything that appreciates what men who died for this country did for you."

"That's not true."

"Of course it's true. Listen to what you're saying. 'Not important, the Civil War.' What kind of hogwash is that? Some of us think it was pretty goddamn important."

"It's not that I don't think it was important. I think we are far away from the reality. Like everything. Reality is obfuscated and cheapened and modified." His voice drifted off.

They all looked at him.

"Your problem," said Cyrus, "is that you don't know what to believe in. Rooster's right. That's the problem with all you people."

"So, I'm supposed to believe in Robert E. Lee? In Grant and Sherman, who destroyed great parts of our country? I'm supposed to believe in this? Gettysburg in California?"

No one spoke.

"You're the one who came here," Bob said. "Ain't nobody forced you to come."

Nicely, who had been sitting cross-legged and playing with grass, looked up and said, "Are you OK, Mr. Reynolds?"

Reynolds was exasperated. There was a man-made hill, for Christ's sake. He caught himself. He didn't need to get angry about all this. Bob was right—nobody forced him to come. He had brought himself here for some reason. Part of the fun was seeing how messed up and fun it was.

The first thing he'd done was order the perfect sword. He'd found it on eBay for $680, sold by someone in Pittsburgh. It was fabulous, he saw, as he took it out of the bubble wrap: long, shiny blade, leather scabbard. Next was the rifle. He'd spent several months doing the research and had pulled the trigger on a Springfield, made in New York. It had been refurbished somewhat, but anything dating from the war that hadn't been would not work, and he wanted to be sure that when the time came he could shoot. He'd waited until Stella was in New York and Bella away for the weekend with her friends and taken it in the backyard and fired one solitary round to make sure it worked.

As he found more of his uniform, he'd rented a storage space in Culver City in which to keep his collection. It was a secret. As the outfit took shape, so did his excitement. It was his own little thing, so disassociated from his world: the lunches with other schmendricks like himself trying to put together projects; Stella's chatter about the studio and its byzantine politics; contracts for the licensing of 126 episodes of *John Iron* to Netflix. The momentum toward doing something about it built. Stella thought it was a little strange when he'd stopped shaving, but he had grown a beard once or twice in the past, so it wasn't out of the blue. He almost told Norman but couldn't. He thought of telling Bella, but she would get worried about him.

When he found the right pair of boots, in November, he bought a hanging lamp from Home Depot and a large floor mirror from a discount furniture store on Pico. He went to the storage unit. It was six by six and he had removed any shelving, so it was just a big closet. He shut the door behind him and hung the lamp on the doorknob, giving the inside of the space a kind of yellow-white feeling against the drywall perimeter. He stood the mirror against the wall so that he could get a full view of himself when he was ready. He undressed, trying not to look at himself in the cheap mirror. He pulled on the breeches and the undershirt. He climbed into the jacket and sat on the floor to put on the boots. He hoisted the sword in its scabbard around his torso. He donned his cap and grabbed his gun.

When he was dressed to regimental standards he looked in the mirror. And for a moment, before his cynical voice took over and told him he looked like a complete jackass, before he was engulfed in terrible shame for being like the kind of moron who wears a football helmet to watch the game on Sunday, he took his own breath away. He looked real. The uniform was authentic in every way. There were touches to it that only he would know, that only he could know. The shade of blue to the breeches, for example, was a bit darker than the standard, because the unit he most admired, the 183rd Pennsylvania, had their pants their own color. They'd been made by a haberdasher in Concordville, and Reynolds had scoured the Internet and run a pair down. To the inside of his cap he had sewn his name and address, a habit of the soldiers now lost to time. He felt a rush of pride when he thought of these things—things that he knew like a special secret, things that gave him an advantage, things that made it so he could be good at this, if he wanted.

He remembered being a boy, maybe at the end of being a boy, maybe at fifteen, when he hadn't yet learned to hate the battle, before his father's views had won him over, identifying, as they did, the horror and stupidity of the battle, the generals, the war.

Before he had learned the now obvious truth that the place where they lived was glorified. But there in the storage space, he returned to a place in memory that warmed him in the same way as crawling onto the couch with his mother or smelling the French fries through a Burger King bag. For him, the battle was home, and he could not change that, no matter what his father said or how far away he went.

"No, Nicely, I'm OK. It's just . . . this is complicated for me."

"For me too, now that you've told us this stuff."

"Yeah. I'm sorry," Reynolds said. After a beat, he continued, "Remember, guys: these armies were full of men who were as hard as steel and as brave as centurions."

The ragtag outfit of Union and Confederate soldiers just stared at the ground around the picnic table sitting off the third-base side of field four.

"It is good that we remember them."

CHAPTER 22

The Battle of the Wheatfield

The company was lying in the outfield grass near third base. The Rebel troops were assembled across the field eight outfield fence, in position to swoop down and turn the Union's right flank. The SCCWA, the Southern California Civil War Association, had covered the outfield's deep green grass in straw for a more authentic setting for the battle of the Wheatfield. There were a few structures made of barn planks and sparse wheat stalks.

"Jesus Christ," Bob said, "We are going to be running for our lives toward a full outfield of these fuckwads."

"Bob," Reynolds said, "I've come to believe you are hiding your light under a bushel."

"For sure, General. You can't sleep on Bob," Stevie said.

"Same goes for you," Reynolds said. "Just know, then," he said, "I've got my eye on all three of you." He winked at Nicely.

"All right, I've given you all the scenario," Cyrus said. "There are three waves of men from our side. We are in the first one. Which is unfortunate. When we get the order, we have to run out, find cover, and try to draw the Rebels to the middle of the field. Try to get behind the shelter at deep shortstop as quick as possible, because if we don't we'll be sitting ducks as soon as we get to second base."

"General Reynolds?' Nicely said. "How does where all of us troops are assembled relate to the real battle of the Wheatfield? Who is coming from where?"

"Sometimes, guys, I don't have any goddamn idea what is going on here," Reynolds said.

"I know, me either," Cyrus said. "All I can think of is that they know the Confederates won the first part of this brawl, and the Federals were shot down like fish in a barrel. So, the authenticity committee set it up as best they could."

A loud boom from the Confederate cavalry started the battle. Cyrus waited for five minutes and then ordered the company to run for the shelter at shortstop. Each of them ran in a serpentine fashion until they reached the five-foot barricade of barn siding and wheat, where they dove and landed on top of one another. Cyrus ordered them to stand up and turn sideways, so they all could be protected.

"OK, Cyrus," Bob said, "Any bright ideas?"

"Look, Bob, we're supposed to get shot," Cyrus said.

Reynolds looked around the side of the shelter and saw that a group of fifteen Rebel soldiers had advanced from the left side and were twenty-five yards away from their shelter.

"We're done for," Reynolds said.

Each of the other guys peeked, to the left or the right, and saw the same thing.

"We have to go balls out and charge them Charlemagne style," Nicely said.

"We're *not supposed to win* this part, you idiots," Cyrus said.

Reynolds looked again and saw the Confederates closing in. "I think it's time we made our run," he said.

"That was a helluva fight," Stevie said. He and the rest of the guys were resting in the shade by the third baseline. "I think they shot me a good nine times."

"That's why they call it the battle of the Wheatfield. You're out there in a field, undermanned, to get killed by Confederates in a superior position. As in flat. As in a place where you get your head blown off."

"I'm not sure about that," Reynolds.

"They called it the battle of the Wheatfield because it happened in a wheat field," Bob said.

"Bingo," Reynolds said.

"If you think about it," Nicely said, "they came at us out of left field."

"Let's not go to battles where we have to lose anymore. I hate losing," Bob said.

"Yeah," Stevie said, "I don't get these fuckers who come to Gettysburg battles to lose every time. And there are always more of them than us. What, to fight for slavery? A little part of me comes to these things to fight to get rid of fucking slavery. To beat the living shit out of those guys. Like for real. Like the actual people over there. Like to eradicate those bastards who want slavery to continue."

"Word," Bob said.

"Easy does it," Reynolds said.

Everyone was quiet for a little while, most staring at Stevie.

Nicely spoke up. "Well, I don't disagree with you, Stevie. You're my boy. But I suppose they could see it as one part of a big production, and someone has to be the bad guys. We are playing a role in a full show that is aimed at being authentic and entertaining. You can't put politics in it. It's a giant complicated production that is fun to be a part of." Nicely went back to playing with his paintball gun.

"Oh, I get it," Cyrus said. "We're all in a big show like actors." He took the back of his right hand and put it on the left side. Then slowly crossed it back to his right, like the lead singer of INXS. "Like a spectacular *musical* with people dancing and singing and crying and dying and with pianos dropping from the roof. That's what you want, isn't it?"

"Um . . . no," Nicely said.

"Damn, Cyrus," Bob said. "Don't be a dick."

Stevie said, "Who hurt you, Cyrus? Can you tell us? This is a safe space."

"OK, enough," Reynolds said. "I think Nicely has it right. We are here to retell the story of one great and horrible event in American history, and you can't hold any real-life grudges toward the men who fought in the war, or men who are out there on the field with you."

"C'mon," Bob said. "You don't believe that."

CHAPTER 23

I Thought You Hated This

When the smoke cleared from the Wheatfield, the crowd began to file out to the parking lots, done for the day. Delaney and Marisol gave Stella explicit directions to the tent, which had now expanded to four tents, through Cyrus's good graces and some legwork by Robert. This would be enough to house Reynolds's growing crowd for the night. Stella was too dazed to correct their simple-headed notion that she was going to join the fun and sleep in a tent that evening herself. For now, she played along and was happy that Bella and Heather were having fun.

Stella stood on the sideline, and the soldiers began to pass her by. They were no longer in any kind of organized group; they crossed before her in clumps of twos and threes, strange concoctions of strange men: fallen soldiers, actors, and construction worker buddies going for a beer after work. They were bloodied and beaten, most of them, and she had the feeling of a farmwoman in a dusty apron on the side of Hagerstown Road or something—a little like *Days of Heaven*, maybe. She was losing it, she thought. Stella had been on enough sets and watched enough extras herd their way to lunch to be able to differentiate between a made-up world and reality. Her job was to help make up the worlds, she didn't live in them. Fantasy was for schmucks—or at least for others. That's what being in the business meant. Making the magic involved not believing in the magic anymore. She was one of the gods. And this was the worst kind of amateur hour. She was glad she had gotten a hold of herself.

And then she saw him, on the rise past the centerfield fence of the field closest to her, talking to Cyrus. He was smiling and chattering, moving his pointing finger against the horizon to illustrate some troop movement. She went toward him, running a bit. He saw her, and his face dropped.

She gave a little wave. "Hi, honey," she said.

Cyrus slipped away. Reynolds said, "I'll catch up with you at camp, sir."

Reynolds stopped and stood ten paces from her.

"I didn't come here to laugh at them," Reynolds said.

Stella felt her heart crash. He was embarrassed. She walked fast and reached out to hug him. She didn't want to look at his face, she didn't need to see him feeling so exposed and gone—like he was looking at someone from the future, as though he had walked off the battlefield and seen something as incomprehensible to the mind of a Union soldier as a studio executive from Paramount who was juggling three pictures.

"I know," Stella said. She put her arms around him and squeezed tight, trying to show him he didn't need to be embarrassed.

"How'd you find me?" he said. "I didn't want *anyone* to see me."

"I can track you by your phone. I'm sorry, honey."

He scrunched his face, "Damnit."

Why didn't you tell me?" she said. "This looks like fun."

"Oh, please," Reynolds said.

"No, I mean it. But, I thought . . . I thought you weren't into this. *Are* you into this?" He didn't say anything. She continued, "I thought your father . . . oh, never mind. I'm so sorry, I've invaded your private thing."

"That's what I thought—my father and all. But, I don't know." He looked around. Most of the soldiers were off the field now, and it was the two of them alone. He avoided her eyes. "I just started feeling *drawn* to it."

She was looking at him now, tilting her head sideways, showing a little bit of a smile, testing the waters to see whether he was available to come back to sanity. To have a laugh about the whole thing and zap them both back to now. Then she could use the opening to get him in the car and back to takeout from the Ivy and home to Malibu. Back to safety, where she could put him back together again, the way she had so many times before with drunken directors and actors off their meds.

"Forget it," he said. He was embarrassed again. He broke away from her and started toward the tents.

"No, Reynolds. Honey, wait." She went after him. "Reynoldsy, I'm sorry." She grabbed the sleeve of his tunic and turned him around. Then she grabbed the front of the garment and looked at his dirt-streaked face. "I'm sorry. I think this is great—it's so cool. I called Bella and she's here. With Heather. We all want to watch you. We want to see you do this."

His eyes widened. "Bella? Oh my God, you *told* her? That's even worse."

"She's into it. You're her father. She wants to see it. I want to see it. We're going to sleep in the tents with you."

"You want to sleep in the tents?"

"Sure. So does Bell."

"Stell, this was not supposed to happen. I didn't want anyone to know."

"Well, we know now, honey, and we want to support you."

Stella said she had to find a bathroom.

Reynolds turned his thoughts to her. His wife. The most beautiful girl in the world. He dreamt of her constantly, before she'd even talked to him. She'd been the unattainable neighbor. She'd led a glamorous life—she went out to premieres and awards shows dressed like a movie star and had big black sedans waiting to whisk her away. She had dinner parties with discreet lists of guests, during which he imagined champagne flowing and piles of coke on glass tables. Stella looked cool and beautiful even going to the airport.

She had hair like Ali McGraw and dead-sexy, dark brown eyes—her skin was just a hint lighter than milk chocolate. She still got tanned at the beach, still had tan lines naked. She was gifted with a perfectly proportioned body with curvy hips, which he loved. It was no accident that she had so many boyfriends picking her up in limos.

Reynolds thought of Stella driving all the way down here. She was probably beyond angry and certain he was having an affair, but she wasn't showing it. That's how incredible she was. It suddenly gave him a chill, this notion that he was hurting her. He wasn't doing that, for God's sake. He'd had a dream about Delaney Bedford, and Delaney Bedford happened to be there. A little suspect, he'd admit. He felt things getting away from him. Stella was the most important thing in his life. He thought, *she is my heart and soul*. Over the years, they'd had bullshit fights. But that was it. The bond between them was truthful and had stood the test of time.

They had been young together. They became more financially successful than they could have ever imagined. As they succeeded, and large and stressful decisions had to be made, each was the other's closest counsel. They had Bella, and the cascade of feelings that comes only with having a child. And Bella was the kind of kid who would tighten the relationship of two entirely devoted parents. As Bella grew, they were a strong and happy family.

With a job and a child, Stella had to work constantly and efficiently. Reynolds could see that the work of being a mom was endless, while that of being a dad was not endless, no matter how he tried to help. Because of all she had to do, Reynolds worried that Stella believed she had become cold, short, and petty. That she had become mean. She was nothing of the sort. She did *everything*. She'd been class parent three times and team parent for Bella's ninth-grade soccer season. Stella had produced three of Paramount's most profitable movies in six years. She was, as Norman said, unstoppable. But she wasn't that way with him. She was always ready to rent a movie, go in the ocean, or run away for the weekends. Most of all, though, they were nice to each other, they protected each other, they were loyal to each other, and they cherished each other.

CHAPTER 24

Between the Battle and the Cotillion

Stella and Reynolds continued to look over the field.

"Oh. Jeez. That's a small battle over there," Stella said.

Reynolds had been watching for several minutes when she said it. "It's a skirmish."

"Where does a skirmish stop and a battle begin?"

"It's all a battle," Reynolds said. "Skirmishes are small parts. Like a subset."

"I'm so confused," Stella said.

"I think they are having little skirmishes because there's not enough people."

Rifle shots rang out. The drummer boy, who had shed his wool tunic, wore what from a distance looked like a concert T-shirt.

"I wonder if he's a drummer in a band in real life," said Stella.

"It would appear they have a small nucleus of hard-core reenactors."

"And then they get the kids to be extras."

"Right," said Reynolds. He contemplated this. "I wish I had binoculars. I'm John Reynolds, three-star general of the United States fucking army, and I don't have binoculars."

Stella was shading her eyes, trying to catch what they were doing out on the field. "That building right there, that's a rec center. It's surrounded by, like, seven softball fields."

"Try not to focus on that."

"I know. I can't help it." Another few moments passed by. Stella stood on her tiptoes for a few seconds before sitting back down. She looked at Reynolds, who was still staring out. Then she gazed out on the action again.

"It's just so *bad*."

His face collapsed, but he smiled. "I know. It's a kaleidoscope of insanity."

They got up to stroll. She walked holding his arm. His uniform was dirty, covered with the mud and blood of battle. There was a blotch of blackening red on his right side.

"Oh my God, what's that?" she said. "Are you hurt?"

"You like that? Cyrus gave me a blood capsule. I think it ruined the shirt, but it looks good. I have to work on the release. I made it kind of obvious when I cracked it. Had to reach in and do it with my hands."

"You're going to work on it? There's going to be more?"

"I don't know. Maybe."

Stella motioned to a stone picnic table where no one was sitting. She sat across from him, wanting to talk. He was distant, like he was caught up in the cannon fire.

"Honey," she said. "Are you OK?"

"I'm fine," he said. Then, catching her look, "What, just because I came to this?"

She shrugged. Then she nodded. "Well, yeah."

"I don't know." He wouldn't look her in the eye. "You know how some people—people who haven't been to church since they were kids, people who rebelled against organized religion . . ."

"People like us?"

"That's not what I'm saying, but yeah, OK. People who haven't been to church for years start to get drawn back to it. Like it's a quiet call from a previous life."

"And that's what you are doing? That's normal. It's normal to want to go back to something basic in your memory. Something fundamental and familiar. People do that all the time."

"But I hate this memory. It's embarrassing. You know when I left home I realized my father was right—he wasn't right about much, but he was right about this. It was barbaric. And *reenactors*? Reenacting it? These people are sickos. This is celebrating a slaughter."

"Hey, no argument here." She felt he was coming back to her.

"But I kept wanting to do it. It's like I had to come back home. Like I am a prodigal son or something." He looked at her to see whether she understood.

She gave him a weak smile. "Sure. I mean, sure, I think I understand." They were silent for a second. "Honey, does this have anything to do with us? Me and Bella?"

"Nooo," Reynolds said. "Of course not." He felt like a man visiting from back in time. Her clothes looked foreign. Her face was pretty, like the face of a porcelain doll. He could see the Golden Arches of a McDonald's near the freeway, and the view brought him back. "You know I haven't been feeling good. Drifty, you know?"

"Everyone goes through that. C'mon. You know that. What would you tell one of your friends who was feeling this way? That's what you always tell me and Bella to ask ourselves. You're going *through* something."

He glanced at her, his look like that of a golden retriever deciding whether to trust a woman with a treat in hand. "Well, we're here."

"Absolutely," she said. "I'm game. We'll have fun."

"No eye rolling?"

"No eye rolling."

"I didn't come to laugh at them."

"I get it."

They got up and walked for a while. Then Stella wheeled and faced him, stormy now. "Ridiculous," she said. "Have you lost your mind?"

"I know, it's quirky."

"Quirky? Quirky? You're going to take these two idiots and pitch it to Lifetime and tell them it's a serious show?"

"Not serious. Fun. I just want it to be unique. It will be different. It's a good hook."

She put her hands down to her sides like she was closing the trunk of a car. "Honey, let's slow down here. You're going *through* something." She waved her arm around to take in the battlefield and the camp. "Let's not let it snowball into something else. Let's do your war thing here and get home and talk about it."

"See," he said. "You don't get it. It has nothing to do with this." He waved at the field and the parking lot the same way she had. "This is something else. I was coming here anyway. They just came with me. It was an accident. I was coming here on my own. I didn't want anyone to know it. *Anyone.* I got drunk and brought those two." He changed the subject. "But it all fits together. What is going on here works on two different levels."

She was quiet for a second. "What are the two levels, baby?"

"I'm working on the past, and I'm working on the future."

She closed her eyes and then opened them. "OK, OK. I'm on your side. I love you. Let's back up. Let me get back to the show, because that's all I can think about. What *is* the show?"

"These aging beauties get in all sorts of absurd but upscale situations. Like *Sister Wendy* meets *The Kardashians*."

"*Sister Wendy* meets *The Kardashians*?" Then she said it again, "*Sister Wendy* meets *The Kardashians*."

"I'm working on it. I don't expect anyone to understand it yet."

"Who knows, it might work."

"Are you humoring me? Don't humor me."

"No." She shrugged. "What do I know? Maybe you're right. Maybe it's for Amazon. Is one Sister Wendy and the other Kim Kardashian?"

"Look, just because you think I'm losing my mind doesn't mean you have to say this is a good idea; maybe it is stupid."

"Let's not worry about it now. Let's have fun. Let's get ready for the party."

"Cotillion."

"Cotillion?" she said.

"Cotillion."

"Is it like a square dance? With fiddles and all that?"

Reynolds looked at her. "Stella," he said, "how am I supposed to know?"

She laughed a little. "You're the expert."

"I'm not an expert on whatever party it is they have at night. I'm an expert on the Battle of Gettysburg. There were no parties with ladies in hoopskirts at night during the Battle of Gettysburg, I can promise you that. The Southern California Civil

War ... Association—whatever they're called—they are pretty far into their own thing with the cotillion."

Her phone buzzed. "It's Bella."

Stella put it to her ear. "Hi. Where are you? Across the fields? Is it good there? No, it's good, I mean it's fine ... He's right here ... You should see how good he looks ... I'm serious. Come meet us at the tents. Delaney and Mari are there already."

She ended the call and looked at Reynolds. "We're friends with Delaney and Mari now. We're supposed to all meet at the tents now for a drink."

CHAPTER 25

Readying

When Reynolds and Stella got to the tents they were met by Delaney and Marisol and Robert, all sitting in the kind of portable chairs suburban parents sit in to watch their kids play sports, navy blue folding things with mesh cup holders in the arms.

Marisol stood up. "Come, come here. We have started the happy hour."

Robert also stood up, not sure what to do. He was still in his General Longstreet outfit. He grabbed two unopened chairs from next to the tent. "Here," he said. "I got lots of chairs."

Like Reynolds, Stella had known Robert for years. "Why, thank you, Gin-eral," she said, *sotto voce*, in a Southern accent.

"Very funny," he whispered to her. She smiled at him. "Not in my entire life . . ." he said.

"We have beer and wine," said Marisol. "And tequila for later."

Stella took a cup of white wine from Marisol and stuck her head inside one of the tents. Not much to it, she thought. The tents were beige-white, but the light inside was yellow. "We have a sleeping bag for you," said Delaney. "And we use the ladies' room over by the backstop of that ball field." She pointed toward the building.

With nothing much else to do, they were soon all seated in a circle nursing drinks. An awkward silence prevailed.

"So," said Stella to Reynolds. "The ladies tell me you are going to be doing a TV show."

Reynolds stared daggers at her for bringing it up in front everyone.

"Oh yes," said Delaney.

"*Sí.*"

"We are sooo excited."

"And it is going to center on your teachings? With the kids? At home?"

"*Sí*, the teachings of the Secret."

Robert said, "Do you mind if I ask you something? What is the Secret?"

Stella whispered to Reynolds, "I asked her the same thing."

"*Shh*," Reynolds said. Then to the group, "I think we can make a great show around these two. Something that hasn't been done before. We can center it both on their lives and on interesting and sophisticated adventures. It can be a hosted show—with Delaney and Marisol as the hosts—and at the same time be a show about them, behind the scenes, kind of. After a few episodes, you don't know if it will be a show about them doing a show, or just the show about their lives."

"It is so exciting," said Delaney.

"Who's the audience?" Stella said.

Reynolds, Delaney, and Marisol all blurted their answers at the same time.

"Older women," said Reynolds.

"Young women," said Delaney.

"Men," said Marisol. Then she added, "And the gay men, especially. They love these shows."

"Mom?"

They looked up from their chairs to see two huge young men standing over them.

"Oh my God! Hello, boys." Delaney and Marisol jumped up to greet their sons.

"*Ay*, Renzo!" said Marisol.

"Reynolds, Stella, I want you to meet my son, Lance," Delaney said.

"And this is my son, Lorenzo."

The kids reached out and shook hands all around. "Mom, what the heck?" Lance waved his arm around to indicate the whole of the campsite and the battlefields. Then he looked at Reynolds and Stella. "What has she gotten you folks into?"

"Oh, shut up, you," Delaney said, laughing at him. "He's such a pain in my rear end. Had a son and got my father." She gave him a playful smack. "Guess what? Mr. Reynolds here is going to produce our show."

The boys looked at Reynolds and he gave an uneasy nod.

Stella whispered to Reynolds, "Dude, you are so far over your skis."

Marisol's son, Lorenzo, looked at his mother, and she nodded. "Wow," he said. Then Lorenzo looked at Reynolds. "Is it about all this?" He gestured with his hands, like Lance, to indicate the campsite.

"No, Renzo," said Delaney. "It's about *us*. Me and your mom. We might use some of this in the pilot, but it's about us. Our lives. You can be in it."

Lance looked at Reynolds. "Is this true?"

"Essentially."

"You see, wise guy," said Delaney to Lance. "Now if you don't behave, I'm gonna tell Mr. Reynolds here not to put you in the show."

Stella backed a few steps away and ducked into the tent. Once out of everyone's sight, she shook her head in disbelief. She fumbled for her secret vape and took a long drag.

Reynolds looked the boys over for a few minutes. They were dressed in what looked like Brooks Brothers casual, and they had short hair. They matched Marisol and Delaney—Lance was blond and Lorenzo dark. They were handsome the way their mothers were pretty. Lance looked at Reynolds's uniform.

"So, Mom, what are you guys doing here? At this thing?"

"Mr. Reynolds was on his way here, and we decided to make it part of the first show."

Lorenzo said, "Where are the cameras? Is this thing being filmed?"

"Oh, he's another one," Delaney said to Reynolds. "Another lunkhead, like my son." She turned to the boys again. "No, Ricky Ricardo, it's not being filmed. It's not a movie. It's a reality program. We're just getting a feel for it. We thought we would all hang out for the weekend, since we're going to be working together."

"And this is Reynaldo's favorite hobby. It is a lot of fun. And so realistic, the fighting. You boys should see it, the guns and everything. *My God.*"

Reynolds looked at the boys. "It's not really my favorite hobby. It's my first time."

"Come, sit down," said Stella, out of the tent, now the host. "Do you want some wine?" Then to their moms, "Can they drink wine? Are they allowed?"

"Oh, no, thanks," Lance said.

"Oh, go ahead, all-American boy," Marisol said. "*Chicos*," she said to Stella, throwing her hands up. "They so goddamn serious, you know?" To Lorenzo, she said, "Go ahead. Don't act like you don't want it." Finally, she said to Delaney, "*Los dos. Tontos.*"

"Bullshit artists," Delaney said. They both smiled at their boys.

Stella laughed and poured the boys wine. "So, you guys are just out of school? Where did you go?" She stopped herself. "Oh, that's right, you go to school at home."

Lance and Lorenzo looked at each other. "We went to Westlake," said Lance.

Delaney finished a sip of wine fast and said, "Now." Everyone looked at her. "You go to Westlake *now*. Before you went to school at home. With us. When we taught you at home."

"That was for, like, two years in junior high," said Lance.

When he noticed that the whole circle was staring at him, Lance said, "What has she been telling you guys?"

"Nothing," said Delaney. "Just that we do some homeschooling of you guys."

"Oh Jesus," said Lorenzo. "What else did you tell them?"

Lance said, "Did you go into all of that Secret crap? Oh my God, mom. You made us do it so much."

"Don't call the Secret 'crap,'" said Marisol, and she kicked at him. "You wanted to be in sports, so we send you to Westlake. And guess what, *chicos*. The Secret training worked, and you became so good that you had to go to school for more hours in the day."

Lance threw a little ice at Marisol, and the four all laughed, as if it was an old joke.

Delaney had an idea. "Reynolds! I just thought of something. Can the boys be soldiers? Can you get them into the battle?"

"Oh *my God*," said Marisol. "*Es perfecto*. Ray, can you do that?"

"I guess so. I don't see why not. Do you guys want to? Do you want to get in the fight?"

"Sure," said Renzo.

"Yeah," said Lance.

Reynolds looked at Stella. "Well, OK then. Let's see what we can do. There's a costume truck for soldiers on the other side of the parking lot. And if that doesn't work, I'll get ol' Cyrus on it."

Reynolds and the boys walked past the other tents, past the soldiers spread out on lawn chairs and blankets, in unbuttoned and scattered uniforms. The nineteenth-century clothes mixed with the occasional Angels hat and Big Gulp. The degree of authenticity varied with each picnic. Some were hard-core, drinking coffee out of cast-iron pots and eating food off tin plates. Others took a more liberal view of the requirements of reenacting, choosing instead to break character for a while and eat out of coolers and drink cans of Coors Light.

The woman who oversaw the soldiers' store—which was separate and apart from Gail's gown shop—looked more like a housewife at the end of a three-day yard sale than a sales clerk.

"I cannot believe how busy it has been down here," she said, as she rustled up the ramp of the rented trailer and into the back, where the merchandise was. Like many of the reenactors, she had a habit of speaking in a Southern accent. "People have plum bought me out of almost everything." The trailer was still full of hardware, rifles and swords and scabbards; there were a fair number of soldiers' hats from varying ranks and marching boots with holes in the soles. Toward the back were the uniforms.

"I'm down to one full Confederate and . . . yeah, there it is, one Union uniform left. One of each." She looked at the boys, measuring them. "Um hmm. These will work. Will fit you fine. Who wants what?" The boys looked at Reynolds. "Doesn't matter," she said. "They're both the same size."

The boys were looking at him again. What a question, he said to himself. How do you assign a side in a war to a kid? How do any of these guys here pick a side? What does someone in the here and now use as their measure in deciding which part to reenact? Is it based on theatricality, on the desire to escape into a foreign character? He didn't think so. No, for anyone it had to be deeper, something more connected to the side you identified with. Which side you thought you belonged to. Which side you thought was right.

For him it was automatic. He was from Pennsylvania and therefore he was Blue. But, what about Lance and Lorenzo, from the San Fernando Valley? For that matter, what about any of these guys out on the burnt-orange infields of Enchino. There were a lot of Rebels. That's a lot of people choosing the side that fought for slavery, he thought. This brought forth in him a familiar but long-dormant feeling: he had always noticed a different reaction among the people visiting Gettysburg from the South. And it made sense. People from the North felt one way, and people from Georgia and Virginia felt another way. He remembered how he always had to be mindful when he was giving a tour. If he had a mixed tour he had to toe the line, making sure not to favor one side over the other. That was the way he was trained to do it anyway. But if he had a smaller group, a family of Texans, say, he could slant his story in ways they didn't even notice, focusing on the genius of Lee's maneuvers and the towering bravery of the Southern troops and how close they'd come to doing in the Union. He would talk a lot about how it all could have been so different.

If Reynolds had an elementary school group from New York, he would talk up slavery, of course. He would stress the gallantry of Buford and Chamberlain and Reynolds and how they saved the Union. He would tell them of Winfield Scott Hancock and how he saved the center of the Union line during Pickett's Charge. He would make it a day the kids would always remember by driving home in dramatic fashion how very fortunate they and the rest of the world were for the bravery of the troops on those three days at the beginning of July.

He reserved a final type of presentation for foreigners, the pensioners from Yorkshire or the Canadians on bus trips from Ottawa or Montreal. He had learned that they wanted the gore, and that's what he gave them. Daily casualty counts; how many died on Little Round Top; the carnage at Devil's Den; what percentage of the Southern army was gone after three days. Theirs was a third-party experience; they were like anthropologists on a dig. These tourists weren't that interested in objective reality or politics—they wanted the bits about how violent and insane this American war was.

Yet no matter how he spun it to the Southerners or to the Northerners or to the foreigners, he felt like he was polishing a stone set in their imaginations. Looking at Lance and Lorenzo, he was reminded of this. He used to think of these things all the time, so much so that he did it without thinking, as it were. It was part of him, just as the battlefield was part of him, this understanding of people. It came from seeing so many of them. It was no more than being alert and recognizing patterns, commonalities among tribe members, differences between people.

For Reynolds, there were two crosscurrents of American culture, and the adherents of each were aware of the others and of the other's *otherness*. Their relationship to the battle told everything.

No matter how sanctified the tone he took with the Northerners, they took it for granted. Of course, they had won. Of course, it was about slavery. There was a presumption of righteousness that came with having won, of having dictated terms, of salting the soil. Victorious, they saw Gettysburg in the same way they saw foreign wars, all part of a continuum to protect the virtues of freedom and democracy. Grant and Patton and Eisenhower were of a piece. The uniform was the same as it was today: the United States Army. Blue.

He understood this the way you understand your family. It defined him, after all. The current flowed into the modern world. Its heirs were the city dwellers, the intellectuals, the New Dealers, blacks. Its touchstones were modernity, evolution, the pursuit of equality, the unquestionable correctness of individual liberty protected by a beneficent government. The Civil War was one of a long parade of military conflicts establishing and vindicating these principles. He saw in the Blue tribe a greater connection to World Wars I and II, more distinct as they were, and less confusing because of the easier characterization of the enemy. Germanic villains and fanatical Japanese were much more easily sorted in the Northerners' common mind than Robert E. Lee.

The Southerners—the true other—were the antagonists, the alter ego. The Confederate flag was red with some blue, the inverse of the American flag. This other current was grounded in antifederalism and Jefferson, in the aristocratic and states' rights. It was never about slavery, and those who didn't believe that subordinated that concern to greater ideals, as Lee did with Virginia. They did not think so much of foreign wars, believing they smacked too much of being beside the point, superfluous to what had gone on here, the later business of the Yankees.

Right below the surface in all of them—every single, goddamn one he'd ever met, then or now—was defeat, honor, and revenge. The feeling of being vanquished. It was passed through the generations in DNA. Honor and revenge were the *condition precedents* of their presence, the *"you" understood* of the grammar of Southern life. The descendants of the Confederacy took with it a dissatisfaction, a quiet boil, a vengeance, which came out in weird ways, like Reagan and country music, Fox News and Rush Limbaugh. The Southern current was more powerful than the Northern and often beautiful: it gave us Faulkner and Flannery O'Connor. It was more romantic: that's why the war's centennial celebrations were much more popular in the South. The War between the States was not part of any continuum.

Anyone from outside the country was confused by Gettysburg and, when you considered that they were *there*, not terribly interested. He remembered thinking the thing about de Tocqueville was that he didn't get bored like the rest of the foreigners who came to America. It was an early indicator to Reynolds of just how ethnocentric the Civil War was. Someone from beyond our continent could not understand how the war's history, and thus the nation's history, and thus the world's history, hung in the balance on that battlefield that day, a fact even the daftest American schoolkid—North, South, Blue, Gray, whatever—grasped. It was a reality that escaped all others.

The thing that united the two tribes and eluded the rest was the requirement of freedom. Take it all away, that's what mattered most. Those times when America can pull together, whenever the two crosscurrents can flow side by side, it's because of freedom— the shared pursuit and maintenance of freedom. Reynolds shook his head, trying to bring himself out of his reverie. He had not accessed that place in his mind in a while. He used to think in that manner all the time when he was younger. But not in an academic or bookish way—again, he was reminded that such thoughts were natural to him. It was like he'd grown up breathing in water and didn't know others couldn't breathe in water. Then he'd gone and lived on land for so long he forgot that he could breathe underwater.

"What do you think, Reynolds?"

He saw Lance's face. He was holding a Union tunic and a worn Confederate cap.

"Tough question," Reynolds said.

Lance made up his mind. "My mom is from Texas. I'll go with the South." He threw the blue jacket to Lorenzo.

"That's as good a reason as any," Reynolds said.

"Can we get guns?" Lorenzo said.

"Let's get you outfitted and go talk to my friend Cyrus. We'll see what he has."

"This is pretty cool," Lance said.

The shop woman assembled the pieces of the two uniforms. "The breeches are the same size. Go over there, I won't look. And here." She gave them both undershirts and boots.

They pulled the clothes on and right in front of Reynolds's eyes transformed into soldiers.

"Are these real? Did real soldiers wear these?" said Lorenzo.

The woman and Reynolds looked at each other and both shook their heads.

"No," said Reynolds.

"No, they make them new. You have to remember, you're big strong boys," said the woman. Then, when she could see they were confused, added, "Men were a lot smaller then, hon."

"Smaller in stature," Reynolds said, correcting her. He gave her his American Express card.

"No need for that," the lady said. "Just give me your name and tent number, chief. You put your credit card on file back when you signed up."

"So, what do you mean?" Reynolds said. "I can just go around and get whatever I want and just give my tent number to pay?"

"Yup."

"God," he said to himself. "It's like the Four Seasons on Maui."

The boys stepped out of the trailer in their uniforms. "Let me look at you," the shop owner said before they left. They stood in front of her a little bashful, but upright and strong, getting used to their new look. She turned to Reynolds. "Mighty fine, wouldn't you say?"

"Yes. Yes, indeed."

They walked toward the camp, the boys getting over their awkwardness. "I hope we can get some guns," said Lorenzo.

Reynolds could tell that something was bothering Lance, who was the more talkative of the two but had not said anything since he put on the uniform.

"Is something bothering you, son?"

"You know my mom was a Playboy centerfold, right?"

Reynolds stopped walking. "Sure, I do. I remember it from—" He stopped himself. "Yes, yes, I know that."

"Is that why you're going to do a show about her?"

"Nooo. Is that what you think?"

"Yeah."

"Of course, he thinks that," said Lorenzo. "And my mom was Miss Spain. And Miss Universe. We get stuff all the time."

"Well, yeah. I mean, yes, to be honest, it is a factor."

"So, you are going to make fun of them, like, 'Here's two old bimbos who are like the mother of the Kardashians, and we're going to follow them around with cameras.'"

"And watch them do stupid shit," Lorenzo said.

"And show how they follow the Secret."

"No, boys, I wouldn't do that," Reynolds said. "I think I—we—can do something different. Something about how people from our memory can become real and how they live today."

"That's what they do with *Celebrity Rehab* and *The Surreal Life* and stuff like that. Everyone is famous for something or other in LA," said Lance.

"Mr. Reynolds," said Lorenzo. "You have to understand something." The brass buttons on his Union jacket shone in the sun. "They're our moms."

"For better and worse," Lance said.

"They crave fame."

"Always have."

"We protect them as best we can."

"And we don't want anyone to make fools out of them."

"Guys, guys," said Reynolds. "You don't know me. I wouldn't do that. I'm a serious guy. I don't do crap reality shows—this is the first time I've ever done something like this." After a pause he said, "Look, if you don't want me to do it, I won't. Done. I have been a bit confused for a while. Maybe this was a bad idea, anyway. Yesterday kind of got away from me. I mean, I didn't expect this." He indicated the surroundings. "I got a lot on my mind. I wanted this to be a complete secret. Next thing I know, your moms and a driver were here. Now my wife and daughter and her friend have shown up. I can drop this, no problem."

They walked on in quiet. "We don't want to ruin their dreams, especially if you are going to do it . . . you know, can make them come true," Lance said.

"But can you do it so you don't make fun of them?" Lorenzo said.

"Listen, guys. When I look at your mothers, both, you know what I see? Two stars. You guys know it more than anyone. Born stars. Beautiful, funny, honest, and very intelligent. Give them more credit. Cameras love them. People like them. And I want to help them be successful. This wasn't my intent when I met them. But I feel that way now. I'm not going to let them get hurt. I won't allow it to happen to you and I won't allow it to happen to them."

CHAPTER 26

Soldier Boys

Reynolds and Lorenzo and Lance returned to the group of tents where the rest of the crew was sitting in the circle of chairs and drinking.

"Oh my God," said Marisol. She and Delaney jumped up and ran over to the boys, all fussy and flustered.

"Will you look at this. Jesus Christ in the morning, look at you two," Stella said.

Reynolds stood next to her.

"Wow," Stella said. "You dressed them up nice."

"Cyrus," said Reynolds. "These boys need rifles."

"I'm the man to see. C'mon back to my truck." He stood up from his chair and led the boys to the parking lot.

Reynolds was left standing alone, while the three or four stragglers in the chairs were embroiled in a conversation about Tiger Woods. He walked through the camp and looked out on the battleground of outfields. He strolled around on the grass, where empty cartridges and torn rags and other bits of war were still strewn about. He stood very still in the middle of the field for a minute. Then he went back to the campsite and returned to his tent and stretched out on his sleeping bag with his hands behind his head.

This was familiar turf for him, being inside a set piece. The Gettysburg he knew in his lifetime was a stage. It was a vessel through which hundreds of thousands of people flowed each year, gobbling up canned information and recited facts about the monstrous three days of war a century and a half earlier. Reynolds first knew turnstiles and museums and bed-and-breakfasts, long before he learned the strategies and causes and stories of the war. The families he went to school with lived on multitudes of tourists the way others fed off trout in a stream.

A general discomfort combined with a touch of his father's misguided entrepreneurialism had led him to a deeper investigation of his hometown. He found it intoxicating the way most American men do, or at least the ones with literary leanings. Coming from such a demythologized and stripped-down point of view, he was a natural to show the folks around. Other people read about Gettysburg in books; he knew it from the inside, the way a Native American knew his land. While they scorned General Dan Sickles for moving his divisions down on Cemetery Ridge, Reynolds understood better the optical illusion the general faced, and Reynolds could take his groups of fourth graders right to the place and show them the rising crest of the hill. You could see why the guy felt vulnerable, why he moved. It wasn't because he was a politician and not a military man—that was just the kind of crap the two-bit and even the silver-dollar historians said with twenty-twenty hindsight. But who could put themselves in the man's shoes? He put his men in about the worst fighting there ever was in the Wheatfield, but what was going on all around them—in the Peach Orchard, in Devil's Den—was not a game of footsie.

And Wheatfield or no, the Union won the day. Another guide and all the books may tell you something else, he told the kids, but I know why Sickles did what he did.

He thought about that fucking Lee. A religious fanatic and a butcher. They were all butchers, it was true, but it was Lee's reputation for greatness that annoyed him in an obsessive way. In what other country would the leader of the rebellious force be so honored? The Confederates had invaded the land with the intention of overthrowing the greatest example of a democratic government the world had ever known. Then Lee had sent most of his army straight into the cannons. You had to walk across that field, already known as a cemetery, to know how stupid that was. There was no defending that move. There was no way it made sense to anyone but a madman who thought God was on his side. And yet, the tourists couldn't get enough of Lee. They worshipped him, bought doodads with his image, key chains, belt buckles of his face, coffee mugs.

Where were the coffee mugs with John Reynolds's picture? Or Hancock's? Those guys saved the Union, saved us all. They were from Pennsylvania, fighting to defend their own soil no less. He felt the rush of old anger at the craziness of that part of it, the lack of recognition of our own. Long ago he had written it off to a deeper interest on the part of the Southerners, of more passion coming from the vanquished. Northerners on day trips from Philadelphia and retired couples from Milwaukee and Maine passed through. But people from the South made it their destination, were more likely to stay overnight. They felt it more. Over time, that passion and that interest fed the historians and writers and enabled them to choose the heroes. And the North, the Blue, the Union moved on—not disinterested so much as embarrassed or just over it. Reynolds felt that the collective consciousness of Northerners saw Gettysburg as a regrettable schoolyard brawl from long ago. They had won and moved on.

Like the country itself, he satisfied himself with that for a while. Slavery was outlawed. Freedom and equality: that had to be the point. It was the punctuation to the sentence about why it all had to happen. It gave finality and a moral to the whole bloody business. It provided the guides like him a way to wrap up their tours. It was the genius of Lincoln that he figured it out way before everyone else, which was the nature of genius, as Norman often said. Equality and freedom were at stake there beneath the bullet-strewn ground of Gettysburg, and the Jennie Wade Museum, and the souvenir stores. That they had prevailed drove the workers in the stores and gas stations forward, drove the town forward, and drove the nation forward. They're at bottom for an American: root, elemental, fundamental, essential. They are founded in Pennsylvania: born in Philadelphia and saved one hundred miles west. The virtue and righteousness of the war was the true religion of the town—you could see it in the faces of the old-timers: they had the peace of the devout. The tenets of America, defended and saved on that hallowed ground, buffered them as the idea of God did a preacher.

But he would come to leave their church. As he approached adulthood, the once-invincible conviction cracked and came apart. The constant churn of tourists wore him down. He began to hate the place. He told his mother that the thing of most importance in the town was the Lutheran Seminary, not any statue or battlefield, and it remained so today. It was more than typical rebellion, and he chafed when she called it that. She told him to go look up callow. It was deeper, he said. The true lesson was twofold: that it was pointless slaughter, and that the post-traumatic carnival show of the town they lived in was farcical. It was also, as Whitman had said, the birth of looking forward. It was the past and the future.

True, like a man's man or a lawyer's lawyer or a ballplayer's ballplayer, the Civil War was a war's war and Gettysburg a battle's battle. But so what? It was senseless and indefensible, and that truth crept over him and like the idea of mortality. Everyone spoke for the men; everyone said they did not die in vain. But would Evander Law, the twenty-nine-year-old general from Alabama whose brigade marched twenty-five miles overnight and in the morning joined the fight on Little Round Top, not have wished to grow into old age? Fifty thousand killed and wounded in three days, countless others dying from infections and disease. In one hour on the third day, all fifteen of Pickett's brigadier leaders were killed or wounded. Fifteen first-class leaders gone in an hour— men Lee knew well, men he had spent years with. He flat out killed them. It was too horrible to keep inside the body of the nation. We had to invent excuses, explanations, mythology. Hence the Gettysburg Address. Lincoln knew it was about the past and the future. How else was he going to meet his maker?

Reynolds was bitter and jaded by the time he left home to live in a dorm room, a few miles away but it could just have well been two hundred. Between the DNA his parents had passed on and just living in their bookish world, he had enough smarts to cruise through college and law school, which he did for his mother. Though she never complained about her own lot, she wanted Reynolds to be a lawyer because she was convinced he would get rich doing it. He retained just enough of his buttoned-down side, diminishing as it was, due to his adventurous side taking over, to maintain the interest needed to get those degrees. He was interested in understanding why it was that lawyers wielded so much power, but that was not enough to sustain him. The real thing he held onto from his roots was his interest in performing, in telling stories.

His visits home for school breaks became more and more like trips back in time. He was done with the tourists, done with the battle. He wanted to free himself of its stench, its decay, its stigma. He wanted to wake up and be from a place—in a place—where an orchard was just an orchard, not a site where nine thousand people had died; or a house was just a house, not someplace George Meade had slept.

It came back to him through strange inroads of recognition—as it had the first time he was in Las Vegas, just after he'd moved to LA. Drunk, after watching strippers put whipped cream on a friend soon to be married, he'd taken a cab back to the hotel. In the smoke and noise of the casino, he'd recognized a familiar look in the eyes of the blackjack dealers and croupiers. He could see they knew what it was like—the ones who live in Vegas and don't give a shit whether you win or lose. It's just a job to them, and you are just chum going through the machine.

"Dad? Oh my God, look at you." It was Bella, sticking her head through the crease of the tent. She stepped toward him as if she were approaching his hospital bed. "Are you OK?" she said.

Her hair was pulled back in a ponytail, and the effect was that the features of her face were all he could see. The light was perfect; it was. Her eyes, her cheeks, her mouth were all in straight, taut lines. She was a beauty, and she made his heart rumble. It snuck up on him, her prettiness, the porcelain doll quality she had taken on. When he looked at old photos and videos of her, he went weak at the younger, pudgier version. When she was a baby and a little girl her face had been the puffiest, whitest cumulonimbus cloud in the world, all curvy and cottony and cute. With age, with each school photo that came home, her countenance had thinned out a shade. It was as though she was coming into clearer relief each year, the roundness yielding to distinct, sharpened beauty. There was nothing about watching a kid grow up that would lead you to believe in white noise overwhelming everything. Kids got more specific every day. But what didn't leave was that she was his little girl. That was permanent.

"Dad?" Bella said again. "Are you OK in here?"

"Hey . . . yeah, wait . . . here." He sat up and embraced her.

She looked him over. "Wow, so . . . yeah, wow. This is cool. So, are you, like, a general? Are you a specific guy? Or are you, like, the general you're named after?"

Reynolds said, "Yeah, I am a certain guy . . . I'm still working that out. Most of these guys pick a brigade, that's how they do it." She nodded as though she were listening to a child or maybe a well-advanced senior citizen. "Do you think I'm crazy?" Reynolds said.

"No, of course not. No. What makes you think that? I think it's great. Why didn't you tell us?"

"I don't know. Because I thought you guys would think it was weird. It *is* weird." He put the back of his hand to the side of his mouth and whispered, "They *are* weird, these guys. They're awesome, I mean, but we're in Enchino doing the Battle of Gettysburg. That's weird, right? I don't think I could've explained that very well to you guys."

She nodded again. Her look told him she was feeling sorry for him.

"I don't know," he said. "I just wanted to check it out a little. Maybe I was embarrassed. Do you think I look crazy?"

"No, you're dashing. Is that a real sword? Where'd you get it?"

"On eBay. Here, feel it." He put the blade in her hand.

She felt its steel. "It's just that . . . Dad, I thought you hated this stuff. You always told me that."

Heather stuck her head through the tent. "Hellooo. Where's the party?" She saw Bella touching Reynolds's sword and busted out laughing. "Whoa. Hi, Reynolds. Is that thing real?"

"Oh my God, you have to feel it," said Bella. She brought it to Heather's fingers and pointed to her dad with her head. "Doesn't he look good?"

"Are you a general?" Heather said.

"Kind of. But I'm kind of a real soldier too," Reynolds said.

"Are you a specific guy, or just yourself?"

"I just asked him the same thing," Bella said.

"Let me show you around," Reynolds said. He led the girls outside, where they met Lance and Lorenzo. The boys stood up from the lounge chairs in their uniforms and, upon seeing the girls, took off their caps. "Lance, Lorenzo, this is my daughter, Bella, and her friend Heather." The four kids exchanged looks and polite greetings. He continued with the girls toward the costume truck.

"Who are they?" Bella said.

"They're the sons of the two ladies who came down here with me."

"Wait, those two are Delaney and Marisol's sons?" Heather said.

"By the way, you brought other people with you?" said Bella. "I thought this was, like, a secret thing you were doing."

"It was. But, well, I was in a meeting yesterday, and their moms wanted to come. We're talking about doing a reality show."

"So, their moms are from a network?" Heather asked.

"No, they're Playboy Bunnies. One of them is, I mean."

"You came down here with Playboy Bunnies?" Bella said.

"One was Miss Universe."

"Cool," said Heather.

"Cool?" said Bella. Then back to Reynolds. "What kind of show are you going to do?"

"*The Surprisingly Smart Playmate and Miss Universe Visit Places Show*. They're like *Dick Van Dyke* meets Anthony Bourdain meets the nun who goes to museums and explains art and makes nothing but classic English food with nothing but meat and pudding. Those were giant hits."

"Don't think the nun show was a show, Dad."

"It fucking-A was. She was called Sister Wendy. Look it up."

Bella put the back of her hand to her mouth, cracking up.

Reynolds started laughing, as well. "What?"

Bella said, "You sound like Norman."

Bella and Heather went off, likely in the throes of cannabis, and Reynolds went back to the campsite. He sat with his crew and tried to get his bearings.

He thought about the impossibility of the night ahead, and a question occurred to him. He turned to Cyrus. "Where around here are they going to be able to hold a square dance for all these people?"

"Cotillion, damnit. It's a cotillion. They have it at the high school on the other side of the freeway."

"How do we get there? Do we drive?"

Cyrus shook his head. "No. Can't drive. People get half shot in the ass and try to drive back. So we have to take the shuttle." He gestured to the end of the recreation center's parking lot, where five airport-style shuttle buses were waiting. Blue and gray soldiers were lining up to board the first. Cyrus held a strange-looking flask in front of him. "Want some applejack? Homemade?"

"Uh. No, thanks," Reynolds said.

"What kind of soldier are you?"

"That's a good question."

"Don't want a drink? What kind of soldier don't want a drink? How about a beer?"

"Yes. I'll take a beer," Reynolds said.

"I'll try the applejack," said Lance.

"Me too," said Lorenzo. They held out the plastic party cups they were holding, and Cyrus poured. Reynolds thought about protesting but didn't.

The boys were carrying rifles Cyrus had provided. "How many of these things do you have at home?" Nicely said. "Do you have, like, a whole mess of guns?"

"I have fifteen Springfield's, and seven or eight Enfield's. I have to be able to outfit a whole company for some of the shows. People don't know this, but the change in weapons decided the whole thing, you know?"

"Those guns are essentially paintball guns, right?" Nicely said.

"What?" Bob said.

"They all shoot a single pellet or bullet—but one projectile —and can shoot targets at long distance," Nicely said. "I think if I retrofit a realistically old-fashioned butt to affix to the gun that enables the weapon to still operate, I will have a break-through of boundless proportions. Every weapon here can be replaced by retrofitted paintball guns. It will enhance the whole experience."

"That's idiotic," said Bob. "Putting that many new weapons on the street. Then cops have to deal with it."

"I don't think a bunch of street-legal pellet guns will upset American law enforcement to the extent our freedom becomes at risk," said Nicely.

"Ignore him," Cyrus said.

Reynolds said, "Guns became much more accurate at the time of the Civil War." Cyrus nodded and Reynolds continued. "Before the war, in those earlier wars that you hear about—Napoleonic Wars, Indian Wars, the Revolution—all there were were muskets. Muskets just shoot out little lead balls. Soldiers had to be pretty much on top of each other to make a kill. There's a quote from Grant . . . What is it, Cyrus? Something like, 'Before the War, a fella could have the enemy shooting at him from three hundred yards away for the entire day and not even know it.'"

Cyrus laughed. "That's about right."

"But then they invented rifled muskets, like the ones you guys got there," Reynolds said. "And things got better—or worse, actually. They were all of a sudden accurate to two hundred and fifty to three hundred yards. So, when these guys got right up next to each other in traditional style, it was a complete massacre."

"Bloody fucking mess," Cyrus said.

Reynolds was warming to his usual role. "That's one of the things that explains what happened at Gettysburg, what we're doing here. Because of a series of events, the Union held the defensive position throughout the three days—which was very different than the early part of the war, which Lee was winning because he could shoot the Northern army to pieces and counterattack once he had them down. But at Gettysburg, he was trying to break them, to shoot them from lower ground, up Little Round Top and Culp's Hill, where they were dug in on top behind rocks and trenches."

"So the Southerners just got obliterated walking up the hills?" said Lorenzo.

"Basically."

"Why did Lee do that?" said Lance. "Why do they always say he was such a great general?"

"He *was* a great general," Cyrus said. "He was just wrong that day."

"No," Reynolds said. He became very solemn. "Lee was a maniac. He had glory in his eyes. He thought God was going to intervene and that his troops were just going to bust the Union line and walk to Washington. He was separated from reality. His own generals knew it. Longstreet didn't want him to attack. Neither did Hood. Or Garnett or Armistead."

Cyrus broke in. "Goddamnit, Reynolds, you got to stop with that ranting and raving about Robert E. Lee. For fuck's sake. Get something new. Lee was a military genius except for that day."

"Why did the soldiers walk right into getting shot, then?" Lance said, getting back to Reynolds.

"They were obeying their commander, son," said Cyrus. "That's what war is all about. That kind of thing gets lost nowadays. Back then they didn't have all these fancy attractions you kids have like video games and iPods. Boys your age were sent into battle, and that's what they did. Ought to make you stop and think."

"About what?" Lorenzo said.

"About life! And your country. And freedom and duty. And all the things you take for granted in this world." Cyrus's face reddened. Lance gave Reynolds a look.

"I don't take anything for granted," said Lorenzo. "I'm just a normal kid."

"Cyrus, don't get going with all that bullshit," said Stevie, sitting nearby.

"Yeah, ignore him, guys," Bob said.

"The point is," Cyrus said, to all of them, "that what we are doing means *something*. These men, your grandfathers' grandfathers, fought and died on this field."

"My grandfather is from Spain," said Lorenzo.

"On this field?" said Lance. "I thought it was in Pennsylvania."

"It's symbolic, son. You have to use your imagination," said Cyrus.

Lance looked at the other guys and at Reynolds. Stevie shrugged. "That's what he always says. If you're a Civil War reenactor and you live in California, you just got to get used to it."

"You're already faking the battle part," Bob said. "It ain't that much harder to fake the place. I mean, movies don't get shot where they happened."

"And stories and novels come out of the imagination," Nicely said. The nodding of agreement that had taken up a nice pace slowed down, and all the men furrowed their brows and turned to look at Nicely. "Wh-what I mean is that if you think about encountering a story, there's a progression. First, you can see a thing from history happen in real life, you don't have to use your imagination. If you see a story reenacted from history at its real place, that requires more imagination and acting. If you see a thing from history reenacted in a different place than it happened, then you need good acting and a tremendous amount of imagination. And if there's no real or fake place, and no acting, and all you have is words to describe something, then that requires the most imagination of all."

There was silence. Then Cyrus looked at Reynolds and said, "Ain't that right."

CHAPTER 27

Relief Work

Norman and Carol pulled out of the gate at the Colony on their way to Nobu, the Japanese restaurant on the beach in Malibu, a quarter of a mile away.

"We are so used to driving ten goddamn feet," she said. "It's terrible."

"Why are we doing this?" Norman said.

"Oh, stop. I canceled on Barbara three times. Buck up."

David and Barbara Mundberg were already at the table when Norman and Carol walked into Nobu. The sun was shining, hotter at two thirty than it had been at noon. Carol sped up to embrace Barbara, while Norman hung back for a second to speak with the hostesses, all beautiful in black, moving the billionaires, stars, and real estate brokers around as they pleased.

"How are you, Mr. Daley?" said a young blond woman who had worked at the restaurant for a while.

"Good, cookie. Did you miss me?"

"You know I did," she said.

He gave her a skeptical squint, which caused her to smile more.

"Are we late?" he said.

"Nope. Right on schedule. Time to see a new dentist."

"Now, c'mon," she said. "Carol will get mad at me if I put up with you for too long."

"OK, but remember," Norman said. "After five minutes you come get me with an urgent call."

He shook hands with David, and they performed a half hug, somewhere between the no hugs of their fathers and the bro hugs of today. He and Carol took their seats across from the other couple.

"Did you watch?" David said.

"I did," said Carol. "I thought the English guy was funny."

"Me too," said Barbara, whispering, like they were sharing a secret.

"He's an idiot," said David. "I talked to him later."

"You went?" said Norman.

"Steven made me go."

How does it get to a point, Norman wondered, where you come from the same neighborhood as a guy, go to the same high school, both work as comedy writers, both make a fortune, both end up in beach houses sitting in the sun all day, but after ninety seconds you want to beat his brains out?

"When did you get back?" said Carol.

"Just on Saturday," said David.

"Good for you. Was it awful?" said Carol.

"It's catastrophic. There is no way to understand it by just watching from the States," David said.

"They have nothing," said Barbara.

"It's demolished," said David. "We were there for a week—I went with George—and we didn't sleep. We were in tents outside of Santo Domingo. The devastation is unbelievable."

"I saw the piece with George on *Good Morning America*," said Carol.

"I got George in with Diane Sawyer," said David. "I said, 'Diane, you have to do five minutes with him. This is a humanitarian crisis we're dealing with here.'"

"I'm sure it wasn't hard to convince George," said Norman.

"Daley," Carol said.

"Still," said David. "They need people directing traffic. I'm very glad we went."

"He's raised six million," said Barbara.

"Let us know who we make ours to," said Carol.

David nodded. "Thank you, Carol."

Norman was cracking up with the valet guy and then gave him a tightly rolled fifty when his boss wasn't looking.

He got behind the wheel, and they headed home.

Carol said, "They seem good."

"Schmuck," said Norman. "Did you hear him?"

"I know what it is about him that gets you."

"They need *him* to go to the Dominican Republic to help rescue people?"

"Oh stop. You're going to complain about that?"

"That's the point. It's perfect. Complete narcissism is at its best when it's done that way. Lots of cameras, complete chaos. If you say anything about it, you're an asshole."

She nodded. "It *is* true."

"Asshole."

"But I figured out what it is."

"What?"

"He's your one. The one."

"Oh, please."

"You know it's true."

He thought about it. Her theory was that every person in the history of Hollywood has one other person who drives them crazy with jealousy. "It fits. The Bronx, NBC, everything."

"You're wrong."

"I am not wrong."

"There's a big flaw in your theory. He's Jewish. I'm Irish."

"Oh, really. Is that so? Gimme a break. You're more Jewish than me." She saw him smiling. "Plus," she said, moving under his arm to get close, "where you and David come from it didn't matter what you were. You ought to be like brothers having gotten out of the Bronx, the both of you."

Carol had had a lifetime of listening to the stories. She kept quiet around all the business talk, relying on Norman to fill her in. Since he was successful so young and had sustained it for so long, she knew everyone that mattered, and she had enjoyed an advantage in each new relationship—namely, Norman. For Norman Daley was a person everyone wanted to know, to be friends with, to discuss matters of great importance with, and to laugh with at a gut-busting inside joke. There were very few people in the world who Carol wanted to meet that she hadn't.

And in all the years of queens and presidents and movie stars, she had discovered that the rule of The One was still the most certain truism about successful people. Brad Pitt had Johnny Depp. Gwyneth Paltrow had Nicole Kidman. De Niro had Pacino. Spielberg, Scorsese. No group was immune. It worked with novelists and with composers, with agents and studio heads. It worked with screenwriters and showrunners. And it even worked with eighty-year-old television creators who sat around and collected checks all day. Everyone had someone who made them nuts with jealousy.

Norman knew she was right. "Well, if I ever tell you I want to go to a disaster area with a movie star, you better shoot me."

"Deal," said Carol. Then, after a pause, she said, "So you and Tom won't be going to any tornado zone any time soon?"

"Tom and I *are* going for a drive tomorrow. To go get Reynolds."

"I hate when you drive so much."

"We'll switch off."

"So, you plan on driving, then?" Carol said.

"Stop with me, for crissakes," Norman said.

"You hate when Tom drives—so you'll drive, and that's it."

"Stop . . ."

She let out a victorious cluck. After studying him for a bit, she said, "Starfucker."

Norman laughed. "You're pretty funny for a girl in her late seventies."

"Seventy-three is early seventies. Nuts to you," she said. "How was your sushi, by the way?"

"Spectacular. As usual. Did I show you what Bella did on Jackie Gleason?"

"You gave her Jackie Gleason?"

"Sure."

"What is the point of that? Jackie Gleason?"

"Jackie Gleason was a great man."

"Ha," Carol said. "He was a drunk and a sleaze."

"Are you kidding? He was among the greatest Americans there ever was. Look at Ralph Cramden: Every day trying to get rich.

Every day a new scheme. Fall down, get up. Jackie had flaws, but man, he was fun. He was the same in real life. And Ralph never left him. He knew people—his characters were the most human I've ever seen. He never stopped. He was kindhearted. He played the clarinet, and he wanted to get rich. What an American."

"Well, fun, shmun. I should have listened to my mother in 1962 before we got married," Carol said.

"What?"

"She told me show business was nothing but a whore's game."

"You got that right, toots." Then he looked at her from behind the wheel and said, "Hey, what are we gonna watch? A show or a movie?"

"I thought we might try more *Westworld*, if you want."

"I'll fall asleep, but you should watch," Norman said.

"It's good," Carol said.

"Let's not get carried away. It's all right."

"The writing is good, you have to admit that," Carol said.

"I don't have to admit any such thing, unless you have a firearm and dental kit right there."

She looked at him and then looked straight ahead. "You're such a baby. When did you become such a baby?"

"Let's watch the Coen brothers' picture again."

She weighed the suggestion and after a second, she said, "OK."

"Sy Ableman," he said.

She laughed.

After a second, he said, "Let me explain something to you. The thing with you is you give people the benefit of the doubt just because you know them. But people you don't know, you assume the worst. You're just like my mother."

"Your mother was a good woman," Carol said.

"You're too suspicious of everyone and not suspicious enough of the ones right in front of you. For example, the man we saw today at the grocery store at Ralph's, the one who went up to the woman, by the deli counter."

"Creep."

"Why? That's my point. Why is he a creep?"

"Because he was coming on to that poor girl."

"First of all, she was almost your age. Second, how do you know he was a creep? Do you ever think about what it must be like for a fifty-year-old man who lives by himself? You know, the way you want a family—the way everyone wants a family and people to be with? Well, maybe that poor guy is just tired of being alone."

"What's your point?" she said.

"The point is, why think the worst of that guy?" Norman said. "He's just trying to meet someone. Imagine what it's like to be alone."

"Now you make me feel awful," Carol said.

"Don't feel awful. Just don't get mad at me for hating David Mundberg."

"What's the creep in the supermarket have to do with David Mundberg?"

"You haven't listened to a word I said."

"Yes, I have," Carol said. "You're mad for some reason that David Mundberg went to Puerto Rico and is getting all kinds of attention for it."

"I'm mad," Norman said, "because it is all transparent. It is for him and not for anyone else. If he really wants to be generous, who has to know about it?"

"But people like to copy movie stars. They are examples."

"David Mundberg is not a movie star."

"Well, he might as well be. And he can get movie stars to do things."

"Oh God. Take me. Take me right here."

"Yeah, OK," she said. "Well, take a moment to remember that I am not having any goddamn Catholic Mass, with the four hours and going up and down and up and down on the knees. I told you—a rabbi at Forest Lawn. Maybe an hour, a walk up one of the paths, and we're there."

Norman parked in the driveway, and they went inside.

She noticed that he was quiet. She softened her voice. "I never said I disagree with you, honey. I agree. David Mundberg is an intolerable asshole. And maybe the guy in the supermarket is lonely—you're right. That's why you are you, honey. You like to think about the little guy. That's why I love you. That's why America loves you. You know what's in a person's heart."

"That's right, toots."

"Let's forget about *Westworld* and just watch the Coen brothers."

"Deal."

CHAPTER 28

The North Came from the Shuttle Buses, and So Did the South

Reynolds wondered how the SCCWA came by six airport-ready shuttle buses. He imagined the chief requisition officer doing the deal with Hertz, or maybe some limo service. They would get a discount, the rate offered to other events. They wouldn't pay more than, say, the Imperial and Riverside AA Roundup, or the Volvo and Audi western region sales managers who were at Pomona last year.

The driver of his shuttle was a braceleted black woman. Her immediate problem was how to get more than half a dozen hoop skirted ladies, along with all the other cotillion-bound passengers, onto one shuttle. A man appearing to be her supervisor leaned into the folding door at the front of the bus and said, "You're going to have to get at least fifteen on here or it's going to take half the night."

"I'm trying, Hector," she said. "They got to squash in. Tell 'em they got to squash." Then she turned back in her chair and half yelled in the direction of two belles in pancake makeup who were making their way to the back. "Push into the back there, ladies. Here, y'all soldiers, you squeeze back in there, too. We gotta squeeze a few of you generals in with the ladies." A trio of Confederate officers followed her orders, sandwiching themselves in as the women pressed down into the seats.

Reynolds guided his entourage of Stella, Bella, Heather, Delaney, and Marisol up the small stairs. He and Robert and Lance and Lorenzo, feeling that the costumes brought a chivalrous bearing to the occasion, escorted the women, supporting each up the steps and into position in the crowded bus. They all had red plastic cups holding some form of alcohol procured at the camp: wine or applejack or beer. Robert had obtained a frozen margarita somewhere. The moment had at some point become one of those times when one concludes that one needs to get completely blotto.

This applied to no one better than Reynolds, who found himself crunched in next to the driver. The mood was happy; it was a party bus. Stella, wedged in between Marisol and Heather, was admiring Marisol's necklace. It was a silhouette of a woman's head in white against a black background. Heather chatted with Lance and Lorenzo while Bella listened. Delaney was the farthest back, enmeshed in conversation with a heavyset woman in a gray gown and a Union cavalry officer whose sword looked ready to tear any ball gown in its vicinity.

For the umpteenth time in the past two days, Reynolds considered the situation in which he found himself. He hadn't planned it this way. For months he'd envisioned a Robert Bly-ish outing, one in which he would get a sort of "Iron John" reconnection to his manhood and his roots. He thought by coming to the reenactment he could commune with the battle, thereby awakening a

sense of self-awareness. He hoped it would be refreshing, center-
ing. He'd seen himself coming home with a clearer look at things,
the same man but adjusted. No one would know what he had
done; they would just recognize his improved manner and, in traditional Hollywood custom, look him over to see if he'd had work
done. They would ask him if he'd been in Hawaii or whether he'd
lost weight. He'd be like the guys in the commercials for penis
enhancement on late night, walking around with a bigger dick and
everyone wondering what it was about him now.

But Jesus Christ, it hadn't worked out that way. He looked at
Delaney Bedford. He wondered whether Stella suspected anything. She *obviously* thought something was up with him, and
she *obviously* would have questions about what possessed him
to bring the two women out to this insane thing. It was like a
puzzle within a puzzle for Stella. Here he was, engaged in bizarre
behavior, and he'd compounded it with a questionable joyride. He
felt in Stella's eyes profound confusion—she didn't understand
the Enchino/Gettysburg of it all. She couldn't even get to the
Delaney and Marisol of it all. It was like one of those events—
like 9/11 or Princess Diana getting killed in France—where you
know as it happens that it will take years and dozens of books to
sort out what went down and what it all meant. All you can do
at the time is go through it.

The shuttle bus passed a series of strip malls on the way to the
freeway. A Kentucky Fried Chicken dominated the first. The next
featured the big three of southern California pan-Asian strip-mall
cuisine: Thai, Chinese, and sushi. The final set of one-story brown-
stucco alcoves was distinguished by a Payday loan center fronted by
a lemon-yellow neon sign that read, "Cal, Med, SDI All Accepted."
From there the Nissan people-mover rambled down the freeway

headed east. In a shuttle bus. In Civil War–era dress. On the way to a Civil War–era dance. At Enchino High School. Just like that.

Reynolds made small talk with the driver. "Are we going far?"

"Aw, no. About ten minutes. Just a few exits."

"Bet you never had this kind of crowd before."

She looked in the rearview. "Oh, I've seen a lot of things. Were you all here last year?"

"No. First year," Reynolds said.

"I think I drove it last year. Was the dance out at the high school?"

He had the sinking realization his self-image as an outsider to the group of nuts in Civil War garb was not evident to his driver. He was just another reenactor to her.

"Oh," he said, "I've never been to this thing before. I'm just checking it out."

She looked at his uniform and then back to the road. Reynolds wasn't satisfied. He had a bad habit when he was tipsy of talking to strangers. It came from his training as a tour guide, a subconscious ability to make small talk, which, in later years, upon the application of alcohol, lent itself to over-gregariousness. "It's the Battle of Gettysburg."

She lifted her eyebrows and nodded, humoring him.

"Do you know much about the Battle of Gettysburg? The Civil War? I know it sounds funny." He rolled his eyes at the rest of the bus. "But, you know, it's pretty fascinating."

Their exit approached, and she maneuvered the shuttle to the right lane. She gave a little snort. "I keep myself busy with the Battle of Busting My Ass to Make Enough Money to Eat."

"Fair," Reynolds said. "That's fair."

Nicely had brought a skinny girl who was half-in, half-out on the Civil War–clothes vibe. She had on a dress, but it had been unbuttoned, showing the jeans shorts and white T-shirt she wore underneath. It was hot, Reynolds thought. She wore granny glasses that didn't help. She might have been slow.

Nicely said, "Reynolds, please meet Jackie."

"Hello, Jackie," Reynolds said, his hand outstretched.

"She's my girlfriend."

Reynolds said, "Terrific—"

Jackie smashed Nicely with a knuckle punch to the triceps. "Ew. I am not your girlfriend."

Reynolds smiled. "Go ahead, Jackie. Be his girlfriend. Be his girlfriend today at least."

CHAPTER 29

White Rasta

The soldiers walked arm in arm with their ladies into Enchino High School, a standard brick and cinder-block building that had concrete walkways and porcelain drinking fountains with rusty-green stains running into the drains. Reynolds noticed a small group of college-age kids moving in the same direction.

"Where are they going?" he said to no one.

"Same place we are," said Heather.

"They're here for the band," Bella said.

"What?" Reynolds said.

"It's a reggae band," said Heather. "This kid I talked to earlier told me about them. They're playing. Supposed to be good."

"Perfect," said Stella.

They were ushered into a large gymnasium. Red, white, and blue bunting hung throughout the space, giving it the aura of a national political convention. The bleachers were pushed in, and the basketball hoops were retracted upward and draped with streamers. Posters of Lincoln, Grant, and Lee, with "Lincoln, "Grant," and "Lee" inscribed in scrolls at their bottoms, were high on the walls.

On the far side of the gym there was a raised stage and a bandstand hung with a large banner reading SCCWA WELCOMES THE BLUE AND THE GRAY. A twentysomething white man with impressive dreadlocks stood at the microphone, singing, in front of a four-piece reggae band. The musicians were black men wearing blue Union tunics and caps. One guy had a bandolier of bullets forming a big X on his torso.

"Awesome," Heather said.

Reynolds saw Bella and Heather look at each other and smile. They began to move their shoulders back and forth, feeling the beat. A steel drum added melody. Delaney and Marisol pushed forward and grabbed the two younger girls by the hands and rushed to the dance floor, which was empty save for an aging couple low clapping along to the music. The lead singer gave the women a nod, endorsing their effort to get the party started, and continued to sing.

> *Said he was a Buffalo soldier, dreadlock Rasta*
> *Buffalo soldier, in the heart of America*
> *If you know your history,*
> *Then you would know where you coming from,*
> *Then you wouldn't have to ask me,*
> *Who the 'eck do I think I am.*

Reynolds, Stella, and Robert stood and watched for a full minute.

"Are they playing that because they think it fits the Civil War?" Stella said.

"I was wondering that," said Robert.

They stood for a while and stared, then Reynolds said to the other two, "Bar?"

"Yes," Stella said.

"Thank God," Robert said.

They went to the bar set up in a corner and downed a drink and ordered another, like teenagers with fake IDs at an "All You Can Drink Tuesday." They found a few seats at one of the card tables set up nearby. "Buffalo Soldier" ended after a good fifteen minutes. The singer addressed the audience.

"Yah, mon. Good evening, warriors. We are White Rasta." He lifted his right arm and extended it to the sky. "My name is Gerald Makimbo. Dis will be a cotillion like no other, mon."

"Woo-hoo. Yay, Gerald!" Delaney said. She and Marisol and the girls were standing just in front of the band.

"Welcome to a symphony of reggae," Gerald said. He was dressed like a Confederate officer. He could lift his right arm high because his tunic was unbuttoned. "We come to bring you peace. We come to bring you the soothing love of Jamaica."

"He's like Yellowman," Reynolds said to Stella. "Remember Yellowman?"

"I think Gerald Makimbo is whiter."

"I'm sure he's not trying to become yellow."

The girls lifted their arms and applauded more. Delaney let out another "Woo-hoo," joined by Marisol. Heather put her hands in her mouth to whistle. The drummer got the beat up again, and the Caribbean sound filled the room once more.

"Hi, Robert." A woman in a dowdy ball gown stood at the table.

"Oh, hello," he said. When Reynolds and Stella looked at him, Robert said, "Reynolds, Stella, meet . . . I'm sorry, what was your name?"

She was disappointed but held out her hand to Reynolds. "I'm Irma."

Stella and Reynolds greeted her and nodded.

"I'm hitting on him," she said. "I saw him today and just could not get over his resemblance to General Longstreet. He is the finest specimen there ever was." Reynolds thought Irma was attempting an olden-times dialect. "General," she continued, "I told my sister I would bring you over to say hello. She has a bad hip. Would you mind terribly?"

Stella and Reynolds were alone.

"Did you fuck her?" Stella said.

"What?"

"Did you fuck her?"

"No. Who? That old lady? Jesus, Stella. No."

"*Who?* Your new reality star."

"Oh, stop."

"Since when do you like reality? You're the person the least interested in it I know."

"Stella, I just did a reality pilot. God, I thought you were understanding me there for a second. I should have known better."

"Yeah, well that was before I saw her tits."

"What?"

"She's hot. Is that what it is? You want to get laid?"

"Were they great?" Reynolds said, and after two seconds he cringed.

"Oh, c'mon. Fuck *off* with that, please," Stella said.

Gerald Makimbo made orchestral signals to the right side of the stage.

"Why don't you just leave," Reynolds said. "Why are you even here? And what the hell is it with following me? You put a tracking device on my phone? You did that?"

"You won't even watch reality. You won't watch *Real Housewives*, you won't watch with us. You won't watch *The Kardashians*

with us. You won't even watch *The Deadliest* Fucking *Catch*, which
is a good show. Now you want to produce reality?"

"Stella, stop."

"This is all about sex, right? It's about boobs! Should have
known—that's always been your thing."

"Cut it out."

On stage, White Rasta finished—or paused, Reynolds thought
was more like it—a number. Their leader stood at the microphone
with a white sheet of paper in his hands. An anxious-looking
woman in a red ruffled gown stood next to him. "OK, OK. Listen
up, mon. We have many things to do at this party. First of all, we
gonna do square dancing. Yah, mon. Line up peoples."

A Union officer and two like-minded ladies materialized on
the basketball court and indicated places for the dancers.

It cut across his mind like a razor blade: *she's scared*. Reynolds
didn't dare turn his head for fear she would see that he knew. In all
the time he had been with Stella, Reynolds had seen her scared once.
That was when she was pregnant and alone. Since then it was all
brass tacks. He'd watched her stare down every mogul and say hello
and no to every movie star. He'd seen her disembowel publicists
while brushing her teeth. *I'm scaring her.* Maybe it was the situation,
with the booze, Delaney and Marisol, and, well, the Civil War. But
there was no doubt; she was shaken. She stood up and left the gym.

Reynolds looked around the room, a scene of mayhem. He
watched his daughter and Heather chatting with Lance and
Lorenzo. They were flirting. He thought for a moment that he
should object, just out of principle, then thought better of it, this
being a time of war and chaos. All rules were relaxed.

"General Reynolds." It was Cyrus. He had appeared in the
seat next to him.

"Cyrus. Hello. I'm no John Reynolds," Reynolds said. "Nobody is."

Cyrus took a sip of his drink and smacked his lips. "Yow. They got a spiced punch. You got to get yourself some."

Reynolds held up his cup to show he was good.

Cyrus crossed a boot over his knee. "You got it all here in front of you, huh?"

"Yeah, right," Reynolds said.

"Well, you got your Civil War, which is in your blood. You got your family here; they've joined you and are having a good time. And you're working on your project with them two fine ladies."

"Cyrus, do you always talk this way? Like you're in the nineteenth century? Or do you just adopt it when you come to these events?"

Cyrus looked hurt.

"I'm sorry," said Reynolds. "That was mean."

"Yeah. It's all right, though. But what I'm saying is that you're a lucky man."

Reynolds paused. "Cyrus, let me explain something to you. This . . ." he indicated the expanse of the gym. He searched for words. "If you think this is my life, I am in deep shit. This is *insane*. Nothing personal, but we're in the eastern part of Los Angeles, at a dance, in the middle of a three-day costume performance—a *bad* costume performance—of a battle that happened a hundred and fifty years ago. I did want to come here, but I wanted to be away from my family, alone. My wife tracked me down through surveillance tactics I don't understand. She suspects me of philandering and is not altogether certain of my sanity. My daughter, the shining light of my existence, has come also, which embarrasses me beyond my power to articulate, and I am sure I have shattered any good image she has of me. And to this add the final ingredient of two attractive and slightly over-the-hill pseudo-celebrities who believe I am going to put them on television, something which I have no power or desire to do. That, my friend, is a mess."

Cyrus took it in. "Hmm. I didn't know all that."

"Well, that's about the way it is."

They watched the soldiers and the ladies in ruffles dance.

"Maybe I should just go home. This might have been a bad idea."

"No, sir. You can't go home," said Cyrus.

"Why not."

"Don't you see? You're like all of Lee's lieutenants right now. It's the second day of the battle, and you're ready to quit. You can't quit. You must get in there and fight. You've come this far. You're doing something. Learning something."

"How am I like even *one* of Lee's lieutenants, man? Explain that to me."

"You want to go around it all because you're tentative. The enemy is right in front of you, son, and you have to strike it."

"Cyrus, that's, like, all wrong." He closed his eyes and then opened them again in exasperation. "Lee was wrong. On the last day, he sent what was left of his army into a slaughter, and the South lost the war."

Cyrus pretended to be surprised. "Lee again. Christ, man. Oh yeah, Reynolds. You're burdened by Robert E. Lee. Oh, that's so insightful, you fucking pedant."

"Well, it's true," Reynolds said.

Cyrus paused. "Well, OK, I'll give you that."

Reynolds said it again. "What do you mean, I'm like Lee's lieutenants? What are you, crazy? C'mon, Cyrus." He tried to calm down, but the exasperated feeling kept coming over him, and he could not stop it. "You see, that is what I mean. Nothing means anything. That war was idiotic. No one even remembers it the right way. The battle of Waterloo, Charge of the Light Brigade. Do you think history is accurate about those? How can we expect *anything* to mean *anything?*

Cyrus responded as he might have to a foolish child. "Do you mind if I explain something to you?"

"Be my guest."

"Well, you know this, but I will remind you anyway. Evander Law's division of Longstreet's army, the First Corps, the Fifth Alabama Regiment, marched twenty-five miles to get to Gettysburg the night before the second day. Marched all night. They hadn't eaten in three days and were barefoot. They'd marched over a hundred miles in the past ten days. They got to the front, and within a few hours they were sent up Little Round Top, where the Federals sat behind rocks and trees and shot the hell out of them. They tried to get up that hill eight times till they had to quit. Almost all those boys got killed that day."

"I know," Reynolds said.

"So, what I'm saying is, how bad do we have it?"

Reynolds didn't say a word.

Cyrus waved toward the gym, as Reynolds had a minute earlier. "This is life, my friend. It's now." He stood up to leave. "And when you compare it to most lives, it beats the living shit out of them. That's why I come to these things. To remind me of that."

After Cyrus excused himself to go bullshit with a group of guys looking at a table labeled "Weaponry Advances," Reynolds wandered outside the gym like a teen on a Nickelodeon sitcom who didn't want to watch everyone else make out. He found Stella on a swing set. He sat next to her and they rocked back and forth.

"You do look very pretty," Reynolds said.

She laughed. "You look good too."

"You know," he said, "Delaney Bedford was the first Playboy Bunny that ever got to me. I would sit on my bed and stare at her for hours. It was the first time I ever realized what a woman was, what all the fuss was about."

"Why are you telling me this?"

"Just listen. So, when Scottie told me about her, I was, like, stunned. And then there I was, talking to her. It was like she came right out of the page. Isn't that weird?"

"She's an ex-party girl who ended up in the Valley. So what?"

"I don't know. It was like she represented something. We are so used to being around all these movie stars, it gets lost. It's like white noise, all the fame and everything. This was different. It was like something coming out of a fog and appearing, real, in front of me."

"And?"

"I don't know . . . That's why I thought it might be a show. Something about a thing coming from the mist of your memory and becoming real. Like, that's what a reality show should be. Like Warhol."

She thought about it. "Maybe, honey."

"I always thought things were being obliterated over time. That they were being dulled by the assault of technology and age. But that's wrong. Think about watches, clocks, time. No one will ever have to wonder if their watch is slow or if a clock is wrong. No more putting your clock radio ahead ten minutes to force yourself to be on time."

"You're losing me."

"It's more precise. Everything's more precise. No waiting for a song to come on the radio. Whatever song you want—now. No more blurry faxes. Exact fucking digital replicas of documents. Our generation is the only one who will ever know about fax machines. They're gone. Poof. More exact now. Delaney Bedford is not in my mind—she's right fucking here. Older, but here. Now."

"She is here now. So am I. So is Bella. So is White Rasta."

He laughed. "I'm drunk."

"Me fucking too," she said.

He took her hand. "Let's dance."

On the floor, Lance had coupled up. Delaney and Marisol had each acquired an officer: Delaney's was a Confederate with a beard, and Marisol got a fat red-faced guy from the North. White Rasta was cranking out what sounded like something from *Hee Haw*, its steel drum now emulating the twang of a guitar. Gerald Makimbo was singing in a voice that was Jamaican-cum-Kentuckian. The group leaders who had organized everyone were now acting as dance leaders. They showed the troupe a very basic do-si-do that could be performed in lines.

Reynolds and Stella found themselves across the newly formed aisle from each other. To her left, Marisol lifted her skirts as she moved like a flamenco dancer, like a José Feliciano album cover. Next to her, Delaney was doing something similar. Cyrus and the boys of his brigade moved into line and clapped. The troupe was supposed to join arm in arm on both sides and proceed in a line dance. Jamaican and country blended into a Motown, wedding-style deal. Lorenzo and Bella danced down the middle like a couple who just got married. Heather and Lance were next, throwing signs like rappers. Marisol did a wavy walk, and a solo Federal officer hopped the whole distance.

Stella and Reynolds gave each other a knowing look. They went forward. Reynolds walked swinging his hand, like a Big Band leader, snapping to the rhythm without moving to the left or right, making a straight line down the middle. Stella bopped and grooved around him in circles. They had done it for years at weddings during line dances and the rowdy, formless moments after the cake is cut and the old people go home, when the parents make asses of themselves and the band gives the impression of going overtime. The crowd doing the Civil War version in the here and now broke into applause.

Delaney was next up. She hooked elbows with a Confederate officer, and they were joined by White Rasta's bassist, in a bushy beard, the bandolier, and a crocheted hat in rainbow colors. Delaney traveled in a circle around the two, and then the Confederate grabbed her from behind and pressed his crotch into her backside. He made a lassoing motion to his troops. Delaney was taken by surprise and lost her balance, whereupon the guy yanked her back toward his midsection again. The effect was a little rough.

Reynolds, a few yards away, didn't like it at all and jumped toward the guy. Lance passed by him in a blur; he *really* didn't like it. He charged the Confederate, separated the man from his mother, and punched him in the face. He then tackled the man to the ground and began to administer even more efficient punches to the head. A confederate of the Confederate officer lunged to knock Lance off. Then it was *on*. Soldiers from both sides jumped in and started wrestling and swinging. Bob took the yellow-shirted guy, the roofer Reynolds had taken out on Little Round Top and held him up while Stevie and Nicely smashed him in the stomach.

Marisol jumped in and began smacking butternuts with her Civil War shoes. Delaney was right behind her, also slamming shoes. At the bar, Heather grabbed an ice scooper while Bella moved in unarmed. Heather saw Stella, who had *her* shoe off, charging at the asshole who had started the whole thing. Reynolds slipped into the middle of the turmoil like he was on a lacrosse attack. He tried to get Lance off the Southern guy who'd mistreated Delaney. Lorenzo joined him. They wrestled Lance away from the pack, and the settle-down types took over. Gerald Makimbo kept singing, and the rest of White Rasta never stopped jamming.

DAY 3

CHAPTER 30

On the Road

It was just becoming light when Norman slipped into his Mercedes. Fine German automobile, he thought. He'd never been one to care about who made the car he drove. He hadn't slept much, and when he had, he'd had weird dreams, the kind you must shake off in the morning. Curse of a creative mind. But these were as weird as he could remember of any dream without sex. Reynolds had been on a horse outside Joey's Restaurant trying to get in. He kept saying, "All I want is a corned beef sandwich." Luis and some other waiters were saying no, patient but firm. Norman couldn't talk Reynolds off the horse. Then Stella came, and she couldn't talk Reynolds off the horse either. Then somehow it became a *Dog Day Afternoon* kind of thing, and Reynolds was surrounded. Norman tried to remember the details as he got in the car in the garage. The horse had started bucking and everyone had backed off; kids screamed. Norman had been frightened for Reynolds. The cops came and barricaded him and the horse at an ATM for a regional bank in between Sigouri Sushi and the frozen yogurt place. The tension mounted. Norman had been scared in that deep, real way a dream scares you. *My God*, he remembered thinking, *they're going to kill me*. Then he woke up.

He shook out the willies as he started the car. On one level, of course, the symbolism was obvious. But there were certain things that didn't make sense. They didn't have corned beef at Joey's, first of all. But on a more important level, he realized, now that he wasn't scared for Reynolds any more, he saw the fact that his surrogate son was out in Enchino in a Civil War uniform as kind of funny. Harmless. He had always had a gift for finding the comedy in things, and at his age found he could take almost nothing seriously. At least not seriously enough to let it scare him. But this dream scared him awake. And as he backed the car silently out of the garage, he was still shaking it off.

Tom's place was on Carbon Beach. Norman rolled up without his lights on and found Tom sitting on the sole bus-stop bench in that part of Malibu, just a little south of his house. He wore a Cal Berkeley baseball cap and had a gym bag. Norman felt a rush of affection. He'd been watching out for Tom for thirty years. The kid had become such a star so young. None of them, least of all Tom, had seen it coming, and by the time it was on him it was too late. It went unspoken between them, but Norman knew what it meant, and he knew Tom knew it too. And Tom knew that Norman knew.

He was dead, is what it meant. His privacy was gone. If Tom chose, anything he thought or did could become known to the world, with the press of the *Send* button or a call to his publicist. If he wanted to go to Africa and call attention to something, the world would listen. If he went to a strip club, all the magazines would know. If his kids got suspended from private school for smoking pot or cheating, it would be in the *LA Times*. Norman was one of the only people who didn't sugarcoat it, didn't pretend it wasn't true. The thing about Tom for Norman was, as young as

he still was and as imperfect as he was, he was the only one Norman had ever seen—and he had seen all of them, since Hollywood
really isn't that big, about as big as a small town in Iowa—who
knew it and had the appropriate amount of sadness about it. Tom
couldn't not love the action and remained a ham bone on the
screen and in person. But he carried around the knowledge of his
Faustian bargain.

Tom, seemingly in a trance himself, came out of it and broke
into a big smile when he saw the Benz. He threw his bag in the
trunk and got in.

"You're the only one who can have this car and get away with
it," he said. "Don't they kill you on the carbon footprint?"

"Ah, they all leave me alone. I'm an old man. How are ya, bub?"

"Good. Now, what's the mystery? What is going on?" Tom said.
"I'm so curious, I can't stand it."

"You know I'm worried about you. I want you to break out of
the clouds. This is a little adventure."

"I will say I love you for worrying about me and bringing me
to this. Now, what the fuck are we doing?"

"It's weird," Norman.

"I love weird, you know that."

"Reynolds is in Enchino, and I promised Stella I'd help go
get him"

"O-kaaay." Tom opened his hands. "Is he in trouble?"

"Maybe. He's at a Civil War reenactment."

"A . . . what?" Tom started to laugh.

"A reenactment. Stella's there too."

"Awesome," Tom said.

"Sure?"

"I'm going, and I'm driving."

* * *

After they rode for a while, Tom said, "With all we talked about, we've never talked about Gettysburg. Do you know much about it? You must."

"I know it. Well, some. Carol and I took the kids years ago. They hated it; Carol hated it." He smiled thinking about it.

"How are your kids?" Tom said.

"Old and living in Europe with my grandchildren, who are also getting older. Thank God for FaceTime. Kathy published another book. Wrote it in French. Don't ask me what it's about."

He looked at Tom. Back to the mission at hand. "Reynolds is from there, you know."

"He's *from* there?"

"Yup."

"Oh, so this is in his blood."

"Yeah. He talks to me a little. But never about something like this. He hates it. At least he did."

Tom was quiet for a minute. Then he said, "Who would you be?"

"What?"

"Who would you be? In the Civil War? If you got to be someone?" Tom said.

"Somebody from New York. Or Lincoln."

"No. C'mon. You can't be Lincoln. You have to be someone in the *battles*."

"Oh, Christ, I don't know," Norman said.

"All right, start with this: Would you be North?"

"North," Norman said in an instant. "Of course, I'm for the North."

"Who cares where you're from? Is that the thing that decides it?" Tom said.

"I can't be from the South. Me, from the *South*?" Norman said.

"OK. I think I would be from the South. They were cooler."

"Cooler? Slaveholders. Remember that?"

"I meant the uniforms, the generals, stuff like that. Of course, I don't mean the slave thing."

"I don't know. Lee was more . . . glamorous than the rest, I guess."

"What are the great Civil War pictures?" Tom said.

"*Gone with the Wind*, to start."

"Yeah, but there are no battles in *Gone with the Wind*. It's all interiors."

"Well, the Battle of Atlanta."

"Yeah, but that's not a battle in the movie. All I remember is fire. What movies have the real great battles?"

"I don't know. They all kind of turn into Westerns. The Civil War is a backdrop. It's going on in the background. There was that book, good book. *Cold Mountain*."

"Great book," Tom said.

"But *not* a great movie."

"Ugh. I hated that thing."

"Me too," Norman said. "Here you have a classic American story—I mean, could that guy be any more American, that character? And he puts all fucking English actors in it. I'm sure it was Grossman. He took over and did that fake literary thing he bullshits everyone into and ruined it."

"And he made the black girl white, didn't he?" Tom said, agreeing. "What's wrong with these people? Can you explain that to me?" He sat back in his seat. "How is it so easy to hate everyone these days?"

"You don't hate everyone," Norman said. "You hate Hollywood."

"I guess. But Hollywood hatred is so hard to lose. Like you said, I do hate Grossman. Such a horrible human. He's a guy who's mean to little people. And a fucking liar."

"Well, I can't defend that piece of shit. But you don't hate Bill Clinton, for example. He's your friend. Have you spoken to him?"

"No, not in a while." After a pause, Tom said, "Isn't it crazy that I always know the president? That I can call him? That I can call him anytime I want to talk about anything."

"Of course, it's crazy."

"I mean, look at life, right? I get up in the morning and go to the computer, my picture is on the front page." He showed a little deep Texas in his voice. "And forget that whoever is in the news—whoever's picture is up there—I will know them most of the time. Have their phone number. I know almost all the famous people in the world." He pointed at Norman. "So do you, by the way."

"So?"

"Well, I'm just saying . . . it's weird. There's not some level of unknowability. Nothing is exciting. There's something that's odd—like *off*—when you aren't excluded from anything."

"Only a person who's not excluded from anything would think that, bub."

"Maybe," Tom said. He thought for a moment. "Do you know who my old man's favorite politician was?"

"Nixon."

"Stop. I'm being serious here. Kennedy. JFK. Do you know why?"

"The wife."

"No. Because he drove by our house. God's honest truth. My dad had an old eight-millimeter camera, and when Kennedy's motorcade drove by our house during the campaign, everyone went down the street and stood by waiting for him to pass. My dad took his little camera and got footage of his Cadillac limousine riding by. He made my brother and I watch it. He got drunk and ran it on a projector against a bedsheet in the cellar. It was like his own Zapruder film. He'd slow down the part when Kennedy passed by the house. He swore you catch sight of him waving out of the window, but I never saw it. He'd just run that back and forth, like it was a picture of God or something."

"Spectacular," Norman said.

"I know. But the point is, my Dad would have never thought of actually meeting Kennedy. It would never even cross his mind. Or being on TV. No one was actually *on* TV."

"I know. I had the same feeling when I went to work at NBC. I was so excited to be in the building. It was like being behind the curtain in Oz."

"Exactly. Now I see someone on TV, or in the newspaper, or in a movie I like . . . and I take out my phone and I call them up. Bang. There's no distance. I can access everything."

"Yeah, but you're a movie star."

"I *know*. But I'm just an extreme case of the way it's going with everyone. It's what Warhol said, for sure. There's reality shows— everyone thinks their life can be a TV show. Or a webcam, or a blog. You, Norman, you have a *Wikipedia* page."

"I have a *Wikipedia* page?"

"You have a *Wikipedia* page. Of course you have a *Wikipedia* page. The eighth replacement character actor on your worst show in the sixties has a *Wikipedia* page."

"Yeah, but that's because it's show biz."

"But it's *everywhere*. You like the Dodgers, you can go be a Dodger for a week in the winter in Arizona. If your goal in life is to be a TV weatherman, chances are you can go to some dipshit school and be a TV weatherman. It starts to make my head explode. I *know* I'm the extreme. I know I'm famous. But the point is, everyone is a little famous."

"Sure, everything is speeding up."

"There's something bad about it. I can't explain it. Maybe I'm just sick of being famous."

"You're just sick of being famous."

"It's like being hooked on something."

"Well, there's nothing you can do about it, kid. And you can't expect anyone to feel sorry for you."

"I can stop working for a while. Go away."

Norman thought about that for a second, started to say something, thought better of it. "Yes," he said. "You could do that."

In the light Sunday traffic, the Mercedes flew.

Tom said, "You know the first thing I think about when someone says 'Civil War'?"

"Booth," Norman said.

"How did you know that?"

"You're an actor. All actors go right to Booth."

"'All actors go to Booth.' Do you play this game all the time? The 'Who do you think of when you think of the Civil War' game?"

They moved down the PCH, and Tom adjusted the visor and switched to sunglasses. After he was locked down under baseball hat and plain black shades, he said, "How is it that a guy who is the biggest star in America gets so distracted by politics that he kills the president?"

"Conviction," Norman said.

"I guess."

"Are you not believing that?"

"No, I'm saying they didn't spoil their stars enough back then." Norman chuckled.

"I mean, c'mon. How can the biggest star in America move around in such obscurity and sneak into the president's box?"

Now they were hitting bad traffic going through downtown.

"Right? Who were they not letting in?" Norman said.

"That's right. I can't sneak in anywhere without a disguise." They passed a VW bus with longboards as it slowed down. He couldn't imagine where they were going in this direction, away from the water.

"Why do you think it is," said Norman, "that Booth is not immortalized?"

"What are you talking about? He *is* immortalized."

"As an assassin. No one remembers he was an actor."

Tom thought about it. "No one remembers his roles . . ."

"Just his real-life role."

A beat passed. "I hope that's changed," said Tom. Then, "Do you think it's changed?"

Norman took note of the sad rumination behind this last bit. In their time as friends, in the hours on location with nothing to do while grips and gaffers moved gels and booms, Norman had come to marvel at Tom. When they worked together, Norman had spent endless hours observing Tom, while the two rode from one location to the next to the next. On set, Tom's hand-picked

Teamster always sat in front of the trailer in a lawn chair, while other members of his team scampered about to put the most current draft in front of him. New changes would be on new colors; pale blue, construction paper red, and yellow pages. Still other assistants walk-ran between the trailer and the set as Tom maintained his position throughout the movies he did. "Maintained," Norman thought to himself. That was the way to put it.

Norman was no romanticizer of the old days, of the bosses and the syndicates. But it could still be said that in an age that—as much as any other, silent films, golden age, no matter—commoditized actors, Tom thrived even as the studios and the audiences rode all good taste off the rails, till the movies were no longer the touchstone at the center of America's mind, the thing that had to be waited for, the thing that had to be traveled to, the scarce thing. Now the big screen was the little one, as Norman had always known. Tom self-guided through the multidimensional puzzle game presented by a world that devalued his opinions, jokes, sensibilities, and politics, and then rubbed it in by aging him. But even through the occasional mocking, strong in his first days as an idol, lessening as his parts changed from rookie to detective, Tom did not fall apart, did not have affairs, jump on couches, or adopt children from Africa. Tom threaded the needle in an art form less about his pauses than special effects, graphics, and rubber comic-book faces.

Tom had done it with two elemental beliefs: he would choose earnest over ironic, and he would prepare but not overthink. He would ask himself whether Jimmy Stewart would do it. He would ask himself whether Gary Cooper would do it. He embraced clichéd decision making, fuck what anyone said, no one needed to know how he decided. He used simple tools: pros and cons on a piece of notebook paper, shy away from departures and never do them in desperation, work in sync with tentpoles and sequels, no writing or directing, promote with quiet presence, treat all the executives and producers, ADs, and DPs with unsolicitous respect. He treated the agents as well as anyone else. Said "thank you," said "no, thank you." He started conversations with everyone on the set over the course of a shoot. He stayed around for coverage to support the other actors.

"Maybe, bub. Maybe he changed it all." Norman shared Tom's contemplative mood. "Booth. What a crazy cocksucker. You know, Reynolds did used to tell me—and he's not one to tell anyone else much, which I like, which everyone likes, it's one of his great qualities—that the Civil War changed everything." Norman put an index finger on the dash. "He used to talk about it more when he was younger but still very rarely. But he's talked to me twice in the last six months. When he does he either talks with a grudge or like he's opening up, letting go of a big secret."

"He never talks about it with anyone else?" Tom said.

"As I said, very rarely," Norman said.

"No projects? Seems like he would find a project."

Norman grimaced and shook his head.

"Sorry," Tom said. "You know what I mean."

"Yeah, it's true. I mean, he did a few things that were good. The John O'Hara piece was better than it got. But no, nothing you would think."

"Sad."

"Makes me wonder what this is all about," said Norman.

Tom looked at him for a long second. "Obvious, no?"

"What's obvious?"

"Reynolds is not doing too well."

* * *

Tom looked at the road ahead as they sped down the interstate.

"What do you think it is?" he said. "Do you think it's like community theater?"

"No. I think it's more connected to a history," said Norman.

"But there's the whole theatrical side of it. They are putting on a show after all."

"True."

"But it's weird. No one else seems to go running around redoing events that went on in history. Do they redo the First World War?"

"Not that I know of. How could you redo the First World War?"

"Maybe we can do the Battle of El Alamein here."

They laughed.

"They don't redo World War Two," Norman said. "I know that happened. I was there."

"It didn't happen out here."

"Well, neither did the fucking Civil War."

"True."

Tom thought for a minute, then he said, "It's like we are driving back in time, going to this thing. It's so . . . weird."

Norman grinned. "It's just weird to you because you are a liberal Hollywood jerk."

"How so?"

"This is what people do, go to things like this. It's bread and circuses in the real world. This is just another circus, a minor league circus. You're engaged in the big circus, so you have no time for the small circus."

"Yeah, yeah. I get that. But it's something different, too. I'm so excited, now that we're going to this." He lifted his hands off the wheel and rubbed them together. "And what do you mean I have no time for the small circus? Those are my people. They're *your* people too, Mister Television."

"Yeah, but making them laugh and wanting to live with them are two different things. Let me tell you something, bubby. There are two cultures in America. Two crosscurrents." He made an X with his arms. "One is race and the other is class. There were terrible losses on both fronts in the Civil War. These people may not understand this."

"Maybe they're not trying to understand it. Do you think an actor is trying to understand something when he does a part?"

"Of course. You're an actor. How can you ask me that?"

"Bullshit," Tom said. "Actors tell themselves that, but they're just trying to get paid and get attention. That's the dirty secret. Then you get the attention and you wish you had settled for just getting paid."

They had been down this road before. All roads with Tom, in fact, led to this point. Norman needed to change the subject. "What I can't figure out," he said, "is Reynolds. That's more interesting. Why did he go to this thing, and why now? The poor fucking guy has always been lost. He's a secret intellectual. He hides his light. His parents are professors, did you know that?"

"I knew he grew up back East. But I had no idea he grew up in Gettysburg until you just told me. So, why's it weird that he should come to this? It's the most natural thing in the world."

They passed the gigantic I-10/I-710 interchange.

"No, that's not it," Norman said. "It's weird that he should come to this, because he doesn't care for it. He'll never talk about it. All he ever told me was that he 'rejected' it."

"Rejected it?"

"Yeah. It has a pacifist feel to it, the way he gets. Or like an anti-death-penalty person." He could tell Tom was looking at him with confusion.

"Like the way most people reject their religion they grew up with, the way Catholics hate being Catholics. Jews are that way too. Protestants, not so much. It must be because the others are so heavy. I have to think about that."

"Most people reject their religion?' said Tom. "Is that true?"

"Not most people. Most people we know. The kind of people we know."

They drove in silence for a few minutes, both lost in their thoughts.

Tom said, "You know what I always have wondered about these things? Who the fuck comes to be a grunt? To be one of the guys who gets shot? I mean, someone said it before, maybe I said it, but if you go to the trouble of doing this—you know, of getting the uniform and the sword and the blood capsules and the musket and everything—wouldn't you want to be a general?"

They were now making good progress down the freeway. Norman remembered they had not been playing their usual driving game.

"Let's play our game. The What Do You Like? game," he said. "Your turn. I went last, Mister National Treasure."

Tom said, "Oh, I'm ready for you."

"Go ahead," said Norman.

"Get ready."

"I'm ready. Lay it on me."

"Baseball fights," Tom said.

Norman closed his eyes in enjoyment.

Tom said, "How good is that? Huh?"

"So good."

"Your turn."

"Let me think about it . . . ooh-hoo, I got it. Breaking free from traffic."

"Niiiice." Tom thought about it. "How about breaking through from traffic that you didn't know why it was there in the first place? Like, when it just goes away, and you're left saying, 'What the fuck was it all for?'"

"Right. When that happens, I try to make up a story about what happened, which is fun," Norman said. "OK, I'm comfortable with that as an improvement. Your turn."

"All right, I have one, but think it through before you judge."

"Go. No preambles."

"The shower after you lose at the Oscars."

Norman exploded in laughter.

"Right?" Tom said.

"It's like *Carrie*." Norman said.

"It's like *Carrie*," Tom said, doubling up so much that he almost couldn't drive.

CHAPTER 31

Sleeping Bags

Early Sunday morning, Lance was startled by a foot kicking him in the back, through the sleeping bag. He turned and saw Heather standing over him.

"Hey, Private. Let me back in."

She gestured to the Prius, where she and Bella had stretched out and had it quite nice in the back seat. Lance and Lorenzo had braved the elements in sleeping bags. Lorenzo moved to the side, and Heather climbed into his spot. Lorenzo squinted at her.

"You guys are insane," Heather said. "Why didn't you sleep in your car like normal people?"

"Please, dear. I haven't had my coffee yet," Lorenzo said, and he rolled away from her and then rolled back, a sleeping bag double take. "Holy shit, I'm in the army. Which army am I in?"

"You're in the South. Someone came over with a fresh uniform for you. I'm just glad we got out of your sleeping bags and went to the car before whoever it was came," Heather said. "Come on, give me room."

Bella came up and got into Lance's sleeping bag.

Next to her, Lance said, "*Hola, chica.* Oh my god, I was so drunk by the end of the night."

"Me too. And stoned."

"Me too," Lance said. After a pause, in a shy voice, he said, "Hey . . . um, can I ask you a question?"

"Sure," she said.

"Did we . . . um . . . did we do anything last night?"

Bella laughed and put her fingertip on his nose.

"You're very cute."

CHAPTER 32

General Pickett

Tom and Norman got out of the Mercedes and took in the vast spectacle. Both had their hands over their eyes like privates saluting as they absorbed the panorama. "Are those soccer fields?" said Tom.

Norman grunted. "A few softball fields too. Maybe all softball fields. That looks like an infield." He saw two spectators to his right speaking with a man in a Federal uniform. He approached and said, "Pardon me, do you know which battle this is?"

"Gettysburg," said the soldier.

"I know that," Norman said, old and from New York. He caught himself and followed up, trying to be calmer and nicer. "I mean which part of the battle?"

"That over there is Pickett's Charge. They're getting ready for it." The man turned to Tom and said, "Are you famous?"

Tom said, "Who wants to know?"

He jerked a thumb back. "Her."

Tom walked to the woman, who was in a plain frock with a blue satin belt cinched at the waist.

"Tom Mack, how do you do?"

* * *

Twenty minutes had passed after Tom had given the amiable greeting. There was nothing blatant, no requests for photographs, no lingering stares as if he were a circus oddity. But Norman felt the usual building of energy in the small crowd, as the conversations became louder and the glimpses at Tom and, to a smaller extent, Norman, out of corners of eyes happened more often. Norman, always a man of the people, started talking to all the folks who started to gather around, which he knew was as helpful to Tom as a third nipple. The crowd, feeling Tom's presence, the sheer fame of him, in the flesh, worked itself into a nonverbal frenzy. Norman just kept on talking to folks, trying not to call attention to any place or thing, and responded to Tom only when he asked him something.

The loudspeaker came on; the announcer was by now instructing the crowd in a conversational tone, what with two days–plus of guiding them as the eye in the sky, and with a sense of what they'd accomplished together, the valiant skirmishes of yesterday and the kerfuffle in the gym the night before.

> *OK, reminder: we're accumulating for Pickett's Charge. If you haven't heard it yet, the battle will take place in fields two, three, and four. Assembly of Union troops will be in field one. Assembly of Confederate troops will be in field five. Union battery will set up field two-three hill and Confederate battery in field four. Batteries will go off precisely at two p.m. and hand-to-hand will follow at two-fifteen. There will be no simultaneous battery and hand-to-hand. Repeat: no simultaneous battery and field fighting. Battery reenactors may join the hand-to-hand fighters. Please carry your rifles and all other materials with you at all times. Use caution with bayonets and stay with your outfits. Horses must be in their locations*

*with officers by one-thirty for final preparations. Remember: there
are only four authorized horses in the battle today, no other horses
that may be on the grounds will be allowed on the field after that.*

Norman noticed a small huddle of senior officers near the
space where all the backstops intersected. All roads from the fields
ran to this dusty space, which on a map or from the sky would look
like a dirty penny. He indicated the group to Tom and said, "I'm
sorry, bub, I think they're coming at you."

"Nah. What would they want from me?" Tom said.

But Norman was right; the men moved their way, smiles on
all faces. The leader was balding and wore an old-time suit with
a bow tie, a cross between Secretary of War Edward Stanton and
the Munchkin mayor, if the Munchkin mayor had been full-size.
Two Union generals and a splendid Confederate cavalryman with
a seven-foot sword made up the rest of the delegation.

"Mr. Mack, how do you do?" said the mayor.

"Hey, guys."

"We are terribly sorry to bother you, but, well, this is a chance
we have a hard time passing up."

"Fellas, we're just here to watch our friend," Norman said.

"Reynolds Stanhope," said Tom. "He's excellent."

The cavalryman charged in. "Top notch, I'm sure. Listen, we'll
cut to the quick. Right now, it is two o'clock on the third day of
the battle. Do you know what comes now?"

"The end of the battle. The big drive by the South," said Tom.

The delegation was pleased. The mayor said, "It is time for
Pickett's Charge. The gentlemen who reenacts General Pickett
has graciously offered to allow us to ask you to do the association
a gigantic charitable favor."

Norman said, "I think Tom is just here—"

Tom interrupted him. "What does it entail?" he said to the military men and the mayor. "I'd need to see the costume."

A Union general gave a quick answer. "We need you to dress like George Pickett and ride up and down the line and tell the Southern reenactors to be brave and do their duty . . . that kind of thing."

"Are there sides?"

"A script," Norman explained.

"Yes," said the mayor. "Very specific to what he said. Lots of yelling and such. We know how important accuracy is to you." He nodded to Norman, "To you both. Big fan of *Artie*."

"Oh, thanks. I'm not sure how important it was on *Artie*, though," Norman said, loosening up and sensing at least a few guys who remembered his work.

"*Artie* was my favorite show," the mayor continued, nostalgic, which seemed appropriate. "I watched it with my brother. We both ended up in the Navy."

CHAPTER 33

Stopped

In the late morning, Norman took Bella's elbow lightly and said, "C'mon, cookie, take a walk with me."

They took a few strides, and Bella said, "Do you have a clue about my dad's weirdness?" She wasn't trying for a laugh.

"Well," Norman said. "I don't really know. I don't think anyone knows that much." They walked on. "I think your dad has stopped being moved by anything other than you and your mom," he said.

"It's OK if you say he has stopped being moved by anything, period," Bella said.

"Well, none of it is like him. He lives for the profound, Reynolds. He is looking for excitement of the mind. He's not shutting down early, like most people—most people are happy to hew to a life of making money and conformity after they see chasms flying by for a while. And your dad had a swell life of conformity if he wanted it. Despite the calm he gives off, he has never been a settler. I think he's had a life so far that has stimulated him, and he could always find excitement. But he wants something else. For him, I think, it's something else." He pointed to a snack stand nearby. "Here, I want to get some coffee. Want some, honey?" he said.

While they waited, he said, "I think he's at a point where I don't think he can find it, this thing that a few people look for more than others—profundity, call it. You know, the profound."

"Don't we all? I know I do. And you do. And Mom definitely does."

"Ah," Norman said. "Always beyond your years." He stared at her. There was not a more perfect girl.

Coffee obtained, they walked to a picnic table.

"I don't know," Bella said. "Lots of times, people are looking for something profound to hit them—so they can be moved even a little bit."

"Yup," Norman said. "Or they look to move other people. I think your dad is in that category, and he's frustrated because he can't get there. He's not been able to tell his stories."

"I guess that's your point on most things, huh? That stories are everywhere. And if you are a storyteller you need to live your life telling stories. You need to get in there and touch people." Bella blew into her coffee.

"It's hard to place this thing. Gettysburg. I can't decide if it's bad community theater or brave outdoor theater—like at Saratoga," he said.

"Above or below performance art?"

"They both show real dedication by the artist," Norman said.

"OK, Chumley. I agree," Bella said.

Holding his coffee in front of him with two hands, Norman said, "You know, about twenty-five years ago, I just stopped. I told your dad to take care of everything. My kids were in Europe by then, so they weren't around. Gave Carol the number to reach me but told her to not use it. I filled my car with books. And I pointed south and drove away.

"I went to a little Catholic retreat—like an inn, really. It was marvelous. Set back from the ocean, with a great panorama of a view. Twisted path down to one of those wide San Diego beaches. They gave me their big suite, which had five rooms: a bedroom, a bathroom, a living room, a nice dining room, and a kitchen. It had a patio where I could read, or watch the sunset, or have lunch. There was a tiny chapel on the third floor. When I arrived, I got my suite situated, unpacked my clothes, and went to a chair on the patio, sat in it . . . and I stopped. Stopped doing anything. Disappeared from the world. Stopped. And I stayed there stopped for four months."

"Wow, Chums, that's a lot," Bella said.

"Yes, it was. I stopped. No forward or sideways or backwards motion. I just read and took long, long hikes."

"So, it happened to you?"

"I don't think it's optional. For men and sometimes women, though women have dealt with the issues long before. And, by the way, I don't think everyone just has it and puts it in the past and goes happily ever after. That's the real crux of it, toots. That's what's sad. Most of the people in this world live lives of quiet desperation. As people, we're at our best when we are trying to lighten that load of others. That's what I found out when I stopped. But who the hell knows? Everyone is different."

CHAPTER 34

McPherson's Ridge

When he heard the announcement that the troops should begin assembling in fields one and five for Pickett's Charge, which would take place in the combined space of fields two, three, and four, Reynolds decided it was time to move. He walked to the backstop of field one, where Cyrus was standing on the edge of the visitor's dugout, while the boys of the battalion sat on the benches.

"Cyrus, I need to borrow one of the ponies," Reynolds said.

"Just borrow my car," said Cyrus.

"No, I need the pony."

"OK, borrow my gun."

"I don't want your gun, I want a horse—or a pony, doesn't matter."

"I'll take your car," said Nicely, eavesdropping.

"I'll take your gun," Bob said.

"Nobody's taking anything," said Reynolds. Then, back to Cyrus, "Please?"

"For how long? I just got the goddamned animal from the higher-ups—an acknowledgement of service. They gave it to me for Pickett's Charge."

"Half hour, tops."

"You better have him back within the hour."

"Thanks, Cyrus."

"And no running him. I need him fresh for the battle."

"Where are you going to run a Union horse during Pickett's Charge when we're defending Cemetery Hill?"

"Let me worry about that."

Reynolds considered the dugout and saw Nicely looking at him as though he were anticipating what was to come next.

"Hey, Nicely," Reynolds said. "Please grab your gun and come with me." Reynolds didn't wait, hurrying instead toward where the horses were kept, a little way past the restrooms, where makeshift stalls had been set up for the steeds. When Nicely caught up, Reynolds was atop a chestnut pony with a Seabiscuit-size hind end.

"We're going around the waterworks . . . over near the cement things," Reynolds said. "To a field of grass out there by the parking lot with the trucks and the service building." Nicely marched beside Reynolds around the aqueduct, carrying his rifle and his paintball gun in a soldier's rucksack slung over his shoulder. The kid soldiered well.

Reynolds started speaking, "I should tell you what this is all about."

"Go ahead, sir. Please. I'll call you, sir."

"McPherson Ridge, where we're imagining this place to be . . ."

"Over by the parking lot for the cable trucks?"

"Yes. Now, what I'm working with is that the ridge is the spot on the first day of the Battle of Gettysburg where the Union cavalry first saw the Southern army accumulating in the hills to the north of town, fifty thousand men."

"That's why you say 'the South came from—'"

" . . . 'the north and the North came from the south.' That's right. Very good." Reynolds continued, "There are ten feeder roads leading into Gettysburg—when you look at a map it makes the town look, well, like an asshole. These feeder roads brought the troops together en masse, and the Confederates got to the area first."

"So, this place, this ridge, is where your man saw the South?"

"No, first it was the cavalry leader, General John Buford," Reynolds explained, atop Cyrus's pony. "He made the critical decision to fight on that high ground that first day. He saw that retreating would allow the massive Southern army to occupy all of the high ground in the area around Gettysburg—you see, the Union Army was not up yet. Eighty thousand men were within fifty miles but just not close enough to the town and its surrounding terrain, whereas the Southern armies were digging in. And high ground was the whole ball game. The South's success throughout the early part of the war, 1861 and 1862, was predominately in battles where they had established the high ground and the Union Army had charged from a lower position and, as a result, been blown away. This is what Lee and Longstreet and Stonewall Jackson had done so often, most recently in Fredericksburg, where the Union lost twenty thousand men in one day."

Nicely nodded, still marching well. "So, who is your guy, Reynolds?"

"I'm getting there. So, on that day, John Reynolds," said Reynolds, "who was a three-star general and the commander of the First Corps, has ten thousand Federal troops, the Iron Brigade, just five miles south of McPherson Ridge. You know, where we're going over there."

"Right," said Nicely, as if getting instructions from a coach. "Wait, we're pretending this is five miles to over there?"

"No, we are there already. John Buford, who was a goddamn good soldier, had the cavalry there. He had sent a message asking for immediate backup, and he, General John Reynolds, me, I, me"—Reynolds pointed to himself—"he said to Buford, 'hold the ground if at all possible,' because he, General John Reynolds, me, was coming. He was ten miles away. They didn't know what to do. Last night, a lieutenant on Buford's staff tried to be ballsy and predicted the Confederates would not attack. Buford said no; he said, 'They will come three deep and booming.'"

Nicely listened.

"And, of course, Lee came three deep and booming, just as Buford said. And remember, Buford only had four thousand men and limited batteries."

"What'd he need batteries for?"

"That means cannons. Cannon, big guns," Reynolds explained. "So, Buford's men fight like hell and hold the ridge longer than they had any right to, but it's slipping away. There's a clock tower at Gettysburg College—still there today. Buford took distance glasses up there and watched his men take on waves and waves of hot iron as the Rebels kept coming, with the sinking feeling that once they had to turn and seek cover, Lee would take the ridge, proceed to overrun the town below and every piece of high ground in a ten-mile radius, and then sit and wait for the slow-moving Union Army. The next day—Buford and Reynolds knew this because they had seen it so many fucking times before—Meade would assemble and the day after that, with Lincoln and Halleck up his ass, would have to attack uphill, and Union forces would get blown away—again."

Nicely nodded. Reynolds was throwing a lot more names in the mix.

"They—in Washington—wanted to get the war over with and couldn't understand why the Confederate Army, this outmanned guerilla operation, could not be squashed in a proper battle. Anyway, the important point for Buford and Reynolds was that Meade would be fucked within a day. Remember, Meade was scared to deploy the entire Union Army, which at full capacity had eight corps and one hundred thousand men. But to amass as a whole army at Gettysburg was very scary—they were out in the open with the capital exposed behind them. A losing effort like Fredericksburg or Chancellorsville at Gettysburg could result in the Confederates having a straight shot at DC."

"Significant," said Nicely, the historian.

"Damn right. So back at the cupola—imagine just over here by the last field." Reynolds gestured at the closest softball diamond. "Buford is ready to pull back. He climbs down the tower, ready to order retreat. But before he does, he looks south, down the Emmitsburg Road, and sees John Reynolds galloping along with an entourage of junior officers and the colors of the United States of America and the Iron Brigade. Reynolds has ridden ahead of his ten thousand men."

"Badass."

"Yup. He rides right to Buford, who has tears in his eyes but can't show it, and says, 'What's the matter, John?' Tough old Buford says, 'They'll be coming again any minute, and there'll be the devil to pay.' Reynolds calms him and compliments his strategy of holding the ridge. 'Damn fine ground, John.' And then, on cue, the drumbeat and colors of the First Division of the Iron Brigade arrive from the south, on the double-step."

"Awesome, sir," said Nicely.

"You have to remember, Nicely, that this was Gettysburg. Today this seems all about high ground and military strategy from warfare made obsolete long ago. But what this all means—the reason it is so important—is that Buford's courage saved the moment, and John Reynolds's courage saved the day. And together they made it possible to win the battle, which saved the Union. So, when you think it through, all that America has become, all that America has given the world, can be traced back here, to these men on this ground."

As Reynolds looked in reverie at the horizon, Nicely shifted his eyes to the left and right, leaving it unspoken that they were in fact in a sports complex in Enchino, California, with five hundred people in ceremonial clothes shooting guns with blanks. He and Reynolds had now made it around the aqueduct and were in the middle of a patch of land outside the fences, as removed as possible from the event grounds on the ball fields without being AWOL. The patch of brown grass and dirt they were in was bounded to the west by a small stucco building with a parking lot filled with white cable-repair vans.

"So, is that what happened?" asked Nicely. "Is that it? Is that why we're here?"

"No, I'm getting to it." Reynolds patted the horse's neck and began speaking again. "General John Reynolds then positioned his troops all around the exposures, spreading his commanders to plug up the defenses in order to hold the ground for as long as possible, giving the rest of the Federal army time to arrive and occupy good ground around the southern side of the town." Reynolds Stanhope was lyrical now. "As he finished organizing the troops, General John Reynolds, commander of the Iron Brigade, guided his horse to the shade of trees on the side of McPherson Ridge. The other officers were going about their business with preparations. When one of them looked up, he saw Reynolds's horse without rider. The general was on the ground with blood rushing from the back of his head."

"What?" said Nicely.

"He had been hit by a Southern sniper from high ground a distance beyond the ridge. He died instantly."

They remained in silence for ten or fifteen seconds, Reynolds staring off and Nicely staring at Reynolds.

"Reynolds, sir, are you doing something with this? Now?"

Reynolds blew air into his cheeks and let it out. "Nicely, it's a little hard to explain, but I was hoping you could just do me a favor."

"Sure."

"Will you please go over beyond the cable trucks and some-where out behind us—where you can see me, but I can't see you—I won't be looking for you, anyway."

"Uh, OK."

"I'll be on the horse facing away from you. I will lift my cap and put it back on. That is your signal. Wait a minute or two, and then fire your rifle at me. Make it sound like a shot ringing out from a sniper if you can."

Nicely knew not to investigate Reynolds's motives any further. He stood up and saluted. "Right away, sir."

Reynolds saluted back. As the kid turned away, Reynolds said, "Nicely, thank you."

"I'm honored, sir," Nicely said. He saluted again.

Reynolds leaned down and patted the horse's neck again. He drew a deep breath and straightened up. After all this time, he was where he wanted to be. His self-criticism was vanishing now. He was doing something he had wanted to do his entire life. This was not just a fantasy, but a powerful personal quest. He thought, as he had so many times before, of the moments on that hot day in 1863 before the sniper blast, when John Reynolds had just evened the tables at the battle, and the feeling of patriotism and honor that must have flowed through the forty-two-year-old at being able to come to the front at such a critical time.

General John Reynolds had not been a self-promoter, but his bravery preceded him, and his good sense preceded that. Here was the man Reynolds Stanhope had always wanted to be: a dependable, sturdy, and brave man. The modern-day Reynolds did not know whether he measured up to his namesake in any way. Truth was, Reynolds didn't know how he could have lived in the spirit of the gentleman warrior who was his namesake. And in some desperate way, this was why he found himself here, sweating in the Inland Empire. He had wanted to respect his nominal ancestor and pray for something to come from it. He made the signal, picking up his cap and putting it down. He kept the pony at a stop. Life had been all in front of General John Reynolds that day on McPherson Ridge near the trees. And then he was gone. Maybe this, too, was what Reynolds had come to find, to appreciate—that he had more time. In some way, Reynolds was here to snap himself out of the paralysis that had set upon him in recent years with the feeling that nothing in Hollywood, and therefore his professional life, and therefore, as awful as it was, his *life*, was worth half a try. He thought, finally, that he sought a communing with the authentic ghost of his better nature and that it would guide him to the elusive path back to living life without question, without negativity, and without the oppressive irony made mandatory by quotidian existence in the world's dream factory.

A squadron of thoughts flew through Reynolds's cranial neurons as he fell from the horse. These disparate thoughts at paintball impact proved that narrow observation and grand enlightenment can occur at once.

First, he thought that the place on the skull between the part of his hair and the ear, where the red paintball struck him, was called the "temple" for a reason: it is there that the brain is most vulnerable, because of the sacred thoughts within. Second, he noted that the eccentric young author and paintball-gun enthusiast had shot him in the wrong part of the head. If there was a blow to begin with, and for Christ's sake there should not have been, to be authentic it should have been delivered square in the back of the head, above the neck, nowhere near the side. This missed detail normally would have driven Reynolds to a state of agitation (wanting your head wound to be reenacted with authenticity was not asking too much), but Reynolds bore no frustration now, both because he wouldn't have wanted Nicely to feel bad and because the reality—that life is precious—rendered it moot. Third, that reality led to the knowledge that his time on earth was ending, he was passing into death, and all explanations, all what-ifs and quibbling about decisions and choices and worrying about insurance and tactics for winning and accuracy and value and love and war were irrelevant, because the deed was done, and this strange and lovely world would be gone.

CHAPTER 35
The Charge

At 2:41 p.m. on July third in Enchino, California, Confederate troops in the shade of the backstops and dugouts were told to line up. Union soldiers stood across the ball park behind the four-and-a-half-foot chain-link outfield fence, their weapons trained and loaded for the upcoming Rebel attack.

Reynolds had drifted down the right side of the field to hear Tom's "do it for the Gipper" speech. He was already horrified to see how things had developed, that Tom was even here. The whole point was that this place—this event—was pure and devoid of connection with Hollywood. Now that was crumbling. They were so happy to crap on their own unique form of devotion. He was dazed and confused.

Tom was aboard a paint pony that looked to be a little small and a little old. He was trying to memorize the make-shift script he had been presented with by the Mayor. which he then folded and put in the side pocket of his coat. Once the troops assembled, Tom rode the paint to the front and began to speak.

"Men, as you can see, our job is to take this field of battle. It may be fraught with danger, and seem impossible, but we will do it!" Cheers went up from the soldiers. "One quick thing," Tom said. "Don't worry if you see me in the field today. In addition to General Pickett, I will also be playing General Armistead!" A somewhat lesser cheer came up from the soldiers.

Tom began to ride toward the side, when one of the other generals motioned that he should take a quick look at his script one last time. Tom took out the papers and read and gave a nod to the general. He rode back out in front of the troops in formation and said, "And today, boys, don't forget that you fight for old Virginny!" A very small cheer went up from the soldiers. Then Tom took his sword out of its scabbard and yelled, "Charge!"

The men had run through most of the infield before the Yankees opened fire. The Rebel troops began falling like sinkers, and a butternut soldier could not be blamed for beginning to question General Lee's plan here.

Behind the fence, at least six Union officers playing Winfield Scott Hancock walked up and down the line shouting encouragement. As the attack continued, more and more Union soldiers bit the dust. The Rebels made progress by the minute, and their leaders began getting close to the outfield fence, all the while shouting the bone-shaking Rebel yell.

Tom had consulted with Norman and done research on his phone and charted his course. He ran down the middle of the field. But about halfway into the outfield, he knelt and took off his coat and his Stetson hat with the feather, thereby converting himself into General Lewis Armistead, the famous Rebel officer who was killed as he jumped the Union barricades at Pickett's Charge.

Reynolds had made his way back to the top of the field and stood with the generals. He was too blown away by the spectacle to get into the fighting. The presence of Tom had taken the battle out of the realm of imagination and into the realm of what things people will do around a movie star.

After partially disrobing, Tom jumped up and began charging, now inhabiting a different role. He pointed himself toward field seven's scoreboard. He kept charging despite the Union soldiers' constant direct, then point blank, rifle blasts to his head and mid-section. He ran ahead of the other attacking Confederates, sword waving. When he arrived at the chain-link fence, he tossed his sword to the other side of the barrier, unburdening himself of the sharp object. He then took five quick steps backward, like a guy preparing to do a straddle jump over a parking meter, and rushed the fence. He scrambled over and landed right near his sword, which he picked up and began to swing.

Once again, Tom was shot by Yankees surrounding him but didn't die. After it became, like, a fucking joke already, the Union soldiers tackled him, took his sword away, and pinned him on his back. Unable to move and barely breathing, Tom said, "Lift me up, lift me up, guys." Once sitting with no one on him anymore, Tom said in a Shakespearean tone, "And with that, the gallant General Armistead died, having broken through the Union defense and on his way to glory." Two seconds expired before Tom was again forced to the ground and pummeled by the Yankees, many of whom were enjoying getting a few in on a movie star.

CHAPTER 36

Speechless

At the direction of the guy who looked like the mayor of the Munchkins and the senior generals who had asked Tom to participate in Pickett's Charge, volunteers gathered the populace of the reenactment for closing ceremonies. A quick stage and microphone had materialized next to the red clay pitcher's mound in the gravelly infield of field three.

Reynolds's ragtag group—Norman, Stella, Bella, Heather, Delaney, Marisol, Robert, Lorenzo, Lance, and Tom—stood around a tree next to the parking lot in the back of the crowd. Reynolds checked out Tom, who kept a smile for anyone who looked his way while still maintaining the gravity of a Virginian general who'd just had his troops blown away. He had decided he couldn't wear Pickett's hat anymore and kept it by his side.

The mayor lifted off into a speech: "We have been especially blessed this day to have the world's greatest actor drop out of the sky to play General ... umm ... a number of generals. We are all speechless." He paused for a moment, seeming to collect his thoughts. "And what a fine battle it was, I should say first. I think it is fair to say, in the words of Edward Everett, that the heavens shone down and lifted up America today." The crowd applauded. Phones were lifted everywhere. The mayor then went on to thank at least thirty people for helping put the project together.

"So, last but not least, Tom wants to say a few words. Tom, come on up."

Tom looked at Norman and mouthed, "I do?" But it was too late.

"Tell them they're the real heroes," Norman whispered, as Tom leaned in for a word. A path cleared for the actor, and he took to the stage, head bowed, with, it appeared to Norman, not a clue as to what to say.

Tom stepped next to the mayor on the infield and took the microphone. "Mr. Mayor, Officers, distinguished ladies and gentlemen, soldiers of the Blue and the Gray, thank you very much." He began to hit his stride. "You know, I had no idea this would be my day today, but I'm sure glad it has been. Like most people, I understand the Civil War as one of the great tragedies in history. I think it is wonderful that a group such as yours keeps the memory alive. Also, as an actor, I am impressed with your attention to detail and commitment to the accuracy of the day. Now, I know I kind of got carried away in the heat of battle, running into the center of the action, but I hope you can look past it." Laughs spread through the crowd. Tom scratched the side of his face. "You kind of get anxious to get in the mix after you've saved the world in eight or nine movies." The crowd erupted in laughter.

"But the best thing I can do right now is thank you good people and fade away. You are the heroes today—you who have worked so hard to re-create such an important part of our heritage. You know, people have an oversize amount of reliance on Hollywood these days. It just . . ." Here, Tom paused. "It's just too damn important. Don't get me wrong, Hollywood has been very good to me. But I'm not sure it is as important or as good as what you folks do here." The crowd applauded.

"In closing," Tom said, "I'd like to invite my friend Reynolds Stanhope up to lead us in the Gettysburg Address. Reynolds actually grew up and attended college in Gettysburg, so he probably knows as much as all of you combined."

There was a mumble of approval, and the senior generals on the makeshift dais nodded. Marisol put her arm on Reynolds's shoulder, as if to encourage him and show she was impressed.

"Reynolds?" Tom said, waving to his friend and offering up the mike.

"Classic spotting," Norman whispered to Bella.

"Huh?" she said.

"That's when you nail the other actor when you don't know what to say in an improv. Put someone else on the spot. Tom's good. Your poor dad."

But Reynolds seemed ready for it, and his face lightened. He had the look of a man resolved. The red spatter of the paintball looked like blood on his neck. As he stepped forward, he whispered in Stella's ear, "Tell everyone to go home when this is done. I'm going off on my own. I will get a way home—I'll get an Uber or something."

Stella nodded but looked concerned. "Honey, please, tell me what's wrong."

"I'm OK."

He started off, and Bella grabbed his uniform cuff. "Dad?" she said.

Reynolds kissed the top of her head. Then he smiled and headed to the podium, where he took the mic from Tom. There was a small breeze. The sun was beginning to set.

Reynolds reached into his pocket and produced a sheaf of notebook papers.

"He wrote this *down*?" Bella whispered to her mother.

"Hello, everyone," Reynolds said, and he took his cap off. "I want to thank you all for this. I have to admit, being from the town where the conflict happened, it is a little strange being here today." There were a few blank stares. He kept going. "What with this being here three thousand miles away." Less recognition from the crowd now, a few eyebrows raised. "And on a ball field . . ." He saw Bella signaling him, drawing her finger across her neck—*Stop, Dad, don't get wound up.*

"Anyway," Reynolds said. "It is good to remember the men. That is what it always came down to for me, growing up in that place so full of ghosts. I know Tom—thanks, Tom, by the way, for doing this—added to the stardust of today. I know Tom wants me to read Lincoln's famous speech from seven months after the battle, and we should. That speech is, of course, one of the most important ever made. But before we get to that—and since I don't know when I will ever have a chance to speak to such an important group of people on this subject—I mean that . . ." He choked up, and Norman looked down at the ground. "I mean, in this day and age, to take this up as an interest and honor our history and recognize its importance in the world that we live in truly moves me." Reynolds was still choking up. Now Stella and Bella looked down at the ground too, realizing he was going somewhere else. "So please don't let what I am about to say spoil your passion or affect your orientation toward the reality of our national history."

The mayor and the generals looked at one another in curiosity, as did the gung-ho reenactors, the ones with bespoke uniforms and swords and accessories. Nicely and the other boys, who had come to appreciate Reynolds, and all of whom and been thinking of getting out of there, listened up.

"Guys, as I think you know, as you think through the complexity of this topic—this battle—the Civil War was a human disaster. Early July of 1863, with Vicksburg falling and Lee losing Gettysburg, guaranteed the rebellion would fail, though it took two long and horrible years to finish the job. When I was in high school and college, I made money taking people around the battlefield—I was just a National Park Service employee, but I came to learn so much. Most of it was about logistics and generals and decisions and war—the kind of stuff historians get off on, and I'm afraid I see that in many Civil War devotees too.

"The most important thing I learned in my time as a guide is that it is almost impossible to understand what happened then. Remember, those people were grandparents of grandparents of grandparents of today's world. There were no phones. The average weight of a Confederate soldier was 117 pounds. Two percent of the population of the United States died in the war. It was a terrible, terrible time. They clung to religion the way we cling to television and clothes and the Internet. The war is believed to be about freeing the slaves, and that is true but not the whole way—and I know you all know that. Living on the battlefield and walking it every day, I became convinced that war was about excitement and ego and, in the end, the evil of this world taking hold for a while, as it always does. We lose that understanding over time—things become glorified rather than understood. And I fear that this is something we don't understand as humans anymore—that history is ugly. That we are making history and much of what we are doing is ugly."

At this point, there was stone silence in the crowd. Reynolds was confusing people. Just as the stitching was about to come off the ball, he began again. "The important thing to understand today—as important as Abraham Lincoln's eloquent statement about the things that make America great and that were preserved in the war—is that a lot of crazy, crazy mistakes were made, and we did it to ourselves. It was the only time, as famous historians have said, that we failed to compromise as a people. So, when you watch these stupid cable channels and all the people that want to scare you into fighting with the other side—whomever that may be—remember that town in Pennsylvania (which is still beautiful, by the way) and this place, this, well, this park in California, where kids come to play and your group has imagined so many things, that fighting all the way leads to dead kids and undeserving heroes and great people cut down too early." He paused. "Too early."

At this point the mayor stepped forward as though he was going to take the microphone and get on with the Gettysburg Address. Reynolds eased up and said, "OK, OK. Before we get to the great speech, there is one other speech that I would like to recite for you that I would give the people on my tours as a college kid. Is that OK?"

"Sure," said a man in the crowd.

"Yes, it is," Tom said.

"Thank you," Reynolds said. "It won't take long. It comes from what we just did—Pickett's Charge. General Longstreet, who Lee trusted very much, except at Gettysburg, was very much in disagreement in what became one of the worst tactical moves ever made—maybe the most significant if you think about it, given what the United States has accomplished as a unified nation and force in this world. Longstreet pouted and did everything he could to talk Lee out of it, but there was no use. Let me ask you a question. What day was Pickett's Charge?

Cyrus yelled out, "July 3, 1863."

"That's right, Cyrus," Reynolds said. "And what lay beyond the Union line at Cemetery Ridge, where Pickett—and General Armistead, who Tom so wonderfully . . ." Here Reynolds's looked at Tom. "Maybe too wonderfully . . . showed almost breaking through? . . . What was in the distance?"

"Washington, DC," Norman called out. Then he added, "Unprotected."

"That's also right," said Reynolds. "So that meant the Confederate Army would be running at Washington, DC, on the Fourth of July."

The crowd was silent.

"So, what people don't pay enough attention to is that the great man everyone thinks of as Robert E. Lee was delusional."

Stevie and Bob grabbed each other's jackets and started to pretend to bash their heads together.

Bob said, "*Fuuuuck*. Lee *again. Again.*"

"I . . . can't . . . take it, Bob. There's no more room in my ass for Lee to be shoved anymore."

Back at the podium, Reynolds went on. "Lee was an Old Testament guy. He believed that the almighty preordained that battle would be the end of the war. As Lee became convinced of this line of attack, at the final moment, Longstreet, who was just about the toughest and the most loyal guy in the war, stood up to Lee and said the following: 'General Lee, I have been a soldier all my life. I have been with soldiers engaged in fights by couples, by squads, companies, regiments, divisions, and armies, and I should know as well as anyone what soldiers can do. It is my opinion that no fifteen thousand men ever arrayed for battle can take that position.'"

Much nodding from the crowd.

"And, to pick up on Tom's thoughts: this might very well be more important than what we do in Hollywood. You see, what's *gone missing* in Hollywood is the commitment to making things that have heart. Not passion, not hard work—those are like table salt. But today, so many of us feel that our lives are going by while we are making shit that doesn't have heart. I have been frustrated by this for years, and I have gotten way, *way* off course, but it took you folks to get me back between the rails a little. Maybe." Nervous laughter came from the crowd, as though not everyone was sure he wouldn't fall apart. "Like you, I have a lot of problems. But I think if we in Hollywood could approach our work the way you guys here do the reenactment of the Battle of Gettysburg, we could all be a whole lot happier."

"So, with that out of my system, I'll finish up," Reynolds said. "The lesson of Gettysburg to me is not a lesson at all. It is that things get out of control, and the spiritual and the practical mix, and all kinds of things happen. I don't know what else it means or meant. The man I was named for, John Reynolds, a general from Pennsylvania, who was a great man, was killed at that battle, and I've spend my entire life wondering why. I came here this weekend to remember him. It seemed important, in a time when so many unimportant and confusing things and so much change are happening, that I do that. So, I want to finish by saying the same thing I started with, thank you for coming.

"And, if I may, please ask you to take one thing with you: it's good to remember the men."

There came a single loud clap, from Tom, which was then followed by other clapping. Heather nudged Bella to show her that Tom had tears running down his face. Bella wiped her own eyes.

"So funny," she whispered back to Heather, her mother listening too. "No one has any idea what he was talking about except Tom."

Back at the stage, the mayor, who appeared relieved, took the microphone and made a motion to the videographer to focus on him. Norman looked down and kicked a rock. The mayor said, "Four score and seven years ago . . ."

Norman said, "Our fathers . . ."

And with that, the crowd continued with them:

brought forth on this continent, a new nation, conceived in Liberty, and dedicated to the proposition that all men are created equal.

Now we are engaged in a great civil war, testing whether that nation, or any nation so conceived and so dedicated, can long endure. We are met on a great battle-field of that war. We have come to dedicate a portion of that field, as a final resting place for those who here gave their lives that that nation might live. It is altogether fitting and proper that we should do this.

But, in a larger sense, we cannot dedicate—we cannot consecrate—we cannot hallow—this ground. The brave men, living and dead, who struggled here, have consecrated it, far above our poor power to add or detract. The world will little note, nor long remember what we say here, but it can never forget what they did here.

It is for us the living, rather, to be dedicated here to the unfinished work which they who fought here have thus far so nobly advanced. It is rather for us to be here dedicated to the great task remaining before us—that from these honored dead we take increased devotion to that cause for which they gave the last full measure of devotion—that we here highly resolve that these dead

shall not have died in vain—that this nation, under God, shall
have a new birth of freedom—and that government of the people,
by the people, for the people, shall not perish from the earth.

When the reading was over, there was silence in the crowd. On the dais, Tom said, "Reynolds, brother, we got to hang out and talk. I have a few ideas for things that might be fun. Love you, man."

"Love you too, Tom," Reynolds said.

"Thank you all," Tom said, and he shook the mayor's hand and went back toward Norman and the others.

"Nice job, man," Bella said.

"Yes, Tom," Marisol said. Tom gave her a small salute, still in Southern general mode.

Reynolds came up to the group.

"Hi, Dad," Bella said, and she walked over and gave him a big hug. The other women lined up to do the same. Stella went last. Reynolds and she stayed in the hug for a few seconds.

Stella broke the hug and took him by the forearms. "Look at me, honey. Look me in the eyes," she said.

Reynolds lifted his head. "I am."

She leaned into him and began to whisper. "You are the most sensitive, beautiful, smart, kind, and handsomest man in the world. You are also a rock—the rockiest of rocks. Bella's and my rock."

She stood on her toes to get closer to his ear. Her whisper quieted. "I love you. I am not letting you get away from me. You are my hero. Bella's too. If you need anything I don't do, I'll fix it . . . Let's travel. Let's get into art and collect more . . ."

Reynolds said, "Oh, Stell, it's not like that . . ."

She pulled back from his ear. "OK, but whatever it is, it seems complicated." She smiled and shook his arms. "Like you." She put her head on his chest, unironically.

"OK, you guys," Reynolds said. "Sorry I dragged you all out here."

"Don't be sorry," Delaney said. "You didn't drag us out here, sugar. We're sorry—*I'm sorry*—for sticking our noses where they don't belong." She wiped a tear away. "You were great."

"Spectacular," Norman said.

"Yes. Very great, Rey," Marisol said. "This battalion will follow you anywhere."

Tom said, "Well, guys, I hate to be a big jerk like this, but I have to fly out to New York. I found an airport nearby so I'm gonna run over there."

"Ontario?" said Stella.

"Like Canada?" said Heather.

CHAPTER 37

Man of Action, Part 2

He dreamed again that he held the long and beautiful gun, the giver and taker of America. When he woke, he was leaning against the outfield fence in field two. The crowds had long since gone; it was magic hour. He was rested and calm, in the way a deep, washing sleep can render the exhausted traveler a new person. Off in the parking lot, just at his vision's end, he could see two lone vehicles, an SUV and a pickup truck with a slouched Confederate flag in the bed. Music came from the back, where a handful of guys still in tattered gray and brown uniforms were gathered. This meant they were Confederates.

He pulled himself up. His Springfield was standing against the fence next to the 305-foot sign set at dead center. The flagpole was right behind it, the Stars and Stripes up top, splendid in the wind. As he crossed the field he stepped over debris from the battle, a torn tunic here, a chewed-up cap there. Nothing like the dead bodies from the real place on the real day that haunted his real home. Just gentle trash on a respectful and well-kept patch of grass blessed not by Lincoln but by a sincere group of descendants who somehow sought to connect with that brutal, uncompromising, and violent time. They had tried to consecrate something, some concept, with respect; they had tried to locate the touchstone of freedom; they had also come to ham it up and make friends and blow shit up. But overall, Reynolds was convinced they thought it as good a place as any to honor that time and that spirit in which their families had been led to kill each other.

He knew he was alone and had no way back to Malibu and the ocean. He felt his phone in his pocket and hoped it hadn't run out of power. He would use it or look for a pay phone, maybe borrow a phone from one of the men drinking in the parking lot, or a janitor or a security guard or a cop. Some man in uniform would help him. He walked past the stands behind the dugout and strode by the few trees planted in the space leading to the lot. The SUV pulled out and the pickup followed. But the pickup slowed before the exit, circled to the left, and swung back around to where Reynolds stood.

"You all alone?"

"Guess so."

"C'mon, get in. I can drop you somewhere."

Reynolds put his gun in the back of the truck and climbed in. The driver had on gray pants with a yellow line down the side, the kind worn by a baseball or football player. He had stripped down to a white T-shirt and wore a full day's face of dust.

"How'd you get left behind?" he said, as they drove along the service road by Reynolds's self-appointed McPherson's Ridge, next to the lot of white vans.

"I told them to leave me."

"Leave you for dead?" the guy said, and then laughed to show he was just playing.

"I guess."

They both became quiet as they drove along the service road for about three miles till they saw an intersection of two large roads. They headed toward a Chevron Station on the opposite corner. They were at the traffic light, and after a pause, the Confederate driver said, "I know how you feel, brother. Tomorrow's Monday."

Reynolds agreed. "Tomorrow's Monday."

He thanked the driver before he pulled away from the Chevron station, having learned his name was Phil, and that Phil imagined himself as a basic Southern soldier because his family roots were in Georgia. "Weird, I know," he had said. Phil drove off, toward Ontario, where he worked at a plant that made small flashlights.

Reynolds checked his tunic and found twenty-one bucks. He bought an e-cigarette and a Diet Dr Pepper and sat on the curb, out of the sight line of the man at the counter or anyone who might stop for gas. He pulled his phone out of his pocket. He did not look at his messages, couldn't bear to. He opened the only app he could stand now: the one that played his music. The song he wanted was already teed up. He set the phone on the curb and leaned back, listening, looking past the gas pumps to the park, the whole of it.

He picked up the phone from the concrete and hit *Pause*. At the main menu he chose the phone icon, tapped the number he needed, and held the handset to his ear. It rang four times and beeped.

"It's me," he said. "I'm OK."

He hung up, put the phone down, and looked out at the intersection. Then, to his right, in a spot in the Chevron parking lot he saw a big black Mercedes. Norman sat behind the wheel, reading a book. Reynolds walked over and tapped on the window. Norman lowered it.

"How did you know I'd be here?" Reynolds said.

"It's the only gas station near the place." Norman said. "And the only place with any food. Made sense you'd get here to figure out your next move. Get in." Then he thought about it. "Wait, I'm getting out. You drive."

Reynolds did as he was told, and they made their way to the I-10.

After about five minutes, Norman said, "What the hell's wrong with you?"

"I know, sorry," Reynolds said.

"Don't be sorry. You didn't do anything wrong,"

Reynolds sighed and stretched his shoulders up and down. "Yeah . . ." he said.

"I think the trick here is riding this out," Norman said.

They drove in silence, until Reynolds said, "Man, I don't know." He looked out at the freeway, "I might be fine."

He took a deep breath, paused for a moment, and exhaled. The relaxed breathing of a well-insured man.

Acknowledgments

I want to thank Morgan Entrekin for his encouragement, advice, and friendship throughout this campaign. Thank you also to Peter Blackstock, Emily Burns, Deb Seager, and everyone else at Grove Atlantic for their professionalism and good work. I am in debt to my eyeballs to my agent, Jane von Mehren, for her guidance and kindness. Thank you to the people who take care of things: my boss Nikole Sullivan, Mark Cleland, Melodie Moore, Nataly Rodrigues, Annett Wolf, Lindsay Wineberg, Alex Kohner, Ailleen Gorospe, Miles Metcalf. Thank you to my wise men, Phil Stutz and Glenn Altschuler. Every writer is lucky to have Terry McDonald in their corner, and my gratitude can't be measured. Thank you to Eric Roth for tough love and inspiration from the first word. And thank you for help along the way to Kevin Yorn, David Krintzman, Karen Green, Stuart Liner, Betsy and John Walters, Max Rudin, Todd Rubenstein, Dennis Morris, Brian Morris, Matt Stone, Anne Garefino, Trey Parker, Gavin O'Connor, James Frey, Matthew McConaughey, Jim Gavin, and the late Herman Goldblatt.

Finally, thank you to the Gettysburg scholar, long ago who gave my family a station wagon tour that opened my eyes to the power, sad poetry, and tragedy of the battle. In these ironic and cynical times, it is good that we remember the soldiers who gave that last full measure of devotion during those early, boiling Pennsylvania days in July 1863.

KM, 2019